WOUNDS

ALTON GANSKY

Nashville, Tennessee

Printed in the United States of America

978-1-4336-7718-2

Published by B&H Publishing Group
Nashville, Tennessee

Dewey Decimal Classification: F
Subject Heading: MYSTERY FICTION \ HOMICIDE—FICTION \ SERIAL KILLERS—FICTION

Publishers Note: The characters and events in this book are fictional, and any resemblance to actual persons or events is coincidental.

1 2 3 4 5 6 7 8 • 17 16 15 14 13

To Reverend Don Venosdel,
Now in glory and much missed here.
Thanks for the decades of wisdom.

PROLOGUE

A bead of sweat trickled down the preacher's spine, trekking south toward a perspiration-soaked waistband. It wasn't the first bead he had felt since stepping on the platform, and twenty years of experience told him it wouldn't be the last. For two decades he had trod well-worn hardwood floors that clad a thousand stages around the world.

The growing rivulet widened and flowed faster with each minute. A similar outpouring ran from beneath his arms and down his sides, gluing his dress shirt to damp skin. Along the hairline, moisture oozed through pores and wetted his dark hair—hair two shades lighter than coal. The skin of his tanned face felt like an over-saturated sponge on the verge of disgorging its cargo of sweat. A round belly proved that his ever-youthful appearance belied his fifty-five years.

On the stage, dressed in a collarless shirt the color of obsidian—an attempt to look thinner than his 220 pounds—a gray suit coat, and black pants, he moved with the energy of a man two decades younger. On stage he still looked more youthful than he was. Television proved a different matter. The camera had no allegiances to men of the cloth. High-definition digital video remained steeped in truth, conveying every wrinkle, age spot, and other epidermal faults. After reviewing his last television interview, the preacher wished for the days when digital detail mattered less than content.

He moved to the lectern again, a handcrafted pulpit made by a faithful woodworker in Tennessee as a gift to the ministry. More than the composite of hard maple with ebony trim, the pulpit held electronics that preachers of a generation before would never have dreamed. A clock gave the local time; a lapse timer showed that he had been preaching for twenty-one-and-a-half minutes. A small plasma screen connected to the television feed served as a video monitor giving real-time feedback about which of three cameras gazed on him at the moment and what the world would see once the editing and distribution had been done.

Somewhere beyond the glare of the spotlights sat an audience hanging on his every word. Hubris did not plant the thought in his mind. Rather, hundreds of sermons in scores of countries and every state in the union had done so.

He had traveled so much that there were times he couldn't remember which city hosted his crusades. Today, however, he knew citizens of Philadelphia filled the sports arena. He had visited the Liberty Bell earlier that day, a special tour granted by the city and the historical society that managed such things.

He paused his machine-gun delivery. Not because he had lost his place but to heighten his point. All good speakers know the trick, and the world had judged him to be one of the most gifted orators of his or any generation. The platform was his throne and he made use of it.

In exactly three minutes, he would bring his sermon to a climactic close. People would stand and sing. Hundreds would come forward, and shortly after he would exit stage right.

Gone were the days when he could spend time with the people who had come to hear words of hope and promise. Gone, too, were the times of shaking hands and personal prayers, of intimate fellowship. All replaced by drum-tight security. Bodyguards were a requirement these days. The ministry spent thousands of donated dollars just to keep him safe.

What had the world come to when a simple preacher-man couldn't step on a stage without first wondering if it would be his last public appearance?

The death threats hadn't helped. Threats that came every week like clockwork. No matter where he was in the world, word would reach him and always with the same message: "THY MAKER AWAITS."

The Reverend Dr. Daniel Templeton's gaze drifted to the audience and he wondered . . .

Did his tormentor look back?

He leaned over the sink of the tiny, dirty bathroom, eyes fixed on the steady flow of water that poured from the chipped, rusted faucet. The water drew him, serenaded him with a song only he could hear.

He leaned closer and watched the colorless cascade. The sound of it filled his ears with a rhythm that matched a heart beating at full throttle. The event had occurred over an hour ago, but the thrill of it fueled the pulsing behind his sternum.

A smile tickled the corners of his mouth.

He bent more and moved closer, closer, until the tip of his nose hovered an inch from the stream. Too close now to focus, he closed his eyes, allowing the sound of the water to become his lullaby. Tiny drops splashed from the bottom of the sink, dotting his face.

It had been so easy. It had felt so right. Every step fell in place. Every motion planned. Every detail observed. The act had been completed just as he saw it a hundred times in his mind.

The smile widened.

He straightened and looked at his reflection. The naked man staring back didn't fit the image chiseled in his mind. That man remained eighteen, full of energy and muscled by unrelenting exercise. The man in the mirror still displayed muscles twice the size of any other man in his late forties, but he also showed skin that looked thinner than it should and was dotted with skin tags and undefined dark spots—the latter the result of too many years of careless sun exposure. He hadn't cared about such things when he wore a younger man's clothes, and he didn't much care now.

He closed his eyes again and saw the body, saw the markings, and relived the unexpected turn.

That didn't matter now. The result remained the same even if the catalyst had been unanticipated. That was the thing with murder. No matter how well planned an execution might be, things could change.

He turned off the faucet.

He couldn't turn off the visions or the voices.

Thursday, March 28, 2013

Flies.

The buzzing bothered her the most. No matter how many times she heard it, no matter the number of times she had seen what drew the insects, the sound still ate at the lining of her stomach.

"Cover him." Carmen Rainmondi frowned and turned away, giving no outward indication of the discomfort within. Was she losing her edge?

A uniformed officer stood to her right. Tall and lanky, he looked too young to shave. He also looked a little green around the gills. "You don't want to wait for the rest of the team?" He followed the words with a hard swallow.

Carmen gave the officer a glance, then shook her head. "It's a public place. It won't be long before parents will be walking by with their children. I don't want letters telling the chief how we scarred their kids for life. Now are you going to cover him or do you want to jaw about it some more?"

"Got it. No problem." He trotted toward one of the black-and-whites, its emergency lights tossing splashes of red and blue in the air. Carmen noticed that he moved with care, following the same path out that they had taken in.

At least the newbie got that right.

She forced herself to face the body again. Face down, arms and legs askew, the victim looked as if he had fallen from a low-flying airplane. She could see he was young. He wore only a pair of brown shorts—no shoes, no shirt, no cap. The same dew that covered the grass dampened the body and clung to his hair. There were no signs of gunshot or knife wounds, but she could see a series of dried blood drops covering his back and the one side of his face she could examine.

Studying the shorts, Carmen saw what she hoped to see: a bulge in the right rear pocket. With a latex-gloved hand she removed the wallet, which felt thin and light. *Right pocket; right-handed.* Nothing earthshaking in that realization, but details mattered. Sometimes the little things turned the whole case.

Like the officer before her, Carmen carefully retraced her steps and ducked beneath the yellow crime-scene tape that cordoned off a quarter-acre of ground. The smell of eucalyptus trees mixed with the perfume of a dozen different flowering plants followed her. The sun crawled up the blue San Diego sky on the same journey it had made millions of times before.

Many considered Balboa Park one of the most beautiful places in the city and Carmen agreed. She spent a summer of her college years working at the historic park. As part of her training, her employers pounded some of the park's history into her brain. She knew more about the fourteen-hundred-acre area—complete with quaint cottages, spectacular Spanish Colonial buildings, museums, and stage theaters—than those living nearby.

The park was the jewel in the Chamber of Commerce's crown. Having a badly beaten body lying on emerald grass dulled the gem.

"I used to love this place."

The words snatched Carmen from her thoughts. "Huh?"

"Wool gathering, Detective?" Bud Tock had come up behind her. Tock worked homicide too, and they were often teamed together. He would be the number-two detective on the case.

"Yeah, I guess I was. I used to work here."

"In the park or at the Botanical Building?" He motioned to the long, wide, wood-lathe structure with a rounded trellis for a roof.

"I worked at the Reuben H. Fleet Science Center. They have a gift shop. Those were some slow hours."

"I'll bet." He paused as he looked beyond the cordoning tape. "Did you take a peek?"

Tock stood tall, lean, and somehow managed to look younger than his fifty-one years. Unlike many men his age, his dark hair had not deserted him, but it yielded to spreading gray. Carmen at forty-six, however, fought a relentless battle against a broadening waist and the appearance of new wrinkles. She did her best to look sharp, professional, and just attractive enough, but she wondered whether a day would come when she just quit caring about such things. Her brown hair showed a tint of red in the sunlight. It always had.

She let her eyes linger on Tock for a moment, like a dieter eyeing a piece of cheesecake, but those thoughts cinched closed. They had history, she and Tock. They had been an item. It began five years ago and ended with brutal honesty thirty days later. Every time she thought of that month she felt the bitterest pleasure and the sweetest regret. Three months later he married another woman. It was his third marriage. She had yet to have one.

"I asked if you took a peek. You okay?"

"I'm fine. Didn't sleep well last night. Too much caffeine or something." The lie came easily. "I'm having the body covered. Too many civilian eyes around here. Or there will be soon."

"We probably have an hour before the crowds arrive. At least it's Thursday, not a weekend. What have we got?"

"Male, white, young, maybe early twenties. My best guess is he's been dead for six hours or so. I'll let the ME give us a better estimate on time."

Tock pursed his lips. "So someone did him in the wee hours? Three or four a.m.?"

"Probably."

"I think we should close the grounds to the public. The Botanical Building is a pretty big draw. I also suggest we have a couple of officers tape off the walkways." He paused. "That is, if it's okay with you. You're lead dog on this sled."

"Lead dog? I see you still know how to sweet-talk a woman."

"My wife won't let me sweet-talk other ladies. She says it just breaks their hearts." He pointed at the object in her hand. "Is that his wallet?"

"I just retrieved it." Carmen opened the billfold. "It looks like he's had it for some time. The leather is worn at the fold."

The first thing she looked for she found behind a clear plastic window. "California driver's license . . . Doug Lindsey . . ." She studied the date on the license and did the math. "Twenty-three. He would have been twenty-four next month." She continued her search through the wallet. "Usual stuff: a credit card, debit card, a picture of his family. Looks like his mom and pop. Twenty-three dollars and . . ."

"And what?"

Carmen removed a thin, plastic-coated card from one of the wallet's compartments. "Student ID. It appears young Mr. Lindsey attended San Diego Theological Seminary."

"Never heard of it."

She grinned. "I'm not surprised."

"Oh, is that how it is? I don't recall seeing you hanging around any churches."

"They see me coming and bar the doors—afraid the roof will cave in." She studied the card. "The address says the seminary is in Escondido."

"What about wounds?" Tock moved toward the yellow tape. "See anything to make our job simple?"

"No holes from a knife or bullet that I could see. I haven't moved the body yet. Still waiting on the team."

Homicide procedures demanded no work begin until the full team arrived on scene. The team members varied but always included a forensic technician, a sergeant, a scene detective, and another homicide cop. Sometimes individuals had to travel some distance to arrive. San Diego County covered more than ıdred square miles, and San Diego City covered d and forty-two of those. The county's population ıearly three million, and a third of those lived in the city proper. Police staff could live in any of eighteen incorporated cities or seventeen unincorporated communities. It might take one team member ten minutes to arrive and an hour for another. In the meantime, detectives like Carmen had to wait and twiddle their thumbs. It made for lousy and misleading news coverage.

"There's something you're going to want to see," Carmen said. "It's a new one on me."

"What?"

"Words aren't going to do it justice. This is one of those have-to-see-to-believe deals."

"I'm feeling impatient. Let's take a look now." Tock moved toward the crime scene and Carmen followed a step behind.

The uniformed officer struggled alone to unfold a thin plastic tarp. Two older officers watched and snickered. As Carmen and Tock reached the tape barricade, one of the officers fast-stepped to help the rookie. Carmen said nothing to the man—the razzing new officers received at the hands of veterans was part of the cop bonding process that turned strangers into partners. It was the price paid to enter the tribe.

"Hold up on that," Carmen said to the young officer.

"But you said—"

"I know what I said. Just hang on a minute. Detective Tock wants to see the body."

Tock approached, careful of his steps.

Less than two minutes later, Tock shook his head. "What'd the guy do? Sleep on a bed of nails? He looks like a pin cushion."

“I assume you noticed his face. Same small puncture marks.”

“They don’t look deep, at least not at first glance. Can a man die from a hundred shallow punctures?”

Carmen shrugged. “I suppose it depends what he was punctured with.”

“A hundred poison darts? Not likely.”

“Agreed. He was alive when it happened.” Carmen gazed at the corpse. The two officers gently laid the plastic tarp over the body.

“Yeah, I saw the blood streaks. Looks like he was allowed to bleed for a while, but I don’t see a pool of blood. Maybe the wounds are deeper than they look and he bled out internally.”

“Torture?”

“Maybe, but who would want to torture a seminary student? And where is the rest of his clothing? It’s still a little cool at night to be running in nothing but shorts.”

Tock stared over Carmen’s shoulder. “Here comes the cavalry.”

Carmen followed the gaze and saw several of the homicide team arriving. “Good. I’m itching to get started.”

“My gut tells me you’re going to have your hands full with this one.”

Carmen’s gut told her the same thing.

2

Contentment. That which Ellis Poe loved surrounded him: books, journals, student papers, and silence. Outside his office window on the campus of San Diego Theological Seminary shone a bright morning sun, which sparrows serenaded with chirps and twitters. He let the morning image paint his mind. The seminary sat on top of one of the many hills in Escondido. Ellis could see the sprawl of the city. At night the sight proved more pleasing than a painting. The daytime view was just as easy on the eyes, especially now that spring had sprung. Here, spring always came early.

Turning his back on the panorama, Ellis settled behind an oak desk that was older than his forty-five years. On its surface rested a Bible, a Greek New Testament, a copy of James S. Jeffers's *The Greco-Roman World of the New Testament Era*, and three stacks of student papers—one for each of the classes he taught this quarter.

There were no students today. Classes were dismissed for the remainder of the week and all of next week. After all, tomorrow was Good Friday and Sunday would bring Easter—Resurrection Day, as he preferred to think of it.

The work might be suspended for the students, but it had just begun for the professors. Most would take a few days off, but midterm exams fell this week and eager ministry students would be pestering the faculty for grades.

That suited Ellis just fine. He held no great love for grading term papers. Most were badly written, rushed, and poorly researched, but occasionally a student showed extraordinary promise. That's what he lived for. Professors loved to intellectually clone themselves, and he was no different.

The drip coffeemaker sputtered like a dying car engine, signaling its work had ended. Ellis rose and poured the Ethiopian blend into a mug. The cup had been a gift from a fellow professor. In a creative flare, someone had researched the insults that appear in Shakespeare's writings and printed them on the cup's surface. "I wish we could be better strangers," and "You flop-eared, beetle-headed knave" were his favorites. He had no idea why.

Returning to his desk, he settled in again, hearing the familiar squeak of his chair. Pulling the first essay from the stack, he opened the folder and smiled to see a neatly typed presentation complete with the proper title sheet and the correct number of pages. It always puzzled him that graduate-level students couldn't follow simple instructions. This one had.

"*Potuit Non Peccare; Non Potuit Peccare*" the title read. The student was showing off his Latin and his research. Ellis liked that. Not a bad topic for a survey of systematic theology course.

"*Able not to sin; not able to sin*," the student wrote, "*the debate has lasted centuries. The impeccability of Christ (His ability or inability to sin) has troubled theological minds*—"

A knock on the door pulled Ellis from his reading. He heard the knob turn and watched the door slowly open.

"Dr. Poe?"

Dr. Allen Dunne, academic dean for the school, slipped in. Ellis liked Dunne. He had moved from the pulpit to the lectern almost a decade ago. In that time, he had gone from adjunct professor to dean.

"Come in, Dr. Dunne."

Allen crossed the threshold, stepped to the desk, and sat in the "student's" chair.

Ellis offered Allen coffee but he declined. It took a few moments for Ellis to realize that something troubled his colleague. Normally gregarious and quick to laugh, Allen looked drawn and thin, like a man at the end of a protracted illness.

Allen pursed his lips. "Back in my pastor days, I learned the best way to deliver bad news is quickly, then deal with the emotions next."

"There's bad news?" Ellis's stomach soured.

"Doug Lindsey is dead. The police found his body early this morning in Balboa Park."

"No." Something twisted inside Ellis. "Accident?"

Allen shook his head. "Murder. The police are sure of it. I'm talking to whoever is on campus. I'll call the other faculty when I'm done."

"Murder? How? When?" Ellis's blood pooled in his feet. "I'm sorry. Apparently I'm incoherent."

"Understandable. It took me ten minutes to get out of my chair."

"I don't know what to say."

"Words fail at times like this." Allen paused. "You knew him well?"

Ellis nodded. "As well as a professor can know a student. Bright, clever, insightful, humorous. A class leader."

"M.Div. student, right?"

"Yes." Master of Divinity, one of the longer degree programs at the seminary—three years for the full-time student. "He planned to enter pulpit ministry, although I overheard him talking to another student about missionary work. I think he was still trying to find his role in the world."

"Most of us go through that, Ellis. I know I did."

"What can I do?"

"When I'm done talking to the on-campus faculty and making my calls, I'm going to pick up Loren and swing by the family's home. You're welcome to come along."

Ellis feared Allen would say that. "I'm not very good at that kind of thing. I-I'm sorry."

"No problem. The police are going to come by. It would help to have someone show them around and answer their questions."

"I'll stay here until they arrive."

Allen stood and Ellis joined him. "If you need me, Ellis, don't hesitate to call."

"I won't. I'll keep you in prayer."

Allen thanked him and left. Ellis returned to the window and looked on the panorama again. A few moments ago he saw beauty; now all he could see was a planet infested with evil—the same kind of evil that kept him withdrawn from others.

The same kind of evil that kept him frightened all the time.

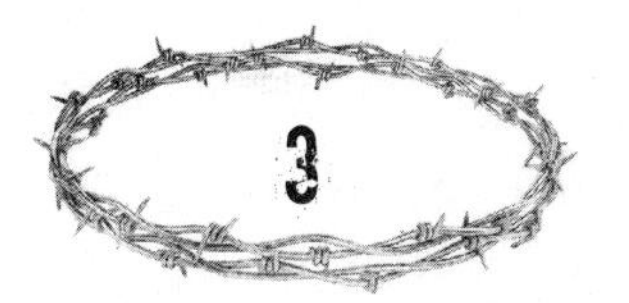

3

Carmen Rainmondi pulled the black Crown Victoria up the grade onto the campus of San Diego Theological Seminary and tried to get her bearings. Several large, uninspired rectangular buildings with red-tile roofs formed a cluster around a broad concrete courtyard. A fountain bubbled in the center and concrete benches provided seating areas.

The parking lot and driveway extended around the buildings and a large open field of freshly mowed grass. She saw no chalk stripes indicating the lawn area was part of a sports field. Did seminaries *have* team sports? She guessed not.

"Nice place," Bud Tock said. "Clean, nicely landscaped. Yup, a man could do some real study in a place like this."

Carmen cut her eyes his way. "When did *you* last crack a book?"

"You wound me, Carmen. I began a new book just last night."

"Did it come with crayons?" She smiled.

"I'm not talking a coloring book here. I mean a real live book. It's a novel."

"Who wrote it?" She parked as close to the courtyard as she could. There were very few vehicles, which struck her as odd.

"I don't remember." Tock opened his door. Carmen did the same with hers and they exited. The air had warmed as the day grew older.

"Yep, you're a scholar all right."

"Oh, really? And what was the last book you read?"

Carmen struggled to look nonchalant. "I reread a Jane Austen novel and followed that with the latest Dean Koontz. I read all his stuff. Before those—"

"All right, all right, I get the picture. Can I help it if I prefer movies and television?"

They walked from the lot and through the center of the courtyard. Large, bronze, block letters marked the buildings. Carmen headed for the one marked "Administration."

A pair of tinted glass doors opened to a lobby of green carpet, white plaster walls, a counter, and half-wall that separated the visitor's area from the offices. Several desks were visible beyond the counter. Carmen could see a hallway a few feet farther on.

A young woman seated at the closest desk rose and approached. "May I help you?"

Carmen judged her to be in her mid-twenties, fawn hair, clear blue eyes, and perfect skin. For a moment, Carmen wished she were twenty-five again.

"Good morning, I'm Detective Carmen Rainmondi and this is my partner Bud Tock. I called and spoke to Mr. Allen Dunne. He said there would be someone here to help us."

"Dr. Dunne is visiting Doug's family, but he told me that I should direct you to Dr. Poe."

"Poe? As in Edgar Allen?" Bud grinned.

"Yes. Dr. Poe is the head of New Testament studies. I'll let him know you're here." She began to turn.

"Before you do, maybe you could help us." Carmen beamed her friendliest smile at the young woman.

"If I can."

"May I ask your name?" Carmen spoke as Bud removed a small notepad from his suit coat. They often worked this way: one asked questions, the other took notes, only talking if something important was overlooked.

"Missy Robinson."

"And you're the receptionist?"

"Just part-time when school is in session. It helps pay the tuition. Since it's Easter break, I'm putting in eight hours a day."

"So you're a student?" That surprised Carmen.

Missy picked up on it. "About a third of the students are female."

"But don't people go to seminary to become priests?"

Missy grinned. "This is an evangelical seminary. Some of the students will become pastors, some will go to the mission field, others will teach."

"Which are you?" Carmen let the curt question hide her embarrassment.

"I'm in the academic track. My undergraduate degree is in archaeology. I want to do field research in biblical archaeology for a decade or so, then gain tenure as a professor somewhere."

Carmen swallowed. She was so out of her element. Time to bring things back to center. "I assume Mr. Dunne . . . *Dr.* Dunne told you why we're here."

The receptionist's expression drooped, as if sadness had just tripled gravity's pull on her face. "He did."

"Did you know Doug Lindsey?"

Her head moved from side to side. "Not really. He is a third-year M.Div. student."

Carmen frowned. "Emdiv?"

"Master of Divinity," Missy explained. "It's a three-year degree track. It's the program you enter if you want to be the pastor of a church or a missionary."

"That's different from what you're doing?" Carmen tilted her head to the side.

"Again, I'm in an academic track. Let me try it this way: You go to the doctor because you're sick. He examines you and gives you a medication to take. The doctor has a doctor of medicine degree: an MD. The people who did the research and designed the medication you take probably have PhDs. Their education is different from the doctor's. Things overlap of course, but the MD is a professional degree. The doctor learns a lot of science, but he or she also learns examination techniques, ethics, and things that will help the doctor serve the patient.

"The PhD," she continued, "may have a degree in chemistry, pharmacology, biology, or something similar. Their education is geared to pure science, while the doctor's is aimed at creating a professional health-care provider."

"So the M.Div. student learns, what? Preacher stuff?"

"Theology, Bible, preaching, counseling, administration,

and the like. That's why it takes three years to get the degree. A full-time student can earn an MA in theology or biblical studies in about two years, counting the time it takes to write the thesis. At least, that's how it's done here."

"So you didn't share many classes with Mr. Lindsey?"

"No."

"What about socially?"

She shook her head. "Sorry." She paused. "Shall I call Dr. Poe now?"

Carmen gave a quick look to Bud. "Questions?"

He shook his head. "No questions for her."

She nodded to Missy. "Then yes, give him a call."

Ellis Poe squirmed in his seat. Having two detectives in his office made him uneasy. He tried to think of the last time someone other than students or faculty had invaded his space. Well, he knew of one reason for being ill at ease—a reason he didn't want to talk about.

"You keep it dark in here."

Ellis watched Detective Rainmondi smile with the comment. He stared at the woman, his heart flopping in his chest like a dying fish. His skin turned cold and clammy. His mind accepted the fact, but his heart refused to believe it.

"Was it something I said?" Carmen's words chilled the air.

"What? Um, no. I'm sorry. I just lost myself in thought. What did you say?"

"I said you keep it dark in here."

"I seldom use the overhead lights. I can turn them on if you like. It's just easier to focus on my work when the lights are dim. I'm weird that way."

"We're all a little weird in some way, Dr. Poe." The woman detective sat in the same chair Allen had used a few hours before. She seemed comfortable and in charge. Ellis wriggled in his seat and felt like a paper wrapper in the wind.

"I can't tell you how horrible I feel about all this." Ellis cleared his throat. "Over the years I've lost students to auto accidents and one to illness, but never murder. You're certain it's murder?"

"We're proceeding under that assumption." She paused and studied him. Ellis could almost feel her gaze crawling over his face. "I expected to see Dr. Dunne, but the receptionist said he went to visit Doug Lindsey's family."

"Yes, that's right. Can I offer you some coffee?"

The detective introduced as Bud Tock looked ready to say yes, but the woman waved him off. "No thanks. We were just at the Lindsey home and didn't see him."

"I'm not surprised. He told me he was going to pick up Loren first."

"Loren?"

"His wife. She's a doctor. It would take him some time to drive to the hospital in San Diego, pick her up, then drive to east county. Doug lived in La Mesa. But I guess you know that since you were just there."

"We know. Dr. Poe, do you know of anyone who would like to see Doug dead?"

The bluntness of the question made his heart stutter. "No. Doug was a good student and seemed well-liked."

"Had he ever been in a confrontation on campus?"

"No. Of course not. As I said, he was a fine student. Not top of his class or prone to higher academics, but a good student in his own right."

"Do you know if he used drugs or alcohol?"

"I suppose it's possible but not likely. I'd be very surprised if he involved himself in any of that. He studied to be a pastor."

"Pastors are human too."

"I won't argue with that, but I stand by my statement."

The woman detective nodded but looked unconvinced. "What about his sexual orientation?"

"That's enough!" Ellis couldn't help snapping at her. "Now you're being ridiculous."

"Why?"

"I imagine you deal with all sorts of unpleasantness in your job, Detective, but that doesn't mean that every victim of a crime has a substance abuse problem or is involved in some sexual misadventures."

"Misadventures?" A sardonic grin crossed her face. "I haven't heard that word in a long time."

"Doug did nothing or said nothing that would make me think that he was anything other than a sincere Christian looking to serve the church."

"There's no need to get defensive, Dr. Poe." Carmen's face grew stern, and it made Ellis shift in his chair. "You're right. We see a lot of unpleasantness—stuff that still curls my hair, which isn't easy to do. We have to ask these questions. It's part of the investigation."

"Still, you go too far."

"I haven't gone far enough. Your problem is that you confuse a question with an accusation. Knowing what young Mr. Lindsey wasn't involved in may be as important as what he was."

The chastisement landed like a velvet punch. "I'm sorry. I'm probably overreacting."

"No problem. It's good to see people stand up for one another. Now, I need to ask a few more questions."

Ellis nodded.

"When did you last see Mr. Lindsey?" The detective leaned back in the chair.

"Tuesday. Monday and Tuesday were exam days. The students have the rest of this week and all of next week off."

"Spring break?"

"We still call it 'Easter break.' Secular schools have migrated away from the religious titles. We're not so inclined."

"Of course. So you spoke to him two days ago?"

"I didn't really speak to him. He handed in a paper and wished me a happy Easter. That was it."

"Did he seem troubled? Worried?"

Ellis let his mind drift back in time. "No. I didn't sense anything unusual in his behavior."

"So he was a good student?"

"Better than most. As I said, higher academics weren't his forte, but his study skills were good and he was dedicated to doing well."

"And he wanted to be a minister?"

That they were using the past tense gnawed at Ellis. Every past participle stung. The detectives stared at him, waiting for his answer. They gave no sign of being disturbed. Another body, another murder—a routine day for them.

"Dr. Poe?"

Ellis forced himself back into the moment. "Yes. Students declare their intent when they enter the seminary. That information is shared with the professors. It helps us understand our students. Doug wanted to enter the pastorate."

"And his behavior was consistent with that goal?"

"As far as I could tell, yes. Look, Detective, if you're hoping that I can tell you I had concerns about him, or that he was a troublemaker, then you're going to be disappointed. Doug came to campus, did his work, seemed comfortable with the other students, and did nothing to raise a flag with me."

"So no disciplinary actions were ever taken?"

"None that I know of."

"Would you know if there had been?" Her expression never changed and it unnerved Ellis.

"If it were serious, I would have known. Word would have reached me from the administration or other professors."

"You shared information on your students?"

"Only if it might affect other instructors or their classes." Carmen Rainmondi looked disappointed. "I know it would make your life a lot easier if Doug had a history of trouble, but he doesn't. At least as far as I know. I wish I could be more helpful."

The woman stood. "We appreciate your time." She handed him a business card. "That's my office number and my cell number. If you think of anything that might help us in our investigation, then call."

Ellis said he would, then stood. The two detectives left, and Ellis returned to his desk chair and wondered who would want to kill a seminary student. Then his mind went where he knew it must . . .

How had Carmen Rainmondi reentered his life?

She hadn't recognized him. No surprise there. It had been nearly thirty years since their eyes last met. There had been no conversation, no dialog, no encounter . . .

Just two people standing on different borders of the same nightmare.

He leaned forward and lay his head on his desk, trying to lock the door to the cellar of his mind, but some beasts cannot be caged.

The image slipped to the forefront of his brain: the smoke, the overturned car, the wide-eyed, brutal, furious-insane driver, and the helpless woman. He could still smell the acrid scent of spilled gasoline on asphalt, of oily smoke. He could still see the overturned car, its tires spinning. And he could still hear the man's curses and the sounds—the aching, marrow-chilling, horrible sounds of him as he—

Alone in his office, Ellis plugged his ears with his fingers, a useless act against noises that came from within his own skull.

He saw it happen.

He saw what the killer did.

He watched a woman die and he did nothing.

Nothing.

A helpless woman's blue eyes had looked to him for help and found only a quivering, spineless, seventeen-year-old kid.

And now, twenty-eight years after the fact, he saw those blue eyes again—the same, yet different—as the detective sat before him asking questions about another murder.

Ellis began to weep into the silent room.

"You're kidding." Tock looked up from his desk. "Seems a little quick to me."

Carmen set the handset in the phone's cradle. "That was the man himself. He hasn't finished the autopsy, but he said there's something we should see."

Tock sighed and looked at his watch. "It's already after six and I promised to be home early."

"That's the surest way to guarantee you'll be stuck on overtime. How much more do you have on the book?" Carmen eyed the file Tock was working on. "The book" was verbal shorthand for the homicide file. She and Tock would add information as they worked the case.

"Not much. Maybe another ten or fifteen minutes."

"I'll swing by the ME's and fill you in tomorrow. Go home to your wife."

Tock looked conflicted. "Is this where I offer a weak and contrived objection?"

"Yes, and this is where I insist I don't mind, then leave you thinking what a wonderful partner I am."

"My wife and kids thank you."

An image of Tock's family flashed in Carmen's mind like a picture from an old slide projector: a blonde, thin woman in her mid-thirties, an equally blonde eight-year-old stepdaughter, and a dark-haired boy of four who already looked too much like his father. Carmen had been to their home on several occasions, usually at some party thrown by his gregarious wife. Tock had never told his wife about his and Carmen's short affair, and Carmen never felt compelled to fill in the blanks.

"Tell your wife I said, 'Hi.' You can also tell her she's too good for you."

"Thanks, but she already knows that."

Carmen forced a smile and left the office, fighting envy with every step.

She drove from downtown and up the I-15 to Clairemont Mesa Boulevard, exited to the west, and pushed through coagulating traffic until she arrived at the San Diego County Medical Examiner's office on Farmam Street. When she exited the Ford sedan, she noticed a small, private airplane banking on approach to Montgomery Field Airport a short distance away. For a moment she watched and wondered what it might be like to be able to fly to other cities on a whim.

Then she shook the daydream off and soon exchanged the sweet, evening spring air for the recycled, tainted air of the ME's offices.

After identifying herself and signing in, she pushed through the doors leading to the autopsy rooms in the back. Each visit she made to the building stirred up a stew of emotions. She always felt a small amount of apprehension, but she had grown used to the grisly sights found in the windowless rooms. Mostly, the ironic resemblance to a hospital teased her. Most people who enter a hospital leave in better shape than when they arrived. Not here. You came in dead and you left just as dead, and with a Y-shaped scar on your chest and detached rib cage.

No matter how clean the employees kept the facility, there remained a vague, haunting odor that reminded Carmen of cold, uncooked chicken.

She pushed through the doors that opened to the wide work area. The scene was familiar: a series of stainless steel tables lined one wall; at the head of each sat a sink. Horrible things drained into those basins every day. On each of the tables rested the unclothed form of what had once been a living person. The medical examiner's office investigated any unusual death. That included suicides, accidental deaths, sudden deaths, communicable disease, and environmentally related deaths. In the end, however, dead remained dead.

Dr. Norman Shuffler stood next to another ME, scrutinizing each move. Judging by the age difference, the senior Shuffler was guiding the younger man in the fine art of cutting corpses. Her eyes traced the scene and noticed that the nude body of her victim reclined on the nearest table as if patiently waiting his turn. She looked back at Shuffler, who pointed to something inside a woman's chest.

"Holding court again, Doc?"

Shuffler shifted his gaze. "Ah, there she is, heartthrob of the SDPD."

"Yeah, right. Heartthrob. That's me."

The ME said something to his protégé, rounded the autopsy table, and approached the lifeless form of Doug Lindsey. Shuffler wore green surgical garb, tennis shoes, and horn-rimmed glasses that looked like a leftover from four decades before. A tuft of white hair crept from beneath the cloth head covering that draped his dome.

Shuffler ranked high on the scale of Carmen's favorite people. He had a quick wit and ready smile. His blue eyes reflected a keen intelligence. Not the kind to rush to judgment, he had provided valuable information on many of Carmen's cases. She considered herself lucky when she drew him as the ME.

"You don't give yourself enough credit, Detective. Many men find you attractive." He stepped to the side of Doug Lindsey's body and gazed at it.

"Now you sound like my father. Whatcha got?" She moved closer to the metal table. Doug Lindsey seemed anything but serene. His pale skin looked more like rubber than human flesh. Eyes that would never blink again stared at the ceiling. The series of red puncture marks dotted his torso.

"I thought you'd want to see this before I opened him up. Everything is still preliminary, but you will find this interesting." He reached for a switch and a powerful overhead light came on, bathing the body in white illumination. "Of course, you've already noticed the puncture marks. They run from belt line to shoulders and, as you can see, cover his chest and face."

"Do you think that those wounds are the COD?"

He shook his head. "I have an early guess about the cause of death, but first I want you to notice the pattern."

Carmen leaned over the body, her face just a foot or two away. "They're uniform."

"Excellent." He pushed on one of the small holes near the deceased's navel. "You'll notice that the punctures are evenly spaced—about six millimeters between each two punctures—a quarter of an inch. The distance between the rows is about the same. Each wound is nine millimeters deep—call it three-eights of an inch."

"There must be a hundred or more holes in this guy's skin. That would take a long time to do."

"That's where you're wrong, Detective. It could be done in moments."

Carmen narrowed her eyes. "How can you know that?"

"Because I love pizza."

Carmen's mind seized. "What?"

"Surely you've seen someone make a pizza. It's quite the art. I worked my way through college slinging dough and dipping out pizza sauce."

"That's a part of your history I would never guess. I thought you came from the privileged class."

"I do, but my father believed his darling son should learn what it means to work for a buck. I had to pay for the first two years at the university. If I did well, he'd pay the last two years, as well as foot the bill for med school."

"Doesn't seem to have hurt you."

"I loved the old man for it. Built character. Well, I didn't love him the first two years of university, but I see the wisdom now. Anyway, part of the preparation for a great pizza is docking the dough."

"I don't follow."

"A dough docker is a tool that puts small holes in the bread. The dough is rolled out and spun to the right size; then the cook takes a tool that is nothing more than a nylon roller with small spikes and runs it over the dough. Then come the toppings."

"Someone ran a pizza-making tool over this guy? Why?"

"Ah, that I don't know. I just read bodies. It's your job to find bad guys and make sense of the clues." He pointed at a string of holes. "Notice that there's a small gap between this set of holes and the adjoining set. The roller you're looking for is about twelve-and-a-half centimeters wide."

"Twelve-and-a-half centimeters—"

"Five inches."

"Got it." Carmen studied the body. "Tell me something, Doc. Would the victim have to be still for the rows to be this even? I mean, three-eights of an inch isn't deep, but it had to hurt."

"'Hurt' doesn't cover it. It'd be excruciating."

"And you think you know how he died?"

"Look here." Shuffler moved to the dead man's head. "See his eyes?"

"Petechial hemorrhage." She shifted her gaze to the man's neck. "I don't see any bruises or marks to indicate strangulation."

"Petechial hemorrhage doesn't always indicate strangulation. When it appears in the eyes, it only indicates vascular congestion in the head that results in ruptured capillaries." He straightened. "Now here's where you rise up and call me a genius." He removed a magnifier with a light from a drawer and held it close to the victim's mouth. "Take a look."

Carmen took the device and again bent over the corpse. "Red bumps. Like a rash."

"Now here." He drew a finger along the jaw line.

"More of the same."

"Right. There are spots on his arms as well."

Carmen handed the magnifier back to Shuffler. "And just what am I to make of all of this? He had a rash when he died?"

"I know this rash." Shuffler returned the tool to the drawer. "I get it all the time."

"Do I want to hear this?"

"If you want to solve the case you do. I'm waiting on the blood work for verification, but I'd bet your next paycheck that our departed friend here has an allergy to latex."

"Latex? Like the gloves we wear?" Carmen knew of several officers who developed an annoying rash each time they donned latex gloves. She also knew of one crime-scene tech who had to quit because of the allergy. He was even allergic to the newer, non-latex material.

"Five- to ten-percent of health care workers have some degree of latex allergy. I'm one of them. I wear one-hundred-percent nitrile, powder-free gloves. If I don't, I'm up all night applying lotions and scratching like a flea-infested dog. I'm not fun to live with when I get that way."

"I didn't know that."

Shuffler grinned. "No need for you to. Latex comes from rubber trees in Africa and Southeast Asia. Some of us develop the allergy over time. Some patients who have exposure to latex because of repeated surgeries can develop the allergy."

"As uncomfortable as that sounds, I don't see how a skin allergy plays into this."

"Hang with me just another moment, Detective. Not all allergies are created equal. What I have is simple irritant-contact dermatitis. Annoying but not serious. On the dangerous end of the scale is latex hypersensitivity. Some people have such a serious response they go into anaphylactic shock."

"You mean like people who are allergic to bee stings."

"Exactly, except the causative agent is latex or some other rubber-based product. I'm betting he used to carry an Epipen of some sort."

"So he could give himself a dose of epinephrine if he needed to."

"Yes. And he needed to in the worst way."

"But someone kept him from reaching it."

The ME nodded. "That's how it looks now. I'll know more when the blood work is back and after I open him up. For now, it looks like someone held the young man down and held a latex glove over his mouth. Most gloves come with latex powder in them. Your victim inhaled some and suffocated shortly after—suffocated by his own body.

"A death that results from a felony is still murder. The death might not have been premeditated, but running a roller with pins in it over the body shows intent—sick intent."

Carmen stared at the body. "You'll get no argument from me."

5

May 4, 1985

The Saturday night seemed darker than usual, heavier with salty ocean air. The street lights along Grand Avenue in Pacific Beach pooled golden light on the asphalt and sidewalks of the beach community. Small shops and houses lined the streets. At an hour past midnight, most lights in buildings were off, but a few glowed in the bars and bungalow homes. Pacific Beach was an eclectic community, filled with young people who couldn't tolerate living more than a few miles from the ocean, and old surfers who had moved into town never to leave.

Ellis Poe saw the view on a regular basis. Several times a week—more often than he liked—he drove from the McDonald's on Garnett Street, to Grand to Balboa, to his home in East Clairemont—and usually did so in the wee hours of the day. Ellis had worked at the burger joint for the last two years, becoming a favored closer. When not exhausted, he was thankful for the late shift. First, it gave him time to do homework before making the fifteen-minute drive to the fast-food restaurant. Much of his shift was taken up with cleaning the grill, mopping the floor, sterilizing the milk-shake machine, and twenty other daily details required to close the place for the night. During those hours, Ellis could focus on his work without having to deal with patrons. Ellis liked people; he just didn't much like being *around* them.

There were exceptions of course. He wasn't a misanthrope. He just liked people he knew, and those in small numbers.

As Grand gave way to Balboa, Ellis let his mind run to the days ahead. A few more weeks of study and then final exams. Soon he'd leave behind the tedious high-school experience and move to the more challenging and, hopefully, mature college life. He wouldn't be going far. San Diego State University would be his collegiate home. He saw no need to leave his hometown. History majors were not judged by their choice of colleges, unlike science and engineering majors.

Ellis kept a light foot on the accelerator. He was in no hurry to get home. His parents would be long asleep. Dad went to bed at ten. Never later. Never sooner. Besides, the drive home was therapeutic. He could forget the pressure-filled work of cranking out burgers and fries and let his mind paint images of his future. His 1967 VW Beetle served as a decompression chamber. To his father, it was a collector's item, but then his father was a mechanic and any old thing with an engine was something to be adored.

Another thought rattled around in his mind as he drove onto Clairemont Mesa Boulevard: Jesus. Three days ago, that would have been an odd thought. Not that he was irreligious. He and his parents were regulars at a local Methodist church. Well, Easter and Christmas. They went to church when there was a need: funeral, wedding, baptism of a friend's child. He couldn't think of a time when one of his parents said on a Saturday night, "Let's go to church in the morning." There was always something else to do, or Dad was too tired from busting his knuckles on car engines.

Then, last week, something happened. Something unexpected. An ongoing conversation with an acquaintance at school turned into something more than jawing about history. He had had little time to think his decision through, something he hoped to do tomorrow. He had been invited to church and was certain he would go—

The headlights in his rearview mirror caught his attention, first because of how bright they were—some moron was driving with his high beams on—then by the speed at which they approached. The first fact annoyed him, but not unduly. At this time of night, local watering holes were disgorging their tipsy customers to swerve their way home. The second fact, however, alarmed him. It was one thing to be drunk and driving, but drunk and speeding was just an accident looking for the right spot to forever change lives.

The car swerved to the left, nearly impacting the concrete barrier that separated the two westbound lanes from Ellis's eastbound ones. Then it veered into the right lane—Ellis's lane.

Ellis pressed the accelerator of the VW Bug and the vehicle's four pistons increased their work. It wasn't enough. He was driving an old car up a persistent grade. The car had never been fast, and it wouldn't become so just because some joker felt he was immune to the quart of liquor he had consumed.

Ellis's heart pounded harder than the pistons he was begging to muscle the car up the hill faster.

The bright headlights grew in the rearview mirror.

"Come on, car."

The headlights moved back and forth in the lane, closing the distance. Each second brought it closer. Ellis cranked the wheel to the left, moving to the other lane, but the human-guided missile behind him did the same.

"You gotta be kidding!"

That's what Ellis wanted to say, but he only managed, "You gotta—!" before snapping the wheel to the right. The little vehicle responded, obediently skipping over the dashed white line that delineated the lanes. An eye-snap gaze at the rearview showed the trailing vehicle doing the same. Ellis doubted he would have time to change lanes again. The driver seemed intent on running him over, a coyote snatching a rabbit while on the run.

"Oh, God." It was only the second time Ellis had prayed.

Nothing but headlights in the mirrors—eye-stabbing glare. Ellis narrowed his eyes and then, at the last moment, veered to the shoulder of the road. A yellow streak passed him on the left, its left tires just a foot inside the other lane.

It jerked to the left as if the driver had just now seen Ellis's VW. The sudden motion turned the yellow muscle car sideways.

It hit the safety barrier with enough force to lift the tail end two feet in the air.

Ellis hit the breaks as the Camaro spun a half turn and rolled three times. Dust and bits of car flew in the air, reflecting Ellis's headlights. He kept his car as far right as possible as he slowed, then stopped. The sight of the new car resting on its top, its tires still spinning, turned Ellis's stomach and made his heart pound as if it were trying to shatter his sternum.

Then he saw movement near the front passenger window. He was out of his VW in a heartbeat.

His first steps were tentative. Images from movies and television shows of exploding cars strobed in his mind. Indeed, fuel dripped from the back of the car. Oil and antifreeze bled from the front. Bits of safety glass and shards of headlight glass and taillight plastic carpeted the black asphalt. These things he saw in the harsh rays of his headlight beams and the soft glow of a streetlight. Ivory light of a one-day-old full moon glistened in the car's fluid and fragments.

Although he tried not to let them, horror-movie images of what must remain of the passengers pushed to the front of his mind. Dare he look? Yes. He had too. It was the right thing to do, to see if by some miracle someone survived.

He had taken only two steps closer when a hand appeared in the shattered passenger side window. A delicate hand. A woman's hand with plum nail polish—a color he had seen before, but was too addled to remember where.

"He-help. Some . . . one . . . please."

The sound of a young woman's voice swept away his hesitation. Not even the sparking of something in the engine slowed him. Eight strides later, he reached the overturned Camaro and dropped to his knees. Bits of glass and pebbles of asphalt gouged up by the overturning car dug into his knees. Small pain, he figured, compared to what this poor woman was going through.

"Take it easy. Try not to move. Help is on the way." He had no idea if the last statement were true.

The hand was followed by a wrist, then a forearm. The skin was scratched and the arm shook. Blood covered much of it. Still, Ellis could see it belonged to a someone around his age. He bent and peered through the narrow opening, an opening made all the smaller by the car rolling over and over at high speed.

Very little light made it into the passenger area. Ellis could make out a form, blonde hair tinted pink by blood, and something twitching beyond. To get a better angle, he lay on the debris-populated asphalt. Pointed things stabbed at his bare arm and tried to press through the McDonald's uniform shirt.

"I have to get out. I have to get out!" Her voice wobbled with fear and wooziness. Her slurred speech made Ellis worry about a head wound. How could there *not* be a head wound?

"You need to remain still—"

The arm retracted. Then something dropped from the inverted seat. The woman had released her seat belt and fallen to the ceiling-now-floor of the car. She was coming out whether Ellis thought it was wise or not. Helping her might limit further injury. He didn't know. Working at McDonald's hadn't prepared him for a situation like this.

"Easy. Take it easy." Ellis smelled gasoline. He pushed to his knees.

He had no idea how she managed, but the passenger crawled on her belly through the opening, then pushed to her knees. Blood dripped from the tip of her nose, a nose that looked several degrees off straight. Her arms shook as if the air temperature hovered around freezing instead of in the fifties.

She looked up and Ellis gasped, first at the sight of the gash that ran from the hairline of her forehead to a quarter inch above her left eye. He could see wet, white skull peeking through the wound. Then he gasped again for another reason: he knew her. More than once in his high school career, Ellis had directed his gaze to the eighteen-year-old beauty. She never looked back. Bright, popular, the beauty of the senior class, she was the desire of every student with a Y-chromosome.

"Shelly?"

She tried to make eye contact. "I have to get out of here. Help . . . help me."

The car jostled. A deep groan emanated from the dark interior.

"Please." She held out a hand.

"I don't understand."

"He's crazy. Please."

None of it made sense, but the pleading in her voice did the impossible: making the urgent even more so. "How many people are in the car?"

"I have to leave. Please, please help me."

"Can you stand?"

The car wobbled on the roof again.

Ellis was out of his depth. He rose to his feet, bent, and set a hand on her shoulder. "Okay, but move slow. You're hurt—"

Something seized the back of his work shirt, yanking back with enough force to pull Ellis from his feet as if he weighed nothing. He stumbled back, landing on his rear. Pain ran from his tailbone to his neck. A man, wide in the shoulders with thick arms, hovered over Shelly.

He shouted at her, fire on his lips, his words rolling up the canyon walls.

The names he called her . . .

The fury he displayed . . .

The hatred in his wide eyes . . .

Shelly raised a hand. "Please, don't hurt me again."

"I *told* you! I told you not to mess with me. This is your fault. Your fault, you stupid—" He kicked her in the ribs, hard enough to lift her off the ground. She crumpled, her mouth open, gasping for air like a fish on a pier. The sight of the cruelty enraged Ellis. He scrambled to his feet.

"Hey!" Ellis charged.

It was a brave effort but short lived. The attacker spun, fire in his eyes, blood running from his mouth and nose. He looked demonic. Ellis hesitated. The man did not. The first punch caught Ellis square on the nose. Fiery pain filled his head. He had never been punched before, never felt such pain. Another punch landed just below his ribs sending the air pouring from his lungs. Ellis doubled over. More pain raced up his back as a granite-like fist slammed into the area over his right kidney. Colors flashed in his eyes. Three more punches. Ellis went down on his knees. Hard.

"When I finish with her, I'm coming after you."

Madness draped the assailant's face. What stood before Ellis was not a teenager, but a man long lost of his senses. A torturer. A killer.

Ellis sprinted to his car.

He never looked back.

After a night of sleepless hours, Ellis heard that the body of

Shelly Rainmondi, student at Madison High School, was found along the side of the road. The police estimated her speed to be close to eighty as she rounded the corner. A tragic accident. An unfortunate result of teenage foolishness.

Ellis knew better.

6

Friday, March 29, 2013

The sun showed up for work at 6:41. As it did each morning, it waged war with the giant fir tree that dominated the tiny front yard of Carmen's Mission Village bungalow home. The tree stood more than thirty-feet tall and had been planted by the home's first owners. That would have been in the early sixties. Carmen would have been a toddler back then, and her sister even younger. She closed her eyes and tried to force the image of Shelly from her mind. Shelly had been dead for going on three decades; shouldn't she be over it by now? No. Shelly traveled with her, lived with her, slept in the same bed, and occupied the same house, no matter where that house might be. Shelly was no ghost. She was worse: a persistent, vibrant memory that could touch each of Carmen's senses. Carmen could hear her laugh as a child and as a teenager who grew more restless and rebellious each day.

Carmen pulled her pillow over her face, a shield against the dim but unrelenting sunlight. A new day. Shelly loved sunrises more than sunsets. No matter how late she stayed out, she would rise early to watch the gold orb kick-start a new day. It drove Carmen crazy, then and now. Why leave a warm bed to watch something that happened every day? Carmen rose early only when her school schedule demanded it, or when she hadn't finished her homework the night before. Any time she did get up early, she often found her sister by the east-facing window in the living room, bathing in fresh sunlight.

That was a different house. That was a different time. That was a different life.

Every sunrise reminded Carmen of her brutally slain sister. Every day at her job she dealt with the families of murder victims, people who would forever associate a day of the week, a month, a place with their loss. The worst were those who lost loved ones on holidays. How do you celebrate Christmas when some lowlife chose that day to kill the center of your world?

Carmen rolled on her back. It was no use. She couldn't ignore that it was Friday. She pulled the pillow from her face and stared at a tan water stain that marred the spray on the "popcorn" ceiling. The house had a flat roof, something popular among mid-century subdivision builders, perhaps as a homage to Frank Lloyd Wright. At one time, the buyers considered the look modern. Today the style looked old and tired.

Just like Carmen felt. It was a good match.

She kicked the covers back, draped her legs over the side of the bed, and stared at her bare feet. The skin around the heels was dry and her toenails were bare. Every woman she knew painted her toenails. Carmen never painted anything on her body. She had makeup—somewhere in the house. Maybe below the bathroom sink. It didn't matter.

She pushed to her feet, feeling the carpet beneath her soles. The padding beneath the wall-to-wall carpet was little more than dust. The house needed new flooring. The thought first came to her five years ago. Why rush?

Clad only in a pair of white cotton underpants and a large, gray T-shirt, Carmen walked from the master bedroom of the two-bedroom, 1,200-square-foot house, and into the small kitchen. The walls were yellow, the top Formica, the cabinets oak. She spent the next five minutes getting her drip coffeemaker ready to brew some Yuban. She returned to the bedroom and the master bath, brushed her teeth, stripped, threw her clothes into the dirty clothes hamper and made for the shower. In this house, it took several minutes before the hot water could be coaxed from the water heater, through the pipes, and out the showerhead. She used the time to retrieve her cell phone—the only phone she had—and set it on the lid of the toilet tank.

The water continued to warm as she slipped beneath the silky cascade, its liquid fingers tracing her shoulders, arms, and back. One advantage to living alone: you could be a hot-water hog. Most days she looked forward to going to work, but there were days when staying home and nailing the door shut from the inside sounded good. Today was shaping up like that.

It wasn't the job. Being a cop proved more satisfying than she'd imagined; being a homicide detective was even better. Although a steady diet of cruelty, blood, guts, and violence took its toll. The gore was bad, but she'd been preparing herself for such sights since junior high school. Then, however, she was planning to be a doctor. She had it all figured out. She would work harder than anyone else, earn scholarships to college, and find a way into a prestigious medical school. It was all a matter of discipline and hard work.

Then Shelly was murdered.

That changed everything. It changed Carmen. It changed her thinking. It altered her values, and most of all, it changed her future. The murderer got away. The police seemed less interested than she thought they should be. Shelly fell through the cracks of justice. Carmen could think of only one way to fix all that: she'd become a cop herself. So she applied the same discipline and effort to making certain she would become one of San Diego's finest. She would help others the way her family should have been helped. That was the goal.

Too bad reality tempered the illusion.

She still worked her sister's case, not that there was much she could do on a twenty-eight-year-old cold case. That didn't keep her from fabricating scenarios in which she recognized some clue, some detail, heard some idle remark that opened the doors to justice again. If that ever happened, then she'd be ready.

She turned and faced the spray, dipping her head beneath it and letting her hair soak up the warm fluid. This was therapy. On the bad days, the days of depression and futility, she would shower until the water ran cold.

Amid the sound of water splashing on the shower pan at her feet, above the gentle roar of the showerhead, rose a sharp, electronic trilling. It sounded again before Carmen attached the sound to the source. She directed the shower's spray to the side, pulled back the shower curtain. The light of the smart phone blazed.

"Figures." She shook the water from her hands and reached for the phone. Bud Tock's number. She tapped *answer* and placed the phone to the side of her head, pulling her soggy hair back from her ear. "Yeah."

"Yeah? Really? That's how you answer the phone these days? Yeah?"

"Um, yeah."

"There it is again. Listen, something has come up . . . What is that noise?"

"Water. You caught me in the shower." There was a pause. "Careful what you say next, Bud, or the first thing I do when I get to the station is shoot you in the foot."

"That, Detective, would be assault with a deadly weapon."

She could hear his smile. "I'll claim it was an accidental discharge. Everyone will believe me and think you deserve it."

"That so? Okay. You're probably right."

"I'm always right. So what's up? I'm not due in for another hour or so."

"I came in early to see what you did with the jacket last night. The captain was here. We got another body and since I was already here . . ."

"That'll teach you to show initiative. Where?"

"Corner of College Avenue and Cresita Drive." He gave her the address. "White house. Fence and hedge block much of the house from the street. I'm sure I'll get there before you. Bring a couple of Egg McMuffins, will ya?"

"Nope. You're watching your weight."

"No, I'm not."

"You should. Everyone else is."

"Funny. Now get out of the shower."

When Carmen pulled her police-issued black sedan to the curb, she saw three patrol cars, the crime-scene van, and Bud Tock's vehicle. Yellow crime-scene tape stretched across the driveway and front walk.

Dressed in her usual detective garb—a pair of black slacks, a gray blouse, and black blazer—she waved her badge at the officer guarding the driveway and walk. He nodded. Since she had seen this officer many times, the badge flash was unnecessary, but she did it anyway. The uniform pointed to the southern part of the property.

"Thanks." Carmen ducked under the tape barrier then heard a familiar voice.

"Over here, Detective."

Bud Tock stood a short distance from the front door and stared at the base of a tree that ruled the corner of the front yard.

"Whatcha got, Bud?"

"Male, Caucasian, thirty-three according to his driver's license. Take a look. And, for the record, I no longer want the Egg McMuffins."

That didn't sound promising. Carmen followed Bud's motion and made her way to a mound covered by a tarp. No question what made up the mound. She pulled a pair of latex gloves from her pocket and donned them; then she bent, took a corner of the tarp, and pulled it back. Women on the police force often feel the need to hold back emotions. At least Carmen did. She had developed the habit of stuffing fear and repulsion into a dark corner of her mind, saving them until she could deal with them in private. This sight, however, tested that determination.

Her first instinct was to drop the tarp.

Her second, to vomit.

She did neither. Instead, she crouched and studied the mangled flesh more closely. The sound of footsteps approaching strengthened her determination to maintain composure.

"Quite a mess."

She answered Bud without looking at him. "Well, I see what took away your appetite."

"It takes a lot to do that these days. Maybe I'm just getting old." He took a deep breath.

"No doubt about that. Help me get this thing off. I need to see the big picture."

They removed the covering. The victim lay on his back, both eyes open—but his left eye socket was crushed, leaving the eyeball staring at what had once been a nose. His jaw hung loose, broken in several places. Carmen could see several holes in the man's left check where his teeth had forced through the skin. The autopsy would give the detailed report, but Carmen could make out other injuries: right arm rested at an angle that indicated at least one break; collar bone looked busted too. The man wore a white shirt, and in several spots blood soaked through—although no holes or slices to indicate bullet or knife wounds. Both legs appeared broken.

"Tell me the guy was hit by a bus."

"I don't think so." Bud took another deep breath. "My guess is someone, or someones—maybe a gang—beat him to death."

"Was anyone home to hear the beating? It had to be noisy."

"The whole family was home. They heard nothing."

She snapped her gaze to Bud. "How can that be? Several men beating another isn't the quietest thing. What are they, old and deaf?"

"Nope. Young family. I think the body was dumped here."

Carmen looked back at the body. "Why would anyone beat a man to death then cart him to another location and offload the corpse? Seems risky. College Avenue is four lanes of constant activity."

"The fence might be one reason. Once on the property, it's impossible to be seen from the street, but I think it's more than that. I think it's a hate crime."

Carmen and Bud covered the body again. "You're going to have to explain that one to me, partner."

"Our vic is one David Cohen."

"Jewish? There are a lot of Jews in San Diego, Bud. Let's hear the rest of it."

"This property is owned by Beth Shalom Synagogue. The guy who lives here is the congregation's rabbi."

"Oh, I see what you mean. Does he know the vic?"

"I haven't told him who it is yet, so I don't know. Wanted you here first. You're good at judging reactions."

"Okay, give me a few minutes to look around. Then we'll cut the techs loose to do their thing. We can interview the rabbi then."

"Gotcha."

7

Rabbi Joel Singer was younger than Carmen figured. She'd expected an old man with a gray beard and a large black hat. What she got was a man in his mid-thirties, with curly black hair, a thin, short beard, and piercing eyes. He was dressed in khaki pants and a dark, long-sleeved shirt. Nikes clad his feet. She guessed him to be close to six feet tall, maybe taller on days when there wasn't a battered body left in his front yard.

The inside of the house was clean and simple. No art on the white walls. The furniture looked less than two or three years old, the carpet was clean. A sofa with cloth, flower-print upholstery sat next to the rear wall of the living room, occupied by a lovely woman with shoulder-length brown hair and brown eyes tinted red and swollen from the flood of tears they held back. To her right sat a girl whom Carmen estimated to be six years old, and snuggled under the woman's left arm sat a dark-haired boy who would no doubt break many hearts when he got older.

She chastised herself for the last thought. The kid looked frightened out of his mind.

Had the parents told the children about the body, or were they just picking up the fear from mom and dad? Police cars on the street and strangers milling around the house would certainly have started a stream of questions, the kind only young children could ask. Carmen smiled at the children.

Bud Tock took the lead. "Rabbi, this is my partner Detective Carmen Rainmondi. We need to have a word with you and your wife, if we may."

The children inched closer to their mother.

"I don't think my children should be left alone at the moment, and I don't want them to hear what we have to talk about. This has been very frightening for them—for us."

"Yes, sir, but—"

Carmen cut Bud off. "We can chat with them individually." She stepped to the children and crouched in front of them. "Hi. I'm Detective Carmen." She looked at the little girl first. "What's your name, darling?"

The child looked at her mother. Mom nodded.

"Neria. It means 'Light of the Lord.'"

"That's beautiful. Neria. I like that." Carmen faced the boy. "How about you, champ? What's your name?"

Like his sister, he looked to his mother for permission and got the same nod. "Aviel."

"Aviel. It's a strong name."

The boy smiled. "It means 'The Lord is my father.'"

"Nice. Listen kids, I need to talk to your dad here for a little bit. You know, grown-up talk. Do you mind waiting in another room? Your mother can go with you."

The woman rose. "Come, children."

Carmen pushed to her feet and wondered when getting up from a kneeling position required a grunt. "May I have your name, ma'am?"

"Naomi. Naomi Singer." She didn't bother to say what the name meant. Instead, she led the children down a hall.

Carmen moved to Rabbi Singer. He motioned to the dining room. Like the living room, the space faced the front yard. Also like the living room, the window shades had been drawn. Carmen couldn't blame him. They sat around a simple wood table stained by craftsmen to look like walnut. They sat. "I can make some coffee if you like."

"No, thank you, sir." Bud took the lead, as Carmen had expected. Her job was to listen and watch. "How did you come to find the body, Rabbi?"

"It's in my front yard; how could I not find it?"

Bud smiled. He wielded a smile that could calm an angry, starving bear.

Singer lowered his head for a moment. "Sorry. I'm a little shaken."

"I imagine you are, Rabbi. I've been in this business longer than I care to admit, and this has put me a little off my game. Start from the beginning."

"I rose early. I usually do. It's quieter then, if you know what I mean."

"I know, Rabbi. I've got kids at home. Boy and a girl. Eight and four. They can make more noise than a room full of monkeys."

Singer smiled at the image. "Anyway. I'm the rabbi at Beth Shalom. I guess I already told you that."

"No problem, sir. My partner hasn't heard any of this. You said earlier you were going to the synagogue. Why?"

"I wanted to pick up a couple of books. It's Pesach and I wanted a few things for my sermon."

"Pesach?" Bud tilted his head.

"Passover." Singer rested his hands on the table. "It's one of the high holidays. An eight-day celebration of the deliverance of the children of Israel from Egypt. The first two and last two days of the Pesach are . . ." He seemed to search for a term that his Gentile visitors would understand. ". . . non-work days. Only work that has to do with health and welfare can be done. Well, that and worship. The days in between allow for more kinds of work. Today is one of those days."

"And you were going to walk?" Bud put his hands on the table, mirroring the rabbi.

"Yes, sir. I almost always walk. It isn't far. Just a few blocks."

"Go on."

Carmen took notes in a small pad. It was old school, but still the easiest way to record comments and observations.

"It was about six. My wife and children were still in bed. I went out the front door and locked it behind me. I was, maybe, three steps from the front stoop when I saw . . ." He directed his gaze to the table. "When I saw the body. It was . . ." His face went white, and for a moment Carmen thought the rabbi would take a header onto the wood flooring of the dining room.

"Take your time, Rabbi." Bud leaned back, and as was often the case in interviews, the subject leaned back too. "I know it had to be quite a shock."

"Shock? The word doesn't begin to cover it. I almost fainted. I don't think I've ever fainted, but that—that just about did the job."

"Then what did you do? Did you go to the body?"

He shook his head. "Should I have done that? I mean, he looked dead to me. Really dead. I've seen lots of dead bodies, but nothing like that."

"Wait a minute." Bud held up a hand. "You've seen a lot of dead bodies? You were in the military?"

"No, I meant—" Singer inhaled deeply, slowly. "It is Jewish custom that family or someone from the synagogue sit with a body until it is buried. It is a sign of respect. I am a rabbi, the son of a rabbi who was the son of a rabbi. I have sat with many corpses."

"I see," Bud said. Carmen wasn't sure she did. Bud pressed on. "You told me earlier that neither you nor your wife heard anything during the night?"

"Nothing, Detective."

"What time did you go to bed?"

Singer thought for a moment. "The children were in bed by 8:30. We retire early. Usually by ten."

"That was true for last night?"

"Yes. I read for about half an hour after that, then went to sleep. I heard nothing. I asked the children if they heard anything last night. They said no. Was he killed in our yard?"

Bud shrugged. "Too early to say, Rabbi. The forensic team is just getting started. Still, I doubt it. He was beaten so badly that you would have heard the struggle, unless you had the television turned up."

Singer blanched. “We didn’t watch television last night. We don’t watch it much. News mostly. Never developed the addiction.”

That was an odd phrase.

“How long . . . I mean . . . before the body is moved?”

“It will be a little while, Rabbi. Sorry. We can’t move the body until we have the whole scene photographed, searched, and documented.”

“I was hoping to get the family out for a while. You know, put some distance between them and”—he motioned to the front yard—“that.”

“I understand.” Bud shifted in his chair. “Is there a back door? Another way to the street?”

“No. There’s a fence all the way around the property.”

“I see. Well, we will be as fast as we can, but it will take some time before we can release the scene. I wish we could do more.”

“You’ve been very kind, Detective. Please let me know once the coroner arrives.”

“Medical examiner,” Bud corrected. “Of course. I have a few more questions, sir. Have you or the people at your synagogue experienced hate crimes of late?”

Again, Singer shook his head. “No, the neighborhood is very respectable. Oh sure, occasionally we hear a slur or there will be a bit of graffiti, but nothing serious. Why do you ask?”

Before Bud could answer, a light went on in the rabbi’s mind. Carmen could almost see his eyes glowing.

“Wait. Are you saying . . . the victim is a Jew?” His blinking increased and his jaw went slack.

"We found identification on the victim. Do you know a David Cohen?"

"*Baruch dayan emet.*" Rabbi Singer pushed back from the table. His hands shook.

"Excuse me?" Bud leaned over the table as if his gaze could fix Singer to his chair.

"It can't be. Not David."

He pronounced the name "*Da-veed.*"

"So you know him?"

"Yes, David is our cantor."

"Cantor? What's a cantor?"

"It's a position in the synagogue. A cantor leads the congregation and music. I-I must go to the body." He stood.

"Wait a minute, Rabbi. We're not quite done."

"Naomi!" Singer's voice roared through the house.

Bud was on his feet and standing between the rabbi and the front door before Carmen could scoot her chair back. "Rabbi, just wait. We don't know it's the same person. David Cohen is a common name."

Singer, who had been slack-jawed and pale a moment before stood with teeth clinched and red-faced. "In *this* neighborhood? Near our synagogue? On my property?"

Naomi appeared in the living room without the children. "What? What is it?"

"Call the *chevra kadisha.*"

"Oh no." She raised her hands to her mouth.

"David Cohen. David . . ." The rest of the words failed to launch.

"*Baruch dayan emet.*"

What did that mean?

Singer spun to face Bud. "I must stay with the body."

"I can't let you do that, sir."

"You can't stop me."

Bud stiffened. "Actually—"

"Bud!" Carmen stood, then approached the two. "Rabbi, you may stay near the body, but you may not touch it, or interfere with our team. Is that clear?"

"There are traditions to be upheld."

"Sir . . ." Carmen lowered her voice. "Rabbi, you can do nothing for the man from a holding cell. I know your traditions are important, but so is catching the person or persons who did this. Do you agree?"

"Yes, but we must prepare his body for burial."

Carmen didn't break eye contact. "Rabbi, there will be an autopsy."

"We bury as soon as possible. Usually within a day."

"Not this time, Rabbi. You must let us do our work. We'll do our best to accommodate your beliefs, but some things are not negotiable. Clear?"

He said yes but didn't seem happy about it. Naomi had come to his side. Carmen let a few moments pass then looked to Bud. "Let's get a uniform to stand with the rabbi so he doesn't accidentally contaminate the scene or interfere with chain of evidence. How's that sound?"

"Fine by me." Tock said.

"You okay with that, Rabbi?" Carmen smiled.

"Yes, I'm sorry. I'm just in shock."

"Who wouldn't be? We'll make sure you can stay near the body, but we have to be careful about our investigation. Understood?"

"Yes." He stepped to a bookcase and removed a black book. "Can we go now?"

"Sure." Carmen addressed Bud. "I'll be out in a second."

"Gotcha."

Once the men had left, Carmen had a question for Naomi. "What was that you said?"

"What I said?"

"Yes. Your husband said it too. Said it when he learned the victim was Jewish. "*Baruch* something something."

"*Baruch dayan emet*. It means, 'Blessed be the one true Judge.' It's something Jews say when they hear about the death of another Jew."

With that, Naomi broke into tears. Carmen had seen such sorrow many times.

It never got easy.

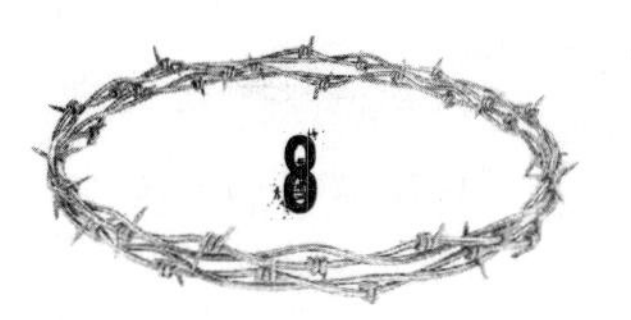

8

Carmen left the rabbi's wife to comfort her children who had, as only children can do, adopted the grief of their parents. Seeing one's mother in tears was unsettling no matter the age of the child. The rabbi's children were very young, unable to understand what had happened, but they knew their mother was beside herself.

As Carmen exited the house she heard the little girl say, "Don't cry, Mommy. It will be okay."

Carmen wished that were true. Such violence committed on the doorstep left wounds that never healed. Carmen knew that for a fact. Tunnel vision was a horrible thing for the eyes, but it could do a world of good for the mind. Focus on the work. Block out anything not related to the investigation. Facts. Evidence. Logic. Careful procedures. Those things mattered. Everything else was a distraction. Think like a laser, not a spotlight. That was her philosophy.

Pity it seldom worked.

Before the door closed behind her, images of her own mother's hysterical weeping washed forward in her mind. A uniformed officer had come to their door late in the night to deliver the news of the tragic auto accident. He looked suitably sad, expressed his regret at the news, and said detectives would be by to ask questions.

The officer left.

The night darkened. Carmen's mother went from weeping in the front yard to screaming. It took Carmen and her father fifteen minutes to get her back into the house. She cried for a full week. Shelly had died on Clairemont Mesa Boulevard; Carmen's mom died that night in a small home in East Clairemont. Not physically. She lived many years longer, but her heart, her spirit, perished that night.

It took a moment for Carmen to realize she had stopped walking. The buzz of a gathering crowd, the drone of slow-moving traffic on a busy College Avenue, a blend of voices hung about her head, waiting for attention.

She raised her eyes and took in the scene. Two uniformed officers stood just on the other side of the yellow police ribbon. A small crowd had gathered, and she recognized reporters from a local radio news station and two television stations. The officers stood tall with shoulders back, beefed up by their bulletproof vests, which made them look thicker and more powerful than they were.

Bud was leaning over the body again. The rabbi stood near by, never moving from the spot Bud had assigned him. No doubt Bud had made it clear that a few careless steps could ruin an investigation and therefore a prosecution. Carmen started Bud's direction but stopped when she saw motion at the barricade. A tall, dapper man in a dark gray suit was pushing through the crowd. He stopped and spoke to the uniforms. Hanging from the man's suit coat pocket was a SDPD badge. He smiled and one of the officers chuckled. Then the unthinkable happened: the man stepped to the yellow tape and lifted it. He was about to enter the crime scene.

"Hold it, Chief!" Carmen raised her voice enough to stop Assistant Police Chief Barry "Butch" Claymore in his tracks.

Carmen hustled his way, doing her best to show no emotion. The emotion she felt, she didn't want to express to the force's newest assistant police chief.

"Morning, Detective Rainmondi." At least he knew her name. She wasn't sure that was a good thing.

"Good morning Assistant Chief. How may I help you?"

"Just doing my job, Detective. Word is spreading about the—let's call it *unique situation*—of the murder. I thought I'd take a quick look." He reached for the barricade again. Carmen stepped in front of him. The two patrolmen moved a few steps to the side, no doubt putting distance between them and what might become a war.

"I'm sorry, Chief, but protocol demands I limit the number of people trafficking the scene."

His smile dissolved. "Do I need to remind you that I outrank you, Detective?"

"No, sir. I congratulate you on your promotion. I'm certain your leadership will be a big boost to the department."

"Are you being sarcastic, Rainmondi?"

"No, sir. I just can't let you on the scene. Rank has nothing to do with it. Protecting the evidence on scene does."

"I've been a cop for twenty-five years, Rainmondi. I know how a crime scene works. I spent many years as a detective."

"Yes, sir. Your personnel jacket is full of awards. I read your bio when you were promoted, but . . ."

"But what, Detective?"

This is where it could all go south. "Forgive me, sir, but you didn't come up through homicide."

"What difference does that make? Never mind, step aside."

"I'm sorry, sir, but I can't."

"Now I know why they call you the Ice Queen." He lifted the barricade and started to duck beneath it.

"Hello, Chief." The voice came from an ebony-skinned man about Carmen's age who sported a shiny head and the build of a redwood tree. He wore a blue suit that must have cost a good two hundred bucks less than the one Claymore wore.

"Finally, someone with a lick of sense. Your detective seems to think I'm too stupid to know how to treat a crime scene. You may want to think about having a disciplinary talk with her."

Captain Ulysses Darrel Simmons was Carmen's immediate superior. He was a by-the-book man who spoke with a James Earl Jones voice. No one called him Ulysses. Ever. It was Darrel or Simmons or Captain. Uttering the "U" name could lead to the dirtiest duty in homicide.

"She's doing her job, Chief. If she had let you in, I would have kicked her fanny all the way to the Mexican border."

"Don't tell me I need to remind *you* of my position—"

"Let's not go there, Chief. Every year, guys like me have to explain why some other cop contaminated a scene. I'm sure you know your way around an investigation, sir, but I drill the principles of scene discipline into my people. If they screw up, they pay for it big time."

"I told Rainmondi I could have her badge. I can have yours, too."

"With all due respect, sir, I don't think you can. If you want to follow that course of action, you are free to do so, but we can't let you in. If it's any comfort to you, I spend more time on this side of the barricade than on that side. At least until the detectives declare it clear."

"Maybe I should talk to the chief." Claymore's face had grown another shade of red.

"Certainly, sir, but just so you know, I have kept him off scenes, too."

Claymore sighed loudly. "When will it be clear?"

Captain Simmons made eye contact with Carmen.

"It's gonna be a while, sir. Detective Tock and I have to finish our first examination. The techs are just getting started. Once they're done, then you can look around."

Claymore opened his mouth to speak but closed it a moment later. Without a word, he turned and left.

Carmen forced a smile. "So should I polish my resume?"

"Nah. He's just trying on his big-boy pants. If he complains, the chief will smack him down a notch. Trust me, he knows how to do that."

Carmen had heard about Captain Simmons's toe-to-toe with the chief. The rest of the details were kept between the two men.

"Thanks for bailing me out. I was pretty sure he would knock me down to make his point."

Simmons shook his head. "He's a bit annoying at times, but he's a good cop. He's also a good politician. Knocking a fellow officer down would look bad. Besides, I'm not sure he could pull it off." He looked into the yard. "Whatcha got?"

"White male. Clothed. Bud found the man's wallet. Name is David Cohen."

"COD?"

"Unofficially, cause of death is beating. He's been worked big time. Of course, we'll let the ME pin it down."

"Whose the civilian?" He nodded to the rabbi.

"Rabbi Joel Singer. The vic was his cantor. A cantor is—"

"I know what a cantor is. What's your take on him?"

Carmen shrugged. "Grief seems genuine. His first concern was to be with the body."

"Jews like to do that. Grew up on a street with several Jewish families. Always treated me good. I assume the uniform is there to keep the man in one place."

"Yes, sir."

"I also assume you explained that his friend won't be buried right away."

"Yes, he seems to understand. Doesn't like it, but he understands."

Simmons put his hands into this pants pockets. "Look, I know you already have a fresh case, but the flu is going around. We're down several detectives. Since you and Bud have got things underway . . ."

"We'll take it, Cap. No problem." *Sleep is for the weak.*

"Right. No problem. I'll help as much as I can. Whatcha need?"

"You could have someone run down the info for the vic. Address. Place of work. You know the drill. I also need these people moved back a few blocks. We think he was dumped here. If so, then we don't have the event scene. The perp may have left clues on the street or sidewalk. Unfortunately, the place is well traveled. Maybe trace can narrow it down for us."

"Okay. What else?"

"You can get some of the uniforms to canvas the block and see if anyone heard or saw anything. They could search for video cameras."

"Will do. Keep me posted. Anything new on our Balboa Park vic?"

"Bizarre death. Seminary kid. He was studying to be a preacher." She reiterated the first report from the ME.

"A dough docker. I thought I'd seen everything. Apparently not. Keep me posted." He started to turn, then stopped and gazed at her for a moment. "Good job, Detective." He walked to a uniformed officer with three stripes on his sleeve and pointed up and down the street as he spoke.

Carmen turned back to the crime scene. This was going to be a long day.

Good Friday. A special day. A day to be remembered. Not necessarily a day of celebration.

Dr. Ellis Poe sat in the cramped confines of his Canadian Sailcraft yacht, sipping coffee and thinking about the day. *Yacht.* The word made him smile. Before inheriting the small craft from an uncle, Ellis thought the word applied only to large craft worth millions of dollars. His 1977, 27-footer was hardly worth seven grand these days. It didn't matter. He had no intention of selling it or using it to impress anyone. The white craft with purple trim seldom left its mooring just off Coronado. He had been overjoyed to receive it and loved the boat most days. On those days when he had to fork over what little money he had for maintenance, marina, and anchorage fees, he loved the boat less.

Poe wasn't much of a sailor. On occasion, he would fire up the Yanmar diesel and motor into the bay, do a few laps, then return and tie up. He avoided open ocean, where the swells could rise and give him more of a ride than he wanted. Still, he kept the *Blushing Bride*. He considered changing the name, but that seemed disrespectful to the man who left the craft to Ellis.

In braver moments, he considered sailing alone to Catalina. He would daydream about it. So far, he had only made the journey in his mind. He had traveled to Catalina Island on one of the ferries. Each time he had to fight seasickness. Better to let the *Blushing Bride* stay in the calm waters of San Diego Bay.

Where some sailors used their boats for adventure and family outings, Ellis used it as a sanctuary, a place to hide from the crush of humanity that made up San Diego. He came here to be alone. He spent his weekdays in a condo in Escondido. He spent those days alone too, but the boat provided something different: a tiny hideaway. He also enjoyed the culture of those who lived on boats. Many were antisocial. No one ever came knocking on the fiberglass hull to ask for a cup of flour.

Ellis rubbed his face and tried to concentrate on the work before him. Not work really. Work implied drudgery. Translating the events that Christians revered as Good Friday brought him satisfaction. Nothing better than losing one's self in the Koine Greek of the New Testament.

Good Friday. Such an odd name for a day set aside to remember the suffering, torture, and murder of Jesus. Scholars debated how the term came to be. Some thought it was a variation of "God's Friday" and the title had changed over the centuries. Perhaps. Ellis thought different. *Good*, in this context, meant *holy, special, unique*.

Good Friday had been celebrated from the fourth century on, probably much longer. The fourth-century Archbishop Ambrose described it as "a day of bitterness on which we fast." Many contemporary Christian holidays got their start a few centuries after the events they celebrated. Some came about as a response to pagan holidays. Easter, although clearly a Christian celebration, still carried the name of the goddess Estare and used pagan symbols such as eggs and rabbits. Not so, Good Friday. It was purely Christian and one of the most poignant times in a believer's life.

Ellis set his coffee cup down and listened to the gentle slapping of water against the fiberglass hull. He had his weekend planned. Most of it involved reading. The seminary was closed in observance of the religious holiday but would open for a few hours for the community Good Friday service. He would take his little skiff to the marina pier, retrieve his car from the parking lot, find a decent restaurant—maybe The Coronado Brewery—then make the drive to Escondido. The last part would take at least half an hour, probably more, depending on traffic. It was Friday. Traffic was guaranteed to be thick and sluggish.

He returned his attention to the Gospel parallels in front of him. It was an older book. There were newer versions of such books. The Gospel parallels laid three of the four Gospels into columns, allowing an easy comparison. John, the fourth Gospel, was included in a column of its own. Since it took a different approach to the telling of Jesus' life and repeated little of what the others had, it had to stand alone. Next to the book was the Greek text he was using for translation.

Determined to make better headway than he had since rising this morning, he focused on the texts, but once again his mind wandered. He had made the same translation every year for the last two decades. It should be easy, but attention undulated like the water around his boat. He had endured two shocks yesterday: news that one of his students had been murdered, and the appearance of Carmen Rainmondi in his office. She didn't recognize him.

For that he was thankful.

Of course there was no reason for her to know him. He had never been to her home. Shelly Rainmondi knew his name, but he couldn't conceive of any reason why she would talk about him to his sister. His fascination with her had been one chained by distance and silence. He wanted to ask her out. Every high school boy wanted to date her. Truth was, he wouldn't have recognized Carmen. He had seen her at school, of course, but they shared no classes. He couldn't recall ever exchanging a word with her. Carmen was a year ahead of Ellis. Theirs were different worlds.

He did, however, recognize the name. *Rainmondi* was not a common name, and after . . .

He had to force away the image of an overturned car . . . the echoes of her pleas for help . . . the violence . . . the pain of the punch he endured . . .

And. His. Cowardice.

Ellis slammed his eyes shut. He wanted to purge himself of the sight, rid himself of nightmares. Forgive himself and know God had forgiven him. His theology told him he was forgiven. He could cite chapter and verse, one after the other, but the feeling of forgiveness never came. For a man of his beliefs, the absence of peace was troubling.

If self-forgiveness were a requirement before God could forgive, then Ellis was doomed. He reminded himself that there was no theology behind the fear.

Fear didn't care.

The usual lunch crowd at Jimmy Chen's Authentic Mexican Cuisine had thinned. Of course, lunchtime had begun three hours before and ended two hours later. The large clock with the image of a cold, frothy Budweiser on it showed ten minutes past three. Carmen hadn't eaten breakfast or lunch, and a sharp-toothed gnawing in her gut reminded her of the fact. That, and a growing sensation of low blood sugar: headache and the feeling that her internal organs were vibrating.

Chen's place was a popular spot in North Park, especially with police. James Chen—once Sergeant Chen of robbery division before a bullet in the hip changed his career path—ran a clean place with an eclectic menu of oriental, Italian, and Southwest food. Cops from all over San Diego County came in, at first to support a wounded comrade, then because he served food worth far more money than he charged. It was a cop restaurant. Like a cop bar that catered to police, Chen's was a safe place where uniformed officers and detectives could let their hair down and not be on. The brass never came in. They understood this was a working cop's place and respected it. Most of them had been in many times before getting kicked upstairs.

Chen had been a better-than-average officer, but he was a better restauranteur, one who knew his clientele and their needs. That meant keeping a back room, one away from the noise and questioning eyes of others. Detectives could discuss cases without other ears listening in.

Carmen and Bud hadn't taken two steps into the place before Chen met them. He limped from behind the counter and into the main dining area, a wide and long space with painted and sealed concrete for its floor. Most of the space looked as if it had been transplanted from Tijuana, across the border, but with art from Asia. The checkered tablecloths gave the place the feel of an Italian bistro. The decor shouldn't work, but somehow it did.

"Late lunch, guys?"

"Yep," Bud said. "Such is the life of the best cops on the force."

Chen grinned. "You're the fourth person today to claim that title."

"Posers, Jimmy. Nothing but posers." Bud slapped him on the shoulder. "You got anything in the vault?"

"I think I can squeeze you in." Chen led them through the near empty front dining area and through a doorless hole in the wall. The room was smaller than the front, holding only six tables. A row of windows on the west side of the room overlooked a narrow garden. Chen's wife was a gardener and nagged Chen into putting in the verdant strip. Something about the "salubrious powers of a simple planter." Chen admitted to having to use a dictionary to look up *salubrious*.

"What's it gonna be?" He sat them at a table next to the windows. A fence blocked out sight of the rest of the world.

"Enchiladas for me." Carmen sat and set a notepad on the table. "Chicken. Green sauce."

Bud sat opposite her. "Tacos, Jimmy. Beef. Let's go with the pinto beans."

"No, you don't, pal. Bring him anything but beans, Jimmy. I gotta spend a lot of time in the car with this guy."

"Hey, you're my partner, not my wife."

Carmen let the corners of her mouth lift. "She'd say the same thing." She shifted her attention to Chen again. "No beans, Jimmy. And remember. I carry a gun."

"So do I," Bud said.

Jimmy chuckled. "True, but she knows how to use hers. No beans."

Bud shook his head. "I get no respect."

"Would you like to know why?" Carmen leaned closer to the table.

"No."

Chen laughed and left. He returned a moment later with two glasses of water, a glass of tea for Carmen and Coke for Bud. He left the room. Carmen sipped the tea, eager for the caffeine.

A few moments of silence passed as Carmen let the hardened cop veneer dissolve. Bud broke the silence.

"Claymore really used the phrase 'Ice Queen'?"

"He did."

"Why didn't you shoot him?"

"It crossed my mind." Carmen sipped her tea. "Besides, it doesn't bother me. He's not the first to call me that. He won't be the last."

Bud's lips tightened into a line. "Of course it bothers you. It bothers me. You could file a complaint."

Carmen huffed. "That might put a dent in my career. I complain about him, and the other assistant chiefs will be waiting for me to do the same to them. Before you know it, I'll be working traffic accidents."

"They wouldn't do that."

"Okay, *you* file a complaint."

"No way. You think I'm crazy?" He laughed.

She joined him. The bit of humor felt good, like a brain massage. "Captain Simmons came to my rescue."

"He's a good man. I have no problem following his lead. He should be assistant chief."

"Then we might have Claymore as our captain."

Bud looked as if he had been chewing a lemon rind. "Nah, he's never worked homicide. He made his name in narcotics."

"Stranger things have happened."

"True that." He lifted his soda. Condensation dripped from the base and splattered on the table top.

"So why do they do it?" Carmen studied the red-and-white pattern of the tablecloth.

"Do what?"

She waved a hand. "It doesn't matter."

"Sure it does. Spill it or I'll make Jimmy bring a double portion of frijoles."

"That's a terrifying thought. Okay, but only because I'm trying to protect the city from your digestive system. Why do they call me 'Ice Queen'?" She leaned back. "I have an idea, but . . ."

"You never asked before."

"I shouldn't be asking now. Knowing doesn't change anything."

"What do you do after your shift?"

"I go home just like everyone else."

Bud shook his head and lowered his voice. "That's it, Carmen. We don't all go home. We pal around. Not a lot, but from time to time, we hit a bar, catch a Padre or Charger game, do a barbecue on the beach. You go home. Always. You did so when you were in uniform. Being a detective hasn't changed that. You come across as aloof."

"Aloof? I am aloof. I'm a loner, Bud. You know that. You know me better than anyone else on the force."

He nodded. "That's why I can say this to you. People like you, but they don't know how to deal with your . . . idiosyncrasies. You've never married. You live alone. You never hang with the crew. You do your job, then go home. People think you have a superiority complex."

"Wow, aloof, idiosyncrasies, and superiority complex. You been going to night school?"

"And there it is, Carmen. First, I have a college degree, so don't act like I just barely got out of high school, and second, stop sidestepping the topic. You brought it up."

She sighed. "I'm not a social butterfly, Bud. I never have been. You know that. We went out a few times. You know what I'm like."

"I do. I know you're usually the smartest person in any room. I also know you have some dark ghosts haunting you. I'm not saying you need to change. I'm just trying to answer your question in a way that won't get me beat up."

Carmen grinned. "I wouldn't beat you, Bud. Not for long anyway." She paused. "Thanks for the honesty. I doubt I will change anything. To quote the famous philosopher Popeye the Sailor, 'I yam what I yam.'" She opened the notebook. "Okay, let's go over this. What do we know?"

Bud opened his own small notebook. It might be the twenty-first century, but note taking at a crime scene was still done faster and better with pen and paper. Besides, having to type the notes into the official report often opened doors to new thoughts.

Bud read from his notes. "Vic is David Cohen, a thirty-three-year-old white male with a wife and three children. Identification was made by ID in his wallet. The wallet contained four credit cards, and eighty-two dollars in cash, indicating robbery was not a motive. Victim was found supine and clothed. No indication that his clothing had been removed or altered prior to or after his death."

"Meaning a sexual attack is doubtful at this point." When Carmen joined the police department she had thought sexual attacks only occurred to women and children. The Academy changed that notion quickly.

"Right, but we leave it on the table for now." Bud flipped a page. "Vic was found in the front yard of Rabbi Joel Singer. We interviewed the rabbi, and he admitted to knowing the vic but had not seen him for a few days. Field exam suggests the vic is a victim of a severe beating, perhaps a crime of passion. Injuries visible to the naked eye indicate he has many broken bones. ME will provide the details on that."

Carmen nodded. "There is reason to doubt the primary crime scene is the initial scene, meaning the body was transported from the murder scene to the rabbi's home. Why do that? Hate crime. The rabbi has an enemy?"

Bud shrugged. "If the perp has more than two brain cells and any experience with cops, he's gotta know that we'd dismiss the rabbi as a direct suspect from the get-go."

"What makes you think it was a guy. You don't think a woman can do that?"

"Sorry, no, I don't. I suppose if she used a baseball bat, but I'll bet my car that the vic was beat to death with fist and foot. Besides, a bruise on the side of the vic's neck looks like a fist mark. A big fist. It's too early to say it was a man or men, but this kind of physical violence by a woman would be rare. Women are far more crafty."

"You got that right."

She studied her notes, although she had already committed them to memory. It kept her from looking at Bud. She wouldn't admit it, but the "Ice Queen" discussion stung. "ME estimates death occurred at two or three this morning. Interviews of homes in the area gave us zilch, and there are no security cameras directed at the rabbi's house, driveway, or yard."

"Do you think the perp knew that?"

"Yep, I do and that scares me."

Bud raised an eyebrow. "I didn't think anything scared you."

"Plenty frightens me; I just don't admit it often. Nothing scares me more than a smart killer. You know how it is: most murders are not planned; those that are, are planned badly."

"Contract killing?

She shrugged. "Maybe, but you heard the guy's wife. He didn't have enemies, wasn't involved in anything illegal." One of the most difficult things Carmen faced in her work was extracting information from family members who had just learned their loved one was never coming home. It was one thing when a spouse keeled over from an aneurism or heart attack, or bought the farm in an auto accident. Knowing that someone went out of their way to murder their loved one conjured up all kinds of visuals and pain.

To make matters worse she had to ask the grieving family upsetting questions like: "Was your husband involved in any illegal activity? Did your husband use drugs? Did he have a gambling problem? Has he always been faithful to you? Did he have enemies? Did he ever mention being threatened? How was your marriage? Was it happy?" On and on. They had to ask, but that didn't mean it was easy. In most cases, anger at the killer was redirected to the investigating officer.

"That doesn't mean he wasn't involved in something he shouldn't be in. It wouldn't be the first time a religious person had been doing irreligious things."

"I know. My gut tells me otherwise." She tapped the table with her finger. "Let me ask this: Do you think the two murders are related?"

"Doubtful. They're very different, although I'll admit two whacked-out killings in two days has alarms going off."

"I know what you're saying, but let me float this across the table." She held up a finger. "First, both vics are related to religious groups." She held up a second finger. "Both were killed someplace then the body dumped somewhere else." Another finger. "Both are men." Finger four. "Both died in an unusual way—one as a pin cushion, the other by a vicious beating."

"We've seen other murders by beating."

"Like this? This guy was pounded on for some time. Okay, I'm guessing here, but I'm thinking the pounding took place over time, stretched out to make it worse. I can't prove that yet."

"My turn. There are differences." Bud held up a finger, mimicking Carmen. "One, there's an age difference of nearly fifteen years; one is a Christian seminary student, the other is a Jewish cantor in a large synagogue; one was found in Balboa Park, the other in the front yard of a home in the College district."

"Yeah, but . . ."

"But what?"

Carmen pursed her lips. "I got nothing but a feeling."

"I don't say you're wrong, but it's a tad early to be chasing what-ifs."

"I know. Okay, after lunch—or whatever this meal is—I say we go back and run traces on their cell phones. I also want to get permission to search their browser history. I'll ask for a warrant if I need to."

"You want to stay teamed up on this or split the load?"

"Let's keep things as they are. You still have a few things to learn."

"I do? I think I've been at this longer than you."

Carmen grinned. "True, but men tend to be slow learners."

"Female chauvinist."

"Here we are." Chen's voice wafted across the room. It was something he did in the Vault. He knew the need for privacy so announced his arrival to give his patrons a chance to change the subject. He set the plates in front of the two.

There were beans on Bud's plate.

10

Ellis Poe's drive from Glorietta Bay on Coronado and up the I-15 to Escondido took longer than usual. The distance wasn't great, just about thirty-five miles, depending on which set of freeways he chose. The problem was the time and day. It was Good Friday, and workers whose day had just ended were jockeying for any position that might get them home—or to the bar or restaurant or party—five minutes faster.

Driving in rush hour in a county of three million people could be daunting. For some drivers it was maddening, but not for Ellis. He long ago learned to take such things in stride. No one won the traffic wars. All a person could do was inflict—or suffer—damage. Better to use the drive as an opportunity to think. As those around him lost their patience and expressed themselves with rude hand gestures and curses, Ellis chose the more noble position: the slow lane.

The spring sun inched its way down the western sky, slowly approaching the horizon. It'd taken on that orange hue, the testimony to the smog and pollutants that hung in the moist ocean air. Overhead, what had been a pristine azure sky had darkened to a slate gray decorated with strips of salmon red clouds. Lights burned in business buildings and shops. It was twilight time in San Diego . . . the perfect match for twilight time in Ellis's heart.

Ellis was a man prone to depression, and he spent no time trying to convince himself otherwise. He accepted the disorder as part of his nature—and his penance. His depression came on its own schedule. Sometimes he woke with a love of life and a keen desire to be about his work. Then it would begin: the darkness, tangible, viscous like oil, percolated up from the center of his being. It spread slowly, leisurely. Over the years he had come to recognize the sensation that heralded the darkness. He knew its every whim, its every path. At times it settled on him like a black fog descending from the sky, filling first the room, then his mind, then his heart. There was little he could do about it, and he had long since given up trying. For a time he considered seeing a doctor. There was medication he could take, chemicals that would keep the ebony mists away, but he always dismissed the idea. His depression was part of him. It helped define him. He took no joy in it, but he accepted it. When it came, he simply acknowledged its existence and continued with his work.

His work. His work was his anchor, his compass, his balm. It was the only medication he needed, the only one he wanted. He was a man of faith and prayer, but in his most honest hours, he had to admit that he needed more than prayer to keep himself sane.

The traffic on the I-15 thinned as he put distance between

himself and the heart of the city. Still, it coagulated at each of the major communities. Not one to listen to music, he made the trip in silence. At times he listened to an audio book. His brain was a ravenous beast that liked to be fed. Tonight though, it was well mannered, letting him think of spiritual things.

Would he have been happier in a more High-Church environment, with its rituals and structure, its creeds and dictates? Such structure was enticing, and while it might fit his temperament, it didn't match his doctrine. The gospel is simple and direct, and he tried to match his life to that pattern. He was intelligent, kind, and fractured. Centuries ago, he would have been a prime candidate for a monastery.

The miles rolled beneath the wheels of his silver Honda Civic, past Kearney Mesa and on north. The clot of cars continued to thin, freeing the asphalt artery to higher speeds. Ellis didn't care. He had plenty of time. He planned to arrive early and spend a half hour or so in his office. It was as much home to him as his condo in Escondido, or his small sailboat that seldom sailed. There were few places where Ellis felt whole and welcome. His office was one such place.

When he pulled onto the property of San Diego Theological Seminary, he saw few cars. Only three. The Good Friday Service was still an hour away. Two of the cars belonged to members of the janitorial staff, who were no doubt cleaning up the worship center. The other belonged to seminary president Dr. Adam Bridger. Bridger was the closest thing Ellis had to a friend. A former pastor, like several of the faculty, Bridger was a man of letters. Unlike Ellis, he was also a man of the people. He loved to be in crowds, something that gave Ellis hives. Like Alan Dunne, the academic dean, his wife was a surgeon.

As he parked, he thought about the difficult task facing Bridger. He had led a community-wide Good Friday service for the last ten years. Normally, it was a joyful time despite the somber remembrance. Today, though, he would have to address the death of Doug Lindsey. Ellis knew that both Dunn and Bridger had visited the family. That had to be rough. He tried not to feel grateful that the job hadn't fallen to him.

Ellis walked through the thickening twilight and made his way to his office.

His depression followed on his heels.

Carmen had spent very little time in the office. She had been called before her shift was to start, and now it was looking as if she would be digging into the overtime coffers of the SDPD's budget. Good for her bank account. Not so good for her stiff neck and growing indigestion. After she and her partner had a three o'clock "lunch," they returned to canvasing the area, speaking to neighbors. She and Bud interviewed Rabbi Singer again. They also ran background checks on Singer, the vic Cohen, and even members of the rabbi's and cantor's families. Not one appeared in the criminal database. Not one had had a traffic ticket in five years. Not even a parking ticket. Spooky.

Based on that and her ability to judge a person by body language, eye contact, nervousness—none of which would be admissible in court—she held high confidence that these people were on the up and up. Just like young Doug Lindsey.

Bud made good sense when he countered her suggestion that the two murders might be connected. She didn't believe it when she brought the idea up, but sometimes thinking out of the homicide box yielded unexpected results. Maybe the thought of chasing one brutal killer was more acceptable than tracking down two.

Her cell phone sounded and she answered. The caller ID revealed the caller. "Dr. Shuffler, did you call to ask me out for a Friday night dinner?"

His chuckle was drenched in weariness. "You know, I would except for two things."

"Uh oh, here it comes."

"I'm having trouble getting away from work these days. It seems a certain homicide detective keeps sending dead bodies over."

She leaned back in her chair and rubbed her eyes with her free hand. "You prefer flowers maybe?"

"A man of my sensitivity can appreciate flowers. They're certainly better than this mess." The hollowness of his tone told her he was calling from the autopsy area.

"What's the second reason for not treating your favorite detective to a steak?"

"If I start dating again, my wife would put me on one of these slabs."

"That would be awkward. At least it would be an easy case to solve." She paused to be polite, then, "You got something for me?"

"Pretty straightforward. Mr. Cohen died from a severe beating. Obvious, I know, but I'm making it official . . . well, official in a preliminary way. There's still toxicology, but that will take some time and I doubt it will change my opinion about COD."

Carmen straightened and grabbed a notepad and pen. "Let me have it."

"First the ugly part. The beating was protracted. Judging by the amount of bleeding into tissue, and the extent of bruising, the guy's heart kept beating long after the attack began. All but two of his ribs were broken. Both arms were pulled out of joint and both sides of his pelvis—the iliac crests—were broken. I can see evidence of a boot print—and before you ask, I can't get a great image of it. I've taken photos. Maybe you can run down the brand, but I doubt it. That'll be your call. Both patellas have been crushed."

"His kneecaps?"

"Yep, just like in those old gangster movies. Three fractures in the left leg, consistent with kicking; two in the right. When I opened him up, I found severe damage to both kidneys."

"And he was alive through all this?"

"Yes, I haven't got to the COD yet. Markings on his wrist and underlying tissue damage indicate his wrists were bound. The skin damage at the site indicates that the victim was strung up by his wrists. Probably explains the dislocated shoulders. It is logical to assume that he was beaten while hanging there."

"Someone used the guy as a punching bag?" The mental image made Carmen's stomach constrict.

"There might be more than one offender. My early examination doesn't reveal that, and I doubt anything I do will tell us if you're dealing with one nut job or several." He exhaled. The man wasn't young anymore, not that a younger man would have endured any better. "I do have a little something for you: the size of the killer's fist. It's big. Heavyweight-boxer big. Knock-a-train-off-the-tracks big. I don't know who the guy is, but you may want to shoot him a few times before you question him."

"Gladly. So what do you think the cause of death is?"

"Crushed larynx. I could be wrong, but I'm pretty sure. The last blow was a wicked punch to the throat, hard enough to crush the laryngeal prominence."

"The Adam's Apple."

"Yes, ma'am. The blow was hard enough to crush the larynx."

Carmen searched for words but none came. Apparently, Shuffler ran low too. The image of a man hanging by his wrists while at least one person pounded on him before delivering a blow that would cause the man to suffocate unnerved her, and it took a lot to do that.

"Bud there with you?" Bud was the first detective on the scene so he got to observe the autopsy.

"Yes, he's still here. Do you want to talk to him?"

"Not unless he has something to add." She heard Shuffler relay the question. "He says no. Frankly, he looks a little off his feed."

"I told him not to have the beans." A second later: "Let me ask something, Doc. Do you think Cohen and Lindsey could have been killed by the same guy?"

"Detective Tock said you were thinking along those lines. At first, I said the idea was ridiculous. Now, I'm not so sure. I have nothing to link them. Lindsey was killed by an anaphylactic response to latex, and an instrument of torture was used on him. I have no trace evidence to suggest that anything other than fists and booted feet were used on this guy."

"But certainly Cohen's death involved torture."

"No arguing that. Still, I can't link them. That being said, it doesn't mean they're not related."

"Okay, thanks, Doc. I look forward to your report and the photos."

"Detective, when you find who ever did this to Cohen, promise me . . . promise you'll arrest him real hard."

"I'll do it, Doc." She hung up. The last time she had heard Shuffler say anything like that was about a brutal murder of a child, and Carmen solved the case and arrested the murderer hard—hospital hard.

Dr. Adam Bridger brought a simple but powerful message. He always did. He was the students' favorite chapel speaker. Although it would be considered unprofessional to say so, Ellis knew the faculty felt the same way.

Bridger, a man of average looks and height, and above-average intelligence, spoke in even tones, more teacher than preacher. He also spoke from personal conviction. He believed what he said; he lived what he taught. His text was drawn from Genesis. Those not familiar with the Bible might think it odd that the seminary president would preach from an Old Testament book instead of the New Testament. The record of Christ's crucifixion was found in the Gospels, but prophecies and allusions to it could be found in several places in the thirty-nine books of the Old Testament.

"Genesis 22 holds an account that makes me furious." Bridger had let the statement land with force. "I cannot read it without a sense of outrage boiling in my gut. God asks for a human sacrifice. Not only that, He demands that His chosen man—Abraham—cut the throat of his only son, the son of divine promise. When I think of Abraham and Isaac crossing the distance from their home to Mount Moriah, the future site of Solomon's temple, I ache for them. What thoughts ran through Abraham's mind? What fears? Imagine the heartbreak. And what of the young man Isaac, who makes the journey with only one question: 'Where is the sacrifice we are to make to the Lord?' My anger grows when Abraham states that God will provide the sacrifice."

Bridger took hold of the pulpit as if he needed to be steadied. "There the scene unfolds. The kindling and wood are laid for the fire to burn the sacrifice. Who set up that altar? Isaac, the one who would be asked to crawl on the wood arranged to burn his flesh to ashes. My fury mounts. At some point Isaac realizes what is being asked of him and based on his father's requests, lays himself on the mound of kindling."

Bridger took a step back, and the emotion in his voice moved Ellis. When Bridger stepped forward again, he leaned closer to the microphone. "Then it comes. The moment when the elderly Abraham lays the sharp edge of his knife to his own son's throat. Did he let it linger? Did his hand shake? Did he close his eyes?

"The muscles in his back and shoulders and arm tense, ready to draw the blade and split Isaac's throat. Isaac, the son he longed for, prayed for, hoped for." He straightened. "Isaac didn't protest. We have no record of him begging for his life or making any attempt to escape. He could have gotten away. He was young; Abraham was old. If Isaac had chosen to fight, Abraham would not have had a chance. Isaac didn't fight back. His father was a man who spoke to God and if this was what God demanded, then he would not resist."

Bridger inhaled deeply. "Then the knife began to move. Only then did God stop Abraham." He nodded. "Furious. Angry. No other passage makes me want to shake my fist in God's face. 'How could you?' I want to cry. `What kind of God does that?'"

He let the questions float in the air. Ellis knew the answer, but the account never failed to move him.

"I'll tell you what kind of God does that: the kind of God who would ask the same thing of Himself. Except for Him, there was no one to stop His hand. Jesus is God the Father's Isaac.

"Do I have a right to feel angry over the passage?" He shrugged. "I think so, but I also have a responsibility to remember that it was God who made that kind of sacrifice for us. We are supposed to be angry about this injustice. We are supposed to be furious about the sacrifice Abraham was called on to make. It is the sacrifice of Good Friday. Jesus went to the cross willingly. He did so for us, and it was no easier for God to see than it was for Abraham. Our life came from Jesus' death. We celebrate Easter—Resurrection Day—but we grieve on Good Friday. The cartoon character Charlie Brown used to say, 'Good grief.' There is a good grief if that grief achieves an eternal difference. We do not have Easter without Good Friday. Out of death came life . . ."

The last phrase echoed in Ellis's mind. Would any good come out of the murder of one of their students? Could anything good come out of the brutal killing of Shelly Rainmondi?

If so, Ellis couldn't see it.

Carmen's late lunch had worn off several hours before. Her head was beginning to ache and her stomach grumbled. She snagged a granola bar from the goody machine and a cup of black fluid she hoped was coffee. She had just taken a bite of the bar when Bud walked into the open detective's area. He carried a polystyrene food container and placed it on her desk. He also set down a folder of material he had retrieved from the ME.

"What's this?"

"A deli sandwich and some chips."

"What kinda sandwich?"

Bud lifted an eyebrow. "What? Now you're getting picky?"

"No, but how do you know I haven't gone out and had dinner?" She opened the container. Ham and turkey on rye. It looked wonderful.

"Because I know you." He pulled a chair close to her desk, a metal contraption that could double for a bomb shelter. "You are a creature of inertia."

"Inertia. You know I love it when you talk all sciency and stuff." She batted her eyes.

"I'm serious. Can't get you out of the house, can't get you to leave a crime scene, can't pry you out of the office. You're a difficult woman to move."

She bit into the sandwich. Perfect. Much better than a six-month old granola bar. "Took you longer to get back from the ME than I thought it would."

"He's a little upset about the nature of the crime. You'd think a man who has seen what he has wouldn't let such things bother him."

"It was especially brutal." Carmen spoke around the food in her mouth.

"That's a fact. You just saw the outsides. His innards were a mess. Blood in the lungs, liver perforated, spleen damaged, broken bones . . . well, you heard that part."

Carmen opened the file and was greeted by a photo of the deceased with his chest cut open. More disturbing was the damage done to the face. Had the man lived, he would have had to endure a number of reconstructive surgeries. She hoped Jews believed in closed-casket funerals. She chewed her food and glanced at the other material in the folder.

"I got copies of the X-rays because I wanted you to see this. I've been thinking about it on the drive back. This is a crime of passion. This man wasn't killed in anger. Doc thinks it was a protracted beating. It was torture. Look." He picked up a print of the digital X-ray.

Carmen saw a rib cage that looked as if someone had taken a baseball bat to the man's chest. "Any trace?"

"Not on the body. We looked for wood fragments . . . we looked for everything. Doc is a thorough man. I was in the room when he called you, so I know he mentioned the fist imprint. A monster fist. We're looking for a brute. King Kong's little brother. Look at the ribs. See how they're busted up? Doc thinks the perp strung the guy up and went all heavy weight on him."

"He told me that."

"What he didn't tell you was the thought that went into the beating. You may want to put your sandwich down for this."

"I can take it."

"Suit yourself. Here's what we think happened. Black Hat abducts the vic, subdues him, maybe knocks him out with a blow or maybe sedates him somehow. Tox will tell us that. Anyway, the guy is hanging by his wrists, arms over head, exposing the rib cage. Our guy starts his workout, first punching the torso in such a way that the ribs snap. There's no indication that he used any blunt instrument other than his fist. But he's not done, see. He then starts aiming at what are now free-floating ribs."

"Why would . . . oh." Carmen set her sandwich down. "You're telling me this guy was trying to drive rib fragments into the vic's lungs?"

"And liver. The guy flailed the chest. He pounded on the sternum so it cut into the liver. So the vic begins to hemorrhage."

"That's sick."

"There's more. Look at this." Bud pulled another X-ray from the folder. This one showed two busted up legs. He then pulled photos of the victim's bare legs. He pointed at several spots on the photo. "See these bruises?"

"The short stripes? I see them."

"Notice the roundish bruise above it. Notice anything weird?"

"No—wait. The skin is broken at one of the stripes."

"Look closer and you'll see that's true for two of the marks. Now, this is where you jump up and sing my praises. The short, rectangular strips are from the protruding sole of a work boot. The semi-round bruises are from the steel toe of the boot."

"You're guessing." Carmen was impressed. "But it's a great guess."

"Great? It's brilliant! We can't prove it—yet, but I think it's on the money."

"So the killer pounds the body with his fists then changes it up to break the victim's legs by repeatedly kicking him?"

"You got it. Leg bones are thick and tough. Aside from using a blunt instrument, they're hard to break by a simple punch."

"Okay, this guy is sick. Really twisted. No wonder Doc is so put out."

"He's a sensitive guy. The vic isn't some gangster who gets beat to death for cheating on his drug delivery. Cohen is an average Joe. No criminal record. Family man. Religious. Well thought of. He didn't deserve this, unless you found something in the background."

"No. I've looked at his cell phone records. Nothing is jumping off the page. In fact, he barely used the thing. I guess he's one of those who carried a cell phone for emergencies or so his family can reach him. That's it. It's not even a smart phone. Can't get bank records until tomorrow, but I doubt they'll show anything. It's possible he's a white-collar criminal, but I won't put any money on it."

"Me either. Anything new on the seminary kid?"

"Nah. Same thing. Clean as bottled water. His phone records are boring. Haven't traced every number yet, but the ones I've done all lead to family and a movie database. The kid liked the flicks."

"So what we have are two nobodies."

"That's one more thing they have in common."

Bud chuckled.

"Here we go again. I don't see any connection. Innocent, nice people get off all the time. Just because these two murders happen within a day of each other means nothing."

"If we were talking gunshot deaths, or murders committed during a crime, then I'd be with you, but two bizarre murders in a row? I don't know, Bud. It doesn't seem right."

"Suspicious minds make for great detectives, but you've got a way to go to convince your good-looking partner."

"True, but have I convinced you?"

"I just said—oh, I see. Having a little fun with ol' Bud, eh? See if I ever bring you a sandwich again."

Carmen's cell phone rang. She answered then said, "Where?" A second later: "Got it. On my way." She stood. "Come on, Genius. They found a car that might be related to the Cohen case."

"Outstanding. This is much better than going home and being with the family."

"Is that sarcasm I hear? You know you love this."

Bud huffed. "I bet I'll enjoy retirement better."

They started from the room, but Carmen stopped suddenly. "Wait." She fast-stepped back to her desk and grabbed her sandwich.

12

Few outside the Force knew it, but many clues leading to the solving of a murder come from the beat cop—the guy or gal in uniform keeping peace on the streets. While the job of collecting and processing clues in a murder fell to the homicide detectives, much of the legwork was done by uniforms and techs. It might take a village to rear a child, but it took a team to solve a murder. Once again, a sharp-eyed patrol officer had found something that might prove helpful.

Officer Joe Heywood was tall and thick and built like an old Ford truck. His brown hair was cut military short, a reminder that he had once been an Army Ranger. He was quick with a smile but had the reputation of being able to intimidate an approaching bullet. He was also a bit of an enigma. In his off time he liked to read popular books about theoretical physics. When Carmen first met him—her last year as a patrol officer and his first year in uniform—she had joked about it: "Having trouble sleeping?"

It had been a mistake, one that forced her to endure fifteen minutes of "quantum entanglement" and "M-theory." She still had no idea what Heywood had said, but he did teach her not to bring up the subject again.

Carmen left the Crown Vic a dozen yards from the suspect car, ducked beneath crime tape, and approached. Heywood had cordoned off the alley. His patrol car served as a barricade on one side. Another officer stood near it, as did one on the opposite end.

Heywood was doing everything right.

As Carmen walked the narrow lane, she took in everything. They were in an alley behind a strip mall at the edge of Mission Valley. Yellow light from nearby high-pressure sodium street lamps, and the back-porch lights next to the rear doors of the shops in the center, cast eerie illumination on the scene.

Carmen and Bud scanned the ground as they approached, looking for anything that might be important.

"Hey, Joe."

"Detectives. You made good time."

Bud shrugged. "It's nine o'clock. The sane people are home watching television."

He grinned. "What's that make us?"

"Protectors of all that is good and right," Bud said. "Whatcha got?"

"Doing routine patrol. There have been several break-ins at this complex. Some of the stores are still open, but some close at eight. I've had to run off kids before. They like to hang back here, smoke, and avoid responsibility."

"Don't be bitter, Joe. They're the future of our country."

"We're doomed." The corner of his mouth tipped up.

"Anyway, I found the car here. You can see the 'no parking' signs. Delivery people can't get their trucks down here if anyone parks in the alley. I also noticed the cargo door was popped. So I thought I'd take a look."

"And?" Carmen studied the vehicle. It was an old Dodge Caravan, blue, and had seen better days.

"I approached. No driver. No passenger. Engine was cold. Since the back was partially open I had cause to look. Someone could have been sleeping or hurt back there."

Carmen nodded. It was as good a reason as any to look inside a car without a warrant.

Heywood moved closer to the back of the car and, with a gloved hand, used a finger to lift the door, revealing the cargo area of the minivan. He then shone the beam of his MAGLITE on the carpet-like cover over the base of the area. It was blue with a large dark stain at one end and several smaller stains to the right. Carmen got a whiff of something sour and rank: fresh blood, urine, and feces. She added the beam of her small Streamlight flashlight, which she had removed from the SDPD windbreaker she wore.

"I'll get the kit." Bud walked back to the Crown Vic. He returned a moment later and set the plastic kit, which looked like a fisherman's tackle-box, on the ground. He removed a small spray bottle and a cotton swab on a long stick, dabbed at the largest stain, then took a step away from the vehicle. A spritz of Luminol and the business end of the swab began to glow blue. The chemical reacted to the iron in hemoglobin. The glow faded within thirty seconds.

"Yep, blood."

Carmen nodded at her partner, then leaned in closer. "There's a dip in the deck. Looks like whatever left the blood was dropped in place, breaking the fiberboard beneath."

"I noticed that, too." No arrogance in Heywood's words. "I ran the plates, and they belong to a 2005 Caddy owned by an elderly couple in Rancho Bernardo. Their car was reported missing two weeks ago."

"I may not be the brightest crayon in the box, but I'm pretty sure this isn't a Cadillac." Bud bagged the swab and closed the kit.

"No arguing about either statement," Carmen said.

"Hey!"

Carmen smiled at Heywood. "Poor guy suffers from insecurity."

Heywood returned the smile with a courtesy grin that said he recognized the attempt at humor, but it didn't deserve a real laugh. "The Caddy was recovered three days later in Otay Mesa. Obviously, the plates were missing."

"Obviously." Carmen directed her light to the ground around the vehicle.

"I found one boot print near the driver's side door. There's a good bit of dust there. After I saw the blood, I withdrew, cordoned off the alley, and called you."

"Good man." Carmen continued to look around. "You used the same path for egress and ingress?"

"Yes. The same one I led you down. No other officers have been within twenty feet of the vehicle."

"What about shop employees? Talk to any of them?" Bud stood with the kit in his hand.

"Yes, sir. Most of the places are closed. There's a small Italian hole-in-the-wall. After I had the alley secured and officers at each end, I chatted up the manager. He said the van had been here since he arrived at three this afternoon. He called the day manager, and she said she saw the vehicle when she opened."

"What time did she start work?" Carmen asked.

"Ten. They open at eleven. She helps set up the kitchen for the lunch rush."

"You got their names?" Carmen started to walk around the Dodge, directing her flashlight in front of her and along the driver's side.

"Yes."

Bud followed Carmen. "Good. What about registration? We know who owns the plates but not the van."

"No, sir. Once I saw the blood I stopped touching things."

"I may need to have you speak with Assistant Police Chief Claymore." Carmen looked in the driver's side window. The interior was neat.

"Yes, ma'am. Um, why?"

"Because I think you could teach him a few things." Carmen moved to the front of the van. The years had taken their toll on the paint and grill. Spots and smears of bug carcasses decorated the exterior. "It's been awhile since this thing has seen any soap and water."

"Reminds me of my former partner," Bud said.

"Cute. You better not be saying things like that about me."

"Never." Bud's playful attitude was one of the ways he dealt with the soul-crushing nature of his work. "I say other things about you."

Carmen returned to the driver's door and used her gloved hand to open it. She looked at the sunshade over the steering wheel. It had a holder for the DMV registration. She pulled down on the shade and noticed two things: one, the registration was missing; two, it had been replaced by a simple typewritten note:

THAT'S TWO

She responded with a string of hot curses.

"That was an excellent sermon, Adam." Ellis Poe sat in a booth in Denny's restaurant. Across from him sat Dr. Adam Bridger and his wife, Dr. Rachel Bridger. Ellis was a bit formal and would never call the president of the seminary by his first name if a student was in earshot, and he certainly wouldn't do so on seminary grounds. This, however, was a neutral place.

"Thank you, Ellis. I'm glad you could join us. I never get to spend as much time with our key faculty as I would like." Bridger took a bite of a tuna fish sandwich. He confessed that through his two decades of ministry he had never been able to eat before speaking. It started when he was in seminary, and he had never been able to solve the problem, so he always postponed eating.

"I don't know how you have time to do what you do."

Rachel sat next to Adam, drinking a cup of decaf. "He's always been an ace at multitasking. I think he works in his sleep."

"Doesn't everyone?" Bridger said.

"No, honey, we mere humans sleep to rest, perchance to dream."

Rachel was in her fifties but still had the radiance of a much younger woman. She was smart, funny, and had a spine of steel—something Ellis assumed came with her job as a surgeon. One couldn't dip both hands into a person's abdomen or chest and have second thoughts about it.

From the outside, they looked like any older middle-aged couple, but they had their own history. Bridger had had adventures he seldom mentioned, and Rachel had spent time in a coma. Ellis didn't have the details, and the couple never offered explanations, which provided fertile soil for rumor.

Ellis admired their banter. Truth was, he envied their relationship. At one time he had seen himself with a lovely, intelligent wife. A young man's dream. These days he worked hard at having no dreams at all. Disappointment followed such idle wishing. Still, he couldn't deny the gnawing emotion that occasionally arose to remind him that he was not as comfortable being a loner as he let on. "You handled the announcement about Doug Lindsey well, Adam. Sensitive. Dignified."

"The whole thing is horrible." Rachel pushed her cup away as if the topic had spoiled the liquid.

Bridger nodded and looked at his plate as if seeing something only his eyes could recognize. "I've been trying to make contact with each of the faculty, checking up on them. Such an—event—can scar a person."

You have no idea.

Bridger looked up from the plate. "I had a little trouble getting hold of you. I left a message at your condo and on your cell phone. Of course, now I know you were on your boat. But the cell phone—"

"I had it turned off." A small wave of guilt washed over Ellis. "I was studying."

Bridger nodded and offered a smile. "I've been known to do the same thing. Great invention, the telephone, but it does mean anyone, anywhere, can ring a bell in your home—or your pocket. Sometimes I think we're too connected." He paused. "Anyway, I'm just checking on the faculty."

"Ever the pastor, eh?"

Bridger shrugged. "True. Some habits shouldn't be dropped." He looked into Ellis's eyes, as if he could read the thoughts printed on his gray matter. "You had Doug in your classes?"

"Yes. Seemed like a nice kid. Not an academician by any means, but genuinely interested in the material. Always respectful. How is his family doing?"

"Horrible." Rachel shook her head. "We visited with them again today. They're holding up—barely. There is no way for a parent to prepare for such a thing." Tears rose in Rachel's eyes, but she held them in check. "They'll come through this. Their church has been with them from the beginning."

"I want to know about you, Ellis. How are you dealing with all this?"

Ellis sat back to give himself another foot or two of distance between them. He thought for a moment. "Dealing with it? I'm not, Adam. What can I do? I only knew Doug from classes. I don't know the family. I'm of no help to anyone on this. Well . . . I spoke to a couple of police detectives but had very little to offer."

"I mean personally." Bridger leaned over the table as if to counter Ellis's withdrawal.

"I know you do, Adam. I'm fine. Bothered? Yes. Troubled?

Yes. Stunned? Beyond words. Still, I'm not in need of grief counseling." He looked away for a moment before returning his gaze to Bridger. "I do appreciate the concern, Adam. I really do."

Bridger pulled back and rubbed his chin. "I'm going to tell you what I told the others. I'm here for you—"

"*We're* here for you," Rachel added.

"Yes, *we're* here if you need to talk. I'm not offering to be your counselor, Ellis, just your friend."

"Thank you, but I'm fine. Really. I'm sad, but fine."

"Okay. Good." Bridger took a sip of his drink. "I plan to send an e-mail to the students. I've asked Rick to make himself available for grief counseling."

Rick—Dr. Ricardo Salinas—taught psychology and Christian counseling at the seminary. Soft-spoken, mild-mannered, the man was considered an expert in his field. This was why Adam Bridger was president of the seminary; the idea of setting up grief counseling hadn't occurred to Ellis.

"We don't have a date for the funeral yet. Much of that depends on when the medical examiner releases the body. Once I know, I'll spread the word to faculty and the student body. Doug and his family went to a small church. I'm pretty sure it can't hold all the family, faculty, and students that will be there. I've offered our chapel. If the funeral is set during the week, I'll cancel classes for the day."

"A good idea. I will be there."

That would be a difficult day.

Especially for Ellis.

13

Carmen Rainmondi and Bud Tock finished their third trip up and down the alley, their eyes fixed on the white splash of light their flashlights made. They waited until the forensic team had arrived before doing a detailed search of the vehicle, something that went against Carmen's nature. Her first impulse had always been to charge ahead and let others catch up if they could, but she was well trained. There were reasons homicide worked the way it did—but that didn't mean she was comfortable with it. In the meantime, she bagged the note and showed it to Bud. He was looking at it again. The small bit of paper would undergo a thorough examination, but there were a few things they could determine.

"Courier type." Bud shone his light on the brief message again. "That's an old-style font, the kind they used on old typewriters." He tilted the paper so he could look at it on end. "Did you notice that each letter left an indent?"

"Yes. Our killer used a typewriter. Maybe an old Royal portable."

"That's kinda specific. What makes you say that?"

"I'm not saying it *is* an old Royal. Could be an ancient Underwood. Who knows? I'm just saying the typeface and the indentation associated with each letter indicate a typewriter not a printer."

"Can't argue with that logic. Now if we only had a typewriter to match it to."

"The rat is taunting us, Bud."

"Which is why you sent Heywood and others to patrol the area. This kind of nut job likes to watch us work."

"Maybe. I got a bad feeling about this. Our perp isn't stupid." Carmen kept her voice low. "He stole a car, changed its plates, dumped the body in an area with no security or traffic cameras, and left the van here, another place with no Big-Brother presence. He also left the back hatch part way open, sure to draw the attention of someone, especially a passing cop. I'd bet money he wanted us to find it."

"It's the only thing that makes sense." Bud handed the plastic bag with the note back to Carmen, who put it in an evidence envelope. "I guess you were right. The murders are related."

"I was just guessing, and technically we can't say they're tied, but I'm betting they are."

"But to what end?"

Carmen released a sigh of weariness and frustration. "I don't know. You're right, there are more differences than similarities. I was ready to get on board with the hate-crime angle. I suppose that's still valid."

"Someone hates Jews *and* seminary students?" Bud pulled at his nose, a clear sign he was puzzled. "I suppose that's possible. One of the New Atheists?"

"New Atheists? What's that?"

"I'm no expert, but I do know that there's a new movement by atheists to make fun of Christians—well, I guess they make fun of anyone who believes in God or gods. Lots of books. Some even hit *The New York Times* best-seller list. They're popping up on talk shows, and some have even taken to holding rallies."

Carmen eyed him. "How do you know all this?"

"Hey, I watch television."

"To each his own. Why would an atheist stoop to murder?" Carmen raised a finger. "Not just murder, but torture. Brutality. Doesn't seem to fit the intellectual type."

Bud nodded. "But then, we're not dealing with a reasonable person here. This guy's elevator has come off its cables."

"We can't underestimate him. He's as clever as he is cruel." Carmen watched as the techs confirmed that the gruesome spot in the van's cargo area was blood. They then dusted the vehicle for fingerprints and "rolled" the seats with something those not in-the-know might confuse with a paint roller. Except this simple device didn't put paint down; it picked up hairs, sloughed-off skin cells, and other items that might hold DNA.

The team worked like a well-choreographed dance troupe, but without the jumps and flowing motions. They needed no instruction, no guidance beyond special requests. This was what they did. Collect evidence. The detectives would build the case. The district attorney would prosecute. The jury would decide.

Carmen could only be responsible for her part: to see beyond the obvious and to avoid mistakes.

"We're missing something, Bud. Something big. I feel like I'm standing next to a rattler and not seeing or hearing it."

"That's not a reference to me is it?"

Carmen smiled. "No, of course not. I wouldn't offend the snake kingdom that way."

"Oh, nice. Pick on the good-looking cop." He let the moment pass. "I have the same feeling"

Carmen chewed her lip for a moment. "How old do you think that minivan is?"

"Heywood said the theft report listed it as a 2001, so twelve years."

"How many people do you think have been in and out of that thing?"

"No way to know, but my guess is lots. You think we're gonna get more DNA and fibers than we can handle?"

"Count on it. Even if the perp left some plump DNA behind, it will do us no good if his DNA is not in the system."

"When we catch the guy, we can tie him to the stolen vehicle—a vehicle with a good bit of blood in the back."

Carmen started to speak when Millie Takahashi approached. She was one of the lead techs of the Field Services Unit. Her appearance matched her last name: light Asian skin, dark intelligent eyes, coal-black hair. She stood only five-two, but her confidence was much taller. Today, though, she looked tired. Field Service techs were on call round the clock.

Carmen angled a look at her. "I don't like that expression, Millie."

"Sorry, Detective, but I bring bad news. Much of the interior has been sprayed with bleach. There's a good chance key areas were treated with hydrogen peroxide." She looked apologetic, as if she had been the one to douse the interior with chemicals.

"That's just . . ." Carmen struggled for a more professional word than the one on her tongue. ". . . swell." Carmen pinched the bridge of her nose. Her weariness grew and the imaginary weight on her shoulders doubled.

"*CSI* effect," Bud said.

"Most likely, sir."

"I don't know why I'm surprised." Carmen's jaw tensed. Bud had called it right: *CSI* effect. Prosecuting crimes had become more difficult since the television show *CSI* and its spinoffs had begun airing in 2000. Murderers and rapists watch television too, and they were picking up hints about how to cover their tracks.

"The bleach can't remove blood evidence, but it can mess with the PCR." Polyermerase Chain Reaction, the process by which DNA is multiplied. "It's odd, because I don't think it was used in the back of the van where the blood is. The killer wasn't trying to destroy the blood evidence. Maybe someone interrupted him?"

"We can't get DNA from red blood cells," Bud said, "but if that blood came from our vic, then there's got to be some white blood cells. Surely there will be hairs—"

"Yes, sir, we're checking that. I just wanted to let you know that we may have a problem." Takahashi started to leave.

"What was sprayed?"

The woman glanced at Carmen. "The driver's seat and the area around it."

"Thanks, Millie."

Carmen let her walk away before turning to Bud. "He's playing with us. He's letting us know he understands the system. He knows how we work."

"We'll get him, Carmen. It's just a matter of time."

She thought of the note. "You got that right. The question is, will others die before we do?"

14

On most nights, Carmen's bed was a place of refuge: soft, warm, thick blankets to provide a night-long embrace. Tonight—or, to be more accurate, this morning—it felt full of sharp rocks. When she was twelve and Shelly was ten, they traveled to Joshua Tree National Park for a camping trip. The concept of camping as fun was lost on Shelly, and Carmen lost interest over the next few years. They were just old enough to want to sleep some distance from their parents. Nature had decorated the desert area with large rocks, some monoliths tipped over and propped up by lesser boulders. Carmen talked Shelly into spreading their sleeping bags beneath a massive stone structure that provided a granite ceiling.

"What if the rock falls on us?" Shelly had always been the timid one.

"Then it will squish us so fast we won't even know it." Carmen had thought the comment funny, but Shelly hadn't seen the humor. That night they slept on naturally decomposed granite.

Right now, her bed felt just like the too-hard ground of the National Park.

She'd arrived home at 2:00 a.m., thrown a slice of cheddar between two pieces of wheat bread, and called it dinner. At 2:30, she stripped and crawled into bed. At 3:00, she was still staring at the glowing numerals of her alarm clock. Sometime after that she fell into a fitful sleep.

At 6:00 she rose, feeling worse for the attempt to rest, showered, donned a dark blouse, black jeans, and a woman's black business jacket. Might as well dress to match her mood. A short time later she headed out the door. She veered from her course long enough to drive through a McDonalds and grab a large coffee and Egg McMuffin. The coffee was tasty, but the breakfast sandwich was unwelcome to her cranky stomach. She downed it anyway. She needed fuel.

She had just settled in her seat when Bud appeared. He looked like a man who had tumbled down a large hill.

He took one look at her and grimaced. "You look awful." He set two Venti-sized cups of Starbucks on his desk. He wore dark slacks, a blue shirt, and a sport coat. Bud's standard uniform, even on a Saturday.

"Wow, you know just what a girl likes to hear. One of those cups for me?" Carmen pointed to the coffee.

"Um, yeah, sure. That's what I was doing. Getting *you* a coffee."

Carmen took a cup anyway. "You're such a sweetheart. Thanks."

He looked like his best friend had just died. "Don't mention it. Seriously, don't ever mention it."

She took a long sip then screwed her face. "Ugh, what's in this? It taste like a candy bar."

"I am a man of refined tastes, and I like my coffee sweet."

"Sweet. Sheesh, man, my pancreas just closed up shop. You got insulin in the other cup?"

He grinned. "No, this one has *more* sugar and caffeine. I needed a jolt this morning."

"That oughta do it." She sipped the drink again. "And they say girls like the froufrou drinks."

Bud didn't reply. He just sat.

A voice rolled down the open office area and over the detectives' desks, many of which were still unmanned. Captain Ulysses Darrel Simmons had no trouble being heard. "Rainmondi, Tock, my office—now." A second later: "And bring your files."

Bud and Carmen exchanged glances. The boss was spending his Saturday morning at the office instead of on the golf course.

Bud rose. "He's in early. I hate it when he's at his desk before me. Makes me feel like a slacker."

"Well, if the shoe—"

"Don't go there, girl. You might hurt my sensitive feelings."

Carmen let it go even though she doubted anything could hurt the man's feelings.

Captain Simmons's office was not spacious or well appointed, but it had walls decorated with photos of him with the chief, the mayor, and a few other politicians. The wall also held a few frames of certificates of merit, including one for bravery. Simmons was a bit of a legend. A fast riser in the ranks, he excelled at everything he did and had little patience with those who didn't do the same. He was loyal to his detectives, willing to take a bullet for one of them, even if the one shooting had the word "chief" in front of his name.

"Close the door." Simmons was also a man of few words. He liked to get straight to the point.

"What's up, Cap?" Carmen stood by one of the two guest chairs in front of the walnut desk, which had been made by Simmons's father. It was a beautiful piece of work, and Simmons made no attempt to hide his pride in the desk or his woodworking father.

"Sit." He waved at the chairs. Only then did Carmen feel it was appropriate to sit.

She settled in the chair, a file folder on her lap. "Sorry for the late call last night."

He huffed. "Yeah, like I haven't had late night calls before. Comes with the turf." He leaned back in his high-back, ergonomic chair, a concession he made to an annoying back muscle he injured tackling a fleeing suspect. He was still fit for duty, but it flared up from time to time—something easy to determine by his "grouch index."

Their superior eyed them for a moment. "How much sleep did you get last night?"

Neither Carmen nor Bud answered.

"Don't make me ask again."

"I logged four hours." Bud's color heightened a fraction at the admission. "I'm good to go."

Simmons's eyes switched to Carmen. She said, "A couple of hours. My mind was logging overtime."

"Been there." Simmons shifted in his chair. Carmen guessed he hadn't slept much either but didn't want to ask. "Okay, here's the deal. I got a meeting with Assistant Chief Claymore in thirty minutes. That note you found just kicked this investigation up a mile or two. He wants a report even if it means he had to come in on the weekend."

"He's not going to pull me from the case is he?" The confrontation at the rabbi's house flashed fresh on her mind. "I mean, it's my job to protect the crime scene—"

"I won't let him do that. I told him then the same thing I told you: you were right to follow procedure. He knows I'd have your head if you hadn't kept him behind the barricade."

"Thanks, Cap, but if not that then—"

"Two murders in two days, both bizarre in nature, and now a note that might indicate a serial killer—well, that's the kind of thing that gets noticed upstairs. I'm going to bring him up to speed, which means I need you to bring *me* up to speed."

"We can go with you if you want, Cap." Bud sounded like a man who had gargled with gravel. Something he did when he operated on too few hours of sleep.

"No. I need you in the field. More to the point, I need to tell Claymore that you're out doing your jobs. So let's get down to it. I know about the van and note, thanks to Carmen's call. I've also read the early ME reports, and I gotta tell you, they sicken me. I've seen some pretty awful things in my career, but I haven't seen anything like the Cohen body—not unless you count the guy who stepped in front of an Amtrak train—and that was done with a man's fists?"

"Best we can tell at this point, Cap. We found no indication of a blunt instrument, and the bruising is consistent with a beating by hand . . . except the legs. We think the perp kicked the man until the leg bones broke." Bud opened the file he carried and removed a photo of the odd marks on the man's legs. "We think the man wore steel-toed boots. We also found a boot print near the van we examined last night. We don't have enough evidence to tie the two together, but I wouldn't be surprised if they're connected."

Simmons crossed his arms and lowered his head—his thinking posture. "But the van was found in an alley, and we have to assume that workers and others have walked back there. The boot could be anyone's." Leave it to Simmons to think like a defense attorney. As a young officer, he often attended criminal trials to learn how defense attorneys worked. A self-education that paid off. As a homicide detective, he held the record for the highest percentage of convictions.

Carmen stirred. "True, Cap, but the location gives us reason to believe that it might be connected."

"Where are you in the investigation?"

"Forensics is going over the clothing of both vics and going over the van again," Carmen said. "I had them bring it back to the station." She took a breath. "We may have a problem though."

"The hydrogen peroxide and bleach?" Simmons had been doing his research. "I heard about that. That might mess up the DNA PCR."

Bud looked at the file as if searching for answers. "I'm sure we'll get some DNA, but it will take time to distinguish bad-guy biologicals from those who had been in the van before. We'll have to collect samples from the van's owners, but if they have had a lot of other people in the vehicle, then we're likely to come up with a ton of useless information."

"Once you catch the guy, you compare his DNA to anything found in the van."

"Yes, sir," Bud said. "We plan to check any DNA we find with the DNA database. If the guy's been in the system, we might get a match."

Carmen fidgeted. "I'm concerned with the guy's psychology. He made no attempt to contaminate the blood in the back of the van. It seems he wants us to connect the van to Cohen. Why? Most murderers try to cover all evidence, not just some of it."

"What's your gut tell you, Carmen?"

"He's playing with us. Let me just say what you're thinking: This guy is a serial killer who is smart, plans his attacks, and wants us to chase him. That or he has some kind of message."

Simmons frowned. "Like what?"

"I have no idea, but the note tells us a lot. He mocks us, and I'm afraid he'll keep doing it until he grows bored with it all or we catch him."

The corners of Simmons's mouth dipped as if trying to touch his shoulders. "I assume you have the techs going over the note."

"Of course, sir."

"I want you to keep me up to speed. Call me when you have info. Day or night. This has the potential of being a public relations nightmare. 'San Diego Terrorized by Serial Killer" is not a headline anyone wants to read, especially the brass. I will report all this to Assistant Chief Claymore, but I can tell that the nature of these cases will require him to brief the chief. I'm sure I'll be in that meeting. We'll have to alert the mayor, too." He paused. "Now the bad news."

"I thought that *was* the bad news," Bud said.

"We have a couple more detectives out with illness and one for a family emergency. To make matters worse, there were three other murders that came over the threshold."

"Three?" Carmen was stunned. "What happened to our lower-than-ever murder rate?"

Simmons pursed his lips. "I'm afraid it's out the window this year. We've had a couple of good years, under thirty murders, but this is shaping up as a record-breaking year, and not in a good way."

"What kind of murders?" Bud pressed.

"A domestic violence case in Allied Gardens, a gang-related shooting downtown—one dead, two teetering on the grave's edge—and a suspicious death in Ocean Beach. You'll want to check on the last one, but I doubt it's related to your cases. Too mundane, if murder can be mundane." He inched toward the desk. "I'm in a tough spot here. If I pull detectives from other cases and the press gets wind of it, then we'll be accused of focusing on only high profile cases."

Carmen knew what that meant. "So we're on our own?"

"No, not entirely. I want you two to stay on course. I've already told the forensic units to give you priority. Also, let's keep the talk of serial killer in-house for now. When I get back from my meeting, I'll call other law enforcement agencies and let them know that there might be something brewing and to keep us informed of anything they might think is related. I'll handle any press calls. You focus on running this guy down before we start making the national news. Clear?"

Carmen and Bud spoke in unison: "Yes."

"I might be able to get some help from the uniforms if you want. If so, got anyone in mind?"

Carmen nodded. "Officer Heywood found the van last night. He did a good job with everything. Sharp guy."

"You good with that, Bud?"

"I am."

"Okay. I'll twist an arm or two, but they're having the same problem with the flu. I'll do what I can."

"Thank you, sir," Carmen said.

"What's your next step?"

Bud nodded at Carmen. "We're working phone records and bank statements. I want to bring the rabbi in for questioning. I don't think he's involved, but I want to be sure. Also he was pretty shook so I'm hoping he will be more forthcoming. I also want to explore any connection between the victims. Maybe they knew each other."

"Keep me in the loop." Simmons stood. "Now get out of my office. I need a few minutes to get my strategy together."

"Yes, sir." Carmen and Bud stood.

"One more thing, detectives. This is the kind of case that makes a career. It's also the kind of case that can end one, if you catch my drift."

"Yeah, we got it, Cap. We got it."

15

Joe Heywood strode into the homicide office and glanced around. Carmen saw the tall man the moment he entered. He was hard to miss. Even so, it took a moment for her eyes to convince her brain that this was the same man she worked with the night before. In the glow of florescent light he looked . . . different. That and he was out of uniform, wearing tan slacks and a blue pullover polo shirt. The short sleeves exposed the pythons most people called arms that his uniform shirt kept hidden. Last night he looked broad in the chest. Most patrol cops did, thanks to their protective vest making them look larger than they were. A nice psychological advantage. But Heywood?

The man had a chest big enough to play table tennis on.

"Officer Heywood. Over here." Carmen waved the man to her desk.

He gave a short, sharp nod. "Detective. My captain said you wanted to see me."

“That didn’t take long.” Bud turned his chair away from his computer screen.

“He called me at home.” Heywood gave no sign of being perturbed by the summons. The man had the Bruce Banner calm. Did he have an inner Hulk to go with it?

“Captain Simmons called your captain. We need your help.” Carmen pointed to the empty desk chair in one of the other cubicles. Heywood retrieved it and sat.

“How can I help?”

“We have a shortage in the department, and there have been several unrelated murders that have tied up other detectives. Our team is thinner than usual. You managed things well last night, and we think you have the chops for this kind of work. Of course, we don’t know that for sure . . .” Carmen wanted to bite her tongue. Why was it so hard for her to praise other people?

“I understand. I appreciate the compliment. What do you want me to do?”

Carmen brought the officer up to speed about the case. “This is the part of detective work they play down on television. Your greatest danger is dying of boredom.”

“I’m willing to risk it. Put me to work.”

“Good. You already know there were no security cameras in the alley, but the driver had to pass in front of some camera somewhere on his way to the location. I want you to find cameras in the area and review the footage. It’s grunt work, but it might lead to something.”

“It’s a shame we don’t have surveillance cameras,” Heywood said. “Even the red-light cameras might prove useful.”

Bud agreed. "Except our guy seems to be more than a little wily. I doubt he'd run a light. He seems to be camera aware."

Heywood rose. "I'll start with Traffic and CalTrans to see if they have cameras in the area, but I doubt I'll find much there. CalTrans has cameras on the freeways." He paused. "I can check the off ramps nearest the area where the van was found. Maybe the perp took the freeway to get to the area. Do you have a time frame?"

Bud answered: "ME says Cohen died about four hours before he was found. That puts time of death around two a.m. You found the van about nine p.m. so that's nineteen hours. Interviews with employees in the strip mall said the vehicle had been there all day."

Heywood considered that. "Doesn't quite add up. I don't think the perp drove straight there from the primary crime scene. Which means he held onto the van for a good number of hours. Or am I wrong?"

"Sounds right to me." He was as smart as she thought. She'd been right to bring him onboard. "But we need more than assumptions."

"Understood. I'll work up a plan."

"It may lead nowhere, but we need to say we chased that rabbit. In the meantime, I plan to interview the rabbi again."

Heywood's eyebrows rose. "Today?"

"Yep. I have more questions. Thinking of asking him to come down."

"May I ask if he's a suspect?"

Odd question. Carmen tried not to sound puzzled. "We're taught to wonder about everyone, especially those who discover the body. Sometimes they're the one we're looking for." She let that hang in the air before continuing. "But he's not high on the list. Too small to have pounded the life out of a man. Of course, he could have hired someone. Is there a problem?"

"No, not a problem, it's just that this is Passover week and it's also the Sabbath. If he's not a suspect, you might get a little further by waiting until after sundown. Of course, it's your call. I'm jus' sayin'."

Bud's brows arched. "You're Jewish?"

"No, sir. I just read a lot."

"Thanks for the heads up," Carmen said. "What about seminary professors?"

"You're good to go on that, Detective. Unless it's a Jewish seminary." Heywood grinned, revealing Hollywood-grade teeth. He gave a nod and started to turn. Bud stopped him.

"I assume you had other plans for the weekend. What'd we pull you from?"

"I was getting ready to head to the racquetball court. No problem though. I always lose."

Carmen tipped her head. Heywood didn't look like the kind of guy that lost any sport. "You're opponent that good, or are you that bad?"

The comment made him smile. "He's pretty good. Especially for a ten-year-old."

"Wait," Bud said. "You let a ten-year-old beat you at racquetball?"

Heywood shrugged and his chest expanded a few inches. "He's my son."

Carmen's eyes hurt. Yesterday, she had obtained a search warrant to look at bank records for her two victims. If the banks felt they were somehow a victim in a crime, they could voluntarily provide the information, but Carmen couldn't make that case. The banks were neutral and therefore required a legal instrument to pry open the databanks. The search warrant came with a nondisclosure directive.

Usually, a bank was under obligation to inform its account holder that it has received a warrant for records. Bank records could be instrumental in outlining the last days of a person's life, especially when there were large withdrawals or atypical deposits. Debit cards left a trail. If a man used a debit card to buy a gun, it might indicate he planned to break the law or was fearful and wanted to defend himself or his family. If someone made fifty thousand a year but deposited twice that in a short period of time, it might indicate a crime. Consistent ATM withdrawals of, say, a thousand dollars might mean a person was being blackmailed. If a victim kept a checking account secret from his or her spouse, then it might lead to motive for murder.

Carmen came up empty on all counts.

She sighed.

"I heard that." Bud had spent the morning reviewing phone records.

"Expect more. I got zilch here."

Bud pushed from his desk and moved his chair across the narrow space that separated their workspace. "Show me."

"You just want to take a break from scouring phone records."

"You got that right. Talk to me. I need the break."

Carmen understood. "Like I said, I got nuthin'." She pointed at the screen. This is Doug Lindsey's bank account. He has only one."

"What do you mean *only one?* I only have one checking account. How many do you have?"

"Are we counting offshore banks?" Carmen tried to keep a straight face.

"Cute. Carry on, moneybags."

Carmen returned her attention to the screen. "It's what you'd expect from a grad student. Very little money, and what little he had he spent on gas, pizza, books, and the occasional movie. He deposited $600 a month for the last two years. When we interviewed his parents, they said he had no job and that they gave him a monthly stipend. I'm guessing the $600 comes from them. We need to confirm that."

"Sounds logical. I don't see a payment to a cell phone company. He has an AT&T account. I know that much."

"No doubt his parents pay some—probably most—of his bills. It looked to me like they made pretty good money." She grabbed the computer mouse and gave it a click. "Okay, Cohen's situation is a little more complex. There are three checking accounts and three savings accounts. First the checking accounts: one is the house account, one is a business account, and one looks like a small account for his wife. Her name is over his on the statements."

"Pin money."

"What?" Carmen turned. Bud had moved closer to the computer and therefore closer to her.

"Pin money. It's an old term. Men used to give money to their wives for pins, clothing, and woman stuff. Not done a lot these days."

"Wow, I wonder why."

"Don't get snippy about it, Carmen. I didn't invent the practice. I'm just saying that Mrs. Cohen may have had a mad money account. Anything interesting?"

Carmen shook her head. "She wasn't a big spender. She gave money to Jewish Family Services. The rest is money spent on the kids, books, and—lady things."

Bud ignored the dig. "What about the business account?"

"No flags. He has some big deposits, but the man was a real-estate developer. He spent money like water then raked it in. The amounts are all different and unevenly spaced. I'll need access to his books to know who was paying him for what, and I doubt I can get a search warrant for that. He's the victim after all; no criminal record."

"Expenditures?"

"All to reputable businesses, best I can tell. Of course, one of them could be dirty. Cash withdrawals are small both for home and business. They seemed to live a simple life."

"The savings accounts?"

"One for vacations, one for taxes, and one for savings. The last one has almost $200,000. They're not millionaires, but they're not hurting."

Bud rubbed his chin. "His phone records look typical. The most frequently called numbers were his wife's cell phone and the synagogue. There are a good number of calls to Rabbi Singer, but that's to be expected."

"Bottom line: we got nuthin' on nobody." Carmen rubbed her face. The lack of sleep, the shocking nature of the killings, the lack of any real leads wore on her.

"Hang in there, partner. We'll get this guy."

Carmen stood suddenly, sending Bud backpedaling. "I need to get some fresh air. Let's go for a drive."

"Where?"

"Let's roust the professor. I want to know if he knows David Cohen or Rabbi Singer. He might give us some info on religious hatred. This has something to do with religion. One Christian, one Jew. What's next, a Buddhist?"

16

"No need, Professor, we'll come to you."

Carmen's voice came over the cell phone calm, professional, polite. Nonetheless, a phone call from a homicide detective could upset anyone.

It certainly did Ellis.

"Well—"

"We show that you live in Escondido." She rattled off an address.

So much for privacy. "That's my home, but I'm not there. I'm in Coronado." Ellis heard muttered curses, then a whispered, "Flip it around, Bud. We're going the wrong way."

"Would you like me to meet you halfway?" Ellis had no idea where that would be.

"No, Professor. Where are you in Coronado?"

"Glorietta Bay. Do you know it?"

"Yes. You have an apartment nearby?"

"Um, no. There are several coffee shops and restaurants nearby. We could—"

"We need something a little more private. Are you staying in one of the hotels or did you just drive over for the day?"

"Neither, Detective. I have a boat here, but it's not big enough for us to meet." He paused. "I don't think you want to talk while sitting on someone's lap." He meant it as a joke but no laugh came. She was probably thinking where to meet. "There's a park here. Would that be private enough?"

"Okay. Yes. We can try that. We'll be there in . . ."

Ellis heard a male voice mumble something.

"We'll be there in about twenty minutes."

The black Crown Vic pulled into the parking lot of Glorietta Bay Park. Carmen slipped from the passenger side of the car and searched the small park for Dr. Ellis Poe. The park was an expanse of grass with a copse of trees just off Mullinex Drive. A small, narrow beach abutted the bay. Just to the north of the circular parking lot were several round concrete tables with arched benches. At one of them, a man stood and waved.

Ellis Poe.

When she first met him in his office at the seminary, he wore a suit. Here he wore well-worn jeans and a plain T-shirt. Few people wore T-shirts that had no message or product emblazoned on them.

As she approached, she could see the tan on the man's thin arms. Apparently he traded his dark office for sunlight enough to fire up the melanin in his skin. His face was less tanned, perhaps protected by sunscreen. His thin frame was a testimony that the only working out he did was hoisting books now and again.

"Detectives."

Ellis sounded nervous. Not all that unusual. The gun, the badge, the title "detective" tended to unsettle people—a fact she used to her advantage. A badge makes a person look bigger and badder than they are. Toss in a little attitude, and most people begin to feel guilty about things they've never done. "Sorry if you had to drive farther than you intended."

"No problem, Dr. Poe. Blue sky, ocean breeze, the smell of fresh-cut grass . . . Much better than the office." Carmen unleashed her best "I'm-your-buddy" smile.

"I think so," Ellis said. "I like to spend my weekends here."

"You own a yacht? I didn't know college professors made that kind of money." Bud Tock, ever the bull in the China shop.

Ellis motioned to the curved benches around the picnic table. The sound of children playing fifty yards away rode the salty air currents. On the water, sailboats plied the boating lanes. Across the bay, Carmen could see several moored navy vessels. This was the place to retire.

Once seated, Ellis studied them. "We don't—well, I don't. I make enough to get by, but I couldn't buy a boat without a mountain of debts."

"But . . ." Bud let the question hang.

"First, I inherited it from an uncle. Second, calling it a yacht is like calling a shed a mansion. Two people can live on it if they really like each other. I live in a condo—well, I guess you know that. It's okay and close to the seminary, but on weekends it can get a little noisy. I don't like noise."

Carmen kept her smile in place. "It must be nice to have a boat you can bring friends to."

"No one else has been on the *Blushing*—"

Carmen cocked her head. Why had Ellis stopped like that?

Ellis started again. "Like I said, it's very small. I don't take guests out to it." He turned and pointed at the small Sailcraft bobbing in the harbor among the larger, more majestic vessels. It looked out of place. "That's it there. The one with the purple trim."

"I can't make out the name on her hull." Carmen said. Ellis had looked embarrassed when he started to share the name.

Ellis face tinted pink. "My uncle christened her the *Blushing Bride*. I can't bring myself to change the name, so I just live with it."

"But only on weekends," Bud said.

"And some holidays. It has a small galley, but I eat most of my meals in town. Coronado has some good places to eat. There's also a Christian drama troupe. They have their own theater. *Lamb's Players*. I go there sometimes." He paused. "But you didn't drive all the way down here to hear about my boat. How can I help you?"

Carmen had brought a large black purse. She didn't like purses, but this one was large enough to hold the two files containing information copied from the official documents. The files were thin and she used them for effect. They had *SDPD Homicide* printed on the cover, another useful intimidation tool, but she wasn't here to intimidate. Just to uncover connections.

"This won't take long, Professor." Carmen pulled a photo from the file but kept the image facing her. "I'm afraid there's been another murder and it might be related to Doug Lindsey." Carmen watched Ellis's face for a reaction. He froze in place and his head dipped. The mention of Lindsey's name hit him hard.

"Another . . . murder?"

"Yes, sir. It was especially vicious." She hesitated, began to lay the photo on the picnic table, then waited one second longer, her eyes fixed on the professor's expression. She could see him tense, fearful of what he was about to see: no joy at the prospect, no curiosity. She set the photo down, the image facing the azure sky. Ellis pulled back, then stopped.

Clearly he had expected something horrible, which was what Carmen set him up to expect. Instead, the photo was of a middle-aged man in a suit and tie, a broad smile of even and near-perfect teeth.

Carmen let a moment or two slip by. "Do you know this man?"

Ellis exhaled slowly. He had been holding his breath. "No. I don't think so. This is the victim?"

Bud leaned over the table. "What do you mean, 'I don't think so'?"

"I don't recall ever meeting him, but I suppose I may have seen him at some seminary function. The seminary has fund-raisers and family nights. I may have seen him at one of those."

"Not likely," Carmen said. "He's Jewish. A cantor at his synagogue. Or should I say, he *was* a cantor."

"That's horrible. Family?"

"Yes." It was the kind of question an innocent man asked. Although Carmen doubted Ellis Poe could be a vicious killer, she had let her mind play with some doubt. "Wife, two teenagers."

Ellis shook his head. "I can't imagine how they must feel." He pulled the photo closer and studied it. "If I ever met this man, I don't remember it."

"Would a Christian have any dealings with a Jewish man?" Bud relaxed his posture.

Ellis smiled.

"What's so funny?" Bud didn't sound amused.

"I'm sorry, Detective. Your question is . . ." Ellis abandoned the sentence. "Jesus is Jewish, so yes, Christians have dealings with a Jewish man." He raised a hand. "I know what you're asking, and the answer is yes. Aside from a few crackpot groups, Christians respect Jews. Christianity was planted on Jewish soil and spread from Jerusalem to the world. There's no reason for your victim to avoid Christians or Christians to avoid Jews. Some of our students visit synagogues to better understand Jewish values and worship. I have done it myself. For a year, I went to synagogue to learn the Jewish perspective on the Tanakh."

That was a new one on Carmen. "The what?"

"The Old Testament," Ellis explained.

"I thought that was called the Torah?"

Ellis seemed surprised she knew the term. "Torah refers to the first five books of what we call the Old Testament: Genesis, Exodus, Leviticus, Numbers, and Deuteronomy. Sometimes the word *Pentateuch* is used. It's a Greek term. Of course, the Jews don't believe in a New Covenant as Christians do, so calling their Scriptures the Old Testament doesn't work." He pushed the photo back to Carmen. "I'm sorry, Detective, I don't know the man."

"His name is David Cohen. Ring any bells?" Carmen retrieved the picture and put it back in the folder.

"Cohen is a very common name, as is David. Your man was named after Israel's greatest king. Cohen means he is related to the priestly line of Jews. So he had the name of a king and a priest. Still, I don't know a David Cohen."

"I have another question for you, Dr. Poe." Carmen set the two folders on the table but left them closed, her hand resting on them as if fearful a gust of wind might send the contents flapping toward the bay or fall at the feet of some mother walking her children around the park. "Cohen was found in front of his rabbi's home—in the front yard. The rabbi found him yesterday morning."

"That's awful." Ellis's face showed his disgust.

"Its worse than you imagine." She opened the file and removed a crime-scene photo and set it on the top of the file.

Ellis recoiled and looked away. "Why would you show that to me?"

"Because, I want you to understand what we're dealing with here. This man was beaten to death. Slowly. By hand. Then the killer, using a stolen vehicle, transported the victim to the rabbi's home and dropped the body in the front yard. The rabbi and his wife have two small children. Why do that? Transporting a body is one way to leave more evidence behind. Most murderers kill and leave. Why kill the cantor and drive to his rabbi's home and toss the body there?"

"How should I know, Detective? I'm an academic, not an investigator." He kept his eyes averted.

"Try and follow me on this, Professor. Your student was in seminary to become a minister, right?"

"Yes."

"He's killed and dumped in a public place. Cohen is a Jewish religious man. He is killed and dumped in a public place. Why?"

"Again, Detective, I don't have a clue. You tell me." Defensiveness edged into Ellis's tone.

Carmen kept her gaze on him. "My partner and I have been talking. We think the killings are related—that they mean something besides the obvious, but we can't figure out what. The fact that both victims were religious people can't be overlooked."

"But Doug was found in Balboa Park, not in someone's front yard."

"True. There are significant differences, but . . ." Carmen looked at Bud, then continued. "We have a very good reason to believe that Lindsey and Cohen are the first in a series of murders."

"How can you know that?"

"The killer is taunting us. That's all I can tell you, and that's probably too much." She shifted on the hard bench. "You know more about the religious world than we do. What ties a Jewish cantor and Christian seminary student together? Why those two?"

Ellis shook his head. "I don't have a clue, Detective. If both were Jews then you might wonder if some anti-Semite, or white supremacist, or a member of an extreme Islamic group did it. But I can't think of any reason why any of those would go after

Doug. If both victims were Christians, then you might suspect a few other groups." He clenched and unclenched his hands. "I don't see a connection. Maybe its just coincidence."

"Maybe," Carmen said, "but that doesn't feel right. Who hates Jews and Christians? Muslims?"

Ellis shrugged. "There are extreme Muslim groups, especially in other countries. Most hate Israel. Christian pastors have been arrested. In some countries if a Muslim converts to Christianity, he or she can be arrested and tried. So that's one possibility. Has anyone taken credit for the murders?"

"No. And just for the record, I'm trusting your discretion in this matter."

"Understood. There's a problem. I'm not an expert in terrorism, but usually a terrorist group wants credit for their actions. They don't act and then hide."

"That crossed my mind," Carmen said.

"I'm at a loss, detectives. I don't know Cohen, and I doubt I've ever met him. I have no memory of it if I have. I don't doubt you when you say there's a connection between the two murders, but I don't see what it is."

Carmen put the graphic photo away and returned the files to her purse. "We appreciate your time, Dr. Poe." Carmen rose. "If you come up with insights, please give us a call. Enjoy the rest of your weekend."

Carmen walked back to the car more frustrated than when she arrived.

Ellis watched Carmen walk away and wished he could avert his eyes. He didn't gaze at her as most men gaze at a woman striding away. He didn't think of her form, her posture, or the breeze in her hair. He thought of how much she looked like her younger sister, Shelly. She possessed the same crinkle of skin around the eyes, the same slope to her nose, the same intelligent gaze—except Carmen's eyes revealed a festering hurt.

Ellis knew why.

17

Carmen slipped into the front seat of the Crown Vic and buckled her belt before Bud could open his door. He noticed.

"We in a hurry?"

"No, but there's no reason to hang around here."

"Boy, you got that right," He slipped the key into the ignition. "Nothing here but clear skies, blue ocean, a warm breeze, fine restaurants, and the best view of the San Diego skyline. Who wants to put up with that?"

"Want me to drive?"

"Nah, I got it."

Bud directed the car from the parking lot, creeping along the asphalt, Carmen assumed, to add a little friendly irritation to the moment. As he turned the car, she caught sight of Ellis walking slowly along the concrete path that lined the grassy area: head down, shoulders slumped, hands in his pockets. He looked to be carrying an invisible, Atlas-sized load on his slight shoulders.

"He's hiding something." Carmen stated it as fact, not supposition.

"You think he's involved in the murders?" Bud applied more pressure to the accelerator as they reached the street.

"No. At least not that I can see. Did you see the way he reacted to the crime-scene photo?"

"I did. I thought he was going to puke on the table. Not that I could blame him. Cohen was as messed up as a man can be. It almost put me off my food."

"Really, I don't recall you missing a meal."

Bud glanced at her. "I said *almost*." He pulled onto the 282 and started for the blue bridge that linked Coronado proper with San Diego. "So what then? You think he knows Cohen?"

"I doubt it. There's something else. Something eating at him."

"Cuz if you think he might be tied in, we could get a couple of warrants and search his boat and his condo."

"We might have trouble with that. We don't have a connection. Not yet, anyway."

Carmen's cell phone sounded. "Rainmondi."

"Officer Heywood here, Detective."

"Found something on the video?"

"Not yet, and I'm doubtful we will, but I'll keep at it. I'm calling to tell you CHP has found Cohen's car."

Carmen had issued a BOLO shortly after identifying Cohen. There was one out for Doug Lindsey's Volkswagen Beetle, too. The "be on the lookout" went to all law enforcement organizations.

"Where?"

"Near Temecula."

Carmen muttered a curse. "Okay, give me the location." She listened. "Rainbow? That's south of Temecula, right?"

"Yes, it's more a village than a town."

"You sound like you've been there, Heywood."

"I broke down there once. It's a long and boring story. I'll let the Chippers know you're on your way. Just so you know, they said there's not much left. It's been stripped."

"Thanks."

Bud glanced at Carmen and raised an eyebrow. "Temecula?"

"Yep. Well, Rainbow. Ever heard of it?"

"I have. It's a berg that used to be important back in the days when the old 395 ran by there. The I-15 has pretty much bypassed the place."

"They found Cohen's car. What's left of it. We got an hour's drive or so, depending on traffic."

"You know . . ."

Carmen closed her eyes. "Don't tell me. You know a great place to eat in Rainbow."

"Nope. See? You don't know me as well as you think." A second later, "It's in Temecula. Mexican place. They have sopaipillas."

"Do they have beans?"

"Of course."

"Then we're not going."

San Diego was in one of its rare moods: northbound traffic was light and the ever-present construction in north county had turned traffic friendly. Returning to the city might be more difficult. Traffic in San Diego was fickle.

Rainbow was a tiny community of two thousand. Most of the homes were World War II era. An old filling station waited just off the side road that joined the I-15 to the community. The buildings looked ready to collapse. Rust covered the metal pole that held a sign that once beckoned travelers to fill up their twenty-gallon tanks so their large V-8s could swill down the juice at twelve miles to the gallon. Carmen could imagine the place and the deserted diner nearby once surrounded by station wagons, Ramblers, and Fords, all with hoods large enough to serve as a landing pad for a helicopter. Only ghosts visited the sites now.

The homes and small businesses were a mixture of well-tended structures situated on large lots next to rundown houses that hadn't seen a coat of paint since Reagan occupied the Oval Office.

The GPS unit in the dash of the Crown Vic led the detectives to the eastern-most part of the town—a place with metal buildings that had once served the orchard ranchers in the area. Their road ended in a junkyard at the foot of a mesquite-covered hill. A black-and-white California Highway Patrol car was parked next to a chain-link fence that looked ready to topple any moment. The officer was a woman with brownish-blonde hair. She stood about five-foot-six and had a fair complexion. Carmen thought her pretty but not movie-star gorgeous. The officer exited her patrol car when Carmen and Bud pulled up.

"I take it you're the investigators from San Diego?" Her no-nonsense way with her words wasn't unusual for a cop.

They sized up most everyone they spoke to. In the field, the goal was to separate friend from foe. With others of the profession, it was to establish professionalism and determine the pecking order.

Carmen nodded. "Carmen Rainmondi, homicide. This is my partner, Detective Bud Tock."

"Lilly Carr." Lilly looked to be under thirty. They shook hands.

"What have we got?" Bud seemed eager.

"We have the remains of a 2012 Lexus LS." The officer started for a gate in the rickety fence. "At one time it was a luxury car. Sixty or seventy thousand dollars. I ID-ed it by the chassis number."

Carmen frowned. "I don't like the sound of that."

"It's just a heap, now, Detective. This is a dumping spot for strip shops in the area. It's far enough off the beaten bath to avoid observation. We patrol the community, but not much. Usually, we show up here if someone calls."

"No LEOs?"

Lily shook her head in answer to Bud's question. "Too little population to pay for a local sheriff. Technically, this place isn't even a town, just a Census Area. County sheriff has the responsibility, but we have patrol privileges. It's one of those handshake things. They handle crime; we deal with transportation and traffic."

Carr led them through the gate. "Auto strippers pay some flunky to do the drop off. Even if we catch him, he knows nothing about the operation. Anyway, I got to thinking that someone might have dropped your vic's car here. It was a one-in-a-million shot, but it paid off."

"You'd be surprised how often a one-in-a-million shot does so." Bud shrugged. "Luck is the part of police work no one talks about."

"There's no lock on the gate," Carmen said.

"Hasn't been one for years. Wouldn't matter. The car thieves just bring bolt cutters."

"Who owns the place?" Carmen glanced around. The place was a graveyard for once-dignified cars. Most were old models looking for someone to recycle them into something useful; others were just chassis, the remains of stripped luxury or high-performance cars.

"My understanding is that question is up in the air. The owner died intestate and had no family. The state owns it, but no one seems to be paying any attention. It's hard to sell property in this berg, at least for a profit."

They didn't walk far, something that made sense to Carmen. It was a dump-and-run. Drive in late at night, drop off the carcass, and go home.

Sure enough, what Carr pointed out was the metal frame of an expensive car. The engine was gone, as were the doors, the seats, the dash, the wheels, the tires, and the brake system. In short . . .

Everything.

Carmen scanned the area around them. "Any idea if the chop shop is nearby?"

"No idea. As I said, there are several. Some are in the hills. There's no way to tie this to any particular shop. They remove what they want and haul it away, so there's nothing to tie anything to them. These guys are pretty sophisticated."

Carr started to move closer.

"Hang on a sec, Officer." Carmen touched her elbow. "I want to take some photos and analyze the lot. We have to treat this like a murder scene."

"For all we know, it is." Bud turned back toward their car. "I'll get on the horn to the San Diego sheriffs so we can bring them into the loop. I'll make sure they know it's our case."

"You may have to argue that point," Carmen said, "but you're right."

Carmen returned to the Crown Vic, slipped on a pair of blue gloves, and grabbed the digital camera. She returned to the heap that had once belonged to the man lying in a cooler in the ME's office. She glanced at Carr. "How much walking around did you do in here?"

"Not much. I had to find the chassis number." Carr squatted. "This is my footprint."

Carmen photographed it and the surrounding scene. Then she approached the metal carcass, taking photos as she did. The interior showed no signs of violence. No blood. No tissue. At least that she could see. The techs would go over it with a fine-toothed comb.

Twenty minutes later, two men, both in their fifties and sporting round middles and graying hair, appeared. After introductions, Carmen brought the county detectives up to speed.

"Our murders happened in the city, but the vehicle—well, what's left of it—is in the county."

The larger of the two detectives eyed her. "How do you want to handle it?"

"If it's all the same to you, I'd like our forensics team on this. They're already working evidence from two homicides that appear related. I know you guys do the forensic work for what, a dozen other cities?"

"Thirty." The man looked at his partner, who seemed to be the junior of the two. "Okay. How can we help?"

"There are a lot of buildings around here. Any one of them could have been the murder scene. We could use some of your guys canvassing the area."

"You think your man was killed in Rainbow?"

Carmen shook her head. "No. It doesn't fit the profile we're developing. But that doesn't mean our killer *didn't* do the deed here. We know he stole, or caused to be stolen, an older Dodge Caravan that belongs to an elderly couple in Rancho Bernardo. That's fairly close to here."

"So he could have stolen the Caravan, killed your vic anywhere, then left the Lexus out in the open where some thieves helped themselves."

"Maybe, but our guy is smart—twisted beyond imagination, but smart. He has a plan. I'm thinking he arranged for the Lexus to be stolen. Let other people tear it up."

"What do you mean the guy is twisted?"

At the second detective's question, Bud jumped in. "Come with us." He led them to the Crown Vic and removed the folder with photos of the victim.

"Before you do that . . ." Carmen made eye contact with

the counties. "This is not a typical murder. We have to keep our cards close to our vest. Keep this to yourselves. Deal?"

"Deal." The lead county detective smirked as if humoring "the little lady." Ah, male chauvinism. It was alive and well in every police force.

"Thanks." Carmen nodded at Bud, who whipped out the gruesome photo of Cohen.

Eyes widened.

"The guy hit him with a Mac truck?" The junior detective turned his head.

"Nope." Carmen watched the men. "Our guy did this with his fists."

The senior officer's gaze hardened. "We'll help any way we can, Detective. Just say the word."

18

Homicide work begins with dread at what the investigator will find, followed by days of exhaustive, sometimes dreary work, punctuated with the occasional bit of useful information and culminating in an arrest. Usually.

Every year, approximately thirteen thousand people in the United States die as victims of murder. Carmen, however, knew what few citizens did: nationwide, one in three murderers got away with the crime. Some cities had it worse. Only thirty-five percent of homicides in Chicago were solved. New Orleans and Detroit were even worse, with only one in five homicides solved. Other cities such as Philadelphia and Denver fared better, closing the book on seventy to ninety percent of the crimes. But San Diego?

They had a closure rate of more than 90 percent.

That was something to be proud about, but it also brought great pressure.

What really depressed Carmen, though, was that a third of the serial killers went unpunished. She took some comfort in knowing that serial killers tended to stay around. It was part of their sick game. The irony wasn't wasted on her.

She steered her car up the I-15 in no rush to reach her destination. Driving was thinking time for her, and since Bud had gone home to his family, she was making the trip alone. The week had been grueling, the slow flow of evidence grinding away layer after layer of her confidence. It had been four days since the CHP found Cohen's car. Forensics found nothing of value in what was left of the vehicle. The sheriff's department had assigned a number of officers to search abandoned or otherwise empty buildings for clues that might tie a pair of deaths to the location.

The negative report didn't surprise Carmen. She didn't expect any revelations. Their killer was too smart to leave something behind that might identify him. He left behind only what he wanted the police to find.

Doug Lindsey's Volkswagen had yet to turn up. DNA from the Dodge Caravan was inconclusive, damaged as it was by the hydrogen peroxide and bleach. A bit of useful DNA made it through PCR, but it matched the swabs taken of the elderly couple who owned the vehicle.

Dr. Norman Shuffler had released both bodies to the families. Cohen was buried almost immediately. Rabbi Singer performed the service, a steady stream of tears lining his face. Carmen had attended, ostensibly to show friends and family that the SDPD cared and did more than ask questions of the family. She also attended because she wanted to scan the crowd. The murderer might just be whacked enough to attend the funeral of a man he beat and kicked to death.

She looked into eyes and stole glances at everyone she could, especially of the larger men. A bruised hand might indicate injury from repeatedly beating a man hanging from the ceiling.

She struck out.

Dr. Shuffler had also found two small puncture marks on Doug Lindsey's body, a miracle since the kid's skin had more holes than the moon has craters. "These holes don't fit the pattern," Shuffler had explained. "Remember, the killer used a pizza docker to inflict the wounds. The docker had evenly spaced pins on the cylinder. That created an even pattern. These two holes don't match."

"What's your best guess, Doc?"

"Taser. Police grade." He apologized for not coming up with more.

Something else weighed on Carmen's mind, something her partner said yesterday when he was seated at his desk, his face bathed in the light from his computer monitor. It made him look anemic.

He'd looked at her. "Hey, didn't you go to Madison High School?"

"Um, yes. Didn't you have eggs for breakfast?"

"What?"

She had shrugged. "I thought it was a game. You know, toss out unconnected, meaningless questions."

"You're a laugh a minute, that's what you are, but there is a connection . . . I think. Did you know that Ellis Poe went to the same school? About the same time as you. Did you know him then?"

"What are you doing?" She moved to his desk and looked over his shoulder.

"I'm doing a deeper background check on some of the people we've interviewed. I just noticed that Poe and you were schoolmates."

"It's a big school. Our paths may have crossed, but I don't remember it."

Bud studied the screen. It was the Web site of the seminary and he was on the faculty page. "Looks like he graduated a year after you. Maybe he knew your sister."

The sentence was a long, fiery sword to the gut. "Like I said, it was a big school. Shelly never mentioned him. She had her own crowd."

"Maybe. I doubt Poe was the kind of guy who ran with a crowd. Probably just went to class, then to the library, then home. You know, the bookworm type."

She did know. She was a bookworm type. Getting into med school required the best of grades, something Carmen worked at day and night—until Shelly's murder. "I'll ask next time I see him." She stepped away, but each step took concentration and more strength than it should.

Carmen pushed the thoughts of yesterday from her mind as she pulled off the freeway and onto the street that led to the San Diego Theological Seminary.

Lindsey's memorial service would be held there, at 6:00, then a graveside at a local cemetery. At first, Carmen's motives for attending were the same as for attending the Cohen service: to see who showed up. But now . . .

With Bud's revelation, she had new reasons.

Darkness cloaked the small school set on a hill overlooking the city of Escondido. Evening was one of Ellis's favorite times. It meant the day's duties were done and an evening of relaxation awaited him. Tonight would be different. Dr. Bridger had offered the seminary chapel to Doug Lindsey's parents, an offer the cash-strapped family accepted. Their small church, Ellis had heard, had made the same offer, but their facility could not hold the student body that was certain to come to celebrate the "home going" of their classmate. "Celebrate" was a misunderstood term. Those outside the faith imagined Christians gathered around the open casket of the departed, swapped jokes and sipped Kool-Aid. Those who attended a memorial service in honor of a Christian who had passed knew better. One celebrated eternal life but wept openly for the personal loss.

Ellis was glad he wasn't officiating. During his career he had been asked to perform a simple graveside or a small memorial service, but he had never been able to do so. He admired the pastors who did this work week in and week out. He had no idea how they did it. Just attending a funeral made his spine quiver.

He waited behind the closed door of his office where he hid from the incoming crowds. From his dark space he could hear voices as people walked past his door; he could hear the solemn tones of their conversation. For a few moments, he listened to what sounded like a young woman weeping and someone—a male friend—comforting her. Then he heard the familiar cadence of prayer. He couldn't make out the words, but the emotion was clear enough.

Five minutes before the service was to start, Ellis rose, slipped into his black suit coat, smoothed his dark blue tie, and buttoned the jacket. Then he straightened his spine and took a deep breath.

As a rule he walked with his gaze down and set a couple of yards ahead of him, but as he stepped from his office and into the darkening evening, headlights caught his attention. The lights went off, the driver's door opened, and Detective Carmen Rainmondi stepped into view. She waved, and for some reason he thought that an odd thing to do. Nonetheless, he waved back.

If it had been possible he would have ignored her, pretended not to have seen her arrive, but their gazes had crossed and he felt obligated to wait for the woman. It was the polite thing to do, the right thing to do. It just wasn't something he *wanted* to do. He gave a smile despite the situation.

"Evening, Detective." Ellis held out his hand to offer a polite shake. "Don't take this the wrong way, but I didn't expect to see you here."

"I hope I'm not intruding." Her tone was even, friendly. "I want those who knew young Mr. Lindsey to know he is still in the forefront of our minds, that we are still working the case."

Ellis motioned toward the open doors of the chapel and started that direction with a slow, even pace. "You're planning to say that publicly?"

Carmen shook her head. "Of course not. I have no plans to bother anyone."

A sense of relief ran through Ellis. He was just beginning to enjoy it when the detective added, "Except you of course."

Ellis's stride shortened, but Detective Rainmondi kept hers even and straight. She reminded Ellis of a battleship plowing through rough seas.

"Me?"

"Yes, sir. I want to ask you about my sister."

Ellis's heart tumbled and for moment he thought it would stop beating. His lungs ceased to draw breath. He had to take two long strides to catch up with the female detective. Questions rattled in his mind: *What makes you think I know your sister? Why do you bring her up now?* But he kept his mouth shut and did his best to act as if she'd begun a discussion of the weather.

Ellis was "a back-pew Baptist." He was most comfortable sitting in the rear of any building. From the rear pew he could see everything. Like an Old West gunslinger, he preferred to have a wall at his back. He slipped onto the rearmost pew on the west side of the chapel and was surprised when Carmen Rainmondi joined him. He smiled, indicating his pleasure—pleasure he felt, so long as they avoided one particular topic.

Try as he might he could not keep his eyes from stealing glances at the woman who sat to his left. She gave no indication of what she was thinking or feeling. She set her purse between them, as if erecting a wall. She unbuttoned the single button of her dark gray women's business coat and pushed back in the pew.

Ellis forced his gaze forward to the large oak pulpit that sat center of the raised dais. Affixed to the front of the pulpit was a simple wood cross, the enduring symbol of Christianity.

The chapel was not large when compared to the worship centers of mega-churches. In the latter, thousands could gather to sing God's praises and listen to the sermon. The chapel seated five hundred, which was more than necessary for the weekly chapel service. The Board of Directors for the seminary had elected to build a larger facility than needed so it could be used as an outreach for the community, and for situations such as this.

Tonight, the chapel was nearly full. Students interrupted their weeklong Easter break to return to campus and offer their support to the family and to seek a measure of personal healing. Ellis knew that some were Doug's friends, a few were little more than classmates, and some didn't know him at all. The latter came to lend their strength and prayers to those hurting most.

There were still a few moments before the service would start, and Ellis struggled to find a line of conversation that did not lead back to Carmen's sister, Shelley.

"Do you . . ." Ellis coughed, as if the words had stuck in his throat. He tried again. "Do you attend many church services?"

"Can't say that I do, Professor. My family is Catholic, but we almost never went to Mass. Oh, we went on the occasional Easter, or if we knew someone whose baby was being baptized, but that's pretty much it. I guess we are Catholic in name only."

"I see."

She eyed him for a moment. "I imagine you think I'm some sort of heathen."

"That may be going a little too far. I wouldn't have used the word *heathen*."

"Oh, really?" She hiked an eyebrow. "What term would you use?"

Ellis would've felt a little more comfortable if she had uttered those words with a smile. The detective didn't seem to smile often. "I'm sorry. I didn't mean it that way."

"How did you mean it?"

Ellis scratched the back of his head as if doing so would push ideas to the front of his mind. "I prefer the term *unchurched*. It's less offensive." He scratched the back of his head again. He was trying to make headway, but everything he said seemed to make the path of conversation all the more slippery.

She kept her eyes on him, as if every insecurity, fear, and regret were scrolling across his face. Thankfully, Dr. Adam Bridger stepped to the pulpit.

"On behalf of the family of Doug Lindsey and on behalf of our seminary family, I wish to thank each of you for coming tonight to do the difficult work of grieving. It is no easy thing that we do today, but few things are as important. One week ago our world was shaken by the news of the death of one of our own. The nature of that death, the suddenness, the brutality of it, has branded our minds, our hearts, and our souls."

The sound of sniffling filled the open space, traveling from the front row where the family sat to the back where Ellis hid. He knew that it would only get worse, and for a few moments his mind put aside his own worries and centered on the family that had been so damaged by an unimaginable cruelty.

"Most of us," Bridger continued, "have been in services similar to this. Perhaps the nature of death was different; perhaps the passing was expected. No matter how many times we have faced the mortality of those around us and of ourselves, we never get used to it. That is how it should be. The theologians remind us that death is unnatural; experience teaches us that no one gets out of this life alive."

Dr. Bridger's tone was steady and strong, and Ellis could feel a measure of comfort from the cadence and content of his words. Bridger was a master communicator, and it was his sincerity that gave his words enduring power and the ability to touch minds and hearts. Ellis was glad to know a man of such high caliber.

Ellis glanced at Carmen. Her eyes were fixed on the front of the chapel. She showed no emotion but seemed to be listening.

"We have come to knit our hearts together for the noble, the dignified, the important work of mourning the loss of family and friend. We also gather to stand with the Lindsey family. Our weakness becomes strength when we stand together." Bridger looked to the front pew. "No words that I utter tonight can remove your hurt or dampen your pain."

Quiet sobs joined the sniffling. Bridger stood straight and appeared strong, something Ellis knew he did to help others through the weakest moments of their lives.

Bridger continued. "The pain you feel—the pain we all feel—is the price and the proof of love. If Doug had not been loved and loved deeply, then this building would be empty. Our tears are our way of expressing our love. Nonetheless, we have gathered as Christians, and that makes dealing with the pain possible. We rejoice that Doug's faith in Christ has assured him a place in heaven, a place paid for by the death and resurrection of our Lord and Savior Jesus Christ. He is in a world of great glory now, a place where tears do not fall, a place where pain cannot be felt. However, we are not so simpleminded as to think that Doug's entrance into heaven has not left many hurting and empty. Tonight, we will call upon God's Word to help us face the future, but first let us stand and pray."

As the congregation stood, Ellis saw a choir assemble behind Dr. Bridger. It was going to be a difficult night, but a meaningful one.

After the prayer, the congregation sat again and directed their attention to the front of the chapel. The congregation joined the choir and sang "It Is Well with My Soul."

Ellis could only lose himself in the service for a few moments at a time, knowing that at the end of the memorial the woman sitting next to him might ask questions he'd spent years not answering. His stomach filled with acid, and he could imagine that it was consuming his internal organs. A bit of lung. A slice of liver . . .

Slowly but surely, Ellis felt as if he were dissolving from the inside out.

19

It had been Ellis's plan to exit the chapel and quietly make his way back to his office while the mourners visited and made their way to their cars for the sad journeys home.

Carmen changed that.

"Don't take off, Professor. A few minutes of your time, please." Somehow she had made the statement sound like a request, but Ellis considered it an order. She waited as friends and family gathered around Lindsey's parents.

When the crowd thinned, Carmen moved forward and Ellis watched as she bent to speak to the still-seated Lindsey family.

He tried to make the best possible use of the time by formulating reasons he couldn't stay and talk. He could tell her that he only had a few moments before making his way to the graveside service—the service he hadn't planned to attend. Maybe he should ask her back to his office, but the thought of being alone with her in a confined space unnerved him. Perhaps they should meet someplace public, where she would be required to keep a professional decorum. But where? A coffee shop? A restaurant?

Maybe if they went nowhere—avoided the office and eateries, and just stood in the night as the seminary campus became more empty—the meeting might be shortened.

Ellis had no idea what to do. His instinct begged to walk into the parking lot, enter his car, and drive home, but then he'd look all the more guilty. Besides, the detective knew where he lived and even where he kept his boat. There was nothing for him to do but stand and endure.

Carmen returned down the center aisle of the chapel, walking with a confidence and assuredness that Ellis had seldom seen in others.

And had never seen in himself.

"Ready?"

He nodded. "You have a question for me?" Maybe if he stood his ground in the chapel, he could keep the questions to a minimum.

"Yes. May we use your office?"

Doom.

"Sure." He tried to sound sure of himself but was pretty sure it failed. If insecurity were a crime, Ellis would've been arrested decades ago.

"Are you going to the graveside service?" Carmen followed one step behind and to his left as they moved from the chapel.

Say yes! "I hadn't planned to. You?"

"No. That would be overkill." She grimaced. "Sorry. That was a poor choice of words."

"If that's the biggest mistake you make in life, you're doing well."

They walked along the sidewalk that fronted the chapel and past the doors that led to classrooms. Ellis's office was only twenty yards from the administration building. The air was cool and carried a tad more humidity than was normal. The coolness seeped into the marrow of Ellis's bones.

Ellis put the key into the lock on his office door and gave it a quick turn. It swung open silently on well-oiled hinges. He flicked on the overhead lights and waited for the detective to enter. He closed the door after her and eyed the chair she had sat in when the two first met a week ago.

Ellis hesitated for a moment as he tried to decide whether to sit behind his desk or in the other guest chair. Sitting behind his desk might lend him a degree of dignity and the slight advantage of being on his own turf. Somehow he didn't think that would affect Carmen. Sitting in the second guest chair might make him look a little more friendly and comfortable. He unbuttoned his suit coat but left it on. He turned her chair ninety degrees from the desk and then did the same with his. He sat, crossed his legs, folded his hands, and tried to look relaxed.

Carmen set her purse on the floor and smoothed her jacket; then she looked up and drilled her gaze into his eyes. "I just learned that we went to the same high school together. I don't recall meeting you. Did you go to Madison High School on Doliva Street?"

The question welded him to his seat. *Calm. It's just a question. Just a twisting, rending, set-your-mind-blazing question.*

"I did. I don't recall meeting you either. What year did you graduate?"

"Maybe you knew my sister? Shelley?"

She'd sidestepped his question and asked one of her own. Was this an interview technique? A way of throwing him off balance?

It was working.

Ellis was beginning to feel paranoid. He paused before answering. Tried to look as though he were thinking hard, searching his memory. "Shelley Rainmondi. I knew of her. We shared a few classes, but that was it. We traveled in different circles." *Not that I had much of a circle.*

He wasn't sure, but Ellis thought he saw Carmen tense. What did that mean? What had he said to trigger that?

"Forgive me, Dr. Poe, but I find it odd that you didn't mention it to me the first time we met."

Ellis cocked his head. "Why is that?"

"Because, Professor, Rainmondi is not a common name. I would think that once you heard it you would've made the association."

Ellis couldn't keep the slight defensive note from his words. "That was a long time ago, Detective. Decades."

"Why didn't you mention you knew my sister?" There was no doubt now—the detective was tensing. Her eyes sparked like struck flint.

Ellis uncrossed his legs, put both feet on the floor, and scooted back in his chair. "Let me see if I have this right, Detective. You're put out with me because I didn't mention your sister when you came into my office to talk about the murder of one of my students. Do I have that right?" It was a bit of bravado he did not feel.

"As I said, it strikes me as odd."

"Forgive me for being blunt, Detective, but you are out of line. I'm a quiet man, a loner, and you probably already picked up the fact that I'm not very social."

"Yes."

"I saw no reason to mention your sister, Detective. First, I remember the names of many of my fellow students, but it doesn't mean that I followed their lives outside of high school. Second, you came into my office with a very specific agenda, and that was to learn all you could about Doug Lindsey. Third, I had just learned that a student of mine had been murdered. Murder might be your stock-in-trade; it's not mine. I was stunned, hardly at my best. Perhaps you picked up on that, too."

"What about the second time we met? In Coronado? Were you still stunned then?"

"As a matter of fact, I'm stunned to this day. It's not the kind of thing a man like me gets over quickly."

The detective inhaled deeply and held it for a moment. "What kind of man are you, Professor?"

Time to gamble on bluster. He bristled. "I'm the kind of man unaccustomed to being accused of wrongdoing. I'm sorry if you thought I should've mentioned your sister, but let's be realistic. High school was a very long time ago." Ellis raised a hand. "Yes, I'm aware of your sister's death. Maybe I should've offered my condolences thirty years after the fact, but the truth is, I was thinking about Doug Lindsey."

The detective broke eye contact and spent a moment looking at the carpet to her right. From the faraway look on her features, her mind was someplace other than in this room.

Ellis sighed. "I'm sorry, Detective, if I come across too strong. I can't imagine the pain the loss of your sister has brought you. In no way do I mean to imply that Doug Lindsey's death is more important than your sister's."

"Too strong?" She chuckled. "Trust me, that wasn't strong. Learning to speak your mind might do you some good." She started to speak again when a sound emitted from her jacket pocket. "Excuse me." She retrieved a smart phone, tapped the screen, and placed it to her ear. "Rainmondi."

"I got a good-news-bad-news thing here."

Carmen held back a smile. Bud Tock kept his sense of humor even when he was dog-tired. "I thought you were taking the rest of the day off." Carmen did her best to deliver the line like a straight man.

"Rest of the day? Really? You're going with that? I worked all weekend and have been logging the same long hours as you. A man has to go home to his family every once in awhile or he gets divorce papers."

"Just razzin' you. What's up?" Carmen looked at Ellis, who seemed to have shrunk several inches after his effort to sound offended by her comments. She raised a finger, indicating she would be with him in a moment. She returned her attention to Bud. "Okay, I'll bite. What's the good news?"

"We found Doug Lindsey's VW."

"Do I want to know the bad news?"

"Does it matter? You're gonna have to hear it anyway. We found the car. We also found a body in it."

Carmen let a vulgar expletive shoot past her lips, then looked at the professor. She mouthed the word, *Sorry*. "How come they didn't call me?"

"They did. You didn't pick up."

"That's crazy, I've got a good signal . . . Oh, wait. The service. I muted my phone because I was in the memorial service." She swore again. This time she didn't offer an apology.

"I sent a text, too. It has the location. I'll see you when you get here. Oh . . . a bit of advice: don't eat before you come."

"Why?"

"Because the body has been submerged for a week."

The image that flashed in Carmen's mind turned her stomach. "Thanks for the warning. I'm on my way. I'll apologize to your wife later." She ended the call and stood. "Thank you for your time, Dr. Poe. Something's come up and I have to leave."

Ellis rose and walked to the door. "May I ask if it pertains to Doug's case?"

She paused at the door. "Yes, but keep this under your hat." She relayed Bud's message. The color drained from Poe's face.

20

What Carmen Rainmondi wanted to do was stew over her conversation with Dr. Poe. In many ways, she liked the man. He was courteous, intelligent, and unassuming.

He also had a secret.

If pressed in court about that last thought, she wouldn't be able to say why she was so sure. It was instinct, something undefined in his tone or manner or eye-movement that made her think Poe wasn't showing all his cards. But instead of thinking about the short meeting in the professor's office, her mind raced ahead to what might be waiting for her at Lake Murray Community Park north of I-8 and east of College Avenue.

The location fit with the Cohen murder but not with that of Doug Lindsey—at least not on the surface. Lindsey's body was found in Balboa Park, which was much further to the southwest. Just one more confusing factoid—unless both men were killed in the same area. She had already established that the bodies had been transported from the murder scene or scenes.

Bud had been precise in the location. Lake Murray, a reservoir really, was a small body of water next to the Alvarado Water Treatment Plant on the south shore. She moved through the 6300 block of Park Ridge Boulevard and turned into a small paved lot next to a recreation building with a blue roof. To her left was a pair of baseball fields, occupied by what she took to be a local softball league. Each team had matching uniforms, but no game was underway. Instead, the athletes lined the fence on the third-base side of the nearest field. Apparently, the activity of the police by the water's edge was more interesting than running the bases.

She pulled from the paved portion of the lot and drove over a dirt island and onto a service road that ran closer to the shore. The majority of the lake lay farther to the south, but that didn't matter. Bud told her the body and car were found in one of the finger recesses that gave Lake Murray it's odd shape. She had no trouble finding the location. Two patrol cars lined the access road, and one had left its light bar flashing in the dark, splashing blue and red swatches on the area. Carmen pulled in front of the marked cars and exited the Crown Vic.

A yellow tape barricade had marked off the length of the inlet's shoreline. Two officers monitored the perimeter. Carmen pulled back her coat enough to reveal her badge and her holster, an unnecessary motion since the Crown Vic said, "Cop." Still, she liked to follow protocol as much as possible.

One of the officers lifted the tape. "Detective."

"Officer." She gave a "we're-in-the-same-club" nod and slipped beneath the crime scene tape.

The scene was surreal. Spotlights from the patrol car shone toward the water, casting long shadows in front of people and plants. Additional light from the lights around the baseball diamond helped, but she still felt as if half her vision had gone.

A tow truck from the company that provided services to the SDPD was parked just inside the tape barrier, and a long metal cable stretched from the back of the vehicle to the rear bumper of an old, beige VW Beetle. That car was old when Carmen was in high school, but the body looked to be in good condition. Someone loved the car.

"Welcome to overtime."

She nodded to her partner. "Hey, Bud." She studied the area and walked carefully to where he stood, several feet behind and to the side of the VW.

"Watch the tire tracks." He pointed. "I'm gonna cast them, even though I'm sure they belong to the Bug. Also, there are some imprints over here that might belong to our man. They look like boot prints."

"How can you tell in this stuff?" The ground leading to the water was mostly desert sand. She shone her flashlight on the ground. "There are prints everywhere."

"Yeah, I know. Public park in the middle of a major city. Throw in a shoreline, and people flock to it like a moth to . . . whatever a moth likes. So where were you when I called?"

"Escondido. I went to the Lindsey funeral." She didn't see any reason to talk about her discussion with Poe. "Why?"

"It took a while for you to get here."

She shrugged. "I had dinner, hit a couple of bars, went shopping, then visited my sweet Aunt May."

Bud's brows creased. "It wasn't a complaint, Carmen, just an observation. No need to get snippy."

"The long hours are getting to me. So what do we have?"

"Shortly before sundown, a mother and her children saw something glinting in the water. She said it looked like a bumper to a car. She called the police. A street unit showed up about ten minutes later. He took a look and recognized the bumper style. VWs have a unique bumper arrangement. He called for a tow truck and let his supervisor know what he was looking at. We have a BOLO out for a VW so they let homicide know. Heywood was still in the office. He's a go-getter, that one." He pointed to a figure a short distance away. Heywood stood back a few steps from the passenger side of the vehicle.

"Yeah, he is. I think he wants your job."

"There are days when I'd give it to him."

Carmen looked him in the eye. "Really?"

"No. I'm fishing for pity."

She smiled. "Getting any bites?"

"Apparently not. Anyway, Heywood got wind of it and phoned me. I guess he likes me better."

"He doesn't know you like I do." Carmen gazed at the VW—she would have to look inside soon.

"I told him to get down here and scope things out, which he did. He oversaw the car's extraction from the lake. He also took a ton of photos. The car was almost completely out of sight. First guess is, our guy killed the passenger then drove here and pushed the car into the water. As you can see, or could see if it were daylight, the water has a great deal of moss and reeds. No wonder it took so long to find."

"Aren't VW Bugs supposed to float?"

"They used to advertise that, but the car is a '67 so it's well over forty years old. I doubt it's as watertight as it was four decades ago."

"And the body is in the car?"

"Oh, yeah. I hope you were kidding about stopping for dinner. Come on, I'll show you."

"I can hardly wait." Carmen swallowed her reluctance and followed Bud to the car.

Moving down the shallow slope leading from the access road to the ebony water, Carmen recognized a man standing next to the open door of the VW and hunched forward, peering inside. She didn't need to see his face to know it was Dr. Norman Shuffler. Why was he here?

"I thought your days in the field were over, Doc." Carmen tried to sound upbeat.

Shuffler withdrew his torso from the car's cab and turned to face Carmen. "Ah, 'She walks in beauty as the night.'" He wore nitrile gloves. As he turned, an odor from the car filled the area. Carmen's eyes burned, her throat constricted, and for a moment she thought she'd vomit everything she had eaten that month. How Shuffler could lean over the waterlogged corpse was beyond her.

"Um, yeah, I always look better in the dark."

"Nonsense. You always look good." Shuffler held his ground as if trying to keep Carmen at a distance. Silence, as thick as the stench, hung in the air. "I left standing orders at the ME office that I was to be notified of any calls that might be related to Lindsey and Cohen. This fit the bill."

Bud had stopped his approach. He apparently had no desire

to see the body again. Carmen had to look at the victim. It was her job. She had seen bad things before: dismembered bodies, brutal sexual assaults, children killed by stoned parents—she could handle this. She kept telling herself that.

Carmen didn't know how other cops did it, but she had a lead-lined curtain in her mind, one she could draw to shut the emotional, reactive part of her brain from the logical, proactive part. She took a deep breath before closing the distance and held it for a moment. Shuffler stepped aside and began talking as if conversation might calm the boiling acid vat that was her stomach.

"He had his wallet on him. Twenty-two-year-old white male. He's been submerged for awhile, so his remains are in bad shape. Really bad shape."

Carmen shone her light on the body. The young man looked like a character from a Zombie movie, only worse. His eyes, what was left of them, were open, revealing fogged orbs half their normal size. His lips were drawn back revealing teeth, his tongue swollen. His skin was pale, almost white. There was evidence that fish in the lake had been dining on him.

She forced down the gorge threatening to erupt from her stomach. The lead curtain closed tight.

Raising her head, she noticed two things: first, the windows were open; second, there was a hole about the size of a 9mm slug in the vic's head. "Did you lower the windows, Doc?"

"No. They were that way when I got here."

"Bud?"

He was close enough to hear the question. "Nope. The thing went in with the windows down."

Carmen returned her attention to the ME. "We know the car belonged to Lindsey, and he was killed about a week ago. Am I right in assuming that . . ." She motioned to the body.

Shuffler didn't need a complete sentence to understand. "His name is Bob Wilton. His license says Bob, not Robert. Yes, I'd say on preliminary examination that the body has been in the water about a week, which fits with the time of death for Doug Lindsey. Of course, it's going to be difficult to prove, but I see nothing that contradicts the assumption."

"Not much guesswork needed for COD." Carmen stared at the swollen bullet wound.

"I can't say officially, but you can probably bet your house on the fact that Mr. Wilton died from a gunshot wound to the head. The other side of the cranium is a mess."

Carmen nodded. "Through and through?"

"Yes. Small hole here." He pointed to the wound. "Big hole on the other side. He's been in the water too long for powder residue, although I might have more luck once I have him back in the office."

Turning, Carmen walked to Bud. Heywood had joined him. Carmen addressed the newcomer first. "Okay, Heywood, what does that gigantic intellect of yours tell you?"

"About the murder?"

"No, about the softball game in the park. Of course, about the murder." She raised a hand. "Sorry. I'm a little on edge."

"No problem, Detective." Heywood straightened. "What strikes me as odd is the gunshot wound to the head. It doesn't fit the other murders."

Carmen gave a nod. "Go on." The three strolled up the bank slowly, still careful about where they stepped.

"Well, Victim Number 1 was tortured and died of anaphylactic shock brought on by latex powder on the murderer's gloves."

"Probably an accident," Bud said. "Not that the man didn't intend to kill Lindsey anyway."

Heywood continued. "Victim Number 2 died of a vicious beating. Both murders were protracted and hands on. The killer here popped the vic in the car with a shot to the head. Impersonal. Fast."

"Why?" Carmen pursed her lips. "Why would he do that? Why change?"

"I'd just be guessing, Detective," Heywood said.

"You'd be surprised how often a guess is right, Officer. Give me your best shot." Carmen stopped at the top of the slope just a couple of feet from the crime scene tape.

"Victim 3 was in the way. He didn't fit whatever the actor is doing, so he just squeezed off a shot. Maybe he did so when he grabbed Lindsey."

"I'm thinking along the same lines. Does that make sense to you, Bud?"

"Yep. Maybe Lindsey and Wilton were out together. Bad guy approaches them somewhere, drills Wilton and takes Lindsey at gunpoint."

"But if he has Lindsey, then how does he have time to drive the Bug here and sink it, unless—"

"—the crime happened here."

"Maybe he sedated Lindsey," Heywood suggested.

"Doc said he found a pair of puncture marks that didn't fit the pattern of the other punctures over the kid's body."

"The Taser thing you mentioned," Bud said. "That's crossed my mind. So he shoots one guy in the car and uses a Taser on the other? That had to be terrifying."

"Wait . . . wait." Carmen's brain had dropped into fourth gear. "Doc says the exit wound is large. If Lindsey is in the driver's seat when his buddy is shot, then why didn't we find blood spatter on his clothing?"

"The bad guy redressed Lindsey after the kid died?" Heywood didn't sound convinced of his own suggestion. "That would mean that he anticipated the problem."

"We gotta go simpler," Carmen said. "Look for the obvious answer."

Bud scratched his chin. "Okay, how about this? Lindsey wasn't in the car at the time. Maybe the perp takes him out with the Taser, then approaches the VW and does Wilton."

That was a real possibility. "Makes sense. But what situation would fit that scenario?"

"Maybe Lindsey needed to use the head, and his buddy stayed in the car." Bud thought for a second. "But that means the perp would know that Lindsey would do that and would have lain in wait. How would he know that?"

"Wait a second." Carmen looked back at the VW. She was going to have to do what she didn't want to: return to the VW. "I'll be right back."

She went to study the corpse again, seeing this time what the hideous condition of the body kept her from seeing before. She returned to the two who waited for her at the top of the bank. She uttered four words as if they answered everything: "He's wearing jogging clothes."

Bud stared at her for a moment, then raised an eyebrow.

The three looked to the park.

"That would explain a lot." Bud gave a slow nod. "A lot."

Carmen waited for the forensics team to arrive, then supervised as they removed the hideous corpse from the small car, placed it on a gurney, covered it, and took it to the ME vehicle. She took her own photos, not because she didn't trust the crime-scene unit or Heywood, but because taking photos focused her attention on details.

She and Bud had interviewed everyone still at the park, and she sent Heywood and a few other officers to search for security cameras. There were no traffic cams in the area, but maybe some security-conscious homeowner had a camera mounted to the front of his or her house. That would be lucky.

Too bad she and luck hadn't been on speaking terms since the first body was found.

21

Carmen and Bud were the last to leave the scene. They drove to the address on Bob Wilton's driver's license—she in her car, Bud following in his. The place was dark and empty. Mail was jammed into the small box. No one had been to the house in days. Which meant Wilton lived alone. The home was located in the town of Allied Gardens, not far west of Lake Murray.

She looked around the small bungalow. Streetlights illuminated the front of the home. Its pale green paint looked newly applied. White trim accented the exterior. The small lawn—far better than what welcomed guests to Carmen's home—was neat, mowed, and looked well attended. Small plants in a dirt strip added visual interest to an otherwise plain wall.

"Keeps a neat yard."

"A week's salary says it's a rental." Bud stepped to Carmen's side. "Not many twenty-something-year-olds spend their time gardening."

"It's not gardening, smart guy, just a few plants and a lawn."

Bud stared at her for a long moment. "You forget, I've been to your house."

"Touché." The comment stung and she couldn't guess why. She didn't care what other people thought of her yard or home or much of anything else. "Let's knock."

"You expect someone to answer? The only person that's been up these porch steps is the mail carrier."

"Still, it's gotta be done. Can't have some suit asking if we knocked or not, and if not, why."

Bud shrugged. "I guess."

Carmen moved up the steps, her gaze shifting from the front door to the living room window, looking for movement or a shadow. It was closing in on eleven. Not a time when people came to the front door of houses. Bud moved to the window and peeked around the jamb. He shook his head, indicating he saw nothing of interest.

A wood-frame screen door opened without a squeak. She knocked firmly but without aggression. She wanted to sound like a friend, not a home invader. As expected, no one responded and she heard nothing. This time she rang the doorbell. The sound of it, a sound that reminded Carmen of her parent's home, oozed outside. Still no response.

Carmen pulled a latex glove from her pocket and used it to turn the doorknob. To her surprise, it turned. She opened the door an inch then drew her Glock 9mm. Bud had already done the same.

"Look," he deadpanned, "the door is open. Someone might need our help." He moved behind Carmen and pulled the screen door wider.

She removed a small flashlight from the pocket of her blazer, pointed it to the porch, and clicked it on. Then she pushed the door open and entered. "San Diego Police. Anyone here?" If she believed she was entering a charged situation, she would have kept the announcement to herself, but she and Bud were entering a private residence without a warrant and on the pretense that someone might be injured. There was no response.

The living room had an old sofa, a coffee table that might have once belonged to the Flintstones, and a small flat-screen television sitting on an old school desk.

Bud moved around her and headed to the kitchen, an open area just off a small dining room. "Clear."

Carmen started down the hall, coming across the hall bath first. It was empty. "Clear."

Bud had already moved down the hall and pushed into a bedroom. "Clear."

It was Carmen's turn at the lead again. The door to the bedroom was closed. Again, she used the glove to keep her prints off the surface of the doorknob. Bud was by her side before she could twist the knob. Carmen pushed the door open and slipped in, afraid she would find someone in the bed. The bed—a mattress on the floor—was empty as was the half-bath of the master bedroom. They holstered their weapons.

"Kid lives a simple life." Bud looked around.

"No bet—" Carmen raised her hand and cocked her head, turning her ear to the master bedroom door. She drew her weapon again. Bud didn't seem to have heard the noise, but he followed suit. Carmen tapped her ear, then pointed out the open door. They separated, each taking a different angle on the door.

They kept their lights off. The pale glow of a night-light emanated from the master bath.

A pair of metal tubes slowly appeared in the doorway. No, not tubes. It took less than two blinks for Carmen to recognize the business end of a double-barrel shotgun. Bud's movements blurred as he seized the end of the weapon and shoved the barrels up toward the ceiling with one hand, then aimed the bore of his handgun at the forehead of the man wielding the shotgun.

Carmen advanced. "Drop it. Drop it now!" Her shout echoed in the near-empty room. Bud pulled the weapon away. "On the ground. Do it now. Face down. *Do* it!" She had enough light to see she was talking to a man.

The man complied. She got a sense that he was thin, even frail. She kept her weapon trained on him until Bud had set the shotgun aside and dropped a knee on the man's back. She heard the wind leave his lungs, carrying a small cry of pain with it.

"Don't hurt me. Please don't hurt me." The voice of an older man. "Who . . . who are you?"

"San Diego PD, pal," Bud said. "Hands behind your back."

"No, wait. You don't understand."

Carmen peeked around the door frame, then entered the hall, handgun leading the way. No one. She closed the front door and locked it. When she returned, she saw the gunman sitting crossed-legged on the floor, his head down. Bud was clearing the shotgun.

"Loaded?" Carmen switched on the light.

"Oh, yeah. If he had pulled the trigger, neither one of us would be as good looking as we are right now."

"Are you guys really cops?"

"We're as real as it get." Carmen took in the man. He looked like a guy who had sixty in his rearview mirror. Gray stubble carpeted his chin and cheeks, his eyes were wide and moist, his frame thin, like a man at the end of a long illness. He smelled of cigarettes and beer. "What's your name?"

"Schirru. Greg Schirru. I live next door. I own the place. This place, I mean."

"You're the landlord?"

"Yes, ma'am. Look, can I stand up? I'm really uncomfortable. Arthritis in my lower spine. Sitting like this is agony."

Carmen was getting the picture. "Sure." She and Bud lifted the man to his feet.

"Maybe the cuffs too?" He sounded childlike.

"Let's wait on that. You were waving a shotgun at us a few moments ago." Carmen tried to sound firm, but not mean.

"Sorry about that. I thought you were a burglar or somethin'."

Bud grinned. "Turns out we were the somethin'."

"I guess so, but I was just trying to protect my property. A man can do that, right? I mean, we haven't lost all our rights."

Carmen didn't want to get into that debate. "Why didn't you call the police?"

"I did. I did, but you know how long that can take."

Bud couldn't let that go. "Our response time is pretty good, sir."

"I guess so. You were here before I called."

Carmen blinked several times, then decided not to unravel that. She looked at Bud.

"I got it." He removed his cell phone and placed a call to the dispatchers informing them of their location and that the burglary call could be canceled.

"I'm Detective Carmen Rainmondi, homicide. This is my partner Detective Bud Tock. We need to ask you a few questions."

"Sure—wait. Homicide? Really? Homicide? But that would mean . . ." He leaned forward like a man about to empty his stomach. He took a couple of deep breaths then straightened. "Tell me you're not here because . . . Bob?" The man looked as if he had been punched. Tears filled already full eyes. "Gone? He's gone?"

"Yes, sir. I'm sorry. Mr. Wilton was murdered."

"How—no, wait—I don't want to know yet. I . . ." He bent again.

Carmen didn't rush the man. She did move back a step. "Are you going to be all right, sir?"

"I think so." Again he straightened. "I just can't wrap my brain around it. Okay. Okay." Tears trickled over his stubble-covered cheek. "What do you want to know?"

"How do you know Mr. Wilton?" Carmen studied the man's reaction, looking for any hint of deception. All she saw was sorrow.

"Like I said, I own this place. He's my renter."

"How long has he lived here?"

"About two years. Good tenant. Quiet. Not like some of those college kids. The only way I knew he was home was if I saw a light on."

"Do you know why someone would want to kill him?" Carmen assumed that Wilton was the wrong guy, in the wrong place, hanging out with the wrong guy.

"No. I mean the kid was a peach. He used to come over from time to time for dinner. He was dirt poor and I'm a widower. A little company was nice. He was always polite. Always good to me."

"Did he have people over?" Carmen asked. Bud was taking notes.

"Do you mean girls?"

"I mean anyone."

"No to the girls. I never saw a girl over there. Not that he was, you know, that way—"

"Gay?"

"Yeah. He was real religious. We talked many an hour about God. I think he was trying to save my miserable, drunken soul." He paused and looked at the ceiling. "Now that I think about it, I did see another guy come over from time to time. But I still don't think he was gay."

Carmen exchanged glances with Bud. "Do you know the name of the man who used to come over?"

"Nah. Never met him. Just saw him from time to time."

Bud looked up from his notes. "Did the friend drive over? Did you see a car?"

"Yes, sir. It was a bit of a classic. An old VW Bug. Brown, I think. Can't tell ya the year. I never could tell those things apart."

"Did you ever see them drive off together?" Carmen continued to study the man's eyes and his body language. So far she saw nothing to indicate the neighbor was lying. It was clear he didn't liked being cuffed, but Carmen wasn't ready to cut him loose. Handcuffed people tended to be more cooperative.

"A few times."

"How were they dressed?"

"You mean, like, was they dressed for a party or somethin'?"

Carmen shook her head. "I don't mean anything, Mr. Schirru. I'm just trying to learn a few things."

"They dressed like guys that age dress. Well, a few times they wore gym clothes."

"Gym clothes? Like what?"

"You know. Jogging stuff. We used to call them sweat suits. Bob was big time into jogging. He ran every morning and sometimes in the evening. He jogged around the neighborhood, but on some days, like Wednesday, he would jog elsewhere. Come to think of it, that's when the other fella would come over. Wednesday."

Doug Lindsey's body was found early Thursday. "How long have they been doing that?"

The man shrugged. "I don't know. I'm retired. Time don't mean the same to me as it used to. A couple of months maybe. Maybe more."

"What about family?" Bud asked. "Did you ever meet Mr. Wilton's family?"

"Kid didn't have one. That's one reason I kept an eye on him. It's also the reason I only charged half rent. Felt sorry for the guy. He told me at one of our little dinners that his parents had been killed in an auto accident up in Riverside. That happened a couple of years ago. He was down here going over to the university."

"San Diego State?" Carmen already knew the answer. Wilton had a student ID card in his wallet. She was testing the witness.

"Yes. He was a graduate student. History, he told me. Wanted to teach college classes, so he still had a lotta schoolin' ahead of him. I guess he had to get a Master's degree and a doctorate."

Bud looked at Carmen. "There are a bunch of books in the first bedroom. Desk. Computer. The kinda stuff you'd expect a grad student to have."

There hadn't been time for Bud to let her know that. Grad school was expensive. Books alone could break the bank pretty quick.

Carmen thought a moment. "Did he have other friends?"

"Not that I know of. At least none that I ever saw. He is . . ." His face clouded over. "He *was* a friendly guy. I liked him. I liked him a lot." Another stream of tears.

"Mr. Wilton has been gone for a week," Carmen said. "The mail is piling up out front. Didn't that concern you?"

"I can't see the mailbox from my house. And it's not unusual for us not to talk for a week or more, especially if he had papers to write or he was crammin' for a test. Now I feel worse."

"You said your tenant was a religious man. Did he mention what church he went to?"

"No. I never asked. Now I wish I had. Someone needs to let them know."

"We appreciate your help, Mr. Schirru." Carmen nodded to Bud, who put his notebook away, then released the man who had introduced himself with a shotgun. "In the future, let the police handle the gun work, okay? This could have gone bad real quick."

"Yes, ma'am. I'm sorry. I hope I didn't scare you none."

Carmen grinned. "You scared me half to death. I'm just glad no one got shot." She retrieved a business card. "Please call me if you think of anything else, or if someone comes snooping around the property." She patted him on the shoulder. "You've been a big help. You can go now."

"Thank you." He started to leave, then stopped and looked at his shotgun.

"I'll bring that over when we leave," Bud said.

Schirru nodded. "Um, listen. I know you can't tell me the details, but was it—quick? His death, I mean."

A wave of pity surged in Carmen. "Yes, sir. Very quick. He didn't suffer."

"Good. I guess that's good." He lowered his head, then raised it a moment later. "Listen, I know the kid didn't have family, and didn't have any money to speak of . . . Man, I can't get my thoughts in order."

"Understandable, sir." Carmen guessed where this was going.

"There should be a funeral. I don't want him treated like a homeless guy found dead in some alley. I'm not rich, but I do all right. Rentals, you know. Anyway, if you'd be kind enough to let me know what I need to do, I'll pay to get him a plot and a decent funeral."

"That's very kind, sir. I'll talk to the medical examiner. I can't speak for him, but if the law allows, he might be able to release the body to you when the time comes."

"Okay. Okay. Thanks." Greg Schirru started for the door. Bud walked with him as a courtesy and to make sure he didn't take anything from the house.

When Bud returned, he looked an inch shorter. "Wow, what a night. First time in my career I felt sorry for someone who leveled a shotgun at my chest."

"I know what you mean; it's a lousy way to start a conversation." She looked around the master bedroom. The sight of the simple mattress on the floor and a yard-sale reading lamp to the left moved her. "This guy had next to nothing. How did he get to SDSU if he didn't have a car?"

"There's a mountain bike in the bedroom, study, whatever you want to call it."

"Show me." Carmen exited the master bedroom. Bud followed. She turned on the overhead light. The old desk looked like it once occupied a 1950s CPA office: black metal body, fake wood top. The wood veneer had pulled away in several places, revealing particleboard below. On the desk was an old Dell laptop that had been used so much that many of the white letters on the keyboard had worn off. Next to the keyboard rested an open Bible. It was open to a chapter—or did they call it a book?—called Malachi.

A notepad with a number 2 pencil rested on the other side of the laptop. Carmen removed a pen from her pocket and used the back end of it to tap a key. The computer came to life. The computer had been "asleep" for a week. She could see the computer was plugged in. A Microsoft Word document appeared on the screen. There was only the title and two paragraphs. Carmen read aloud. "'Early Twentieth Century Changes to Presidential Elections in the United States.'"

"Gripping," Bud said.

"I'm sure it would have been a best seller." She thought for a moment. "I think we can rule out money as a motive, unless that mattress is stuffed with cash."

"Looks like the guy chose poverty to fund his education. I wonder how he paid for his school and books."

Carmen frowned. "I don't know. I should've asked that when Schirru was here. Scholarships, maybe. Small trust fund? Student loans? Insurance from his dead parents?"

"Or combination thereof." She turned from the computer. "We'll get the techs to go over the computer, but I doubt they'll find anything useful. Maybe something in the e-mail or photos."

"I'll make the call."

"That will give us a little time to look around."

It was close to midnight when Carmen crawled into her bed. It was just the way she liked it: warm blankets, cool pillow. She longed for sleep. She *needed* sleep. The way things were going, she and Bud were going to break the overtime budget by themselves.

She'd allowed herself to relax a little the last few days, but only a little. Two murders in a row had her imagination creating unlikely scenarios, like a murder a day. Since it was now Friday, it had been a full week since Cohen's body was found on the rabbi's lawn.

Of course, finding Bob Wilton's body in Doug Lindsey's submerged VW threw a wrench in things, but technically speaking, it was part of the first murder, now a double murder. Add Cohen, and the total so far was three. Maybe that was the end of it.

As she settled beneath the covers, she worked at convincing herself that, despite the enormity of the problem, the killings might be over. She was fooling herself and she knew it.

What did a week without a new murder mean? Nothing. The killer had a plan. That much was clear. She just didn't have a clue yet what it was.

The search of Bob's house hadn't revealed anything new. There hadn't been much to see. The kitchen was stocked with Top Ramen, canned fruit, soup, crackers, and instant coffee. The place was Spartan in every way. Clearly, Wilton was sacrificing for his education.

When Carmen and Bud left the residence, she felt as empty as the house she had just searched. In some ways, she admired poor Wilton. The young man knew what he wanted and was willing to sacrifice for it.

Now in her bed, her mind finally grew tired of rehashing the day. With any luck—No. Strike that. Forget luck. She would have to rely on exhaustion to bring her a few hours sleep.

22

Hector Garcia was a squat man with a hairless dome and a round middle that tested his leather belt. He was also one of the sharpest people Carmen knew, fearless when the occasion called for it, gentlemanly the rest of the time. Carmen found the detective waiting for her when she rolled into the office a little before eight. She had slept, but not well, and for her, a bad night's sleep was worse than no sleep at all.

"Hector, you're back." Carmen tossed her small purse into the drawer of her desk and unclipped her holster. "Enjoy your vacation?"

"Vacation. I spent three days puking up my toes."

"Not my idea of fun, Hec, but if that floats your boat—"

"Just wait until this stomach bug gets you. I'll send over a large glass of raw eggs for you to drink."

"Whoa, that's an image I don't need." She sat. "Feeling better?"

"Yes, thanks. A little off my feed, but at least I'm not spending my days and evenings sleeping next to the toilet."

"Man, you are quite the conversationalist."

"I'm a plainspoken man. Listen, I hear you've had a tough few days. Long night last night, too."

"All nights are the same length, Hec. Something to do with Earth's rotation."

"You know what I mean."

"It was a tough one. I'm running on fumes."

He sat on the edge of her desk. "Then I really hate to do this to you. I got a call-out for a found body. When I reported it to the Cap, he said I needed to talk to you."

Carmen groaned. "Don't tell me. Something is weird about the body."

"You could say that—"

"Hang on." Bud had just walked in. He looked like he had just finished a fifty-mile hike. "Hey, partner. Wife kick you out?"

Bud shook his head. "Of course not. She's always supportive."

"Uh-huh."

"Seriously. I just slept on the sofa so I wouldn't wake her." He slipped off his coat and hung it on the back of his chair, then looked at Hector. "Hey, look who's here. I thought they fired you."

"You're not that lucky." Hector didn't move from his perch on Carmen's desk.

"Well, it's good to see you back . . ." His gaze bounced between Carmen and Hector. "Why has my stomach just taken a dive?"

"Hec was about to tell us about his new case."

Bud squinted at Hector. "Is your new case going to be *our* new case?"

"The Cap thinks so."

Bud dropped into his seat. "How about sharing that disease you had. I could use the rest."

Hector looked at Carmen. "Really, it's been that bad?"

"It's a challenge. What have you got?"

Hector dropped a file on Carmen's desk. "Thirty-five-year-old male, found on the site of the old Navy barracks just north of Miramar. ME gave a tentative TOD as four hours before discovery. That'd have been about three this morning."

Carmen opened the case file and studied the freshly printed digital photos, then handed each print to Bud. Hector continued.

"As you can see, the vic was found facedown on the asphalt, dressed only in his skivvies."

Bud squinted at the photo. "What are the marks on his back?"

"ME thinks the guy was beat with dowels before being choked to death."

Carmen studied the long red, black, and blue marks that covered the corpse from shoulders to his feet. "Bruising."

"Yep, wounds were inflicted while he was alive."

She rifled through the photos until she found a close-up of the victim's wrists. "He was bound. They look like Cohen's wrist wounds." Carmen wanted to walk away, get a job as a waitress. "Horrible way to die."

"They have all been horrible," Bud said.

Hector looked from Bud to Carmen. "Okay, I'm in the dark here, probably because I've had my head in a toilet for a few days, but the Cap said you were the guys to talk to. What's up? Is this part of the serial-killer thing people are whispering about?"

"It looks like it." Carmen couldn't believe how weary she was. "Who found the body?"

"Some old guys using the abandoned barracks as a place to race their motorcycles."

"Old?" Carmen asked.

"You know. Bud's age."

"Cute, Hec. You're a laugh a minute."

Hector smiled, but only for a moment. "They were retired men trying to pretend they were still twenty. The body was lying in the open."

"Let me guess—the motorcycle jocks go out there every week." Carmen didn't bother looking up.

"True. How'd you know?"

"Let's go to the conference room and I'll regale you with a tale you don't want to hear."

"Swell. Just the kind of welcome back I was looking for."

Carmen held up a finger. "But first . . ." She picked up her phone and dialed Captain Simmons. He picked up on the first ring.

"Simmons."

"Hey, Cap. It's Carmen. I want Hector on our team."

"You asking me or telling me?"

"Asking, of course, sir."

"I figured this was coming and I agree. I assume you think the case is connected."

"I would be surprised if it isn't. Bud and I have our hands full. We need the help."

There was a pause. "You sending Heywood back to patrol?"

"No, sir. We need him too." Carmen hoped she wasn't pushing too hard.

"Do you want the rest of the force on this case too?" His voice carried a hint of humor.

"Thank you, Cap. That'll be great."

"Forget it. You can have Hec and keep Heywood. I'm still dealing with cutbacks, you know. And remember, Hector is a senior detective, don't treat him like some shavetail."

"Understood, sir." She hung up, then looked at Hector. "Welcome to Team Nutcase, Hec. In about an hour you're gonna wish you were still dumping your guts in the toilet."

"Gee, how can I turn down an invitation like that?"

The three filled their coffee cups and slipped down the hall to one of the small conference rooms. The room was equipped with a whiteboard, held a table and chairs that could seat eight. Carmen sat at the head of the table near the whiteboard; Bud and Hector selected opposites sides of the well-worn work table so they could face each other.

"Okay, Hec, bring us up to speed on your case."

"Not much more to add." He pulled his chair closer to the table and wrapped his hands around his coffee cup as if fearful it might fly away. "You've seen the body. Bizarre. We canvassed the scene looking for vehicle tracks but came up empty. While the ground around the old barracks is dusty, there's just not enough of a dirt film to leave tire or shoe impressions. Besides that, it's a popular place for off-road cyclists to tear up the place. We found plenty of rubber marks, but they were all from motorcycles. I doubt the perp gave the guy a ride on the back of his Honda."

"That's the old Navy barracks, right? Near the Marine Air Station." Bud looked more rested than Carmen felt, but he still looked a little wrung out.

"Yep. It was built during World War II and stayed active until the end of Vietnam, when the Navy abandoned it. They never sold it because they used to store some nasty chemicals and fuels there. That was after they stopped housing reservists there. Clean up would cost more than the property is worth, even in San Diego."

"If it's a dangerous place, then why do they let cyclists ride out there?" Carmen leaned back.

"They don't *let* people ride out there, bikers just do it." Hector sipped his coffee, then grimaced as if the strong brew had awakened his irritated stomach. "We're lucky the guys who found the body called it in. By doing so, they had to admit to riding on government property without permission."

"Did you bust, 'em?" Bud grinned.

"Nah. Would you? They did us a favor."

The door to the conference room opened and Carmen stiffened. Assistant Chief Barry Claymore entered. Captain Darrel Simmons followed, an apology on his face.

"May I join you?" Claymore moved to the end of the table as if answering his own question.

No. "Of course, sir. Glad to have you here."

His expression said he was doubtful. "Captain Simmons tells me there's been a couple of developments. I need to be brought up to speed. The chief is at an IACP-related meeting in Denver. He told me to stay on top of this and keep the mayor briefed."

The International Association of Chiefs of Police held several conferences throughout the year, the annual conference being late in May.

"Yes, sir." Was it better to stand or to remain seated like the others? "Detective Garcia was filling us in on this morning's case."

"I don't have any details." Claymore leaned back in his chair like the CEO of a large corporation surrounded by his minions. "Maybe you can start from the beginning."

"Yes, sir." Carmen looked at Hector. "Floor is yours, Detective."

Hector broke it down from the time he received the call and laid out everything he had just told Carmen and Bud. "I was just saying that there is almost no physical evidence—"

"What do you mean 'almost'?" Claymore kept his voice low, but the comment seemed abrasive.

"No physical evidence apart from the body, sir. I was just getting to this part. The riders get in through a double-wide gate. The Navy secures it with a chain and padlock, but the chain gets cut nearly every week."

"How do you know that?" Claymore asked.

"I spoke to the department responsible for the property. That took an hour to unravel."

"And the vic was beaten to death?"

Carmen was impressed that Hec didn't show any irritation since he'd just covered that. "Technically, he was suffocated, according to the ME, but that's not official yet." Hector opened the file and slid it to Captain Simmons, who glanced at it before pushing it down to the assistant chief.

At the sight of the body, the chief cringed.

Hector didn't let up. "If you look closely, you can see that some of the stripes have cuts in them. We think the perp was using wood dowels—probably a half-inch in diameter—and he used such force they broke."

Claymore grunted. "One man did this? It looks like it would take two or three to do this kind of damage."

"It's probably one guy doing the beating, sir." Hector nodded at the picture. "Notice the angle and direction of the marks. They're all the same. We're certain the vic was hung up by his wrists, and the perp had at him. Not to be insensitive, but the guy used him like a human piñata."

"This fits with one of the other murders." Carmen opened one of her files as if checking it for information. She didn't need the file. Every word and image in it were committed to memory. "Cohen had marks on his wrists consistent with a man tied and suspended with his arms over his head. From first glance at the marks on our newest victim, I'd say the width of the binding is the same."

Captain Simmons broke his silence. "This guy have a name?"

Hector nodded. "Yes, sir. We found his wallet nearby. As you can see, the guy is wearing nothing but his chones. Vic's name is Rolf Brady, thirty-five years of age, single, lives in Mira Mesa, which is far from where his body was found. No criminal record apart from a traffic citation for rolling through a stop sign. No photos of family. He had one credit card, one debit card, and forty-three dollars in cash. Still trying to track down his employer and search his home as soon as we get done here . . . if that's okay with you." He looked at Carmen.

"It is, but we'll get to that in a minute."

Claymore studied Carmen for a moment. "You're taking lead on this?"

Carmen tensed.

Simmons answered. "She is. She drew the first case, and she and Bud have been running the investigation of the four murders."

"Four?" Claymore snapped his head around. "There's a fourth?"

"Yes, sir. Carmen was about to factor that in for us." Simmons motioned to Carmen. "Go ahead."

"Late last night a body was found in a VW bug that was submerged in one of the small bays of Lake Murray. The car belonged to our first victim."

"Oh, this is a mess." Claymore's face reddened. "Four murders in what? A week?"

"Yes, sir. A little over a week." Carmen leaned on the table, pushing her coffee cup to one side and resting her hands on the case files. "Bob Wilton—the man in the car—was a friend of our first victim. They had been seen in each other's company, and Wilton's neighbor had seen them drive off together in the VW. We're very sure that Wilton was killed when Doug Lindsey was abducted. They jogged in the park next to Lake Murray." She explained about the two punctures that were consistent to a police-level Taser.

She continued. "Here's the kicker: Wilton was killed outright. GSW to the head."

"Why?" Claymore said.

"The very question eating us, sir. Why torture three people to death, one at a time, but pop the guy with Lindsey?"

Claymore thought for a moment. "Could he have been a threat to the attacker?"

"Doubtful, sir. Evidence indicates he was shot while still in the Beetle. I doubt he even got out of the car."

Claymore pinched the bridge of his nose. Carmen hoped he was getting the same headache this case was giving her.

"Again I ask, why?"

The room was silent. It fell to Carmen to respond. "He's delivering a message."

"What message?"

"Sir, I have no idea."

After Assistant Chief Claymore excused himself, the air in the room seemed a little easier to breathe. He was not a bad man and was an able and conscientious cop. He had earned the decoration he wore on his dress uniform. Still, the man knew how to suck the life from a room.

Simmons stayed behind. "How do you plan to proceed, Carmen?" His tone was even, professional. The fact that he used her first name indicated he was setting a more relaxed tone. Of course, that courtesy only went one way. She would never call him Darrel with other cops around.

"Too be honest, Cap, I'm feeling overwhelmed. I mean, four murders in just over a week, and very little to go on. The amount of work is daunting." Carmen was being honest, but she tried to sound solid, confident.

"Are you over your head?" There was no accusation in Simmons's tone. Sometimes a question was just a question. "Can you lead this team?"

"Of course, sir. I didn't mean to imply I was looking for a way out."

"No need to defend yourself, Carmen. You're on my good list, but I have to ask. This case is the kind of thing that can make it to the national media. We're in the spotlight here, or will soon be. The weight is going to come down on the chief and the mayor, and that will trickle down to you and me. Clear?"

"Crystal, sir."

"Okay, so I'm going to ask a few questions, and I want the straight skinny. Got it?" He looked each detective in the eye; each indicated agreement. He looked back to Carmen. "I ask again: Do you have what it takes to deal with a serial killer, or do I need to pass this on to someone else?"

Carmen lifted her chin. "I am ready and able, Cap. I want to stick with this to the end."

Simmons stared at Bud for a moment. "I said straight-skinny, Bud. Are you comfortable with Carmen taking lead in this?"

"Absolutely, Captain. She has my full confidence. I joke around a lot, Cap, so let me get serious: Carmen is the one to fly this plane."

Simmons turned to Hector. "What about you, Hec? You're going to have to roll your case into this mess."

"I'd have to do that anyway, sir. I'm good to go with Carmen in the lead. She's a team player. So am I. I just want to catch this guy."

"We all do," Simmons said. "Okay, I'll get whatever help and resources I can. I've made sure the forensics department gives you guys priority. I'll rattle the chief medical examiner's cage to do the same thing. We got a real nut case running around the city. I want to see him in prison—or someplace else."

Carmen didn't need to guess the place Simmons referred to: a grave.

"Understood, sir." The votes of confidence felt good, but her stomach roiled at the fact that all this could come down on her like a brick wall in an earthquake.

"Tell me your plans."

She took a breath. "Hector is going to stay on his case. Bud will focus on Cohen, and I'll stick with Lindsey. That's only for information gathering and sorting through evidence. We'll work together on the serial aspect of the case. I want to keep Heywood as a field investigator and liaison with the uniforms. He's still part of the clan. I'm going to need Millie Takahashi to coordinate the forensics. If we get too many hands working trace, DNA, etc., then we could end up like a kid trying to fly a dozen kites at one time."

"You got it."

"If you would, Cap, we may need another detective. We're good right now, but I'd like to know I can call on another experienced investigator if we need it."

"I'll make it work, even if I have to do it myself. What else can I do?"

"We need lines of communications open with the sheriff's department, CHP, and maybe the FBI. We might need some extra forensics tools we don't have in-house. But most of all—"

"Keep the brass off your back?"

"Yes, sir. Sooner or later, word is going to get out to the media. So far it's just been the usual coverage of a murder, but if they learn there's a link, then people with cameras are going to be following us around. Of course, there will be public announcements. I'm not good at those kinds of things."

"Done."

"Thanks, Cap." Carmen looked at her team. "Okay, guys, it's time for a little game of contrast and compare; then Hec, I need you to do legwork on Brady's background."

"Will do, Boss."

"And don't call me that."

"Okay, Chief."

The group laughed for a moment. They needed it.

Carmen, Bud, and Hector hammered out a plan of action for the day. Carmen would visit Doug Lindsey's parents to see what she could learn about Wilton. If she were lucky, she might learn which church the student went to and pick up some worthwhile info there. Bud would head over to San Diego State University to see what he could dig up about Wilton from his professors and friends, if he could locate any. Hector would observe the ME's exam. They would reconnect before the end of the day.

Before leaving the conference room, Carmen did something she seldom did. "Listen guys, thanks for standing behind me with the captain. It's good to know you trust me."

"Trust?" Bud feigned surprise. "I'm just setting things up so you will feel obligated to pick up the check next time we're at Jimmy Chen's."

"Gee, thanks. A girl likes to feel special."

"I do what I can." He stood and walked from the room, Hector a step or two behind him.

Alone in the conference room, Carmen took a few moments

to draw a deep breath and quiet a mind that spun like a jet turbine. In an ideal world, she would only concern herself with solving the murders, but there was much more at stake: the media, which were sure to catch wind of things. Four murders—scratch that—*she* was concerned with four murders, but there had been several others. If the media got busy on this, it would have an impact on the force in general, as well as the public, the chief and other brass, and the mayor. A mistake could ruin her otherwise spotless career.

She let the concerns stew for a few moments before reminding herself that what really mattered was bringing down the madman who was taking life for reasons known only to him.

Carmen gathered her files and walked from the room. "I'm coming for you. I'm coming for you, and nothing can protect you."

Carmen moved through the detectives' work bay, her head down, her mind bearing down on the questions in her mind.

"Detective Rainmondi."

A glance up showed the voice belonged to Joe Heywood.

"Hey, Joe. 'Sup?"

"Two things. First, I've struck out on the video camera search. I found one guy in the Lake Murray area who has a security camera mounted to the front of his garage. He's been plagued by taggers, but that turned out to be a goose egg. The recorder he uses only keeps the video a few days before writing over the previous material."

"If this were London, we'd have tons of video to look at. They have security cameras everywhere."

Heywood nodded. "Good for police work. Not so good for privacy rights."

"I wasn't aware we had a right to privacy."

"That's still being debated." Heywood looked serious. He always looked serious. "Second thing: there's a reporter from one of the local television stations looking for you."

"Did you tell him I was here?"

"Her, and I haven't spoken to her. The call came up from reception."

Carmen did nothing to hide her disgust. She didn't hate the media. They could be useful, but she didn't have time for this.

She stepped to her desk, picked up the receiver of her phone, and punched in an extension. "Hey, Cap? I need a favor." She told him about the reporter. "Do you mind handling that? You're better at that kind of thing, and I don't want the killer to know who's tracking him. If you know what I mean."

He did, and Carmen hung up, then addressed Heywood again. "Thanks for the heads-up." She paused. "You miss the patrol car?"

He shrugged. "Some, but not much."

"Good. We need the help . . . What are you doing now?"

"I was about to ask what you needed."

After a moment's thought, she nodded. "Ride with me. I'm headed out to visit the Lindsey family. I've got more questions."

"Do I get to drive?"

She hiked an eyebrow. "Absolutely not. Is that a problem?"

"Not at all. Just trying to make a funny."

"I see. You failed. Let's hit it."

24

The Lindsey home in La Mesa looked the same as the last time Carmen visited. Small, quaint, brown with beige trim and a neat lawn—except the lawn wasn't quite as neat as a week ago. Carmen noticed last time that it was due for a mowing. An additional week had made it more noticeable, not that Carmen was being critical. After her sister was murdered, Carmen hadn't wanted to do anything, not even shower. Letting the grass grow was to be expected.

Carmen had called ahead to make sure Doug's parents would be home. Karen Lindsey opened the door to her home a moment after Carmen and Heywood closed their car doors. She had been waiting for them.

These moments were always awkward. Does one wave? Smile? Carmen had been trained to be sensitive but neutral. It made sense, but it was also close to impossible to achieve. Times like this, Carmen felt more like an actress than a detective.

Karen pushed open the screen door. From a distance, the fifty-four-year-old woman looked twenty years younger. Brown hair, parted in the middle, hung to the top of her shoulders. Her skin, naturally light, looked corpse-like. She wore no make up.

As Carmen approached, the age erased by distance became apparent. The woman was far from old, but wrinkles had appeared around her eyes and on the skin beneath her chin. Grief had sided with the wrinkles.

"Mrs. Lindsey, thank you for seeing us on such short notice." Carmen kept her voice firm but soft around the edges. The woman's son had been abducted, tortured, and killed. She had a right to teeter on the edge of an emotional abyss.

It was a feeling Carmen understood well.

Carmen extended a hand, one to be friendly and two to keep the woman from embracing her. Grief-stricken people have been known to do crazy things: transfer their anger to the police, strike out, even snatch a weapon from a holster.

They shook hands for a moment. The woman's hand felt like a freshly caught fish: cool, clammy, squishy. "This is Officer Joe Heywood. He's helping with your son's case."

"What happened to your other partner?"

"He's working a different angle." Carmen wasn't ready to tell them about the other murders. "May we come in?"

"Of course. I'm sorry. Where are my manners?"

Buried with your son. Carmen couldn't blame her. She buried things with her sister. "Thank you."

Heywood let Carmen cross the threshold first. The inside of the home was decorated in cheery yellow, flower-print sofa and love seat, beige rug. Prints of cities—Paris, Rome,

London—adorned the wall. Cities, Carmen knew from a previous visit, the family had never seen. They were not wealthy, just optimistic. *Had been optimistic.* A handcrafted wooden cross hung on one of the walls.

A tan, leather easy chair rested opposite the sofa. It didn't fit the decor. Eric Lindsey was a man's man: broad in the shoulders, muscled from work on construction sites. He didn't rise when they entered, but he did grace them with a nod. The room was dim, the thin curtain drawn, letting in only a little light and even less of the outside world. Dim as the light was, there was enough to see that the man hadn't shaved since the funeral, and, based on his oily, wayward hair, he hadn't showered.

"They're here, hon." Karen stated the obvious.

Carmen had been around the block enough times—professionally and personally—to know murder kills more than just a person; it assassinates the souls of the family and friends, stripping away every sense of security and often leaving only a husk of humanity. Oddly, it was the men who seemed to suffer more. Carmen had no idea why that was true or why it would be the case, but her years of experience said it was a fact.

"Mr. Lindsey." Carmen nodded, but didn't invade the man's space.

"News?" His voice sounded like it was coated in gravel.

Carmen sat on the sofa. Heywood followed her lead. She noticed his eyes capturing every detail of the room. It was what cops did. Was there a weapon nearby? Empty cans of beer or bottles of Jack Daniels indicating the person was intoxicated? Drug paraphernalia? An ashtray of discarded joints? A dirty hypodermic? The list was endless. She had made the survey the first time she interviewed the family, and she did it again the moment she walked into the twilight of the room. She saw nothing of concern.

Carmen looked Eric in the eye. "There have been developments, Mr. Lindsey, and we're doing everything we can. I want you to know that I have brought on more detectives, and my captain has made your son's death a priority with forensics and other departments."

"I've heard there have been other murders. Why is my boy getting more attention?"

It was an odd question but a fair one. Apparently the man sensed something was up.

"Shouldn't we be glad about that, honey?" Karen spoke to her husband like a woman who never had reason to fear the man. It was a good thing to see.

"Of course it is, but I don't think the police usually work this way. The newspaper runs a crime column. Not much information in it, but I know there have been other murders."

"Yes, sir, there have." Carmen shifted on the sofa, scooting forward and resting her arms on her knees. "We need your help with something, but first I have to ask that you not relate what I'm about to say to the media. I don't want anything messing up the prosecution when we catch your son's killer."

"Don't you mean *if* you catch him?" Mr. Lindsey was curt but not cruel.

"We're going to get him, Mr. Lindsey. I can promise you that."

"Is every murder solved?" He tilted his head.

The question hurt like a slap to the soul. "No, sir. Not every one."

"Then please don't blow smoke our way, Detective. We are wounded, we are middle class, we don't have college educations, but we are far from stupid."

"Yes, sir. I know. I meant no offense." Carmen felt the room cool.

"Don't be rude, Eric." Karen put fire in the words.

Carmen looked to the love seat where Karen sat. "He's right, Mrs. Lindsey. I have to deal with different people and have to guess at the best approach. I've guessed wrong." She directed her gaze to the man in the easy chair. "Straight talk?"

"We've been coddled and cooed over by everyone who sees us. We're busted up, Detective, busted up real bad, but I'd prefer facts. Straight talk."

"Understood. First thing I want to say goes beyond my work as a detective. Truth is, I probably shouldn't say it, but this case has taken on a special meaning for me." She took a breath. She was about to break one of her own rules. She hesitated. Was there any way to back away from the statement she had started? No, not when she was seeing something in these two that set off alarm bells. "I know what you're going through."

"Do you?" Mr. Lindsey's eyes filled with tears. "Everyone says that. I know they don't. They can't—"

"My sister was murdered. It was years ago. I was still a teenager. No need to get into details, but I've buried a loved one. Not a child, but a family member nonetheless."

Karen gasped and raised her hands to her mouth.

"She died a brutal death, like your son. I never share this with anyone, but I'm telling you so you'll understand that when

I say I'll catch the murderer, you can believe I will do so or go to my grave trying."

Mr. Lindsey spoke softly. "Did they catch her killer?"

"Not yet, but I will."

Eric Lindsey nodded. "I believe you."

An awkward moment settled on the four. Carmen's heart was doing jumping jacks. Her emotions, usually stuffed so deep she barely knew they existed, percolated to the top, threatening to rush out with tsunami force. She focused on beating the unwanted feelings back to the dungeon of her mind.

"Thank you. I'd appreciate it if you would keep that to yourselves."

"Count on it." Mr. Lindsey relaxed his shoulders, and his face softened. She was no longer a public employee; she was a fellow traveler on a steep road of sorrow.

"What I share now is confidential." Carmen pushed back on the sofa. "I tell you because I need your help. There's been another murder that is associated with your son's killing." She swallowed then launched into the details like a woman jumping into cold water. "We found your son's car. It was submerged in a small bay of Lake Murray. Did he go to Lake Murray often?"

"He went once a week with a friend of his." Karen's voice wavered. The news had hit her hard.

"Jogging," Eric said. "He was determined to get in shape. His friend was trying to introduce him to the joy of physical exertion. Doug was never much for sports. Jogging was something he could do that didn't require a competitive spirit."

"May I ask his friend's name?"

Karen answered the questions. Eric looked like he had

already made the connection. That was the only reason Carmen could think of why the man's face had lost all its color.

"Bob. Bob Wilton. Nice young man. Full of faith and hope. He goes to SDSU. Grad school. History, I think. Doug didn't have many . . . friends . . ." She looked at her husband, then back to Carmen. "Oh, no. Blessed Jesus, no."

Carmen couldn't count the number of times she had heard people use the name of a deity when faced with danger or pain. For most, it was a form of swearing. For Karen Lindsey, it sounded more like a prayer.

"No . . . no . . . he's not . . ." Tears rolled from the woman's eyes and her face reddened. "Tell me I'm wrong."

"I wish I could, Mrs. Lindsey. I'm afraid Mr. Wilton was murdered. Since he was found in your son's VW, we think he was killed at the same time your son was abducted."

Karen's gaze turned distant, as though seeing something in the past. "Bob . . . was so . . . poor. His whole life was tied up with school." She drew a hand below her eyes. "We used to have him over for dinner at least twice a week. I used to buy extra groceries for him. I—" She dissolved into tears. Crying turned to sobbing. Carmen let the woman grieve. Heywood, who sat on the end of the sofa closest to the love seat, reached to the woman and lay a large hand on her shoulder.

Carmen focused her attention on Eric. "Sir, your wife said Mr. Wilton was a man of faith. Does that mean he went to church?"

"Yes. He taught the junior-high boys Sunday school. Doug would go to his church sometimes to help out. It's a small church. Maybe a hundred people or so. Bob said he preferred small churches. More ministry is done in small churches than mega churches, he used to say . . ." He choked.

"That fits with what Mr. Wilton's neighbor said. Do you know the name of the church?"

"Um, yes." He wiped his eyes. "One of those nondenominational churches. The Bridge Community Church, I think."

Heywood withdrew his comforting hand and did a search on his smart phone. "There is a church by that name not far from Wilton's home. He could bike there easily enough."

"Mr. Lindsey, do you know anyone who might wish to harm Mr. Wilton?" Carmen watched his expression and saw the look of a man stunned into disbelief.

"We didn't know him that well. Just enough to know he seemed like a great kid and that he was good for Doug. I didn't know Karen was buying groceries for Bob." He forced a tiny smile. "I guess she didn't know I was paying his electric bill."

Carmen asked a few more questions, then rose to leave. When they arrived, Eric hadn't budged from his chair. When Carmen stood, he bolted to his feet and walked the detectives to the front door. He moved like a man who had been at sea for six months trying to regain his land legs.

As they stepped onto the front porch and into the light of day, Eric asked a question of his own, one uttered in soft tones. "I have to ask. I'm not sure I want to know. Was Bob found in the car in the lake?"

Carmen had promised straight talk. "Yes, sir. He had been there a week."

He grimaced. "And . . ."

"Gunshot wound to the head."

He looked down as if his head had become too heavy to hold erect anymore. "Thank you for not pulling your punches."

"Thank you for your help. Please know that we're on this."

"I know you are, Detective. We'll pray for you."

He disappeared into the house, closing and locking the door. Carmen heard Karen wail, and a moment later a deep, gravely voice joined hers.

Back in the Crown Vic, Heywood spoke softly. "Do you know the problem with being a higher-order animal?"

"Higher-order animal?" Carmen started the car.

"An animal with high intelligence, like humans."

She pulled from the curb. "I've seen plenty of humans that I would be hard pressed to call intelligent."

Heywood wouldn't leave the track of conversation. "I didn't say intelligent people acted intelligent, just that they have advanced brains compared to other animals."

"Hmm-hmm. Is there a point to this?"

Heywood nodded. "The price of intelligence is sorrow. Our brains allow us to do more—create, appreciate beauty—but they also make emotions more intense."

"You've been watching PBS again, haven't you?"

He ignored the quip. "Humans are one of the few species that understand sorrow. Elephants and dolphins have been known to show some signs of grief, but humans take it to a new level. It forever changes us."

"Like the Lindsey family."

"Yes. You too."

She snapped her gaze his direction. "What do you mean?"

"You deal with death on a daily basis, and not just any kind of death: murders. Vicious violence. As a beat cop, I see the same things. We're usually the first on a murder scene, but we get to walk away after you guys show up. We make our notes, we write our report, we testify in a trial, but mostly we move on to the next problem: domestic violence, robbery, public intoxication. You know what I mean. You patrolled the mean streets."

"That I did, Heywood. That I did." She let his comments marinate in her mind. Television cops seemed immune to the crimes they investigated. Sometimes the writers would give the pretend-detectives a heart, but they had to be well by the next episode. Life didn't work that way. It never had.

"Murder is always personal."

Carmen couldn't believe she'd said that. It sounded like something from a fortune cookie.

But Heywood nodded. "Yes, it is." A second later he added, "Grief is the worst of all diseases."

She couldn't argue.

"Detective?"

"What?"

"I'm sorry about your sister." He showed no emotion, but the sentence was saturated with sincerity.

"Me, too, Joe. Me, too."

25

Ellis Poe was not an arrogant man. He knew no self-centeredness. His humility was real, not like those who appeared humble to garner the praise of others. His meekness came from a festering emotional wound that had gone gangrenous decades before. His disease was not apparent to others, although some suspected an injury lurked in his past, one that remained fresh and painful.

He did his best to appear confident but never gregarious, kind but never engaging, friendly but never a friend. Where other men admired the successful, the icons of business or the media-loving politicians, he admired a different group of men: monks.

At first he told himself that he respected their faith, their determination to avoid all secular involvement so they could spend their days in prayer and meditation; souls so devoted to God they surrendered all desire for love and companionship. Ellis's brutal self-honesty sank that lie in short order. He envied the monks because they didn't deal with life as he had to. They had no social entanglements, and if they were driven to the monastery by some sin known only to them, then they could suffer for it alone.

Alone.

Some feared that word. Some would go to any extent to avoid being alone. Ellis hankered for it. For the most part, he had spent his adult life alone, interacting with people only when it was unavoidable. A few had grown from strangers to acquaintances. People like Adam Bridger, the president of the seminary, made inroads into Poe's self-erected monastery, but he could count on one hand the number of those who found cracks in the walls.

Since his last days of high school, Ellis had found a measure of comfort in empty rooms and books. Theological texts, ancient grammars, scholastic journals, and lesson plans. Even in his classes, he had erected an invisible barrier that spanned the width of the classroom: on the one side the students; on the other, Planet Ellis Poe.

When teaching, he spoke with passion rooted in his love of the New Testament and the times of Christ. That was when he felt whole, complete, human. In those moments, his mind could only embrace the topic of the day.

In his office, in his home, on his tiny boat . . . things were different. The demons rose unbidden; the dark clouds rolled overhead like a desert thunderstorm; the cold, lashing wind of regret tore at him. He let it. Not because he liked it. He didn't. He did so because he deserved it.

He was a coward.

He was unprincipled.

He had been faithless and timid.

He deserved his isolation and so much more. So very much more.

The *Blushing Bride* rocked in the water, and Ellis turned to see a cabin cruiser gliding across the blue waters of the bay—faster than it should. The voices of young men and women joined with loud music as it rolled across the waters. The weekend was beginning a day early for some. Not unusual. San Diego was many things, including a party city. There was always something to do somewhere, and the weekends were the most active of all.

This was the last weekend before classes resumed at the seminary. Normally, the Easter break was one of relaxation and reflection, but Doug Lindsey's murder had changed that. Learning Shelly's sister was investigating Lindsey's and other murders had made things worse. The sight of her, even the sound of her, brought back that night—a night he had tried so hard to forget but couldn't.

He let someone beat and kick Shelly Rainmondi to death.

He had been attacked too, and at the time he thought it was the worst pain a human could feel. But it was nothing compared to what Shelly Rainmondi had experienced that late night. He used to rationalize his emotional pain away by telling himself that her pain lasted only a short time, while his lasted a lifetime.

Nonsense. What kind of man thinks that way?

He could come up with only one answer: a coward.

When Detective Rainmondi asked him about knowing her sister, he skirted the issue the best he could. He couldn't erase the subtle but real sound of pain in the detective's voice. She was still hurting. Oh, she had hidden it well, but Ellis could hear it. Could see it in her eyes and the way her shoulders dipped when she said Shelly's name.

He should have told her everything then, but the decades had not given him any more courage than he had as a traumatized teenager.

Gutless. Useless. Worthless.

He closed his eyes, tilted his head back, and let the late-day sun touch his face and the salty breeze finger his hair. It was his therapy. His way of applying balm to the festering wound on his soul. The sound of small waves slapping the hull was a lullaby he had come to love—sometimes come to need. The *Blushing Bride* was his Fortress of Solitude. Even Superman needed a place to hide, to refresh.

But tonight, it wasn't working. The sounds, the smells, the gentle rocking motion of the craft brought no relief. It too had turned on him.

Tears pressed free of his closed eyes and charted a course down hot cheeks. Mucus filled his nose. He tried to fight it, to think of other things. He began a technique he had created while a student in seminary in Texas: form a complex academic question, then argue both sides. It was what he did when he couldn't sleep.

Arguments for the Pauline authorship of Hebrews followed by counter arguments.

The tears grew hotter.

One, the simple lack of author attribution does not negate the traditionally held view of Pauline authorship.

His breathing grew erratic. To open his eyes would be to open the floodgates.

Two, the book argues for the supremacy of Christ over the law, a topic a rabbi like Paul would undertake.

Something welled within him, like magma in a volcano seeking release.

Three, the arguments in the book are deeply Jewish, requiring an expert knowledge of the Old . . . Testament.

His stomach roiled, burned, and twisted. The car. The dark night. The late hour.

Four, there are mentions of several of Paul's companions, most significantly . . . Tim . . . Timothy, Paul's son . . . in the ministry.

Shelly would never have children. No son. No daughter.

His heart began to beat as if trying to pummel him from the inside out. As if trying to punish him.

Fifth . . . fifth . . . fifth . . .

A sob escaped. Then a gasp. Then an uncontrolled wail. He could hear it roll across the water. He rose from the chair on the stern deck and slipped into the cabin before tenants on the other boats could identify him as the source of the gut-wrenching sound. Inside, he dropped to his knees.

"God, I am so sorry. I shouldn't have left her. I should have stood up. Should have been a man. Should have . . . Should have . . ."

God didn't seem interested.

Carmen paced a side room of the homicide offices. She had set it up so the primary detectives could lay out material and talk without disturbing others around them. She was in the room alone, looking at the photos of the bodies and other items on the wall. She had arranged them in a time line starting with Doug

Lindsey, Bob Wilton, then David Cohen, and the latest victim: Rolf Brady. She paced the room and, after a moment, moved the photo of Wilton's bloated corpse a little lower than the others. His mode of death . . . the fact that his body was hidden . . . He didn't fit the emerging pattern. It was like he was a bystander rather than a target.

Above the unsettling photos of each corpse was an 8x10 picture of the victims taken under normal circumstances: family photo, business headshot, the kind of photos that reminded her that these people once walked, talked, laughed, and loved. She never knew where a clue would come from, and that included the appearance of the victims when alive. Some serial killers targeted only dark-haired prostitutes, or young boys, or college kids. Perhaps there was a similar connection. But if there was, she wasn't seeing it.

The photos formed columns. Beneath each was a photo of the primary crime scene, followed by detailed photos of the injuries. So far, there were no photos of murder sites, just those where the body had been found.

There were notes about time of death, cause of death, age, family relationship, criminal record (those were cards that said, "None"). To the side of the grisly columns was a city map, with a pin identifying each location where a corpse was found: Balboa Park, Rabbi Singer's home near College Avenue, Lake Murray, and the abandoned barracks near Miramar Naval Air Station.

"It's a mess." Thank heaven no one was there to hear her despair.

The door to the room opened, and her team entered, led by Bud. "It's late. We're hungry. So we've decided that you, great leader that you are, would naturally suggest we conduct our meeting at Jimmy Chen's."

She looked at the men. "Is that what you decided?"

"It's what Bud decided." Hector was the last to enter the room.

"Coward," Bud said.

"Just so we're clear, Bud: Carmen scares me more than you do." Hector laughed, and a moment later Bud joined him.

Jimmy Chen's sounded pretty good to Carmen. She had skipped breakfast and had a granola bar for lunch. About an hour ago her stomach began to feast on itself. "Sounds good to me, guys, especially since one of you is buying."

Bud started. "No one said—"

"I'll call and ask for the back room." She started for the door.

"Um, wait," Bud said. "About that whole buying thing . . ."

Carmen kept a straight face as she snapped open the door, then jumped back a foot. Someone was standing on the other side of the threshold. That alone was startling, but seeing the chief of police standing there was more staggering. She could count on one hand the number of times she had had a conversation with the head of the force.

"Chief. You startled me."

He smiled. Chief Mark England was a tall man—six-four—broad shoulders, dark hair tinted with just the right amount of gray, and a lined face that indicated he was a man who was used to smiling—and a man who had seen the worst life could deliver. Carmen had always thought the man could stand in for Tom Selleck. They weren't dead ringers, but in the right light they could pass for brothers.

"I have that effect on people. Sorry." He looked weary, most likely from his travels. "I know you and your team are busy, but I have to brief the mayor tomorrow morning. The poor guy is hunkering down for a media storm."

"There hasn't been a media storm yet, sir." She started. Was the weakness in her voice as apparent to them as it was to her?

"There will be, Detective. Trust me, there will be. The media is putting it all together. Incorrectly, I assume, but all that means is that we'll have to straighten them out. Am I interrupting?"

Carmen glanced at the others. "We were just headed over to Jimmy Chen's for dinner and a change of scenery. We were going to talk things over, but we can cancel that—"

"Ah, Jimmy Chen's." The corners of the chief's mouth inched up. "I haven't been to Jimmy's since I got kicked up stairs. Does he still serve that New Mexico-style green chili stew?"

"Yes, sir. It's still the best this side of Santa Fe." A second passed. "Would you care to join us? Detective Tock is buying."

"Is he now?" England looked at Carmen's partner.

"I-I . . . Yes, sir. It would be an honor." Bud looked a shade more pale than he had a moment ago.

"I appreciate the invitation, and I'd love to join you, but I'm buying." England grinned. "I make a little more than you guys."

Carmen saw Bud relax. This was going to be a story for the ages.

As Chief England turned, he said, "I love their beans. Best in the city."

Bud didn't have to speak.

His grin said it all.

26

Jimmy's was filled, as usual, with a mix of citizens and cops. The latter were easy to identify. They were the ones whose heads snapped up the minute Chief Mark England stepped into the place. Carmen and the others moved through the front dining space and headed for the back room. England glad-handed his way through the crowd, slapping cops of every rank on the shoulder and calling them by name. The man's memory was impressive. The SDPD had more than twenty-seven hundred employees. She didn't know if England knew them all by name, but watching him work the crowd made it appear so.

The back room was empty, unusual for a Friday evening. They passed through a small crowd waiting for seats. Jimmy must have cleared the room for them. She wondered how many meals he had to comp for that.

Two tables had been pushed together. Their number had grown by one, with the addition of Captain Darrel Simmons raising their number to six. The table was set with chips and salsa and glasses of water. Carmen's fanny had barely touched the seat when Jimmy Chen appeared, his Asian face lit like a kid's on Christmas morning.

"This is an honor, Chief!" Jimmy looked ready to split at the seams. "We haven't had the pleasure of your company for a long time."

"And I've missed this place, Jimmy. They tell me you're still making that stomach-blistering green chili stew."

"Oh, yes, sir. We've hospitalized six just this week."

"That's what I want to hear."

Jimmy took the orders by memory and disappeared, interrupting only once to bring sodas and teas. Carmen wanted a beer. She *needed* a beer, but they were on the clock. She settled for water with lemon. While they waited for their drinks, England filled them in on his latest trip to a police chief's conference. "I used to patrol the streets; now I patrol conference centers."

"Do you miss the street, Chief?" Bud asked.

"Some days, yes. There's something about doing police work. When you go home, you feel like you really did something. My work is now all administration and politics. I thought I'd put in thirty or thirty-five years in uniform. Before I knew it, I was wearing a suit, which was fine when I worked Robbery and Gangs, but once you crawl up the ladder, you get a bigger office, more pay, and a sense that you're losing touch with the work you signed up for. Other days, I'm glad I'm chief. I lead the best police force in the nation. We have a crime rate far below cities our size, and our close rate is the envy of every major metroplex in the world."

"I don't want to sound like I'm brown nosing here," Hector said, "but you get the credit for much of that."

"Not really. Some maybe, but we had good leadership long before I came along. Oh, we've had our problems, but in the end we came out stronger. Okay, enough of that. I need to elbow my way into your work." He lifted a hand. "I'm not going to interfere. I have full confidence in you and your captain. Assistant Chief Claymore speaks highly of you."

"He does?" Carmen let the words slip before she realized they had formed in her mind. "I mean—"

"No need to explain, Detective," England said. "He comes off a little strong at times, but he's a good cop. Okay, fill me in." He looked at Carmen. "I understand you're lead on this. Let's start with you."

"Yes, sir." Carmen took a moment to gather her thoughts then started from the beginning. By the time she had finished the explanation and related their approach, the meals had arrived.

"If it's all right with everyone, I'd like to continue our chat through the meal," England said, but only after taking a moment to admire the large bowl of green chili and pork. He looked like a happy man. "I have some paperwork to deal with after this. The problem of being away from the office for a week."

No one objected. No one would. This was the chief, and he lived and worked in a ratified air.

Carmen finished recounting all they knew. England listened, nodding from time to time as he shoveled food in his mouth with easy, precise movements. A man who wore expensive suits had to learn to eat carefully.

When she finished, England set down his spoon and dabbed at his brow, removing the spice-induced perspiration. "Your man is smart. Methodical. Has a hidden purpose. Wants to be noticed. He might even want to be caught, but under his own terms. Does that sound right?"

"Yes," Carmen said. "He seems to avoid any place with a security camera. That means he scopes out his drop spots ahead of time."

"All the injuries occurred before death?"

"The ME says so."

"So he's sadistic. Smart and sadistic. That's the worst. Stupid and sadistic is easy to solve. You've got nothing on video?"

Heywood answered. "I've been working that with a couple of the techs, sir, and I've come up empty. Somehow he evaded cameras in Balboa Park. That was our best opportunity. Some of the museums have security cameras, but I came up with zilch. Since he stays on surface streets, the Cal Trans cameras have been of no use."

England shook his head and stared at his stew as if an answer would bubble to the surface. "What drives this guy? Any indication of male rape or mutilation?"

"None," Bud said. "The ME was specific about that. None of the wounds were sexual in nature."

"And every death is different? Every body found in a different part of the city? Any idea how he's abducting the victims?"

"No, sir. With the Lindsey kid, we know a Taser-like device was used. We haven't found that to be true on the other victims."

"The guy knows the system," the chief said. "He kills in one place then dumps the body elsewhere, yet he's careful enough to make sure there's no trace on the body that can lead to his killing location. All the bodies were bound?"

"Yes, and strung up by the wrists," Carmen answered. "Well, all but Bob Wilton, who died from a GSW to the head."

The chief swore, then apologized to Carmen. He was an old-style gentleman. Clearly he'd never heard Carmen when she was angry. She could curse the leaves off a tree.

"So he has a killing field. Were they gagged?"

Carmen hadn't thought of that. She had studied the photos of the bodies enough to be able to call them to mind in vivid detail. "No. I haven't seen any indications of that, nor has the ME called it to our attention." She looked at Hector.

"No on my guy."

The chief sat silently for a moment. He was known to be a special kind of genius, the kind of smarts that allowed him to process information that would overwhelm lesser humans. "Ask the ME to check that. If he tortured his victims but didn't gag them, then you'd have to assume he has some place in an outlying area where a scream wouldn't draw attention."

How stupid could she be? England said it with such calm assurance that it seemed a fact before he had finished the statement. Of course, no one had an idea where that might be.

"There's meaning in all of this, people. Serial killers usually kill in the same fashion. It's what they practice; a skill they hone. Jack the Ripper didn't use a knife one time and a gun the next. So why is the guy doing things the way he is? What does he want the world to see? To notice? No one goes through this much trouble unless he has a need to be noticed or a cause to promote. You say there is only the one note?"

Carmen answered. "Yes, sir."

England pursed his lips. "The way he hides trace evidence . . . This guy has been working on this for a long time, planning, prepping, and if we don't catch him soon, he'll do it again and again until we figure out what his message is."

"If so, sir, then he's bound to make a mistake somewhere along the line."

"Don't bet on it, Detective. Even if what you say is true, he might not drop the ball until several more are dead. We can't allow that."

"Yes, sir." Carmen tried to imagine the pressure the man was under.

"What about the bullet used to kill . . ."

"Wilton, sir. Bob Wilton."

"Wilton." He said it as if filing the name in his mind. "Any good news on the bullet front?"

Carmen sighed. "Not much, sir. It was a small caliber and a head shot. It blew out the skull before expending its energy and lodged in the interior door panel. The slug is highly deformed. Based on weight we make it out to be .25 calibre. Ballistics was able to get enough information on striation to make us think it's from an older Walther PP series. PPK maybe."

"James Bond special. Database match?"

"No. We ran it, but it was pretty much munched. A soft tissue shot would have been better, but such a small bullet, at such close range and passing through bone then ricocheting around . . . Disappointing. We're still working it."

The chief took another bite of his stew but did so as if in slow motion. He put his spoon down. "You told me you assume he's a big man."

"Yes, sir. Based on the size of the bruising, the damage done by the beating, and the force necessary to kill a man by punching."

"Big man, small gun. Why?"

No one answered, so England offered an idea. "Small bullets deform more easily. Also a small gun means what?"

"The need for a close shot," Carmen said.

The chief nodded slowly. "So . . ."

"He likes to be close when he kills," Bud offered.

"Yes, yes, I think that's true." England poked at his stew, seemingly lost in thought. "It fits, doesn't it? The guy is smart. Did he know that Wilton would be with Lindsey? If he did but didn't want Lindsey, then he knew he'd have to off the witness. He'd be worried about a traceable slug. A small round in the head would deform just as you described it. Did you find the shell or gun?"

"No, sir." Carmen's mind was racing. "We had a team of divers search the lake. No gun there."

"Wise. No, he'd take it with him. Dispose of it later. Or keep it if he's confident the slug can't be traced. If it's never been used in a crime, then the round won't match any of the databases."

"That's my thinking, Chief." Carmen hated agreeing. Life was much easier when the murderer was stupid. A highly intelligent killer was a different ballgame.

And not a good one.

The chief folded his napkin and set it on the table. "Okay, I appreciate the challenge before you. Let me know how I can help. I need to let you know this: There's a good chance I'll be doing a press conference tomorrow. If I know our mayor, he's going to insist on it. Think of it as a preventative media strike. I can't give you an exact time yet, but think about midafternoon tomorrow. Captain Simmons, I want you there."

"Yes, sir," the captain said.

"You, too, Detective Rainmondi."

"Sir, I'm not all that great with the media."

"No problem, Detective. You have all night and a good hunk of tomorrow to become an expert." He smiled.

Carmen didn't feel the humor. "Yes, sir."

"I want you to think about how the public might help." He motioned to Jimmy Chen, who stood just outside the back room. He approached. "Yes, chief?"

"I forgot to ask about your family. Everyone well?"

"Yes, sir. Doing great."

"Wonderful. Good to hear. Could you bring me the check, Jimmy?"

"What check?"

"For the meal. I promised to pay."

Jimmy grinned. "I don't know what you're talking about, Chief? What meal?"

England laughed. "Thanks, Jimmy. You're the best."

"My pleasure."

Jimmy slipped away, and Chief England rose, removed his wallet, and withdrew a hundred that he tossed on the table.

"The least I can do is leave a good tip." England thanked them and walked away. Carmen could hear him chatting it up with the off-duty cops out front.

Carmen looked around the table. "Did we just get schooled?"

"Yep," Bud said. "We got schooled big time."

The *Blushing Bride* shifted on its anchor, pushed by a breeze. Ellis Poe adjusted his cheap beach chair on the tiny front deck so he could stare east at the skyline of San Diego. Few things were as beautiful as the lights of buildings on the water of the bay. One America Plaza, Harbor Club West, Pinnacle Marina West and East Towers, the Marriott Hotel and Marina, with it's curved buildings designed to look like sails, and a dozen or more other tall buildings cast white and colored lights onto the undulating water. At night, the already stunning skyline took on an eerie beauty.

As was his custom when he stayed on the small boat, Poe had spent hours staring at the sight.

Other cities had taller buildings, but all buildings in downtown San Diego had a 500-foot limit because of their proximity to the San Diego International Airport. The height restriction did nothing to stem the creativity of the architects and builders. No matter how many times he saw the sun surrender the night to the skyline, he was impressed and hoped he always would be.

There was another building that could be seen in the skyline: the Metropolitan Correctional Center, a mid-rise prison run by the Department of Prisons. The joke in the city was that it was the only federal pen with an ocean view.

He wondered what the view was like.

If he followed the course he was considering taking, he just might find out.

27

Her cell phone buzzed and chimed. Carmen had been dreaming, and her dream incorporated the sound. She was a young teenager at home, trying to pick up the receiver of the family's rotary-dial phone. No fancy push-button phones for them, her dad had decreed. "These work just fine." Except this one didn't work. Someone had glued the hand-piece to the body of the phone.

Something else was wrong. Their phone rang when someone called. This phone was buzzing like an angry bee and emitting some kind of electronic tone.

"Answer it, Carmen." Shelly was always so impatient.

"I can't, stupid. It's stuck." Carmen tugged at the handset again. Nothing. Not only would it not come out of the cradle, but the body of the phone seemed attached to the table. If this was a joke, she didn't like it.

"You are so lame. Here, let me."

Carmen could feel Shelly step near to her back. A hand reached around her and took hold of the handset.

A skeletal hand.

Fleshless.

Bright white bones.

Carmen screamed and pulled away. She would have been better off had she not looked. Shelly looked at her as if her older sister had lost her mind. She smiled, but since she had only half a face, it didn't work well. A half-smile was more a grimace.

The receiver lifted easily in the boney hand, and Shelly placed it to her skull. "Hello." Another fifty-percent smile. "It's for you, dumdum."

Carmen's knees went hollow. Her heart scrabbled about in her chest like an animal that had gnawed its way to freedom. Her bladder felt ready to let go of its contents. She wobbled back a step.

"It's the police station," Shelly said through the corner of her mouth that had lips. "Don't you want to talk to them?" She held out the phone. A bit of flesh dangled from her wrist . . .

Carmen was out of bed before she knew she had moved.

A light on the nightstand thinned the darkness—the light from her smartphone. She snapped it up. "What?"

A tentative voice. "Detective Rainmondi?"

The words on the caller ID sank in. She was talking to someone from dispatch.

"Yes. Sorry. I was sleeping. Dreaming. Never mind. What's up?" She listened. Memorizing the information as she turned and sat on the edge of the bed. The sheets were wet. She had been sweating. "Understood. I need you to make a few calls . . ."

She ended the call, set the phone down, and rubbed her face. "Someone make it stop."

Then she realized fate had made her the "someone."

The clock on the nightstand read 4:03.

The clock in the Crown Vic read 4:27. The sun had yet to show for work. She moved slowly down Corona Oriente Road west of Crown Point Park. The park had a long stretch of sandy beach bordering Fiesta Bay, a popular boating place. The park was a popular destination for those who preferred the quiet waters of the bay over the crashing waves of Pacific Beach and La Jolla Shores. The trees and grass reminded Carmen of the park in Coronado, where she had interviewed Ellis Poe.

The ocean park was well known to Carmen. She spent many hours here with her family. Old-style streetlights cast a glow along the side of the road bordered by houses built just after World War II and larger, newer executive homes. A fifty-year-old, 1,200-square-foot house could share a block with a much newer 5,000-square-footer. Her interest, however, lay elsewhere: the middle of three parking lots. She pulled to a stop on the apron leading to the large, empty expanse of asphalt. It was an easy spot to find. Four patrol cars were parked nearby, as were two other Crown Vics.

Carmen exited her car and joined two men standing by the yellow barricade stretching around the entire lot. The responding officers must have run through a half-dozen rolls of the tape.

She glanced at Bud and Hector. "You got here quick."

"I was just wasting the night by sleeping." Bud looked as weary as Carmen felt. A field of stubble covered his cheeks and chin. He hadn't bothered to shave. During the half-moment they spent as a couple years ago she learned that he was old-fashioned about shaving. Still used a double-edge safety razor. No cheap throwaway for him.

Hector looked a little more refreshed. His chin was clear of stubble. Probably an electric-shaver man. Much easier to shave quickly.

"Me, too." Carmen fought a yawn. "Why sleep when we could be standing by the ocean on a breezy morning before sunrise?" A Hyundai pulled up, an older sedan. Joe Heywood exited. Since he wasn't a detective, he hadn't been issued a car, so had used his own vehicle to make his way here from home. They waited for him to walk to their location. When he arrived, Carmen took the lead.

"Okay, who was here first?"

"That'd be me." Hector raised a hand. "But Bud arrived right after me."

"Have you looked at the body?" Carmen scanned the parking lot.

"Yes. It definitely fits. Bizarre. This time—"

Carmen cut him off. "Don't destroy our first impressions." She took a deep breath. She had a feeling that she'd rather read about this case than see it. "Lead on, Hector. Let's see what the new trend in crazy is."

Tactical flashlights appeared and scanned the ground as Hector led the group over the lawn to a copse of three trees. The ground was firm, no doubt hard-packed by thousands of park visitors. Carmen saw no shoe impressions or anything else that might be associated with the murder. She didn't expect to. The subject of their search was a meticulous man, which made him all the more dangerous.

"And there he is." Hector motioned to a tree.

A nude male stood with his back to a tree. No, not stood. He was dead. He hung on the tree, his naked form tied to the trunk with long strips of cloth. Carmen trained her light on the corpse, starting at his head. Like some of the other victims, the man had been pummeled. His right eye was swollen closed, the lid of his left eye hung at half-mast. A piece of cloth was wrapped around the man's throat. His hands were bound by the same material, and another strip was tied around his abdomen and the tree trunk and pulled tight with such force the belly fat puffed around it.

"Lovely." Carmen shook her head. "What is that? Purple silk?"

"You asking a bunch of guys if it's silk?" Bud moved closer and shone his small light on the material around the man's throat. "It's shiny. Maybe silk, maybe something similar." He shone his light in the half-open eye. "Petechial hemorrhage consistent with strangulation." He stepped back.

Carmen continued to move her light from head to feet. Severe bruising, especially around the ribs. The light continued down. No trauma to below the waist. The man had voided his bladder and bowels. "Well, this is different." She let the light linger on the waste.

"Killed here." Bud looked at Carmen. "That *is* a change."

The victim's feet and hands were bound with the same

purple material. This time Carmen moved the body and with gloved hands lifted the man's bound wrists. "No rigor. Fresh kill." She directed the beam of her flashlight at the man's left rib cage, which had been covered by his arms. "Deep bruising." She gently lowered the arms. "He was beaten before he was tied to the tree." She wanted to untie his hand to see if the ligature marks matched the other victims, but the cloth was too wide. She would have to wait for the ME to tell her.

"So the guy was beaten elsewhere, tied, and strangled here?" Hector shook his head. "Why?"

"Part of the game. Part of the message." A heavy wave of weariness washed over Carmen. She felt fifty feet below the surface and sinking fast. For the first time in her career she wanted to spin on her heels and walk away.

She didn't. "Okay, no clothes means no wallet, so for the moment we have a John Doe. Let's spread out and survey the area. The wallet may be nearby." She looked at Heywood. "Joe, I want you to get a few of your uniform buddies to check out the area around the park. Keep an eye out for blood spatter." She directed the flashlight back to the man's face—there were streaks of coagulated blood from his nose and mouth. "Also, see if there are any security cameras around. Doesn't look like we have any in the park, but maybe one of the bigger houses has a camera trained on the street. Rich people have more to be paranoid about."

"Got it." He turned and walked back the way they entered.

Carmen continued. "Dispatch has notified the ME's office and the crime-scene techs. They should be here soon." She studied the scene once more. "Let's assume he parked in the lot.

Pulling a body from a car while parked on the street seems too stupid for this guy. Let's move from the tree to the lot."

Hector rubbed the back of his neck. "This is gonna be a long day."

"Could be worse," Bud said. "One of us has a press conference this afternoon."

Carmen swore. "I wonder who I have to shoot to get a cup of coffee."

On the street, a van with a retractable microwave tower mounted to the roof pulled to the curb. Carmen saw Joe Heywood head them off. It was to be expected. Captain Simmons's short press conference the other day had become chum for the sharks. Some detectives liked the limelight.

Carmen wasn't one of them.

Carmen had gone to bed a little early the night before, but being jarred awake had left her feeling like she just came out of major surgery. The long hours of the last two weeks had worked her like a heavyweight worked a body bag. Every few minutes she wondered what it would be like to take a long nap and then take a leisurely drive up the coast. Instead she stood with Captain Simmons and Chief England. They were in the media room of the central station. Before them were several rows of seats, each filled with a reporter. At the back, several video cameras were set up on tripods. In the seats were representatives from every major radio station and newspaper—mainline and independent. To

Carmen, they looked like a school of piranha eyeing a cow that had wandered into their river. The dinner bell was about to ring.

Chief Mark England stepped to the lectern, the top of which sported a dozen microphones. "Thank you for coming in on a Saturday. I appreciate your dedication." England wore his dress uniform, stood straight, head up, and displayed an expression of determination. "Normally we would wait until the work week, but we feel the public needs to hear from us sooner. Thank you for making that possible."

Some of the reporters nodded as if the praise were meant just for them. Several held digital recorders forward, as if the extra foot or two their outstretched arms provided would make the recording that much clearer. Maybe it did. What did Carmen know about reporting? She shifted in her seat, a padded folding chair that seemed unusually hard and uncomfortable.

"A few days ago, the head of our homicide department—Captain Darrel Simmons—informed you of several murder cases the department has been investigating. These crimes are unusual and appear to be the work of one man. Since then there have been more cases. As it stands now five bodies have been found. All male. We want the good citizens of San Diego to know that we are on the job. A special team of detectives has been formed and is being led by Detective Carmen Rainmondi, who reports to Captain Simmons and to me. I've asked that Detective Rainmondi bring us up to date. I must inform you that there are many details she cannot reveal. This is, after all, an ongoing investigation."

England nodded at Carmen, who stood, glad to be out of the chair. Unfortunately, standing at the podium was even less comfortable. She cleared her throat. "On Thursday, March 28, the body of a single, white male was discovered in Balboa Park near the botanical center. He was a student at the San Diego Theological Seminary. The next day, Friday, March 29, a second body was discovered in the College area north of Interstate 8. During the week that followed, we found a third victim in Lake Murray. That victim and the first knew each other and were friends. They had been seen together that evening."

She took a moment to breathe, then continued. "Two other victims have been found this week, one at an abandoned military barracks facility near Marine Corps Air Station Miramar. Today another victim was found at Crown Point Park. As in the three previous cases, the men were severely beaten before they died."

"Can you give us those locations again?" The woman who asked the question looked as if she should be in high school.

"At the end of the conference you will receive a fact sheet with all the details we can release at this time."

A man who looked close to retirement age and projected the same short-timers attitude asked, "That's five bodies in two weeks? Isn't that a lot?"

"It is for San Diego. Most cities this size have that as an average."

The man persisted. "You think they're all related?"

"Yes." Carmen spoke with an ease she didn't feel. "We have several reasons to believe that there is one culprit."

"Such as?"

"I'm sorry, I can't answer that. This is an ongoing investigation, and we must be careful to build our case in a manner that doesn't help the perpetrator. I can tell you the deaths were violent and, in all but one case, occurred someplace other than where the bodies were found."

A female reporter waved her hand. Most were content to simply raise theirs. Carmen called on the woman.

"You mean the killer is transporting the bodies from one place to another?"

Wasn't that obvious from what she just said? "Yes."

"How?"

"That's a detail I can't discuss at this time."

"Can't or won't?" The woman looked like she had just been left at the altar.

"The result is the same, ma'am."

Carmen took questions for ten minutes before moving along to the appeal Chief England asked her to make. "We are calling for the help of the citizens of San Diego and are asking for two things." She looked at the video cameras. "We ask everyone to remain calm but to be on the alert for unusual behavior by a stranger or neighbor. We believe the perpetrator to be a large man. We also ask that if you were in Balboa Park late on the night of March 28 and saw anything unusual, then please contact SDPD. Also if you live in the College Avenue area north of SDSU, or if you live around Lake Murray, Crown Point, or any of the other places we mentioned and have a video security system that might have recorded activity outside your house, then please review recordings for the last two weeks and let us know if your system captured something that might be useful to us." She doubted anyone had a system that kept two weeks' worth of video, but it couldn't hurt to ask.

Carmen thanked the reporters and stepped aside for Chief England to continue. He talked for another ten minutes. Carmen couldn't remember any of it.

He sat in a dimly lit room, drinking beer after beer. It helped keep the voices quiet, and he needed a bit of diversion. His body hurt, his muscles complained about all they had been asked to do. No matter. Pain was a friend, and he had to give it its due.

On a small table sat a cheap, flat-screen television. He was limited to over-the-air channels, but that didn't matter. He had his work to keep him busy, and there was plenty of that. He drew long and deep on the beer, belched, and watched the news. He was getting their attention. Finally. He leaned forward, hanging on every word of the newscast. It was what he expected. Little information. Just a dog-and-pony show. Then the detective stepped to the lectern. What had the chief of police called her? Rainmondi.

Rainmondi?

It couldn't be. He moved closer. Yes, yes. He could see it now. A lot of years had passed, but he could see the resemblance. So, Shelly's big sister grew up to be a cop. A homicide detective at that.

He laughed.

"Adequate. Satisfactory."

The voices were pleased. A good thing. When he left that note in the minivan they had been unhappy, and if they weren't happy, no one was happy. Especially him. They wouldn't let him sleep for two days and made him vomit every time he took a sip of beer. Unfair. A man like him needed his beer.

"Rainmondi."

The name tickled his tongue. "Rainmondi. Raaaaaiiiinmondi. Man I enjoyed your sister. A memorable night. Pity she didn't see things my way." He chuckled. There was something about the first kill. The power of it. The joy of it. The sense that he could do whatever he wanted to anyone. He was a god. The voices told him so. They told him time and time again.

"This is going to be interesting."

He emptied the bottle and set it next to the five other empties near his chair.

"Very, very interesting."

He laughed. Loud. Long. Manic. He laughed until he could barely breathe. "Shelly's sister. This . . . is . . . rich."

In his joy, he felt the urge to kill something.

28

Carmen was getting paranoid. Every time a phone rang, she imagined the grizzly remains of another victim had been found somewhere in San Diego. Saturday night turned into Sunday, and Carmen accumulated almost six hours of sleep before her mind kicked into high gear. This time there were no gruesome dreams of her sister. Hers had been the dream of the dead: imageless.

She was thankful for that.

There was no day off for her. She couldn't justify sitting home, watching television, when a man who had long ago left sanity behind was stalking another victim. Of course, she had no idea if the killer were doing that, but her gut said it was true. The message hadn't been completed. At least she assumed it hadn't. Since she had no idea what the message was, she could be wrong.

Doubtful.

She settled at her desk for a few moments, read e-mail, then reviewed a few written reports by those screening the "cranks," emotionally needy people who confessed to anything that would garner attention. Her favorite was an eighty-eight-year-old woman from Spring Valley who told Hector she had committed the crimes. The image of the senior citizen hoisting an adult male up by his wrists, then pounding him with such force that bones broke, almost made her smile.

Almost.

The news conference ran on the evening and late-night local news. She had heard that CNN and Fox picked it up. There were several calls from reporters and producers wanting interviews and more information. She had no stomach for that. Let Captain Simmons take those. She could either spend her day quenching the curiosity of the media or trying to solve a string of murders. There was no contest.

Bud strolled in five minutes after Carmen.

"You're looking good this morning," he said as he removed his blue blazer. He wore a white business shirt but no tie. He had made it clear over the years that he hated ties. He kept a clip-on in his desk for emergencies.

"Sure I do. My mirror must be lying to me. The woman I saw this morning looked like a cross between a vampire and a zombie."

"A vampire-zombie. I like that. They suck the brains out of their victim. It'd make a great movie." He sat at his desk and leaned back in his chair. The chair protested the action with a loud squeak.

"No, it wouldn't." She rubbed her face, glad she wore no makeup to be smudged, and raised her arms. "I vant to suck your skull." She shook her head. "Dumb."

They shared a smile, but the humor gave way to the gravity of their task.

"I've been thinking."

"Bud, I've asked you not to do that."

"I know, but it happens when I drink too much coffee. So last night I started wondering if we should be asking what we're missing. I mean, we know what we have, but what's missing?"

"Besides a suspect, a witness, a bit of video surveillance, a weapon, the location or locations of the murders?"

"Exactly, but there's more." He leaned forward and the chair seemed relieved. "We have five victims, all male, young to middle age, two Christians, one Jew, and two guys with no religious connections."

Hector had learned the name of the last victim: Max Mulvaney, a teacher at a local traffic school. Hector discovered the man had no family and few friends. He had an apartment in Ocean Beach.

"Go on," Carmen said.

"We have no idea how the abductions took place. We've identified cause of death, but other than the evidence that a Taser-like gun was used on Lindsey, we got nuthin'. Nor do we have their cell phones. We have Lindsey's VW and what's left of Cohen's Lexus. The techs found nothing on any of the computers we brought in. Cell phone calls are the kind we would expect from the victims. None of our vics has a record, so it looks like the killer knows enough about his victims to select those who wouldn't be in the system."

"Except we identified Mulvaney by his fingerprints."

"True, but only because he had been in the military and we searched that database. He's not in the criminal system. All squeaky clean. It's like he's looking for . . . sinless people."

"I doubt they're sinless."

"You know what I mean. Not one of them has ever been in the system. Anyway, we need to figure out how this guy is selecting his victims."

"How?" Carmen appreciated the point, but it also bothered her. It was just more proof that their adversary might be smarter than all of them combined.

"I have no idea." The confession seemed to take a little air out of her partner. "The more I think about this, the less sense it makes." He rubbed his freshly shaved face. "What is the motive? Why do this? Does he have means? Clearly. He kills with his hands—"

"Wilton was shot in the head."

Bud nodded. "I know, and it was you that said he was killed because he was in the way of the other murder."

"Well, I didn't say it like that."

Bud pressed his lips into a line. "Bear with me, Carmen. I'm not trying to quote you, but we all agree that Wilton was an obstacle, not the target. Now back to my point. Lindsey didn't have much money. Cohen had more, but the cash was still in the man's wallet. The killer didn't even try to make it look like a robbery. Why? Because of the time spent killing the vics. No robber would do that. Shoot and grab, sure, but not torture, kill, and transport the body. No armed robber would do that. He's got the means, he creates his own opportunity by studying his vics and planning the killings, but his motive is missing. Why do this?"

"The guy's wacko." Carmen had wondered the same thing. Hearing it from Bud confirmed her thinking.

"No doubt about that. Nothing more scary than a genius nut job. Still, why? We learn that, and we'll be halfway home instead of standing at the starting line tying our shoes."

Carmen agreed. The case was eating away at Bud as much as it was at her. She started to speak when she saw a familiar form at the entrance to the homicide wing.

"What's he doing here?" Carmen motioned Dr. Ellis Poe into the room.

Ellis's eyes burned from lack of sleep. He had spent the night on the *Blushing Bride* trying to rest, but not even the gentle rocking of the craft could lull him into slumber. Instead he stared at the ceiling of the small cabin. Every sound seemed amplified, as if someone had turned the world's volume up.

He tried praying but couldn't. Truth was, he hadn't been able to pray properly for days, the last few days being the worst. Twice he had risen and tried to read his Bible, the one thing that had been his joy and strength since giving his life to Christ in 1985. The practice had seen him through every difficult time. Prayer and Bible study got him through the death of his parents when he was just twenty-five. Last night, that warmth of spiritual focus went cold. He could not string enough words together to pray and couldn't focus long enough to read his favorite New Testament book—Colossians.

At 10:00 p.m. his neck began to hurt. At midnight, his stomach soured. At 2:00 a.m., his mind began to spin like a tornado, ripping up every fragment of self-esteem and confidence he had, sending them crashing into the inside of his skull. At 3:30, his stomach turned on him. And at 4:00 he began to weep again—alone in the small cabin.

On Monday he was due to start teaching. He had never missed the opening of a semester and seldom took a sick day. He had to be there. The thought made him feel worse. He began to sweat and his breathing grew shallow. For long, fearful moments he thought he was having a heart attack, but he felt no pain. He replaced the fear of a coronary with the terror of insanity. Maybe he was losing his mind, but that hypothesis died shortly after it sprang up.

At five that Sunday morning he knew what he must do, if only to save his life. God was squeezing his heart and wouldn't let go until Ellis did what was being demanded.

"Yes, Lord."

That prayer was heard, and peace filled his empty soul.

Now, standing at a doorway leading to the homicide division, a new set of anxieties flooded his being. No matter. He had come to confess, and confess he would, even if the stress of it killed him on the spot.

Detective Carmen Rainmondi waved him in. He smiled, but it felt unnatural. No doubt he looked like a clown. A guilty clown.

Carmen stood. "Dr. Poe, this is unexpected."

"Yes, I-I'm sorry." Great. Stuttering. No way to begin a conversation.

"You remember my partner, Detective Bud Tock." She motioned to him.

"Of course. My office, then in Coronado." He struggled with complete sentences.

"Are you feeling okay? You look pale."

He summoned a smile. "I didn't sleep much last night."

"I hear that," Bud said. "Not much sleeping going around here, either."

"What can I do for you, Dr. Poe?" Carmen's eyes narrowed. She suspected something.

"Well, um, I've been thinking about our conversation . . . you know . . . the one after the funeral—"

"I remember. I was there."

He chuckled, but it sounded plastic. "Of course, otherwise it wouldn't be a conversation. To converse means to . . . Never mind. Detective Rainmondi, may I speak to you in private?"

Carmen and Bud exchanged glances. Ellis felt certain they were thinking he had lost his mind. Both ran their gaze over him, no doubt looking for a weapon. Made sense. Police work had to make people paranoid.

"Sure. Let's go to a side room. I was going to work in there anyway." She turned her attention to Bud. "Where's Hector?"

"He's sitting in on the Mulvaney autopsy. Said he had questions for the ME."

Carmen nodded. "Heywood?"

"A couple of private security videos came in after the press

"A couple of private security videos came in after the press conference. He's checking those out. He said that based on the addresses, he doubted they were valid but he needed to apply due diligence."

"Okay. I want us to meet when everyone gets back. You got stuff to do?"

Bud laughed. "Funny girl. Yeah, I got a few thousand things to do. You go have your chat."

"This way, Dr. Poe." Carmen led them from the room.

29

Carmen twisted the doorknob and entered what she had come to think of as the "case room." A lot of work was done at her desk and in the field, but this was the place where the jigsaw puzzle was worked.

"We can talk here." She left the door open for Ellis.

"I appreciate this."

Poe didn't sound appreciative. He sounded . . . scared.

She stepped to the head of the table and sat, motioning for her visitor to sit to her left. As he rounded the table and lowered himself into the conference room chair, he reminded Carmen of a slowly deflating balloon. His face was pale and moist. His hands fidgeted, and he was having trouble looking her in the eye. He had always seemed a little shy, withdrawn, and easily intimidated. Still, he had always answered her questions without hesitation. Now he looked like a man sitting on a hot stove.

"Okay, Dr. Poe. I'm kinda busy. What can I do for you?"

He looked at the table, then at his hand. "You remember

when you came to my office. I mean, after the funeral. You know, at the seminary."

What had happened to the professor? "Yeah, I already said I remember. It wasn't all that long ago."

"Well, I know that. I mean . . ." He sighed. "I know you have a lot on your plate." He glanced at her, but only a glance. "These horrible murders. I-I don't know how you do it. I mean . . ." He looked up to the wall Carmen had attached photos and fact cards to.

He stopped talking.

For a moment, she thought he had stopped breathing.

"Is . . . that . . ." She saw him looking at the photos to the left of the time line—the place where the photos of his student had been mounted. One of the photos showed the damaged skin made by the dough docker.

Carmen, you're an idiot. You shouldn't have brought the poor man in here. "Yes. That's Doug Lindsey." She stood. "Let me find another room. I wasn't thinking when I brought you here. I've spent so much time in here and . . . Doesn't matter. Come on, I'll find a better place for us."

"Wait." He rose and walked to the wall and studied Lindsey's set of photos. He then looked down the line. "Five murders?"

"Yes. You didn't see the news or read about the other cases?"

"I never watch the news. Too depressing." He moved to the next column and gazed at the corpse of Wilton, who had spent a week submerged in Lake Murray. He seemed to shrink a few inches. "Shot?"

She wasn't sure if it was a question or a statement. The answer was obvious. There was a sizable hole in the kid's head.

He moved to the next column and looked at the battered body of Cohen. He raised a trembling hand and touched the image. “Beaten?”

“Yes.”

“By hand?”

“Yes, but . . .” Carmen didn’t know how to finish the sentence.

Ellis Poe moved to the next photo, that of a man with long marks over his body. He pointed at one of the stripes, opened his mouth. No words came out, leaving his expression to ask the question on his mind.

“Wood dowel. We found bits of wood in some of the wounds.”

The scholar’s face blanched, but he turned to the last set of photos in a column shorter than the others. He gazed at the image of the naked man tied to a tree with strips of purple cloth, including one around the dead man’s throat.

Carmen didn’t wait for a question. Her guest was seeing something she wasn’t. “Found yesterday. Strangled. Still waiting on the ME report, but we believe he was choked to death.”

Poe staggered back from the wall and steadied himself with one of the chairs. “Jesus!”

“It’s shocking, all right.”

“No . . . I . . .” He went milk-white. “I’m going to be sick. Bathroom. Quick! Bathroom!”

Carmen was at the door before Poe could finish the sentence. No way did she want him puking in her case room. “Down the hall a few steps. On the left—”

Poe was on the move, bolting through the door, into the hall, and into the restroom. Carmen let a few moments pass, then followed, entering the same lavatory. He was in the first stall, his face deep in the toilet bowl, vomiting from the toes up. She ignored the sound and the smell. When it seemed the violent stomach purge was over, she pulled a few pieces of paper hand towel from a dispenser then handed them to the white-faced scholar.

He reached to flush the handle, then transitioned from his knees to sitting on the tile floor. Carmen drew another paper towel, wet it, and handed it to Poe. A little color had returned to his face.

"Thank you." Then his eyes widened. "Should you be in the men's restroom?"

Before she could answer, someone entered and paused by Carmen. The woman—small, thin, with dark hair—looked at her. "Everything okay in here, Detective?"

"Yep. Just peachy."

The dark-haired woman nodded, then motioned down the bank of stalls. "Um, do you guys mind?"

"Go ahead. Knock yourself out."

"I won't be long."

Carmen smiled. "Don't rush on our account."

Poe leaned his head back until it rested against the stall divider. "I didn't think a man could embarrass himself in two ways simultaneously." He wiped his mouth again. "I guess the lack of urinals should have been a clue."

"True, well that and the blue placard with the stick figure in a dress and the sign that says WOMEN might have given it away."

"Sorry. I didn't think to check."

"Don't apologize. At least you didn't toss your cookies in my room."

He smiled. "A small victory."

A toilet flushed and the dark-haired woman reappeared. She looked at Carmen, then Poe. "Sure you're okay, Detective?"

"Yep. My friend here just made a wrong turn in the heat of the moment."

The woman shrugged again and exited the bathroom.

"Jesus." Poe stared at the opposite wall.

"Now you see, that surprises me. I didn't think guys like you said things like that. I mean, isn't that some kinda blasphemy or taking God's name in vain?"

"What?" His eyes widened then filled with understanding. "I see. No, I'm not swearing. I'm being literal." He struggled to his feet, wobbled, then found his balance.

"I don't understand."

"You're looking for a link, right? I mean, the wall is organized like someone looking for connections."

"So?"

"Jesus is the connection."

She frowned. "Dr. Poe, I'm not looking for a sermon—"

"No, you're looking for a killer, and Jesus is your answer. Really. He's the link."

Carmen stared at the wobbly man in the stall of the women's restroom. More color returned to his cheeks. Suspicion became Carmen's dominant emotion. She had dealt with her share of religious wackos on the street—from apocalyptic sign-carrying wanderers announcing the end of the world and then asking for a handout to preachers caught fleecing the flock or becoming too intimate with underage parishioners. Was she looking at another nut case?

Her doubt must have been obvious.

"I know it sounds strange, maybe even impossible." Poe rubbed his forehead and took a deep breath then let it out. His breath smelled sour. "Just let me talk it through, then you can toss me out on my ear."

"It won't be your ear, Dr. Poe." She crossed her arms. "Are you sure you're done in here?"

"Yes, I was just a little taken aback. I-I'm fine now. I think."

A tall blonde walked into the restroom and paused. "Are—"

"We're good. Thanks."

"Um . . ."

"We're leaving. Come on, Doc." Carmen heard the woman sigh with relief.

Back in the case room, Carmen stood on the wall opposite her time line and watched Ellis Poe work his way through the photos again and read the notes. He mumbled as he did. Ten minutes later he turned and stared at her. "I'm even more convinced, but I need to ask a few questions."

Carmen held up a finger and moved to the phone on the conference table. She punched in a number. "Bud, I'm in the case room. Get your fanny in here. Oh, and grab Joe. Hector still out?"

"Yes. What's up?"

"A spasm of genius, or maybe just a spasm. I want you to hear something." She hung up, then decided to make another call. Before she entered the numbers she glared at Poe. "You had better be onto something, Doc, because I'm about to put my reputation on the line. Would you risk your reputation on your idea?"

"I'm already doing that. Right?"

Carmen didn't answer. She punched in another button. "Hey, Cap. If you have a few minutes, there's something I want you to hear in the case room . . ."

30

Ellis Poe had come to the station for a one-on-one confession. But that intent had tumbled to the back of his mind. Now he was facing the captain of the homicide division, two detectives, and someone introduced as *Officer* Joe Heywood. He didn't know the difference in police ranking and didn't much care. His heart was doing gymnastics, his stomach churned, and his palms were moist. He also felt light-headed, as if helium filled his cranium instead of brains.

The homicide team sat. Captain Simmons, whom he was told was doing overtime on Sunday like the rest of them, was well dressed and looked trim in a suit Ellis couldn't afford. Heywood looked like his father might have been a Buick.

Carmen settled in her chair and brought the others up to speed. "Dr. Poe thinks Jesus is the link in our case."

"Jesus?" Simmons stared at her. "*The* Jesus? The Son-of-God Jesus?" He looked liked a man trying to understand the punch line to an arcane joke.

"I think that's what he means, Cap." Carmen faced Ellis. "That is the Jesus you mean, right?"

"Yes. Of course . . . Look, I know it sounds crazy, but I haven't lost my mind. Not yet anyway. If you'll bear with me while I ask a few questions, I can then present a cogent response."

"Cogent?" Carmen arched a brow.

Heywood jumped in. "It means logical, clear, orderly—"

"I know what it means, Joe." Carmen frowned. "Okay, let's not waste the captain's time. Ask away."

"First, I confess I haven't been following the news, so I may be missing some information."

"Not so much, Doc," Bud said. "We've kept most of the details out of the media."

"Okay. Well. Um." Poe sighed, thought for a moment. *This is a chance to do something good for a change. Get to it.* He cleared his throat and straightened, as if he were about to lecture one of his classes. He pointed at one of the photos of Doug Lindsey. "I know his body was found in Balboa Park. This is the Botanical Building. Am I right?"

"Yes." It was clear Carmen was going to be the spokesperson for the group. "He was found outside of the building."

"Doesn't matter. The building is significant, but so is the whole park." Ellis tapped a close-up photo of the puncture wounds. "He died from these . . . perforations?"

"No, he died from anaphylactic shock. He was allergic to latex."

The information felt like a punch, but Ellis pushed on. "He died by accident?"

"We believe the murderer would have killed him, but the kid died before he could. In case you're wondering, it still counts as murder."

Ellis rubbed his chin and looked at the photos. "Many of the wounds bled so the injuries . . ."

"It was torture." Carmen stated that face with a calm Ellis envied.

He moved to the next column. "This victim doesn't seem to fit. This is the only thing I'm confused about."

"His name is Wilton. He was with your student when he was abducted."

Ellis scratched the back of his neck. "So he's an anomaly. Someone who was in the way. Is that right?"

"We think so."

"I see." Ellis moved to the next column and pointed at a card beneath one of the photos. "Victim's name is Cohen. I see a note here that he was found at the home of Rabbi Singer. Jewish."

"Most rabbis are, Dr. Poe."

Ellis ignored the jab. "Beaten to death?"

"Yes."

"With an object or by someone's hands?"

"We covered that earlier. He was pummeled."

"I see. That makes sense." Again, he moved down the line.

"How?" Bud sounded impatient.

"Please bear with me. My statement won't make sense until I lay the foundation. Forgive me, but it's how academicians think." Next victim's column. He looked at Carmen. "You said these marks came from a beating with wood dowels."

"The ME thinks so. I said bits of wood were found in some of the wounds. Trace identified it as the kind of wood used to make dowels, so the supposition fits."

"Where was the body found?"

"Near Miramar. There is a set of old barracks on the east side of the freeway."

Ellis was feeling sick again. His initial hypothesis was holding up, and it was unsettling. He moved to the fourth victim. "This column has fewer notations than the others."

"That's because the body was found just yesterday. Crown Point." Carmen leaned on the table. "That part of the investigation is just starting."

"He was found tied to a tree? With purple cloth?"

"Just as you see in the photo, Doc.

"Is there a Jewish home nearby? A large home."

"What's that got to do with anything?" Bud was growing increasingly fed up.

"Yes."

At Officer Heywood's answer, the others looked at him.

He shrugged. "I helped with the canvassing. I noticed a mezuzah on the door frame on one of the houses. I didn't think anything about it."

He gazed at Heywood. "Was it a big home? A mansion?"

"It was pretty big. It might be a stretch to call it a mansion, but it was one of the largest homes on the street. Houses along there aren't especially large. This one stood out."

"You noticed a what on the door frame?" Simmons asked.

Ellis answered. "Mezuzah. It's a small container with a bit of Hebrew Scripture in it. Practicing Jews mount them to the doorposts of their homes. They're being obedient to a couple of passages in the Old Testament. Deuteronomy 6:9 and 11:20, if memory serves. God commands the people to keep His word before them at all times, even to the point of binding it to their doorposts and at times to wear phylacteries—small boxes holding bits of Scripture. The word *mezuzah* used to refer to the doorpost. It's an ancient practice. An admirable one."

"I'm not following you." Carmen's brow was furrowed. "So what if some religious Jew puts up one of these things. San Diego has many Jews. There's got to be thousands of these things."

"Not with a body like this"—Ellis pointed at the photo of the trussed-up corpse—"nearby."

"Wait." Heywood's eyes widened. "You're not suggesting . . ." He slapped his forehead. "I should have seen this. It seems so obvious now."

"*What's* obvious?" Carmen snapped the words.

"I'm with her," Captain Simmons said.

Ellis returned to the front of the time line and tapped the image of Lindsey's dead body. "Garden setting. Drops of blood." He paused. "Gethsemane, where Jesus sweat great drops of blood." A step to the side. "Rabbi's home. Jesus was pummeled by Temple guards at the High Priest's house." He moved down the line again. "Military barracks. Pilate had Jesus beaten by soldiers. It included beating him with reeds. Don't think soft, pliable reeds along a riverbank. Think wood sticks."

"And the latest victim?" Carmen said.

"Contempt. The Roman soldiers dressed Jesus in purple and mocked him by saying, 'Hail to the King of the Jews.' The only reason the Romans were involved was because Jesus' accusers said Jesus claimed to be a king. That was punishable by death in Roman-controlled Jerusalem. The soldiers and temple guards entertained themselves by beating and mocking Jesus. Purple was a sign of wealth and royalty. The mockery took place in or around King Herod's palace."

"That's where your question about the Jewish home came from?" Carmen pushed back in her seat, like she needed the additional support from the back of the chair.

"Yes."

Carmen rubbed her face. No one spoke. It took a full minute before she broke the silence. "So you're telling us that all this lines up perfectly with what the Bible says about Jesus."

"Well, no, not perfectly. I don't know enough criminal psychology to pretend to understand what's going on in the killer's brain, but he's definitely following a biblical pattern . . ." A slap of realization hit Ellis. "Doug Lindsey. He died on a Thursday. Maundy Thursday. That's the day Jesus instituted the Lord's Supper, then went to the garden of Gethsemane where He prayed with such fervor he sweat blood."

Simmons shook his head. "How can a man sweat blood?"

Ellis had heard the question countless times. "Hematidrosis. It's a rare condition. Blood mixes with sweat. It happens when a person is under tremendous, life-threatening stress. From there, Jesus would be captured and tortured. It looks like the killer picked that day to start his killing spree. Of course, he's not torturing and killing one man, so he needs more time. That seems to make sense."

"So he's working his way through the events of Jesus' suffering," Heywood's comment was more statement than question.

"It seems so." Ellis wondered if he should feel proud about his discovery. He didn't. He felt ill.

"Why?" Carmen asked.

Ellis shook his head. "I don't know."

"Let me ask this," Simmons said. "Is there a time line here? I mean, is he working on a schedule?"

"A schedule. I don't know." Ellis turned back to the wall of information. "He's not replicating all that Jesus went through. He seems to be pulling notable events and staging his murders based on them. So, I can't say I see a schedule . . . unless . . ." He closed his eyes trying to tempt the thought to the forefront of his mind. "Easter."

"Easter has passed," Bud said.

"*One* Easter has passed," Ellis countered.

Bud frowned. "Well, just how many Easters are there? I'm not a church expert, but I'm pretty sure there's only one Easter a year."

"I'm sorry, Detective, but you're wrong. There are two. Let me explain. Most Christians celebrate the Western Easter. The Eastern Church celebrates later. Theirs is based on the Julian calendar, not the Gregorian—the calendar we use today. Easter floats. This year it was on March 31, and the Eastern Easter will be celebrated May 5. Next year they will coincide. I wonder . . . could the killer be working between the Easters?"

Carmen narrowed her eyes. "So he's working toward a goal?"

"That would be my guess." Ellis studied the board again, searching for anything he might have missed. He turned back to the group when Carmen spoke.

"Just how many other events are there in the . . . what do we call this?"

"Passion Week is a good term." The things he had avoided thinking crashed like a storm-driven wave. He put his hands through his hair. He felt his knees shake. "Oh my." He moved from the wall, pulled a chair from the conference table, and plopped in it.

"Are you all right?" Simmons asked.

"I'm . . . I'm . . ."

Carmen inched closer to the table. "Do you need to go to the women's restroom again?" A moment passed then he heard her say, "I'll explain later."

"No, I'll be fine. I just need . . . the next murder. It will be horrible. I know what's missing." He closed his eyes against the images that knowledge sent through his mind. "The crown of thorns and the flogging."

"Flogging, like Rolf Brady—the guy beaten with the wood dowels?"

"No. Worse." Ellis raised his head. "Flogging was done with a Roman flagellum, sometimes called a cat-o-nine tails. It's a whip with several strands attached to a wood handle. The strands were weighted on the ends with small, lead weights and bits of metal and glass. It was designed to remove the skin from a man's back. There are historical accounts of the victim being beaten so badly that bits of bone could be seen. Many prisoners died from the beating." He leaned his head back and stared at the ceiling. If only he could slip back to his tiny boat and never leave. "And that's not the worst."

"What could be worse than that?" Carmen's voice was hushed.

"Your man is planning to crucify someone. I can't even describe how horrible that will be. It's beyond imagination." Ellis jerked to his feet and swayed. He looked at Carmen. "The *correct* door is just a little farther along the hall?"

"Yes. Heywood can go with you—"

Ellis raised a hand and belched. "No, I prefer to do this alone . . ."

He ran from the room.

31

The problem with having voices in your head is the inability to be alone, to have a thought, an urge, a home, a dream that isn't known to the invaders. Sometimes they complimented him, but more often they mocked him, discouraged him, even threatened him, twisting his emotions, analyzing every thought.

Then there were the images: grotesque figures. One was the shape of a beautiful woman in a flowing, white wedding dress, moving as if floating an inch above the ground, closer, closer, nearer still until he could gaze beyond the veil at her faceless features.

Others were dark, insectlike. At times he would wake in the night and see them scampering on the ceiling like cockroaches, falling on the bed next to him—falling on him, scrambling, clambering, scrabbling over his petrified body.

Still others hovered just outside his peripheral vision. He would detect the motion of something black-red approaching, but it never arrived.

The sensations bothered him most. The caress of an invisible finger on his ear, its skin like sandpaper; the feeling of hot breath on his neck, and when he would turn he'd find nothing but empty space.

Space. It was one thing the voices did for him. They knew he had a breaking point. He was never afraid. He was incapable of it. Nor could he feel regret. Physically, he was better than any man he had ever met—powerful, agile, dense, tall, broad, with the build of the largest heavyweight boxers—but he had been short-changed in the emotion department. He had never known love. His parents didn't use the word and didn't express kindness. Certainly not when they would lock him in the bathroom for a week at a time. No food, only water from the sink to drink, only the tile floor or bathtub for a bed.

He was small then. When his father abandoned them and his mother died of a drug overdose a week later, he was handed off to a string of foster homes. Two were abusive, one kind, the last three didn't care what he did as long as they received their money from the state.

Pain, he knew. He had felt it; he had delivered it. There was joy in both. He remembered his first school fight. A kid two years older, a sixth grader, and his pals had snatched him after school. They called him names. They stripped him naked, then laughed. Then the large boy punched him in the stomach. He expected excruciating pain. Instead, he felt—joy. Another punch confirmed it. This was new. As a younger child, the beatings his father delivered hurt and left marks. Now . . . it was different.

Then he found an even greater joy.

He clenched his fist and let it fly, catching the other boy on the side of his head. The kid went down, his head bouncing off the pavement in the alley where they had dragged him. He turned to the kids. They fled.

Calmly he dressed himself, smoothed his clothing, gathered his school books, then stepped to the unconscious twelve-year-old. He raised a foot and brought it down on the boy's abdomen. Even unconscious, the boy moaned.

That felt pretty good, too.

This led to his first stint in a reform school.

Work. Work. Work.

There was no sense in arguing with the voices. They had been with him continually for the last year and he had come to know their habits. They would repeat the word until he complied, or make it so he couldn't eat or drink.

"I'm going. I'm going."

The small office of the abandoned warehouse had become his home. His place of work was the empty expanse of the storage area. He walked through the space, his boots echoing off the concrete floor and hard walls. Today's task was easy:

Mount the large Douglas-fir crossbeam to the upright member of the twelve-foot-high cross in the making.

Ellis Poe didn't know whether to feel good or bad. He had gone to the police station to confess what he knew about Shelly's murder, to admit that he was a coward, to apologize, and then take whatever came next, even if that meant arrest. It had taken him all night and most of the day to conjure up the courage to make the trip and to ask to speak to Carmen.

He didn't know if he could do it again.

He steered his car north toward his Escondido home. Traffic was coagulating along the Interstates, something he expected. It didn't matter. His class for tomorrow was ready, requiring only a little review. He'd pick up fast food, go home, eat, read, and hopefully sleep.

He did have one odd sensation. Earlier, while on his boat, he had tried to pray, but God seemed so distant. He thought he'd feel the same way after failing in his confessional mission. Instead, there was a warmth in him. He could imagine Jesus sitting in the passenger's seat. Maybe he had done some good today. That would be nice. He desperately needed to feel that he had done something useful.

Just once in his life he would like to feel valuable instead of cowardly.

The slow traffic gave him time to think. Normally a good thing, but his mind kept running to the sickening wall of murder Carmen had erected. He was certain of his interpretation.

Interpretation.

That was his skill, his superpower. To understand the teaching of the Bible, the reader had to understand the context. When was it written? By whom? Under what circumstance? To whom was the author writing? What did the writer want to achieve? Hermeneutics was not the same as criminal investigation, but there were points of commonality. All events happen in context.

What was the killer's context?

As usual, Ellis steered into the far right lane to take his time. Let the other drivers race home. He had nothing to race to. Once settled into the flow of traffic, he returned to his thinking.

Context. Why kill people to replicate the passion of Christ? And to do it so brutally? Was it a hatred for Christians? Did the killer have an axe to grind with God? Maybe he was trying to hurt God by killing Christians and Jews.

No, that couldn't be it. Carmen had revealed more of the details. Only two were Christians, and one—Wilton—didn't fit the killer's pattern at all. Only one victim, as far as the police knew, was Jewish, although two of the crimes were somehow tied to a Jewish home. Sometimes scholars worked on instinct, and his instinct was telling him he had gone off-course. If every victim had been an active Christian, then the supposition might make sense. The same was true if each victim were Jewish. Neither was the case.

Clearly, the killer had some biblical understanding. At the very least he knew a little about the physical abuse Jesus suffered at the hands of his accusers and the Romans. Maybe he knew more than Ellis supposed. Maybe Ellis hadn't looked deep enough. For example, the man tied to the tree with the purple fabric. Was the killer thinking of Paul's letter to the Galatians? He paraphrased the verse aloud: "Cursed is everyone who hangs on a tree."

Maybe. He couldn't be sure. Who could guess what a crazy man was thinking? The best thing to do was to let it go. Let the police handle everything. It was their job. They had been trained for such work. Just forget it.

If only he could.

Carmen brought Hector up to speed on their meeting with Ellis Poe. They sat in the case room.

"Wait a minute. He ran into the women's restroom." Hector laughed. "That's a good one."

"Funny as it is, Hector, you're missing the point. He's on to something. At first, I thought he'd rounded the bend or was something of a holy roller out to save all our souls, but his logic is unassailable. It seems obvious now. Maybe if I were a churchgoer, I'd have picked up on it myself, but I wasn't even close."

"None of us were close, but let's be honest, Carmen. What good does it do us? So what? Maybe the killer has a biblical bent, but how does that help us catch him?"

"I don't know. I suppose we can canvass all the churches in the city—"

"Do you know how many churches that is? Hundreds. Maybe a few thousand. He may be doing this because he hates churches. If so, he won't be attending one."

Carmen had to acknowledge the wisdom in the comment.

"Did your guy have any ideas about when all this might stop?" Hector leaned back in his chair. He looked worn to the bone. The case was taking a toll on her team. On her.

"He thinks there will be a least one more murder, maybe two or three, depending on how the guy breaks down the Passion of Christ. He thinks the next one will be a guy wearing a crown of thorns with the flesh whipped from his back."

"Ouch. Where does one get a crown of thorns these days?"

"I don't know, but remember, much of this is symbolic. Mulvaney was strapped to a tree with purple cloth. Poe tells us that the purple mentioned in the New Testament would probably have been a robe Jesus' tormentors threw over him, not strips of cloth."

"I guess."

"You look bad, Hector."

"Thanks, Boss. I love you, too."

Carmen chuckled. "You know what I mean. I'm beat. When we find this guy, I may just shoot him over all the sleep I've lost."

"I'll cover for you." He closed his eyes and sighed. "Ready for the preliminary ME report?"

"Sure. Can't wait."

"Max Mulvaney died of strangulation. Had been dead for three hours when he was discovered. He showed bruising from a beating, and there were also two puncture marks indicating a Taser-like weapon was used. The ME thinks he was beaten unconscious after that. I checked DMV, and Mulvaney drove an old GMC pickup. I've put out a BOLO for the vehicle. I got his address, and I'm heading there as soon as we're done. For all I know, the car is there. Or it could be in a ditch." He stood.

"I'll go with you. I've had it with this place." Carmen rose and stretched her back.

"I appreciate the company." He studied the floor for a moment. "I've seen horrible things, Carmen. That includes stuff I saw in the military that I can't talk about. But this stuff? It's making me sick. I may have laughed at your professor buddy, but there are moments I feel like tossing my cookies, too." He paused and lowered his head. "Sorry. I'm feeling sorry for myself."

"You don't have to apologize to me, Hector. I've been thinking about selling flowers on the street corner."

He snickered. "I know what you mean. There are days when I think those guys really have it going on."

She put a hand on the man's shoulder. "We'll get 'im, Hector. You, me, Bud, Joe, the cap—we'll get him. One way or the other."

"I hope you're right."

So do I, buddy. So do I. They walked from the room.

32

Mulvaney's apartment building was a dump, a one-bedroom on the second floor of an apartment building on Del Monte Street in Ocean Beach. The apartment building looked a century old, but Carmen was sure it had only been around since the '40s or '50s. The building was small, with stucco walls that someone thought would be improved with lime-green paint. The windows, double-hung affairs that dated the building, were trimmed in an off-white that could do with a good sanding and fresh gallon of paint.

Carmen and Hector identified themselves to the landlord, informed him he was now shy one tenant, and asked to be let into Mulvaney's apartment. The manager was an old surfer with long, stringy, sun-bleached hair. His skin was dry, with traces of salt. Carmen guessed the man had been surfing a short time ago.

Old surfers never die; they just wash out to sea.

"Dead? Really? Murdered? Whoa, dude." The guy was well

past his fiftieth birthday, but he spoke like an eighteen-year-old from the seventies. "Bummer."

A part—a large part—of Carmen wanted to search the man's apartment for drugs. The air was perfumed with the stench of marijuana. Nothing like a relaxing toke after a few hours in the Pacific. She took a couple of sniffs but said nothing.

"Um, yeah. Sure. His apartment. Glad to help. Just let me get the keys."

"Leave the door open, please." Carmen smiled. A simple message saying don't bail out the back window. To the man's credit, he returned in fifteen seconds, crossed the threshold, and closed the door behind him as if the damage hadn't already been done.

Carmen had no desire to bust the man. She had bigger fish to fry. Surfer dude led them up the exterior stairs. The concrete treads and wood runners bounced with their steps. The stairwell held.

"What kind of tenant was Mr. Mulvaney?"

"Max? He was all right. Stayed to himself. Didn't bother nobody. When he rented the place, he mentioned he had been in the military. I think the war affected him in the head, if you know what I mean."

"Did he do any entertaining?" Hector walked directly behind the manager.

"Nah. Not him. I'd see him go to work and come home. Most nights he went fishing on the pier. Always went alone, came back late, then he'd start the whole thing over."

"So you never saw anyone going to his apartment?" Hector pressed.

"You mean like . . ." He started to use a term then changed his mind midsentence. "You mean like, um, ladies of the evening?"

Hector's voice took on a sharper tone. "I mean anyone."

Surfer dude shook his head. "Like I said, I never saw anyone go to his place. No one complained about the guy. He was jus' a lonely dude, doing his own thing."

They walked down a porchlike walkway. Carmen had a question. "Did he pay his rent on time?"

"Oh, yeah. He was always good about that. Never late. Never had his utilities cut off. You know the utility companies inform us when they cut someone off. They must think we'll cover for the tenant or somethin'." He chuckled "Like that's gonna happen."

Mulvaney's apartment was a street-side corner unit with a fine view of the apartment building directly across Del Monte. The manager started to insert the key into the lock.

"Hang on a sec." Carmen pulled on a pair of latex gloves and twisted the doorknob. It turned easily. The door was unlocked. A closer look at the lock showed scratches around the key slot, perhaps the result of years of use or from being picked. She looked at Hector, who had already pushed the manager to the side. Carmen and Hector drew their weapons.

Carmen already had the doorknob in hand. She would be the one to open it. Hector stepped to her side. Carmen pushed the door open and Hector charged in. "Police!" Carmen followed so close she almost tripped over Hector's trailing foot.

Hector veered to the right, Carmen to the left, their weapons extended before them. There were only two doors in the apartment, one slightly narrower than the other. The smaller had to be the bathroom; the wider, the bedroom. Hector positioned himself next to the bedroom door and opened it with a fluid motion, waited one second, then disappeared. A second later, "Clear."

Carmen moved to the bathroom door as Hector came to her side. She opened the door fast and hard, stepping into the small space. Empty. The shower curtain was drawn. She pushed it back but saw only brown stains on white fiberglass. "Clear."

A voice from behind them. "Cool."

Carmen turned to see Surfer dude smiling.

"Just like television."

"I told you to stay outside," Hector said.

"No way, dude. You told me to move out of the way. You didn't say nuthin' about staying outside."

"Um, Hector . . ."

"I see it. I think we're gonna need Field Services here."

Carmen nodded. "You think?"

Hector moved closer. "Is that lipstick?"

Carmen had been paying attention to the message, not the medium.

She holstered her weapon, leaned forward, and fought the urge to use every swear word she knew.

THAT'S FOUR, CARMEN

They walked the manager from the apartment. Carmen knew her anger must show on her face—it radiated heat. After Hector jogged down the stairs, she spun on the manager. "I thought you said women didn't come up here."

The scraggly haired man's face went white. "No, I didn't. I said I never saw anyone come up here. At least that's what I meant to say. I never saw the guy with a chick. Maybe he's a cross-dresser or somethin'."

This guy was a total waste of time. "Okay, sir. We have some work to do here. I want you to go back to your apartment. We may have more questions."

"Yeah. Sure. Whatever you say. Glad to help. Just ask—"

Carmen turned her back on the man and reentered the room just as Hector was coming up the stairs with a roll of crime-scene tape. While he taped off the second-story walkway leading to the apartment, Carmen took a slow look around the room. What was she missing?

The place was neat, orderly, but plain in every other way. No ornamentation. The kitchen counters were clean, no dishes in the sink. The only decorations on the walls were a triangular wooden frame holding a folded US flag and some medals.

Hector walked in and looked at the display. "I hate to see a guy like this end up this way."

Carmen studied him. "What do you mean?"

Hector pointed at the display of multicolored ribbons. "These tell a story." He pointed at a ribbon with several colored vertical stripes of various widths. "He served in Afghanistan." He pointed at another. "Iraq. This one means he earned a Bronze star. Our vic is a war hero."

A war hero. And he died like that? The news made Carmen's anger boil.

"It's the sad thing about war." Hector sounded heartbroken. "Some go from zero to hero in war, then back to zero when they leave the service. War can make an ordinary man great and a great man something less than ordinary." He pointed at a medal. "Purple Heart. He was wounded while on duty."

Carmen moved to the closet and searched through the man's clothing. No suits, no uniforms. Just jeans and work shirts, a windbreaker, a sweatshirt, and a few sports caps. No female clothing. The manager's suggestion was off the beam. Still, that left the question: "Why lipstick?"

Hector shrugged. "Have you searched for the stick?"

"Yes. Nothing. He may have flushed it."

Hector thought for a moment. "What about other makeup?"

"You think the manger's idea the guy was a cross-dresser has merit?"

Hector shook his head. "Doubtful. Not out of the question, but unless you find a pair of triple-wide size-15 pumps in the closet, I choose not to believe it."

Carmen studied the message. "Something's odd. What's with the lettering? Every other letter angles a different way."

"Beats me . . . Wait, you don't suppose the guy used both his right and left hands to write it? You know, to throw us off."

"Could be. Could be." There was something else about the message that bothered her.

"Odd shade." Hector cocked his head to the side.

"You an expert on lipstick, Hector?"

"Expert? No, but I do have a wife and two teenage daughters. Trust me, I know about things I never thought I would."

She chuckled. "Okay, Mr. Makeup Artist. What's wrong with the shade?"

Hector looked at her. "Shouldn't that be your area of expertise?"

"When was the last time you saw me with lipstick on?"

"Okay, you got me. I don't think my kids would go out in public with that shade of pink. Well, I take that back. My oldest went to an '80s party. She wore something like that."

"Eighties." Carmen mulled that over. "I know enough to know you can get just about any color these days, but you're right. You know, in some ways, it looks familiar."

"Shall we talk about the elephant in the room?" Hector eyed Carmen.

"My name?"

"That'd be the elephant."

"It surprised me at first, but then I remembered the press conference. I was up-front. I'm sure the television folks put my name in the lower third of the screen, and the print media listed me as the lead detective. It's no surprise that the killer watched or read the reports."

"No surprise, eh? Frankly, I expected you to be a little more freaked-out about it."

"He taunted us once before." Carmen turned from the mirror.

"Not by name he hasn't. Why do that? Why come back here and write the message?"

She stopped in the middle of the small living room and gazed at the Spartan furniture, none of it younger than a decade. Even the television was an old CRT style with rabbit-ears. *Rabbit ears,* of all things. This guy lived on the cheap.

Carmen organized her thoughts. "The place is clean and

orderly. No sign of a struggle. No blood spatter, and we know the vic was beaten. The body showed signs of bleeding from the mouth and nose. I'd expect to see some blood in here. The crime scene techs will make a more thorough check, but I'd be surprised if they find anything. Furniture is in place." She pointed at the bottom of the sofa. "You can see the feet of the sofa are in the carpet indentation. True for the rest of the furniture. I'm betting Mulvaney was abducted and killed elsewhere."

"His truck isn't in the parking area of the complex. I checked when I went to get the crime-scene tape."

"Good. That was next on my list." She moved through the apartment again. There had to be something. Anything. Some small clue she'd overlooked before.

The man lived a simple life. His refrigerator held a six-pack of beer, milk, cheese slices, and some lunch meat. One of the kitchen cabinets held a half-dozen cans of Hungry Man soup, and at least a dozen packages of Top Ramen. There were three boxes of off-brand cereal.

He must have eaten out a lot.

"Something is missing." She knew it, just couldn't pinpoint it. She continued through the apartment once more.

Hector snapped his fingers. "Fishing gear. Did you find a pole or tackle box?"

"No." An idea popped into her mind. She moved to the kitchen and opened the trash can. Fish bones. "He ate what he caught."

"A true sportsman." Hector rocked on his heels, then fixed her with a stare. "I'm just going to say it. I think you need to assign a couple of uniforms for your protection."

Seriously? Didn't he think she could take care of herself? "Nonsense. He got my name from the press conference."

"Do you think Captain Simmons will see it that way?"

"I don't know, Hector. I seem to know less with every day that passes."

"You can stay with me and the family. Two guns are better than one."

"Chivalry lives, Hector. Thanks, but I'll be fine. I'm not part of the killer's pattern. Besides, having the killer come to me might be easier than chasing him down."

"That's dangerous thinking, Carmen. Real dangerous."

"Face it, Hector, this guy has the advantage. He isn't a few steps ahead of us, he's miles. We got nothing. No initial crime scene, no DNA, no fingerprints, no trace, no surveillance video, no witnesses, nothing, zip, zilch, nada. Five dead, and all we've learned is that he's replicating scenes from the Bible. That, and he's smarter than we are."

"Still—"

"Let it go, Hector. I'm not going to do anything stupid."

"Wait. The message mentions four victims, not five. Why?"

Carmen chewed on that for a moment. He doesn't count Lindsey's friend. "Wilton was an obstacle not a target."

"I guess that makes sense. Somehow, that chills me all the more."

They spent the next thirty minutes looking in every corner of the room for something that might pass as a clue.

They found nothing.

"Detectives?"

Carmen turned to see Millie Takahashi in the doorway. Two other techs stood behind her. "Hey, Millie." She walked to the head of forensics. "You got here quick."

Millie didn't smile. Like the rest of the team, she looked beat. "We pretty much just follow you around these days. I've been thinking about sleeping in the trunk of your car. It would save time."

"Sorry, but I make Detective Tock ride back there."

"Lucky man," Millie said. "What have we got?"

"I don't think you'll find much, but maybe your magic will come up with something. I want lots of pictures of the bathroom, especially the mirror. There are a lot of smooth surfaces in there, so give it a good dusting. I doubt our man left anything for you to find, but he may have slipped up."

"Got it." Millie took her kit to the bathroom.

"Let's get out of the way, Hector. Knock on a few doors. Maybe another tenant caught sight of our guy."

"Are you kidding me!" Millie's voice poured from the bathroom. She appeared a moment later. "He's calling you by name?"

Great. Another alarmist.

Carmen shrugged and exited the apartment.

The voices were so loud. The words had sharp spines that punctured his brain. "I'm sorry. I'm sorry!" He held his hands to his ears. Futile. The voices lived inside him, between his ears. "I just wanted a little fun. That's all. Fun."

The voices screamed. Cursed him for breaking the rules. He should never have gone to the man's apartment. Should never have written the message on the mirror.

Never.

But he had.

And the voices were making him pay for it.

33

The sun had dropped behind the horizon. The lights of San Diego painted the darkness with an eerie glow. Outside, cars plied the streets, some with owners heading home, some with occupants headed to work. San Diego slowed, but it never slept.

The team had called it a night. There was little more they could do. They turned over every rock they could see and found nothing. Carmen knew they were like her: a homicide detective might go home, but his work went along for the ride. Some of the best mental breakthroughs came when the detectives were home resting or watching television. The subconscious mind liked to be left alone to process what the conscious mind couldn't. That was its function. It had worked for her on several occasions.

Carmen didn't want to go home. There was nothing there but her bed. That sounded pretty good, but she had no desire to be alone just yet. Something was eating at her, churning her stomach and making her head hurt. She was missing something.

She knew that, but such knowledge was useless. Knowing there was something she didn't know only brought fierce frustration.

While she'd never admit it to anyone, she was depressed. The condition began in her teenage years—a darkness, a heaviness, a void that seemed to suck in her soul, leaving her hollow, cored out. Teenage angst was part of the normal maturing process, but Carmen's depression never fully went away. It ebbed and flowed like the tide, lifting her to feelings of euphoria and empowerment, only to withdraw, leaving her an emotional husk. She was no good to anyone in those hours and certainly not pleasant to be around.

Sure, there were medications she could take, but her blues were part of her, defined her, and in a strange way, strengthened her. Odd as it was, she felt more alive when down. Her depression was tied to her grief, and grief was a way of expressing love. A painful, corrosive way to express it.

There was no logic to it. It just was. *She* just was.

Once home, Carmen pulled out one of the drawers of her desk. A special drawer. One containing a small wooden box six-inches on a side and three-inches deep. The lock was a decorative style meant more to look pretty than to thwart snoopers. She kept the small key in the change compartment of her purse. She looked around the empty office area, removed the key, and unlocked the box. Slowly, she opened the lid, something she hadn't done in months. A slight odor of cedar rose to her nostrils.

Mementos. Remembrances. That's what some would call the items in the box. A comb with a few strands of blond hair. A high-school ring. A pair of earrings. A school photo. A photo taken before Junior Prom.

Carmen gazed at the image of her sister. Gone so many years now. So popular. So full of life.

So dead.

She ran a finger along the image, touching the cheek of the young lady in the photo. Carmen smiled. Big hair. Heavy makeup. Yes, the '80s were gone and the world was a better place for it. Shelly wore a pink-and-white prom dress. Carmen remembered her mother arguing about the amount of eye makeup she wore. At least Shelly had picked a unique pink lipstick, a lipstick she would wear frequently after that night. Granted it was a darker pink than was popular for the time—

Carmen bolted to her feet, sending her office chair toppling behind her. Her hands shook. Her stomach tightened into a knot. "No." She shook her head. "It can't be. No. I'm insane." She scrutinized the photo, her eyes boring into the image. Her lips. The lipstick. Too much of a coincidence. She was letting her emotions run away. "Get a grip, girl."

Then a thought: She had another photo from that prom. One she carried in her purse. She retrieved the Polaroid and eased the photo from its plastic enclosure. The photo was too large for a wallet. Polaroids were great, but they didn't take wallet-size photos. It showed Carmen and Shelly, side by side. Shelly was kissing Carmen on the cheek. Carmen remembered that night. She had to use soap and hot water to get the lip marks off her face. She recalled being annoyed.

Shelly also kissed the photo. She was playful.

Something Carmen had never been.

Carmen marched into the forensic department and found Millie still working, sitting at a computer monitor. Millie's husband was a Navy man and had been out to sea for four months. The forensic tech passed the lonely hours working overtime. This case gave her ample opportunity.

"Detective Rainmondi," the young woman said. Slight in build, she had a magnificent mind. "I didn't know you were still around."

"Okay, you're going to think I've taken leave of my senses, but I want you to do something for me, and I need you to do it as quickly as possible."

"I'll do what I can."

"First, I need an evidence bag."

Millie retrieved one from a storage locker and handed it to Carmen, who dropped the photo into the clear, plastic bag.

"Whatcha got?"

Carmen took a deep breath. "This is a one-in-a-million chance, but I want you to test the lipstick on this photo."

"Which case does this relate to . . . Wait. You think the lipstick on the photo might match what we found on the mirror?"

"I doubt it, but the shades are the same, or a least close."

Millie studied the photo. "That's you. Younger, but it's you."

"Right."

"Who is . . . your sister?"

"Yes. It was taken a long time ago." Her voice softened.

"You think there's a connection." Millie thought for a moment. "It looks similar. The lipstick on the mirror was fairly dry. Age could explain that."

"Can you tell if they're a match or not?"

"Yes. I can do a visual comparison of texture and tint. I can arrange for a spectroscopic analysis and see if the profiles match, but you know the chance they're a match is slim at best. Even if they are, all it means is that the perp had access to a product that was produced by the thousands."

"Produced decades ago. And remember, it was used to write my name. The color. My name. There's something there."

"Maybe. Just maybe. I'll get to work on it."

"As soon as possible, Millie. This is important."

"Everything in this department is important, but I get the point."

Carmen thanked her and walked from the room. Her mind was in 1985.

And in the police file of her sister's death.

Ellis Poe sat in his nearly dark office, a converted bedroom in his condo, and reviewed class notes for the new semester. He had two classes on Monday, Wednesday, and Friday: Synoptic Gospels and the Pauline Prison Epistles. The first class was for first-year students, the second for third year. He had taught both classes many times, so his attention kept wandering from his lesson plan and to the problem facing Carmen and her team. Was he on target? The pattern certainly matched, but the "why" remained.

He was no criminologist, no psychologist, but there had to be a reason. Surely the man had lost his senses sometime in the past. It was the only way to explain such brutality. As far as Ellis knew, the killer was targeting and attacking unarmed people. He was doing so in order, and each death was a message.

Was the message complete? He doubted it. Ellis had already estimated one or two more deaths. He pulled a few sheets of blank paper from his desk drawer and moved his lesson plans to the side.

A blank page. Always a formidable foe. Was there something more he could offer? Could he guess where the next body would be found, or at least narrow the possibilities? He doubted he could pinpoint a place, but he might be able to identify a trend.

First, he made a list based on the columns of information he saw in Carmen's case room. The thought of the place made him recall his embarrassing behavior. He would replay the ladies' room thing for the rest of his life. Maybe someday he would consider it a funny event, but he doubted it.

Two things seemed obvious. Each murder was done in a fashion similar to physical torment endured by Jesus: sweating drops of blood; beaten with fists; beaten with reeds, in this case rods; and strangulation. The last one didn't fit. At least not the method of death, although the purple cloth did. The second set of relational points dealt with where the bodies were found: in a garden, at a rabbi's house, by barracks, near a Jewish-owned mansion that he assumed was meant to represent Herod's palace. Jesus didn't die after each abuse, but that didn't seem the killer's point.

If Ellis's assumption were correct, the next death would be someone whipped to death and the body would have a crown of thorns. He had no idea where a person would get such a thing.

He paused, then turned to his computer. A quick Internet search for "crown of thorns" revealed several places one could buy a replica. Would a mass murderer buy something like that from an Internet store? It was worth noting. He imagined that some Christian bookstores—and San Diego had plenty of them—might have a crown of thorns on hand. He made a note to tell Carmen.

He spent the next few hours recreating what he had seen and learned, and then trying to skim new truth from the facts. At first, he told himself that he was wasting time, that he had no special training or gift for this kind of work, but then a more optimistic part of his brain kicked in. In some ways, he had skills that the typical police officer didn't have. He doubted they taught hermeneutics—the ability to properly interpret documents and history in general and the Bible specifically—at the police academy. He had spent his academic career gleaning information from the details in the biblical accounts. It was what theologians did. At least his kind of theologian.

Most people read the Bible; some study it; a few analyze it in depth. Why did Paul use that word instead of a different word? What is the underlying story behind an event? A few years ago he had read a book called *40 Days,* examining the resurrection appearances of Christ, and was overjoyed to learn the unspoken message behind each appearance. There was an old maxim: "The devil is in the details." For Ellis, God was in the details, the things preachers overlooked and liberal scholars ignored. Maybe he did have something to offer.

Then the doubt returned. Still he pressed on into the night.

It was close to midnight when Millie Takahashi phoned Carmen. She had just arrived home. "I hope I didn't wake you." Millie's voice always sounded like that of a young girl.

"Nope. Just walked into the house. Grabbed some fast food for a late dinner."

"Ugh, that stuff will kill you." Millie was a devout vegetarian.

"I should be so lucky. Did you come up with anything on the lipstick?" Carmen's cases were given priority in all departments. Serial killings tended to do that.

"Some. Here's what I've got. I've sent a sample out for another chemical background. We should have those results by noon tomorrow . . . er, today. I did make some headway. I used our scanning electron microscope and did a few more magical incantations. Bottom line: there is a better than an 80-percent chance that the lipstick recovered on the mirror at Mulvaney's place is a match for that removed from the photo you provided."

"So it's from the same stick?"

"I can't go that far. I can say that it is most likely the same brand, same shade, and about as old. So on the science side of things, I'd have to say it is *similar* and might be a *match*, but the statement won't hold up in court. Not yet. Microspectrophotometry and spectroscopy may nail that down for us."

The news unsettled Carmen but also gave her a moment of exhilaration. Could it be? After all these years? A clue?

"You still there, Detective?"

"Yes, just thinking."

A sigh came over the phone. "Okay, I'm gonna ask, and if

I'm out of line, just tell me. Does this mean that the killer you're tracking is related to your sister's murder?"

Shelly's murder was no secret. Carmen seldom spoke of it, but the grapevine kept the story alive. No one came into homicide who wasn't taken aside and briefed. The case had long gone into the cold-case files. Twice a team of detectives had been assigned to the case, but nothing came of it.

Carmen sent her own sigh over the phone. "It must, Millie. I don't know why, but the killer is taunting me."

"Because you did the press conference?"

"Most likely. There are a lot of Raimondis in the world, but not many *Rain*mondis. Some, but not many. He could have associated my name with my sister."

"And the lipstick, if it is your sister's, is his way of saying he's back."

A wave of fury washed through Carmen. "Yes, and I'm going to do to him what my sister couldn't."

Millie went silent. Cops were known for a tendency toward hyperbole and braggadocio. It was a part of the culture that Carmen embraced wholly. Still . . .

Had she crossed the line with Millie or maybe upset her? Hinting violence against an unknown perp was bad form. She was about to apologize when Millie spoke up.

"I'm with you on this, Detective. I and my department will do everything we can to run this guy down. You call me anytime, day or night."

"And I'll probably find you in the lab."

"Yeah, well, until my husband gets back from sea tour, I might as well be here kicking bad-guy backsides with science."

"You get 'em, girl."

"You too, Detective."

Carmen disconnected the call. The greasy food she ate in her car, the lack of sleep, and the news Millie had just shared all upset her stomach. She crawled into bed in an attempt to do the impossible: sleep.

34

Carmen arrived at her desk a little after seven, having managed close to five hours of sleep—four of which she considered good sleep. Exhaustion had kept her from dreaming. That and the sleeping pill she took before crawling between the sheets. To her surprise, she found Millie's report waiting for her on her desk. Nothing more than what she had been told over the phone. She would have to wait for the other tests.

"A little light reading?" Bud slipped into his desk chair. He seemed alert but also looked drawn. The long hours and stress were beginning to show.

She held up the papers. "Millie's preliminary report on the lipstick."

"Hector told me about that. The perp wrote your name? I don't like it."

"It is what it is."

Bud grinned. "That's what makes me like having you as a partner. Where else can a man get a lesson in philosophy like that? Apart from a fortune cookie, I mean."

"Wow, the compliments never cease."

"Admit it, my humor is irresistible."

Carmen met her partner's eyes. "Not the word I'd choose. Wanna hear my term for it?"

"Of course not." He pointed at the file. "So, is it lipstick?"

"Yes . . . look, there's something you should know." She told him about the lipstick on her sister's photo. "It's a close match with what was on the mirror. Waiting on more science, but it is almost certainly a match."

Bud's face hardened as if he had just made eye contact with Medusa. He looked away. Looked at the ceiling, then his desk, then the floor. Carmen had seen the man angry before, but this time he looked as if he were going to explode, sending chunks of himself all over the room. "You're saying . . ." He shook his head. "Can't be. The odds. I mean . . ." He whispered a long string of invectives.

Carmen let him vent.

"I'm sorry," he said. "This must be tough on you. I hated this guy before, but now I want to . . . well, never mind."

Bud was the only person she had ever allowed to see her broken side during their short relationship—and that was a lifetime ago. "Thanks, partner. I appreciate the empathy." She pulled a photo from the file. "What do you make of this?"

He took the photo of the message. "Angles on the letters vary. No, they switch back and forth. He wrote some words with his left hand, others with his right."

"Millie's team thinks so, too."

"He's not wanting to give us even that much. The guy thinks ahead."

Carmen thought for a moment. "That switching hands seems consistent with his cautious nature, but the message is far from what I expect from the guy. Why call me out by name, unless—"

"Unless he's connected to your sister." Bud swore more. This time a little more loudly.

"Of course, but what if he is? So he sees me on TV or reads my name in the papers. He connects the names. Why call my attention to my sister's death?"

"He's taunting you."

"But why?"

"The guy is nuts, that's why."

Carmen shook her head. "I agree his train derailed a long time ago, but he's still smart. If not smart, then criminally clever. I'm sure he has a plan. This doesn't fit his MO. Think about Wilton. He didn't fit the scenario, so he got a bullet in the head and a week underwater. Our man has been on a single mission: kill people in such a way that it delivers a message. I don't think I was on his radar until the press conference. Until that time, there was only one note. And I wasn't mentioned, it was just a generic statement."

"That's two." Bud quoted the note.

"Now I'm in the picture, and somehow that's made him change." She leaned back in the chair. "Think about this: We're pretty sure that Mulvaney was killed somewhere other than his apartment. No blood where we found him, and we know he had been bleeding from his mouth and nose. There is no evidence of a struggle at the man's apartment. None of his neighbors heard or saw anything."

"So the guy went out of his way to go to his victim's apartment and leave the note for you?"

"Yes, and that's a huge departure from everything he's done in the past."

"I'll give you that, but what does all that mean?"

Carmen shrugged. "I don't know. Not yet, but I'm thinking."

Bud's face clouded over. "You better not be thinking of doing something stupid."

"Truth is, Bud, I can't even come up with a *stupid* idea."

"Somehow I don't believe you."

"Your lack of trust wounds me. I may never be the same." She reached for the phone.

"Yeah, I can see how I've crushed your spirit."

Carmen checked her messages and was surprised to find one from Ellis Poe. She listened, jotted down a few items, then hung up.

"That was Poe. Says he wants to talk with me." Carmen looked at the times on the paper.

"What about?"

"About the case, that's all he said. He gave me a list of times he is unavailable. I guess classes have started again at the school. He's got a couple of classes this morning and a faculty meeting."

"You gonna call him in?"

"Nah, I think I'll go out there."

"I'll go with you."

"No need. The poor guy will just throw up on your shoes."

Carmen pulled the Crown Vic into one of the parking slots in the lot closest to the main building. It seemed months since she was here to attend the Lindsey funeral, and even longer since she and Bud first met Poe, when they arrived to ask about Lindsey. Despite her commitment to be cold and prickly to everyone, she was developing a warm spot for the sensitive professor. He was bright, insightful, and cooperative. Not courageous in the least, but at least he had convictions, and men with convictions tended to be worth a little more patience.

Usually.

She locked the car, walked to the admin building, and asked where Poe's class was. An older woman had replaced the young front-desk clerk she met when this whole mess began. The sight of Carmen's badge didn't faze her. She was of an age where she could claim she'd seen everything. Besides, the murder of one of the students was still recent enough to be fresh on everyone's mind. No doubt it was still the topic of the day.

The campus was quiet, but Carmen could see students sitting in classes, professors in front lecturing or writing on a whiteboard or using a computer and projection system. Seeing young minds at work made her recall her love for school and her dreams of being a doctor. She missed those years—and the ones she never got to live.

Placards mounted to the wall next to the doors identified classrooms by number. She looked for 227 and found it easily. A peek in the window showed a full room. Ellis Poe's voice drifted through a slightly open window. She caught a glimpse of him. He wore a suit. The other profs she saw were dressed in casual clothes. This was Southern California, after all.

Poe paced the front of the room, head down, hands behind his back. He was asking question after question, driving his students to think broader and dig deeper. Carmen was familiar with the Socratic method: teach by asking questions and forcing the students to think and counter each other.

She looked at her watch. According to the schedule Ellis had left in his message, she had about a five-minute wait. She used the time to do something therapeutic—stand in the sun and feel the hilltop breeze on her face. The air was still cool but, typical of the inland city of Escondido, was edging up to warm. The sound of birds floated on the air; the smell of nearby eucalyptus trees filled her nostrils.

The weariness she had been fending off settled over her. The urge to get in the Crown Vic and chart a course north until the tank was empty was almost irresistible. The problem with running away was worries traveled along. How unfair. A woman should be able to leave a place of pain and move to a place of pleasure.

Life was unfair.

The sound of soles on concrete made her turn. Ellis had let his class out. She watched the stream of students, mostly male, pour through the door. Their ages surprised her. Most seemed to be in their thirties, some in their twenties, and at least four students looked old enough to be grandparents.

A few caught sight of her and smiled. Most moved with their heads down as if in deep thought. When the door closed, Carmen approached and entered the class. Poe stood behind a wooden lectern, his head down, his hand moving across some papers. "You must be rough on the students. Some of them looked old enough to be my father."

Ellis Poe looked up and smiled. "A couple of them are. Some

people start seminary after they finish their careers. Some come straight from college."

"So you weren't tough on them." She walked to the front of the classroom.

"I didn't say that. I wasn't expecting you."

Carmen cocked her head.

"I mean, I was expecting you to call first."

"Sorry, it's an old detective trick. Show up unannounced."

He blinked several times as if he didn't understand the dynamics of a surprise visit. "I've been thinking about the case you're working on. Couldn't sleep last night."

"That's going around."

"I suppose so. Anyway, I told you and the others that the next victim might parallel the scourging and ridicule of Christ."

Carmen hiked an eyebrow. "Ridicule?"

"The crown of thorns. The Romans crucified Jesus for claiming to be a king. Under Roman rule, only Caesar could be called king. Jesus rode into Jerusalem to much fanfare, like a king. The religious leaders told Pontius Pilate and others that Jesus had been claiming He was King of the Jews. Pilate insisted that the phrase be hung over Jesus' head while he was on the cross."

"So Pilate agreed Jesus was a king?"

"Hardly. He did it to annoy the Jewish leaders. They didn't get along. The crown of thorns was likely made from the acanthus plant and shoved on Jesus' head to mock his self-proclaimed kingship."

"Sounds painful."

Ellis agreed. "More than most people know. Anyway, Roman generals and leaders sometimes received a civic crown made from oak leaves. They called it the Corona Civica."

"A laurel wreath?"

"Yes. That began with the Greeks and, of course, was made of bay laurel."

"Is this going anywhere, Professor?"

"Sorry. We academics like to talk about things no one else is interested in." He took a breath. "I began to wonder where one could get a crown of thorns. I mean, if I'm right, then the killer will need one. I did a little research. Turns out you can buy them online and in some Christian bookstores."

"You're kidding, right? Why would anyone buy such a horrible thing?"

"It's symbolic, Detective. Christianity is very symbolic. Some people wear crosses, which is odd since they've made an instrument of torture and execution into a bit of jewelry. Crosses and crucifixes adorn the walls of many Christians'—"

"Aren't those the same thing?"

Ellis shook his head. "Not technically. A crucifix usually shows Christ on the cross. A typical cross—the kind Protestants prefer—has no corpse. Roman Catholics prefer the crucifix because it emphasizes Christ's sacrifice. Nothing wrong with that. Evangelicals prefer an empty cross because it represents Jesus' victory over death. The word *crucifix* comes from the Latin *cruci fixus*—'one fixed to a cross.' Some people use a crown of thorns as religious art during the week before Easter; pastors sometimes use them as instructional art. The symbology of Christianity is fascinating because . . . I'm doing it again, aren't I?"

"Yep."

"Do you want to sit?"

"I'm fine."

"I'm just saying that your man may have ordered something online or purchased one from a Christian bookstore. If not directly, then through a catalog."

She gave that some thought. It was a long shot, but she could run down orders for crown of thorn replicas and get a team out interviewing employees at Christian bookstores. Long shots were all they had now. "That might be useful. Thanks."

"No problem. I tried to narrow down where the body might be left based on the Antonia Fortress."

"Antonia's what?"

"The Antonia Fortress was a structure built near the temple about two decades before Christ's birth. There's some debate about it, but it probably served as a military barracks. Jesus would have been scourged there."

"By scourging, you mean whipping."

"Yes. As I said in your office, it's a horrible thing that strips the flesh from a man's back. Because Jesus was Jewish, there was no limit to how many stripes He would receive. Some people died under the lash. The only thing that saved Jesus' life was the order that He be crucified."

Carmen tried to imagine the cruelty, and it wasn't hard. She had seen too many battered bodies over the last two weeks. "Did you come up with anything?"

"No, nothing definitive. Based on the information mounted to your wall, we can conclude that the killer is more allegorical than literal. He's not following the Passion events to the letter, just alluding to them. I approached it from a construction point of view. The fortress was built of stone, but I don't know of any military facilities like that. I could be wrong. I only have the information I can get off the Internet. I'm hoping you can find more."

"He's not going to get on an active-duty military base. Our guy is camera shy. He couldn't get past security, not without being seen."

"I don't have answers for you, Detective. I'm just trying to be helpful. I could be wrong about all of this, but I'd regret not bringing it up, then learning I was right and important information could have been obtained."

"Much appreciated, Dr. Poe. Is there anything else?"

Poe squirmed. "Not at the moment."

"You know, we never talked about whatever it was you came to the station to chat about."

Ellis's face paled. "I got distracted by the crime time line you created. The connection to the Passion of Christ knocked me for a loop."

"I picked up on that. Well, I'm here now—"

The door opened and two students entered. "I have another class." He looked away.

"It's your choice, Professor. If it's not important—"

"I'm not saying that . . ." He ceased making eye contact.

An odd thought rolled to the forefront of her mind. She lowered her voice. "You're not going to ask me out, are you? Because—"

"No. Of course not! Nothing like that."

She feigned shock. "Are you saying I'm not worth dating?"

"No. I . . ." His pale face reddened. "I didn't mean that either."

"Relax, Dr. Poe. I'm just giving you a bad time." *And testing your response. What are you hiding?*

"Look. We should talk. I need to talk. This class will run about an hour, then I have student appointments. After lunch, I have a short faculty meeting—"

"You gave me your schedule on the phone. I wrote it down."

"How about four? Classes will be over by then. Do you want me to come to the station?"

"Yes, I don't want to have to drive up here again. So what . . . 4:30 or so?"

"I'll be there." His red cheeks turned pallid.

Carmen studied him for a few moments. He looked guilty.

Very guilty.

But about what?

35

The day passed in a contradictory way: fast and slow. At times it seemed as if the clock had stopped; at other times it seemed the hands of the clock were racing each other. It took all his mental energy just to get through his classes, consultations, and faculty meeting. His mind was a Ping-Pong ball in a tornado.

His body had turned against him as well. His stomach cramped, released, then cramped again. The muscles in his chest constricted as if his suit coat were shrinking around him. He felt feverish, agitated, afraid—everything he felt the other day when he first attempted to tell Carmen what she had a right to know. Would he be able to follow through this time?

The normal half-hour drive was taking longer. Traffic was already clogging the freeway arteries of the city. He couldn't decide if he should be grateful.

His mind alternated between concocting excuses why he shouldn't do this and rehearsing what he was going to say. Mired in the sluggish traffic, he wondered if he would be sleeping in his own bed tonight or as the guest of the county jail.

He tried to pray for courage, for wisdom, for direction, but his prayer life continued to be impotent. Normally prayer was his joy; now it seemed unfruitful. He had long ago lost respect for himself, but he always felt loved by God. He wasn't so certain now. The spiritually warm feelings he had after his last visit to Carmen's office had evaporated. Maybe God had lost respect for him because he once again failed to do right by poor Shelly. His theological mind argued against the supposition, but it lost the argument. Nothing can outshout the heart.

He parked and removed the keys from the ignition. They jingled in his trembling hand. "No turning back now," he said aloud. "Time to man up. Whatever comes of this, at least you'll know you did the right thing."

Right thing. Twenty-eight years late.

The walk from the parking lot was tough. Every five steps he fought the urge to turn around, return to his self-imposed exile, keeping the world at arm's length, hiding in books and ancient texts.

An officer escorted him to the homicide division, and he found Carmen and her team in the case room. They looked weary, worn, but determined.

"Hey, Professor," Bud said.

"Hello." Ellis stepped into the room. This time he avoided the wall of grisly photos and facts.

"You had a couple of good ideas." Bud sat at the conference table. "We're running down leads on the crown of thorns thing. We've also alerted all the military bases and sites about the situation and asked them to up their security. More eyes means a greater possibility of seeing something . . . You okay?"

"Yes. Of course. Why?" Ellis hadn't been able to look at Carmen.

"'Cuz you look like you're ready to blow chunks again."

"No. I'm fine. Just tired."

Hector chortled. "I hear that, Doc."

Ellis lifted his head then did the impossible. He looked at Carmen. She seemed able to read his mind.

"Give us the room, guys. The professor and I have to chat over a couple of things."

They exchanged glances but didn't speak. The team left like children being led to the playground, closing the door after them.

"He's right, you know." Carmen set some papers on the conference room desk. "You look like you might need to hurl. Shall I show you to the ladies' room?"

"Funny." He looked at his shoes then back at Carmen.

"You wanna sit?"

"No. I think I'd better stay on my feet." He cleared his throat. "You may have noticed that I'm a bit of a loner, a little timid, and in general, not all that strong. Truth is, I'm only a few short strides from being a hermit."

"Sounds like you're being rough on yourself." Carmen moved to a chair and pulled it from the table. "We are what we are, Doc. We can't all be the same."

"Well, there's a reason for my reticence." He sucked in a lungful of air. "I want to talk about your sister. There's something you should know. Need to know."

"My sister?" Her face hardened and she stepped back from

the chair—apparently the idea of sitting had fled. "How'd you know about the connection? We haven't talked about it outside this building."

"What?" Ellis's mind shuddered to a stop. "Connection. This doesn't have anything to do with the—" He noticed two new photos on the wall. These were not of bodies, for which he was thankful. One was a photo of Carmen and Shelly when they were young, and one was a photo of some odd writing on a mirror. He noticed Carmen's name. He shook his head. Tempted as he was to ask about the photos, he had determined not to get distracted like last time. If he did, then he would never be able to muster enough courage to give this a third try.

"You're confusing me, Professor."

"Look. Let me get this out. If I don't do it now, I may never be able to do it." Another deep breath. "In 1985, I was a senior at Madison High School. I worked nights at McDonald's in Pacific Beach. I was returning home . . ."

Bud paused a few steps down the hall and turned his attention back to the conference room door. "That was strange."

Hector and Joe Heywood stopped a few steps farther on. Hector shrugged. "Maybe Carmen's got a thing for the professor, or vice versa."

"Ha, that'd be stranger still." Bud screwed up his lips. "No, something else is going—"

An angry voice escaped the confines of the case room. A voice filled with venomous curses. Then came a wet sounding thud, a grunt, and finally the sound of something hitting the wall.

Bud was moving before his next breath. He barged into the room, Hector and Joe on his heels. He stopped two steps in. Dr. Ellis Poe lay on his back staring at the ceiling, a large red mark spreading up the left side of his jaw. He looked half a step from being out cold.

Carmen stood a couple of feet back from the supine form of the seminary professor. She shook her right hand, repeatedly contracting her fingers into a fist then releasing them. Bud didn't need an explanation. Carmen had cold-cocked the professor. What he didn't know was why.

"You son of—" She started for Ellis again.

Bud didn't think; he just acted. He wrapped his arms around her middle and picked her up, her feet kicking at the semiconscious man. "No, you don't."

"Let me go. I'm gonna finish him!"

"No you're not." He carried her to the opposite wall. He set her feet on the floor but pinned her against the wall, his forearm spanning her shoulders and just below her neck. He muffled her mouth with his other hand. "Stop."

Carmen fought back with surprising strength and fury. Her eyes blazed. Then came the kick to the thigh. Fire raced up his leg into his belly, but he refused to let go.

"I think I'll just shut this door," Hector said.

Bud turned his head to the side. "Joe, take a post outside the door. No one gets in. Clear?"

"Got it."

"Hector, check on our guest."

"Already doing that."

Bud leaned into Carmen. She had become a wild woman, and he endured several more knees to his legs. At least she wasn't trying to ruin his ability to have children in the future. "It's over, Carmen. Relax. I'm trying to help you."

She struggled again but with less strength.

"Trust me, kid. I'm trying to save your career. Chill. When you do, I'll let you go, and then you can tell me why you've suddenly lost your mind."

He could hear her sucking air in through her nostrils. She closed her eyes. When she opened them again, they were flooded with tears.

"He's coming around," Hector said. "Doesn't appear hurt too bad, but the swelling in his jaw tells me he'll be on a soft-food diet for a while.

The fury in Carmen's eyes faded, replaced by sadness. Then Bud saw something he had never seen before: Carmen weeping. He took her in his arms and held her as she dissolved into sobs that broke his heart.

Voices from the hallway pressed through the walls and door. He recognized Joe's. "What? In there? Nope, no problem. Just a private meeting. Everything is fine. Hey, how 'bout them Padres?"

Captain Darrel Simmons sat behind his desk, glowering. His black face had darkened, his eyes, often stern, looked like bits of flint. Carmen had seen him angry before, but always at someone else. She didn't like being in his crosshairs.

Someone alerted Simmons to the problem in the case room. He had charged into the place like a one-man SWAT team. Joe Heywood had been willing to keep others out, but no one was keeping Simmons at bay. He had a reputation for kicking uncooperative detectives out of homicide, most of whom ended up writing parking tickets for a year or so. A few minutes later he ordered Carmen and Poe to his office.

"Close the door." It wasn't a request.

Carmen started to do as ordered when Bud Tock entered. "Sorry, sir."

"I don't recall inviting you in here." Simmons rose to his feet.

"You didn't, sir, it's just—"

"Get out. If I want you I'll call for you."

"But, sir—"

"Having trouble with English these days, Detective Tock?"

"No, sir. I . . . Yes, sir." He turned and slipped from the office like a scolded child.

Simmons looked at Carmen. "Sit."

She did without a word. Her heart continued to pound so hard she could hear it. Adrenaline. The captain turned his attention to Ellis Poe. "Dr. Poe. Please have a seat."

Like Carmen, he sat without a word. The left side of his head had swollen, giving the academic a lopsided chipmunk look. She second-guessed her decision to use a fist instead of an open-hand slap. Still she couldn't conjure up enough pity to feel sorry for the man. As far as she was concerned, the man needed more hitting.

Simmons stared through the glass wall at the front of his

office. Carmen turned to see half the division looking back at her. When they noticed the captain's gaze, they diverted their eyes. Several left the bullpen.

Slowly Simmons lowered himself into his seat. "All right, Detective, let's hear it, and I want it fast and accurate."

"I can explain," Ellis began.

"I'm not talking to you, Dr. Poe. You'll get your turn."

Carmen waited a moment to see if Simmons would spontaneously combust. Unfortunately, he didn't. "I lost my temper. I—"

"Sir—" Ellis began.

"Poe, I told you I'd get to you later—"

"No, you'll hear me now. I don't work for you. At the moment, I'm a free citizen, although that may change soon."

A spine? *Now* the man grows a spine. Carmen's fury increased.

Poe continued. "I saw Detective Rainmondi's sister killed."

Simmons blinked several times, his head swiveling back and forth between them. "You what?"

Ellis explained again, and Carmen was forced to listen to the description one more time. She closed her eyes and focused on controlling her temper. A few moments later, Ellis finished. "You see, Captain, I had it coming, and much more."

"Why now? Why tell her now?"

Ellis leaned forward and rested his elbows on his knees. "I can't live with it anymore, Captain. When Detective Rainmondi came to my office a few days ago, I was caught off guard. I didn't know what to do. I froze. I'm good at that. I had been keeping this secret so long, and then she walks through my door. It's almost thirty years later, but I could sense that the event changed her, continued to hurt her like it has changed and tormented me."

That was too much! "Tormented you?" Carmen snapped. "Really? *Torment?* You don't know what torment is."

"That's enough, Detective." Simmons voice had lost some of its edge.

"Not by a long shot, Captain." Carmen felt the volcanic rage near the surface again. "I should have hit you harder. I would have if you didn't hit the ground so quick—"

"ENOUGH!" Simmons's voice rattled the windows. He took several deep breaths before speaking again. "Dr. Poe, I have nothing good to say to you. Your unwillingness or inability to notify the police of what you saw let a killer get away with a murder." He sighed. "I'm in a bind here. On one hand I have an officer who, by her loss of composure, has opened this department to legal action on your part. On the other hand, I'm having trouble not sympathizing with my detective. What a mess."

"There will be no legal action on my part, and if I am to be arrested—"

"Why would you be arrested? There's no law that says you have to testify. Did you remove evidence or do anything to impede the investigation?"

"No, sir."

"Then your crime is one of cowardice and stupidity. However, Dr. Poe, you have the right to swear out a complaint against Detective Rainmondi for assault and battery since she injured you for personal reasons."

"I won't do that."

"That is your choice, but since I'm such a straight shooter I need to advise you to seek the advice of an attorney."

"No, sir. I won't be doing that either."

Simmons leaned over the desk and addressed Carmen. "Does he know about the lipstick?"

"Not from me. I think he saw the photos in the case room." She couldn't look at Ellis. Every time she did, she had the urge to throw a few more punches.

The captain turned an icy gaze on Ellis. "Do you know who killed Carmen's sister?"

"No. I don't know him."

"Here's something else you don't know. The serial killer we're tracking may be the same man. You think about that, Dr. Poe. You think long and hard. Your witness testimony might have helped solve that case. If so, then we might not be trying to track down this guy today." He explained about the lipstick message. "Kinda makes a man wonder how many other people are in the grave because this guy has been running around for . . . thirty years!"

Ellis seemed to deflate even more.

Someone knocked on the door. Simmons snapped his head up, then relaxed a bit. He waved the visitor in.

"Here ya go, Cap."

Simmons took the files. "This is Detective Donovan from missing persons. His captain told me there had been several missing persons, possible abductions. I asked to see the files just in case they might be related." He opened the folders. "That'll be all, Donovan—Wait. These are all women."

"Yes, sir." Donovan looked young and inexperienced. "Does that matter?"

"All our victims are male and were killed the same day they were taken. Some of these have been missing days, and we have no bodies." He flipped through the pages. "One known prostitute, a woman in her fifties, another woman. I don't think they're related to what we're doing." He handed the files back. "Thanks anyway."

"No prob."

"Close the door on the way out, Detective."

"Yes, sir."

"Wait." Ellis sat up. He tilted his head. "The abductions are recent? And one is a prostitute?"

"You got it," Donovan said.

"What are you thinking, Poe?" Simmons said.

Carmen watched the professor. He had the same look when he first saw the photos of the victims. His brain must be trying to make connections again.

Ellis raised his head. "Are any of them named Mary?"

Donovan stared at him. "How did you know that? Two of them are named Mary."

Ellis raised his hands and covered his face. "Oh dear God." He slumped in his chair, as if all his bones had just dissolved.

36

I don't understand."

Ellis didn't respond to Captain Simmons. The pain in his head had been replaced by another in his mind. Why hadn't he seen this coming?

"Dr. Poe, are you okay?" Simmons stern voice had lost its edge.

"What? Yes. No. I mean . . ." Ellis lowered his hands and pushed up in his seat. "I should have thought of this. The moment I saw the wall in the case room. I should've . . . I am so stupid." He couldn't look at any one. His mind painted images of three women with their photos hanging on the case room wall next to the bloodied and battered victims. Nausea rolled through him. His greatest desire was to flee the office, to run.

It was the only thing he was good at.

"Dr. Poe. Look at me." The earlier firmness returned to Simmons's voice. "Look at me!"

Ellis snapped his head up.

"That's better. Are you telling us the abductions are related to the murders?"

Ellis nodded then looked at Carmen. Her jaw was still tight, her face red, and her shoulders tense. She was a frightening sight. "Two Marys and a woman named Salome or something close. Am I right?" His question was for Donovan and Simmons, but he kept his eyes on Carmen.

"Yes. How did you know?" Donovan's words were saturated with suspicion.

"The prostitute angle is wrong. She wasn't a prostitute."

Donovan stepped to the side of Simmons's desk and faced Ellis. "I don't know who you are, buddy, but I can assure you the woman I described is a longtime hooker. She has an arrest record going back ten years."

"Not here, Detective. Mary Magdalene. It's a myth that Mary Magdalene was a prostitute. There's no indication of it in the Bible."

"What?" Donovan looked at Captain Simmons. "Who *is* this guy?"

"Dr. Ellis Poe. He teaches at the seminary in Escondido. He's . . . consulting."

Carmen huffed but said nothing. She looked like a boiler ready to blow.

"A Bible thumper—" Donovan cut himself short. "Sorry, Dr. Poe. What I mean is—"

"I know what you mean, Detective. No need to apologize."

"Carmen, bring Donovan up to speed."

"Do I still have a job?"

Simmons's black face darkened all the more. "That largely depends on what comes out of your mouth next."

She inhaled deeply. "Dr. Poe has convinced us the murders are following a biblical pattern. Each victim was killed in a way that mirrors an assault Jesus endured."

"You're kidding."

"Trust me, Donovan, I'm not in a kidding mood."

Donovan bounced his gaze from Carmen to Ellis and back to Carmen. "Do I want to know about the bruise?"

"You do not." Simmons made it sound like an order. "Go on, Dr. Poe."

He didn't want to. He was embarrassed about his cowardice, he was traumatized by Carmen's attack, he was fearful of going to jail, and he felt adrift from God.

"Poe." Simmons raised his voice.

"When Jesus was crucified, there were several people at the foot of the cross. Three of them were women. Mary the mother of Jesus, Mary Magdalene, and Salome the mother of James and John. Her son John was there, too."

"Wait," Carmen said. "Jesus' mother was at the cross?"

"Yes, Detective. It was not unusual to make the family watch the beatings and crucifixion. It would also be their job to take care of the corpse. If they didn't, the executed person's body would be thrown outside the walls of Jerusalem and left on the city's dump—a burning pile of refuse. Jesus used the burning garbage heap as a metaphor for hell."

"They made the family watch?" Simmons said.

"Romans had no love for Jews. They cared nothing for the torment they caused." He paused. "May I ask when the abductions took place?"

"All over the last few days." Donovan looked defensive. "It takes forty-eight hours before we can open a missing person's case."

"He's making them watch." Ellis leaned forward and lowered his head like someone attempting to avoid fainting. "He's making them watch the flaying and is planning to make them watch the crucifixion."

"Who's getting crucified?" Donovan sounded puzzled.

"We don't know." Carmen's expression changed from fury to concern. She was thinking about the case now. "Were they taken from their homes?"

"Yes," Donovan said.

Carmen turned to Ellis. "Does this mean he'll abduct someone named John? You said John was at the cross, too."

"Maybe. Maybe." Ellis touched his swollen jaw. "Not necessarily. There is not a one-to-one correspondence to the biblical account. For example, he's stretched out the killings over a period of days. What happened to Jesus happened in a single day. The killings are symbolic, not literal."

"They were literal enough for the victims," Carmen snapped.

"Of course. I'm saying the message is not literal. He's parceled out the clues. Maybe to buy time. I don't know. The point is, he may or may not have abducted a male named John." Ellis looked to Donovan, who shook his head.

"None reported."

Donovan exchanged glances with Simmons. "The guy put all this together just by hearing that two of the women were named Mary?"

"He's made a lot of connections we've missed." He turned

to Ellis. "You know this makes you look pretty suspicious, don't you?"

"What? You suspect me to be the killer? Do I look like I could beat the victims like that? Detective Rainmondi just knocked me on my backside. I'm neither a lover nor a fighter. I'm just a guy who spent nearly thirty years finding some small semblance of courage."

"Yeah, about that, Doc," Carmen said. "There's something else you should know. I saw you looking at the photos on the wall. Do you know which ones I'm talking about?"

"The one of you and your sister. The one with the lip prints."

"Nothing gets by you, Professor." Her sarcasm was almost as damaging as her fist. "Did you notice the one next to it?"

"Some kind of writing. It looked like lipstick on glass. A mirror, maybe. I didn't look closely."

Carmen smiled, but he could see no joy in it. "Since you're so good at putting pieces together, maybe you can tell me—"

"Wait, why would a photo of you and Shelly be on the wall . . . the lipstick? It's the same?" He thought for a moment. "The lip prints—are they Shelly's?"

"Bingo."

Ellis's put a hand to his mouth. "The message—that's recent?"

Carmen nodded.

Simmons cleared his throat. "Detective—"

"Let me have this, Cap. I may have just slugged my way out of a job, but you owe me a little something for my years of service."

"I owe you—"

"No . . . no . . . no . . ."

Ellis Poe began to weep.

The next few days passed like months. Ellis continued to teach but often lost his train of thought. A few people asked how he had hurt his face, but he waved it off and said it was embarrassing. No one pressed for an answer. Dr. Adam Bridger looked concerned but respected Ellis's privacy.

Teaching was his tonic, his balm. When in front of the class, he could lose himself in the topics he loved and knew so well, but he couldn't teach twenty-four hours a day. When the breaks came, when the day's work was done, he was left alone with himself, company he didn't like. The bruise darkened before the skin began to lighten. His soul was another matter. His only relief, and it was thin, was learning that he had broken no laws. He had not been part of the murder, didn't know the attacker, never interfered with the investigation. Apparently cowardice was not a crime.

Silence was his enemy. He stayed at work as long as possible, chose to eat out where the noise of others could dilute his acidic thoughts, and began watching television to occupy his mind. He had moments of success, but mostly he spent his alone time submerged in churning guilt.

On the plus side, his prayer life returned. He prayed for Carmen and the other detectives, he prayed for the family of the victims, but he never asked for forgiveness. He deserved punishment and would accept whatever came his way without complaint.

He had lived with his cowardly decision to run for nearly thirty years, but learning that the killer that night might be the same man brutalizing so many now had left him a husk, the form of a man without being a man.

Then, on Thursday, his cell phone rang at 6:00 a.m.

At 6:30, he was in Carmen's Crown Vic. The conversation was minimal and missing the preamble of "How are you doing?" Instead, Carmen spoke without looking at him.

"New body. I want you to see this one in the field."

"I'm afraid I won't be much help. I don't have the training—"

"I'm not asking for your help, Doc. I'm punishing you. You need to see the unsanitized version of homicide."

Ellis didn't know what to say, so he kept his mouth shut, opening it only to leave a message at the seminary that he was going to be out for the day. Someone would cancel his classes.

He didn't know whether it was protocol or not, but Carmen placed a pulsating red light on the dashboard and sped south on the I-15.

"How's the jaw?" Carmen changed lanes to pass a driver who didn't seem to understand the purpose of an emergency light.

"It hurts."

"Good."

No other words were spoken. Ellis thought of apologizing again, but such an act seemed foolish. How do you apologize for what he did—more accurately, what he didn't do.

She took the I-15 to the 163 to the I-5 to Pershing Drive, ignoring all speed limits. She slowed on Pershing and turned left on Florida Drive then made her way to Bob Wilson Drive. Ellis could see a string of patrol cars and two other black Crown Vics. His stomach constricted and twisted like someone wringing out a dishrag.

"You stay with me, Poe. You do not wander off. You touch nothing. You speak only when spoken to. Got it?"

"Yes."

"The media is there. You will not talk to them. You are not here in an official capacity. Is that understood?"

Ellis doubted she had the right to make such demands, but he made no protest.

She parked at the end of the line of police cars. Several television vans were present, as were those from major radio stations in San Diego. There was also a crowd of onlookers stacked near the crime-scene tape.

"Get out." Each of Carmen's words landed like a bomb. "I want you close enough to touch."

"Understood."

They exited the car and pushed through the crowd. Carmen wore her police ID on a strap around her neck. "Coming through. Make a hole." The crowd parted and Ellis followed her. At the barrier tape she made eye contact with one of the uniforms. "He's with me." She snapped her head around. "Walk behind me. No place else. Got it?"

"Got it." Ellis envied those restricted behind the tape.

Ten yards to the north of Bob Wilson Drive was a crowd of men in suits. He recognized them as members of Carmen's team. Dutifully, Ellis followed Carmen step for step.

"Get lost?" Bud asked Carmen.

"I made a detour."

Bud looked at Ellis like a man studying someone with advanced leprosy. "What's he doing here?"

"He's been so helpful, I thought he deserved to be on the ground floor of the investigation." She motioned to a blue tarp on the ground that was clearly hiding something. "Remove the tarp."

Bud and Hector each took a corner and slowly pulled back the covering.

Bile raced up Ellis's throat. He gagged and covered his mouth.

Carmen raised a finger. "So help me, if you puke on my crime scene I will shoot you."

Ellis struggled to keep his gorge down. Being shot sounded pretty good.

"What I want to know is this: Is this what you meant by scourging?"

He wasn't looking.

"Look at the body, Dr. Poe. *Look* at it!"

He did. On the ground was a nude man who looked to be in his thirties. He lay prone, his head turned to the side, his back facing the early morning sky—a back with no flesh, just muscle tissue, and even some of that had been whipped away to reveal bits of rib and vertebrae. The shredded flesh ran from the shoulders, over the back, and down to the back of the man's knees. Just as startling was the razor wire wound around the deceased's head—a poor man's crown of thorns.

"Is it, Professor?"

Ellis nodded.

"I'm sorry, Dr. Poe, I can't hear you."

"Y-yes."

Carmen folded her arms. "Such a young man. If only there had been a way to stop the killer . . . oh, I don't know, twenty-eight years ago."

Ellis couldn't speak. He could barely breathe.

"ID?" She directed her question to Bud.

"No. We'll run prints. Hopefully he's in one of the systems."

Carmen stooped by the body. Ellis had no idea how she could do that.

"Ligature marks on the wrists similar to the others. Wait, this is different." She turned one of the victim's hands so she could view the knuckles. "The skin is busted." She examined his face. "Bruises. Jaw may be broken. Swelling around the eye. This guy fought back." She stood. "I want those wounds examined closely. Maybe we can get some perp DNA."

"Will do."

Carmen faced Ellis. "See, Doc. I went easy on you." She waited for a response. He didn't offer one.

The crime scene was at the bottom of a hill and the intersection of two well-traveled roads. Not main arteries, but busy enough that someone would find the body not long after sunup. Carmen pointed up the hills. "See those buildings, Professor? Know what they are?"

The sight of the body had so unnerved Ellis that he hadn't thought to look. "Naval Medical Center." The Navy's hospital was a landmark in the city.

"Yep. Been around since 1917. Did you know that the grounds had once been a part of Balboa Park? Did you know that when the US entered World War I, the city of San Diego offered property to the various branches of the military? Did you know that in the early years, part of Balboa Park was used as military barracks?"

"No. I didn't know any of that."

Bud Tock stood close to his partner. Ellis wondered if he was protecting her or him.

"She used to work in the park." Bud offered a humorless grin. "She knows everything."

"Seems you were right about the next body being found near a military facility." Carmen looked down at the shrouded corpse. "Kinda got the crown of thorns thing wrong."

He hadn't, but he didn't correct her. True, he hadn't anticipated razor wire being used, but he had been right that the body would have a crown of thorns on his head.

Carmen looked as if she had more to say but decided against it. She turned to Bud. "Where's Officer Heywood?"

"Scouting the area for surveillance cameras. We know the hospital grounds have cameras, but it's doubtful that they track what's going on here. We're too far from the buildings and there isn't much else around."

"Who found the body?"

"Joggers." Bud pointed down Bob Wilson Drive. "Access to the hospital passes through a checkpoint about a quarter mile down. It has a surveillance camera. Joe went there first and talked to the people there. No one on duty saw anything. It looks like our man just pulled up to the curb on Florida Drive and dumped the body."

"It just gets better and better." She looked toward the thin crowd and the media. "The ME is here. Let's canvas the area; then I want to talk to the joggers."

"Hector and I'll check the grounds." Bud stepped away.

"I wish I could help." It was a sincere statement, but Ellis doubted it softened Carmen's opinion of him.

"You can. You've been right about so much of this, maybe you can apply that great intellect of yours and figure out who the killer wants to crucify."

"I don't know how . . ." He thought for a moment. He owed her an effort, even if the odds were impossible. "Maybe . . . I need a place to work. Something with a computer and a phone. I have no idea how to start, but I'll give it my best."

"You do that, Professor. You do that."

For almost three decades, Ellis Poe had believed he couldn't feel more guilty.

He had been wrong.

"That was a pretty special thing you did." Joe Heywood steered his patrol car south to the city.

Ellis looked at the big man. "Special good or special bad? I only ask because I excel in the latter."

"Special good."

Joe smiled and seemed genuinely amused. Ellis hadn't seen many smiles of late. Too bad he couldn't find much comfort in it.

The comment puzzled Ellis. "I don't follow, Detective."

"First, I'm not a detective. Normally, I'm a uniformed officer, but I've been pulled up the ladder to help with the case. I oversee the uniforms during canvassing, review countless hours of video, and pretty much everything else that frees the detectives to do their job. When this is all over, I'll be back on the streets. Not that I mind. I was born for this work."

"You don't want to be a detective?"

"Sure I do. I'd like to rise to captain, but I'm still paying my dues and learning the work."

"It's important work. Not everyone can do it." Ellis gazed out the side window at the passing scenery. Cars in front of them slowed, unsettled by the site of a black-and-white behind them. Several times, Heywood had to decelerate suddenly. He showed no irritation. Apparently he had grown used to such things.

A few moments of silence passed. "I was referring to your refusal to press charges against Detective Rainmondi for popping you one."

Ellis rubbed his jaw. "I had it coming. That and more. I didn't see any reason to ruin her career. I already ruined an important part of her life."

"Not many men would see it that way."

"I can't see it any other way." Ellis kept his gaze out the window as they transitioned to Broadway.

"It must be hard to live with. No doubt."

Ellis didn't respond, and they finished the drive in silence.

The white-and-blue building loomed before them. The headquarters station had come to represent things Ellis didn't want to remember: the wall of death, the ceiling of the case room as seen from the floor, the inside of the homicide captain's office, and most of all, the look on Carmen's face when he came clean about Shelly.

"Detective Rainmondi said I should help you in any way I can." Heywood parked the car.

"I don't know what good I can do. How can I figure out the target? I'm no detective."

Heywood killed the engine. "Look, Dr. Poe, this is gonna sound strange, but Carmen believes in you. True, she hates your guts, but she knows that you're the one who put some of the pieces together. None of the trained detectives saw the connections. You did. Sometimes insight comes from unexpected places."

"I appreciate the thought, Officer, but I don't fool myself. I'm a seminary professor and nothing more."

Heywood's smile became a frown. "It's not my job to cheer you up, Dr. Poe, but I must admit that you surprise me. I've been assuming you're a spiritual man. I mean, you teach New Testament, right?"

Ellis finally faced him. "Yes."

"Do you not believe what you teach?"

"Of course I do." Ellis was surprised at the emotion in his own voice. "It's not just academics with me."

"Well, I'm sorry, Doc, but I don't buy it." Heywood slipped from the car. Ellis did the same. "I was brought up in church and was led to believe that spiritual men were men of prayer."

"I pray more than you can imagine." Ellis rounded the car, his anger growing.

"Let me guess, you spend your prayer time mewling and begging for forgiveness."

"What's wrong with that?"

Heywood stopped and faced Ellis. The man stood six inches taller and was at least fifty pounds heavier. Ellis heart stumbled to a stop. It was one thing to be slugged by Carmen, but if this guy hit him, Ellis would be hunting for his head beneath the parked cars in the lot.

"We're talking murder here, Doc. Not *a* murder, a series of them, and it isn't over yet. We don't know how many people this guy plans to kill. If you're right, there's at least one more. Add to that the abduction of several women. Who knows what he's been doing to them? Frankly, Doc, *that's* what I'd be praying about."

Ellis couldn't decide if he was furious, chastised, convicted, depressed, or something entirely different. His emotions had become a mixed-up stew. He had no response, but he had a sense that Heywood was right.

Heywood started walking again. "Who knows, maybe this is God's way of helping you make good, for your sake as well as others."

The officer's words smoldered in Ellis's brain.

Twenty minutes later, Ellis was in the case room, surrounded by images and details he didn't want to see or know. In front of him was a laptop computer that Heywood set up and entered a password allowing Ellis access to the Internet. He had no access to the police department servers, nor did he want them. If there were details he needed, Heywood would retrieve them, or so he said.

For the first ten minutes, Ellis stared at the screen. He was well acquainted with computers, often using them for detailed translation work and the reading of online theological journals. Still, he was a man who appreciated a blank sheet of paper. He asked for one.

"Sure. There are markers for the whiteboard. I'll help you brainstorm." Heywood stood.

"Okay."

"I don't know where to begin," Ellis said.

"Let's talk about what we know." Heywood regurgitated the

details of each death and the location of each body. He did so quickly. Those facts were already well known. Next he brought up the painful connection between Shelly's murder and the message left by the killer for Carmen.

"He's taunting her," Ellis said. "I know, that's obvious."

"The first note was a general statement. No personal reference. The mirror message was directed at Carmen." Heywood stood at the marker board, but had yet to write anything.

Ellis's mind wasn't cooperating. Too much emotion. Too much regret and self-loathing. He pressed the emotions back and tried to conjure up the academic in him. He had no success until he started praying. His mind relaxed and the gears began to roll again.

"In 1985, I saw the man—the teenager. I know he was big. Bigger than you. At the time, he seemed twice my size. I remember that clearly."

"But he was a teenager? Older than you?"

"Maybe, but not by much. I was a senior. My guess is he was a senior, too."

Heywood wrote *teenager* on the board. "So . . . eighteen?"

"Yes. That seems right. I don't recall seeing him at Madison."

Heywood turned. "That was your high school. Madison High. On Doliva?"

"Yes. The campus was full—fifteen hundred students or so—but I think I would remember someone like him. I remember he drove a yellow—"

"That won't help. Carmen told me the car had been stolen and traced back to a car lot in Mission Beach."

"Well, if he is about my age, then he must have attended high school somewhere. Clairemont High? Mission Bay High? Kearney?"

Heywood picked up the phone and dialed a number. "Hey, Cap. Heywood here. I'm working with Dr. Poe on a few things while Detective Rainmondi and the others are in the field. I need a few errands run. Can I call up a couple of unis for awhile?" He paused. "Thanks." He turned his attention to Ellis. "Yearbooks."

"School yearbooks is a good idea. Have them get year books for '83 to '87."

"It will be at least an hour before we see any of them, so let's stay on track. We've got a little mental momentum so let's focus on who might be the ultimate victim. Are you sure the killer is planning to crucify someone?"

"Sure? I can't be sure of anything. I have to believe that each murder reflects part of the physical abuse Jesus endured. It seems obvious now. Jesus went to Golgotha, where He was tied and nailed to a cross in front of His mother and a few others. The facts of the case all point to my conclusion."

"Except that Jesus was one man. The killer did his torture to several people, not one. He killed them, so obviously he has someone else in mind."

Ellis nodded. "That's my conjecture."

"Who?"

"I don't see how we can . . ." He paused; an idea was inching forward in his mind. "So far the killer has been fairly close to the biblical account. Not completely accurate. I don't think that's his purpose. Still, he's done some research on his victims."

"More than that, he's been able to avoid surveillance cameras, not leave behind trace evidence. The guy might not be an intellectual giant, but he is a thinker, at the very least, a schemer."

Ellis stood and walked to the whiteboard, standing next to Heywood. "Two columns. Let's start with the obvious." Ellis wrote *Jesus* near the top left of the whiteboard with one of the markers.

Heywood got the idea and wrote *Perp*.

"No, not perp." Ellis rolled the marker over in his hand. "The killer isn't matching himself to Jesus . . . but he might be matching himself with the ultimate victim."

"Got it." Heywood erased his first title and replaced it with *Target*. The term made Ellis uncomfortable.

Ellis wrote, *Jesus, Yeshua, Joshua* in a line then pointed at each one. "*Jesus* is the New Testament name, His Greek name. *Yeshua* is His name in Hebrew. *Joshua* is the transliteration of Yeshua."

Heywood wrote a question mark.

Ellis: *Jewish*. Heywood: another question mark.

It took a moment before Ellis continued. What they were doing . . . it didn't feel right. Like they were headed down the wrong road. "Okay. I don't think the killer is being that literal. Jesus was about thirty-three when he was executed, but it would be a mistake to think the target is the same age. We need to be more abstract."

He stared at the whiteboard. Why couldn't answers just appear? How was he supposed to figure this out? "Okay—" He wrote a list of items in a column. *teacher/rabbi, peripatetic, preacher, healer, associated with sinners, critical of RLs, crowds . . .*

"Hang on. Peripatetic?"

Ellis looked at the word. "It means traveling, wandering, itinerate."

"And RLs?"

"Sorry," Ellis said. "Religious leaders."

"Got it."

Ellis stepped back, stood for a moment, then began to pace. He reached the far end of the room and stared at the column. "In your column write 'pastor' in line with 'teacher.'" Heywood did. He also wrote *traveling* across from *peripatetic*. "What about preacher?"

"Evangelist. That works with traveling—" He fell silent and lowered his head in prayerful thought. "Could that be it? An evangelist. There are hundreds of them."

"Any well-known ones coming to town?" Heywood asked.

"I don't know. I don't follow that kind of news. I'm the ivory-tower type. However . . ." He sat at the computer. "I'm doing a search for evangelists and San Diego." His heart sank. "Nothing. Best I can tell, there are no revivals or crusades in the city any time soon."

"Outside the city?"

"Maybe. Checking. I'm going to try crusades and revivals, California." He began typing. "There are three in the next thirty days: Fresno, San Francisco, and Los Angeles."

"L.A. is close. Less that two hours."

Ellis nodded. "But why do his killing in San Diego if the final target is in L.A.? I'm looking at the evangelist's schedule. He's busy. Six crusades in six months. That's a lot. Still, L.A. is the closest, and it just might fit the pattern." Ellis sighed. "We don't even know if our supposition is valid."

"It's all we have at the moment. We're looking for connections. So far, it's all been connected to—"

"What?" Ellis straightened. Could it be . . .

Heywood frowned. "I said we're looking for connections—"

Ellis stood, his mind spinning like the blade in a blender. "Connections. I wonder . . ."

He sat down again and pounded on the keyboard. "Daniel—a Jewish name; Templeton—Temple, the structure central to ancient Judaism. Here it is; he has a bio at his website: 'Reverend Dr. Daniel Templeton started his ministry in a small church, where his speaking skills were immediately recognized. In just a few years he became a much sought-after speaker. Full-time evangelism was the natural outcome. For more than two decades he has traveled the world preaching a solid, uncompromising gospel in crusades that draw tens of thousands each night. His popularity continues to grow. He is the confidante of presidents and world leaders. *Time* magazine dubbed him, "The world's chaplain."'"

Ellis glanced through the evangelist's Web site. There were photos of him in large churches and in stadiums, with movie stars and power politicos, in foreign countries.

Heywood sat at his computer and did a search of his own. "He's in Wikipedia. 'Dr. Daniel Joshua Templeton is an evangelical crusade preacher—'"

"His middle name is Joshua?"

"According to this it is." Heywood looked at the whiteboard. "That part fits, but he's not preaching in San Diego, right?"

Ellis clicked on a link. "They have his schedule posted. L.A., Topeka, Orlando, London. No San Diego . . . I wonder . . ." Ellis was on his feet again, pacing the room.

"What?"

"Let me think. Just give me a second." He placed his hands behind his back and lowered his head. "Does the bio give a date of birth?"

"Yep, but not a place. He was born in 1966."

"A year older than I am. Tell me you can access birth records."

"Not directly, no, but . . . I think I see where you're going. You think he's from San Diego?"

"Yes."

"Then where he was born doesn't matter. My family moved here when I was three. I was born in Texas. What we want to know is, did he go to school here?"

Ellis closed his eyes, and ideas rolled in like the tide. "We can get phone numbers from school Web sites. They all have them. I'll call Mission Bay High; you take Kearney. We'll keep going until we find something."

Ten minutes later, Heywood whooped. "Bingo, Doc! Clairemont High School. The school office there checked their files, and a Danny Templeton graduated in 1984."

"Okay, okay . . . now what? Can you throw your badge around and find out what airline he's flying in on?"

"Yes, but I have a better idea. Let's just call his company. They'll know. Besides, he might not be flying commercial."

Ellis felt stupid. Of course, that was a better approach. Faster. More direct. He returned to the Templeton Web site and clicked on the "Contact" link, found a number, and read it to Heywood. A moment later:

"Good morning. This is Officer Joe Heywood of the San Diego Police Department." He gave his badge number and asked to speak to someone about "the Reverend's travel schedule." There was a pause, then, "I understand your suspicion and commend you for being cautious. Are you able to put me on hold?" He listened. "Great. Please do so and call the San Diego Police Department Headquarters on Broadway. You'll need to know its on Broadway, since we have quite a few stations. I can give you the number or you can look it up online if you wish." Another pause. "Yes, I'll hold."

Heywood looked at Ellis. "She's a cautious one."

"That makes her smart in my book."

Heywood nodded. Minutes passed, then Heywood signaled that the woman on the other end of the line was back on.

"When? Thank you. No ma'am. We think he might be able to help us with something. That's all I can say." He hung up. Before he could speak, the door to the case room opened. Captain Simmons walked in.

"I just got the strangest phone call from some lady in Chicago, and it was about you, Joe."

"Sit down, Cap. We need to talk, and talk fast." Heywood turned to Ellis. "He's already landed. Came in yesterday."

38

Doctor Norman Shuffler looked like a man who had just finished a quick walk across the country. His shoulders slumped; his back was bent; dark bands of flesh accented the space beneath his eyes. Carmen felt bad for him; she felt bad for herself. Her last look in the mirror told her she didn't look much better.

It wasn't death that bothered the ME. He had said as much. It was the manner of death. This from a guy who spent his days cutting open bodies. His eyes lingered on the twisted band of razor wire that rested on a small metal table next to the counter. Nasty, nasty stuff.

Carmen had arrived at the ME's office ready to fight for a quick preliminary autopsy. There had been no fight. Shuffler was waiting to start the moment the corpse was on the metal table. Clearly, he wanted the killer caught as much as Carmen.

She spent ten minutes bringing Shuffler up to date, laying out Dr. Poe's ideas. Shuffler nodded as if he had been thinking the same thing. He hadn't; she was sure he would never sit on an idea. He never had in the past. When she told him about the lipstick connection, he seemed to deflate. "I can't imagine how that has affected you."

"It's made me more determined to find this piece of trash, and I was fully committed before. Now it's personal." She wished she could retract the last sentence. It sounded like something from a movie trailer.

Once the body was removed from the body bag, Shuffler stepped close. An aide took photos with a digital camera. Shuffler gave the woman some room but couldn't conceal his impatience. He bounced on the balls of his feet and gazed at the gruesome remains. The victim, unlike most "visitors" to the medical examiner's theater, lay face down, his raw-hamburger-like back awash in light from overhead fixtures.

"He was found prone?"

"Yes." Carmen stood a step back and to the right side of Shuffler. "We think the killer wanted to display his handiwork."

"No clothing? No ID?"

"We searched the area. Nothing. We're running his fingerprints."

Shuffler nodded. "Did your professor have anything to say about that?"

"He said the display fits. Apparently, the Romans would strip the prisoner before breaking out the whip. He said ancient Jews found this especially embarrassing. He said rabbis wore sleeves that reached to their hands and a cloak that reached their ankles. Being stripped in public would be mortifying. He also said the fact the victim was found near roadways might be significant. I guess scourging was a public torture."

"Unbelievable. I've heard of killers mimicking other murders, but never following biblical history. Sounds like your consultant is a smart man."

"Whatever."

Shuffler looked at her as if her emotions were written on her face, but said nothing.

The first part of the preliminary began with Shuffler recording his first impressions of the body. "The victim is a John Doe, found in an exterior environment. Victim is a male of 165 pounds"—the body had been weighed—"five-eleven-and-a-half inches . . ." He continued, estimating time of death based on liver temperature. He studied the body closely. ". . . appears to have endured a scourging . . ." He turned off the recorder. "Your man was alive during the beating. Just like the others. I can't imagine the pain. It takes time to do damage like this. The epidermis is almost completely removed."

He studied the wounds a little longer, then pulled out a large, lighted magnifying glass. "Hello." He took a pair of forceps and removed a bit of debris from the raw flesh near the left scapula.

"What is it?"

Shuffler studied it in silence for a few moments, then reached for a small sample jar. "Glass. Looks like ordinary bottle glass. Maybe a little thin for that. Perhaps from a glass tumbler."

"Poe said the whips the Roman's used had multiple strands embedded with small lead weights, bits of broken pottery, and shards of metal."

"A cat-of-nine-tails. I've heard of it. Never seen one, and after seeing the damage it does, I never *want* to see one. . . . Hang on. There's something more." He used the forceps to remove another bit of debris. "Wood?"

Carmen stood shoulder-to-shoulder with Shuffler and peered into the magnifying lens. "Another element in the whip?"

"Maybe, but then again . . ." He pressed his lips together. She could tell he was puzzled. "At first, I thought the red color was blood absorption, but it's not. The wood is red . . . closer to purple."

"Meaning what?"

He looked at her. "Meaning it is a sliver of purple wood." He returned his gaze to the sliver. "I think I know what this is."

"You gonna share your insight?"

"Take a breath, Detective. I'm thinking here, and that requires focus. I'm not a young man anymore."

"You will always be an Adonis to me, Doc."

He laughed. "That's why we should marry and sail the oceans on my yacht."

"Except you don't have a yacht."

He kept his eyes on the piece of trace. "There is that."

"And you're married."

"True, and my wife won't let me date. Go figure." He placed the sliver in another small glass jar. He looked up and called to a young woman with red hair and freckles. She looked like a high school student, but the creases around her eyes snitched about her age. "Judy, I want to see this under the microscope. Let's start with the stereoscopic."

"Yes, Doctor."

"There's going to be more." He leaned closer to the shreds of what had once been a man's back and frowned. "There's particulate matter in the wounds. I'll sample it. It's soaked up a good deal of blood. You know . . ."

Carmen could tell the man had something on his mind. He used a swab with a plastic container that moved up the wood stick. It was similar to the swabs used to take DNA samples. Then he moved his gaze down the man's body. The scourging covered the entire back, the buttocks—a mass of difficult-to-define flesh—and the thighs. The man's calves were untouched. Shuffler studied the undamaged flesh of the lower legs and the bare feet. Again he took samples with a swab. "I'm pretty sure I know what this is: sawdust."

"Sawdust."

"Yes, and not just any sawdust. I see a mixture of shades and colors." He returned to the upper torso, this time searching like a man with a mission. He plucked more glass and bits of lead from wounds; then he removed a short, curled, flat piece of wood about the size of a thumbnail. "And I definitely know what this is." He fell silent as he examined it.

"Care to share it with the armed detective in the room?"

"Of course. Sorry. See this curve?" He pointed at the fragment. "I'll bet you a chicken dinner that it's a wood shaving. The kind you get from a planer."

"Like in a wood shop."

"Exactly like you would in a wood shop. I'm pretty sure that was fine sawdust I collected from his feet. We'll know after we run tests."

Carmen started to speak, but Judy the Redhead interrupted. "I have the sample and microscope ready."

"Thanks." He reached for the container holding the glass

fragment. "I want to get a closer look at this, too." He moved from the exam table to a counter sporting various styles of optical microscopes. Judy, as requested, had set up the stereomicroscope. Shuffler bent and placed his eyes over the viewing lenses. A moment later he straightened. "Take a look, Detective. Purple wood."

Carmen did. The microscope gave a clear image. "Can we see this on the monitor?"

"Sure." Shuffler nodded to the tech. The image appeared on a computer screen nearby. "Much of it is covered in blood and tissue, but you can see the base color is purple."

"Someone stained a piece of wood purple?" Carmen was thinking of the purple material used to strangle the last victim.

"No," Judy said, then cut her eyes to Shuffler. She looked like she had interrupted her parents in an important conversation. "Um, I believe it might be purpleheart." When no one responded, Judy continued. "It's an exotic wood. When I was young, my father took up woodworking. He liked the exotic woods. Expensive stuff. He made an Art Deco clock with purpleheart. When you put the finish on it, it turns from pale to bright purple. It's also really hard. My dad bought a piece of the stuff, held it between two fingers, then tapped it with his knuckle. It rang like a bell. Oh, okay, not like a bell, but it rang a little."

"Come with me, Judy." Shuffler led the tech to the mangled body. The small wood shaving and forceps rested on a metal tray. "Can you identify this? Unofficially of course."

She took the forceps and peered at the shred of wood then put it under the magnifier. "I'm not an expert in exotic woods,

Doctor, but my guess is bird's-eye maple. It has a distinctive marking that looks like a bird's eyes, hence the name."

"Thank you, Judy. We'll get more definitive information, but I have a feeling you're right."

Carmen's mind flooded with ideas. "So how do bits of exotic wood get embedded in the vic's back? The glass makes sense; that was part of the torture."

Shuffler straightened as if an erect posture freed his thinking. "I'm just spit-balling here, but the guy is using a whip, right? He starts the flogging, and bits of flesh, fat, and blood collect on the ends of the whip. As he draws the whip back for another strike, it drags along the floor, picking up debris."

The logic was sound, but something bothered Carmen. "Seems careless. The perp has gone to great lengths to erase any evidence. Why do shoddy work now?"

"That, my dear, is *your* problem." Shuffler moved to the man's head and examined the wounds caused by the razor wire.

Carmen couldn't let go of the fact that trace evidence had been found. Was it a mistake? Had he been rushed? Or—was it intentional? A message? A way of taunting Carmen?

"Puncture wounds are deep." Shuffler didn't look up from the corpse. "They go all the way onto the skull. I can't imagine the agony that caused."

Blood streaked the man's face—scalp wounds always bled profusely—indicating he had been vertical when the wounds were inflicted.

Shuffler pressed on the wounds. "Blood in the wound scabbed over. These wounds were inflicted before the beating." He paused, then, "Your man says Jesus was beaten like this?"

"Yes."

He took a step back and gazed at the body again. "And he lived long enough to be crucified?"

"I guess. I'm the wrong one to ask."

Shuffler spoke softly. "I'm going to have to revise my image of Jesus. The pain, the shock . . . Okay, preliminary COD is shock and blood loss. I'll know more when we measure his blood volume, but I've seen enough to make the statement. I'll have something official in a few hours."

Carmen's cell phone rang. She answered, listened, then said, "What?" Thirty seconds of silence were followed by "I'm on my way."

The Reverend Dr. Daniel Templeton rose to consciousness like a bubble rising from the ocean depths. He first became aware of the pain in his side, then the pain in his jaw and the left side of his head. Then came the realization that his hands were bound above him. He was standing. No, not standing. He forced the fog from his brain. Hanging. He was strung up by his wrists. Heat, like hot coals buried beneath his skin, burned in his shoulders. The agony was beyond words.

He raised his head, directing his eyes to the ceiling, and saw a rope wrapped around a rough beam. The rope had been looped through a cloth band wrapped around his swelling wrists. He closed his eyes then opened them again. Something was wrong. His right eye wasn't working. The skin on his cheek felt taut to the point of splitting like overripe fruit.

How did he get here? He couldn't recall, but a terrible memory lurked in the back of his mind and he wasn't ready to face it.

He pointed his toes and found he could touch the floor, but only with the ends of his feet. He could push up a couple of inches but couldn't lower himself enough so his heels touched the floor. With each moment, his mind cleared a little. He had always been proud of his quick thinking, his ability to assimilate information and make cogent conclusions. That skill had gone missing. Was it the blow to the head? Had he been drugged? Maybe he was only semiconscious. He couldn't decide.

A noise caught his attention. A whimper to his left. He swiveled his head to see what kind of animal made such a pathetic sound. The animal was a woman. One of three. The noisy one looked to be in her fifties, and her face bore the marks of a beating. Next to her, lying on her side, was a young woman, also bruised and battered. The swelling around her face made what he assumed had once been an attractive appearance hideous. The first woman was conservatively dressed in jeans and blue pullover blouse. The unconscious woman wore a tight skirt hiked to the top of her thighs. Makeup, run by tears, left tracks on her swollen cheeks. The third woman looked closer to the first in age. She sat crossed-legged, rocking, her mind in some imaginary world, no doubt one more preferable than the reality she was in. He started to speak but managed only a mumble.

He was gagged.

As his mind began to clear, his fear grew. The more he saw, the more he knew, the more terrified he became. Where was he? He looked around the room. It was large and dirty. It looked old and abandoned. Large machines dotted the space, a space he judged to be three or four thousand square feet. He recognized two of the devices: a band saw and a large table saw. A commercial wood shop, or what used to be one. The thick layer of dust on the concrete floor and the tools told a story of neglect. Light pushed through a bank of windows, each of which had been covered with butcher paper.

He used his toes to make a ninety-degree turn and saw things that fueled his confusion: stained wood dowels. He also saw a long, wide sheet of translucent plastic hanging from the overhead beams. A paint room? Maybe where workers used to apply stains and paints. He was no craftsman, but he understood the need for a dust-free environment. His working eye focused on the plastic sheets. There were dark dots and streaks on them. Best he could tell, the stains were on the inside.

Then a thought occurred to him. What if the marks weren't from a sloppy woodworker applying stain? What if they were . . . blood. His stomach turned and he felt the need to vomit, something the tape across his mouth made impossible. The brief image of him aspirating vomitus made him turn away and focus on controlling his stomach. When he opened his eyes, he saw two things that nearly drove his sanity from his mind: A large wooden cross, and a twisted crown of what looked like barbed wire.

Ellis gazed out the window as Carmen drove the Crown Vic over the San Diego-Coronado Bay Bridge. The city lights, which he had always considered a comfort, seemed dull, as if they felt he was unworthy of their beauty. The thought was nonsense, but depression was seldom logical.

Carmen had shown up at the station and entered the case room like a cannonball.

"Fill me in." Her order was cold, concise. Ellis could swear the temperature in the room dropped a dozen degrees.

Bud and Heywood tag-teamed the report. Hector sat quiet, seemingly happy to be one degree removed from the center of attention. Captain Simmons sat at the head of the table, Ellis at the foot. It took five minutes to give her a rundown of why and how they settled on Daniel Templeton and what they had done since learning that he had gone missing.

"Has anyone reported him missing?"

"No," Heywood said. "His office told us that he changed

his agenda a few days ago. His sister is in the hospital. He was planning to visit. We've contacted her, and she said he had called to say he was coming in early to spend time with her but didn't know when he was due."

"Do I want to know why she's in the hospital?"

Heywood didn't hesitate. "She was attacked during a robbery. Took a beating, but not enough to endanger her life."

"Bait?"

"That's what we're thinking." Bud sounded calm and professional, but Ellis thought the man resembled a watch spring wound to the breaking point. He didn't want to be around when the spring gave way.

The conversation fell into police talk that Ellis had trouble following. He deciphered enough to know that an alert had gone out with Templeton's description.

"How did our guy nab him?"

Captain Simmons motioned to Hector. "Detective Garcia was already on the street. Detective?"

Hector leaned over the table. "I took a quick run to the airport and looked at security video."

"They caught our man on camera?"

"Yep. You know how security conscious the airport is. Bud and Joe got the arrival time from Templeton's office. We used that as a starting point and were able to follow him through the terminal. He skipped baggage claim. He had just a carry-on. Most likely his other luggage would arrive with his evangelism team."

"I want to see the video," Carmen said.

"I figured you would. I brought a copy with me, and it's ready for viewing." He tapped a few keys on a laptop. A digital projector hanging from the ceiling came to life and showed the crowds moving through a terminal. It was typical airport pandemonium. People in a hurry raced around those who seemed to have all the time in the world. Parents held the hands of tots overwhelmed with the strange environment.

"This is Templeton." Bud pointed at a middle-aged man with a round middle. He carried a shoulder bag and moved through the terminal like an experienced traveler.

"Nothing happens here." Hector advanced the video. "Another camera picks him up here, as he passes by the TSA checkpoint. Of course, he's an arriving passenger so he doesn't go through security again. Now to the heart of the matter." The video advanced more.

"This is our perp." Bud pointed again.

"He's holding a sign . . . he pretended to be a chauffeur?"

"Yep. Templeton's office arranged for an executive car. Not unusual for executives." Bud continued the narration. "The driver takes Templeton's bag. As you can see, the perp is a big man. He's 280 if he's a pound."

"Hang on." Hector advanced the video. "Okay, this is outside the terminal."

"Where did he get the Lincoln Continental?"

"It belongs to a local firm. The firm had been contracted to pick Templeton up. I spoke to them. They said someone called to verify the pickup. Identified himself as 'Dr. Templeton's advance man.' The firm confirmed the pickup and the time. We don't know what happened after that. The car and the driver are missing. I have a feeling we'll be called about another body soon."

"I don't recognize the perp."

"We think his name is Mitchell Finch," Heywood said.

Carmen looked stunned. "How did you figure that out?"

"I didn't. Dr. Poe did."

"What? I don't believe it."

"Let him explain," Simmons ordered.

Thankfully, the *him* Simmons referred to was Heywood. From the storm brewing on Carmen's face, Ellis wanted to stay as quiet as possible.

Heywood went on. "It took a few hours to get everything in place, so let me just hit the highlights. Dr. Poe made a few conjectures about who the perp wanted to crucify." Heywood explained about the comparisons to Jesus and His passion. "Admittedly, we took a few leaps of faith, but it was all we had." He then explained why there were high school yearbooks on the table. "The doc can explain it better than I can."

"I want to hear it from you," Carmen snapped.

Ellis was about to affirm what a good idea that was when Captain Simmons spoke up again.

"And I want you to hear it from Poe." Simmons's rank and tone trumped Carmen's. She frowned but said nothing.

Ellis had to clear his throat twice before his vocal cords would work. "Daniel Templeton went to Clairemont High. For years I've wondered if I knew the person who . . . attacked . . . who killed Shelly. I never came up with anything, but I've been pretty sure he was about my age. Officer Heywood sent people out to retrieve yearbooks from local schools. They cover the years Shelly was in school."

Heywood nodded. "We established Templeton's school by calling the records department of all the high schools in the city." Heywood motioned for Ellis to continue on.

He did so. "Officer Heywood learned that Templeton had gone to Clairemont, so I started there. I went through the yearbooks and came up empty, but like all yearbooks there were a number of people whose names are listed but for some reason never had their photo taken. We discovered that was true for someone named Mitchell Finch. We found him listed in a group photo, one of the wrestling team. Officer Heywood made some calls."

"And I learned that Finch never graduated. He was expelled for attacking a gym teacher. That would have been his senior year. It also happened about two weeks after your sister's murder. Didn't do any real harm to the teacher. Just a shove, but it got him booted. He disappeared then. We can't find any record of him. We got his Social Security number, but that's it. He's never paid taxes, and, as far as we can tell, never held a job. A legitimate job, that is."

Carmen's gaze bored into Ellis's eyes. "Is he the man who killed my sister?"

"I can't be sure until I see him in the flesh, but I am as sure as I can be based on surveillance video."

Carmen began to pace. "We got an image. We've got a connection. What about a motive?"

"All we know is that Templeton and Finch went to the same high school at the same time. They don't seem to be the kind to kick it together. Templeton was an A-student, Finch not so much."

"Wood shops."

Ellis frowned. Wood shops? What did Carmen mean by that?

Heywood gazed at her. "I didn't ask about shop classes—"

"Not shop classes." Carmen stopped pacing and explained what she learned at the ME's. "Let's get on that. Let's assume Shuffler is right and that the wood comes from a wood shop of some kind. A cabinet maker's shop."

"It would have to be inactive," Bud said. "I doubt he'd torture and kill people in a place of business."

"I've been thinking the same thing." Carmen crossed her arms. "It would need to be set apart from other businesses."

"Some of these places set up in concrete tilt-up buildings, but that would mean other businesses would be around and people would be coming and going." Hector thought for a moment. "It would need to be a place out of earshot of others, so something outside the metroplex."

The ideas began to flow, but Ellis had nothing more to add. He sat in silence and watched the teamwork. But at the back of his mind, something ate at him. Something he didn't want to consider but hadn't been able to escape.

What horrors were those three women and Templeton enduring?

"You sure you don't want me to drive you back to Escondido?" Carmen's words were ice-cube hard. "That's where I picked you up."

Ellis turned to her. Darkness had settled, and only the street lamps lining the bridge and the glow of the dashboard instruments provided illumination. The darkness matched both their moods. "Thanks, but that's an hour of driving for you. I can stay on my boat tonight and catch a cab back to the seminary tomorrow."

One of the harbor cruise boats plied the waters two hundred feet below. It must be nice to have a night out with friends. As they drove, he caught sight of one of the signs attached to the bridge listing the phone number of the suicide hotline. This bridge ranked number three in the country for suicides. Ellis had never been suicidal. It wasn't part of his faith. Still, there were many times when he would have accepted an early death as his due.

Tonight was one of those times.

"I want to be clear on something, Dr. Poe."

He liked it better when she called him Professor or Doc. She used the formal title like a club.

"I hate you. Yes, hate. True, deep, hot hate. I will never forgive you."

"I don't expect forgiveness, Detective. I don't forgive myself; why should you?"

"I say this because you have proved to be useful. You may have helped us crack the case—not that it's anywhere near over. There are going to be those that think I should thank you for your insights and for not bringing charges against me for abuse of power and aggravated assault. My captain could have buried me in an I.A. investigation—"

"I.A.?"

"Internal Affairs."

"Of course."

"I just want you to understand that though I deserve to be brought up on charges, I still hate your guts."

"I know you do, Detective. I wish I could rewrite the past . . ." The heavy cloak of depression lifted for a moment to give room for something new: anger. "And just to be clear, I accept your hatred, but don't think for a moment I haven't been paying for my cowardice. I pay for it daily. For almost three decades I've lived with the memory of that night. You've seen my life. I live in a small condo and on a tiny boat. I hide in my office. I haven't been out of the city as an adult. I go nowhere. I do nothing. I have no family, no wife, and no self-respect."

"I dream about my sister—"

"And so do I. Once, I spent my days trying to work up enough courage to ask her out."

Carmen snapped her head around.

"That's right, Detective. I was enamored with your sister, but I was a realist. I wasn't her type. I was a gangly, geeky, high-school senior who enjoyed books more than people."

"You never asked her out?"

"Of course not. She was way out of my league."

Silence flooded the car. "I had just become a Christian before she was killed. I knew so little and wanted to know so much. I was a blade of grass in a tornado." Tears rose. "I still am. I know more, and my faith is the most important thing in my life, but that one night and my inaction have kept me from becoming more than what little I am."

"You expect me to feel sorry for you?"

"No. Hate me. It's your right."

They reached Coronado, and Carmen followed the familiar path to the park near the small mooring area where the *Blushing Bride* bobbed in dark waters. The park was empty except for a hunched, homeless man walking along the sidewalk marking the edges of the park and lot. Ellis watched him, one of the many homeless who lived on the streets of San Diego. He moved with his head down, his back bent, and walked with a limp. One arm dangled at his side.

Carmen parked across several stalls of the empty lot as if planning a quick getaway. Ellis hoped he could get both feet on the ground before she peeled out. He turned to her but couldn't think of what to say . . .

I'm sorry. Already said, repeatedly.

Have a nice night. Ridiculous.

He decided to slink away like a dog, his tail between his legs. He opened the door, then turned back for a moment. "Be careful, Detective."

"Hey, buddy."

Ellis turned to see the homeless man. Something didn't fit. His eyes were clear and his face freshly shaven. He didn't look like the other homeless people who traveled through the park—

Something hit Ellis on the side of the head. His ears rang, pain shot through his neck, and his vision blurred. Before he could react, he felt another impact in his belly doubling him over.

"Hey!" Carmen's voice rang out. "Police! Step back!"

Through diminished senses he caught a glimpse of Carmen exiting the vehicle and reaching to her side. Her weapon? He felt his feet leave the ground, and before his addled brain could make sense of what was happening he found himself facing Carmen as she drew her weapon.

The attacker was using him as a shield.

She hesitated.

The attacker didn't.

A gun appeared in the hand Ellis had assumed was paralyzed. Something flew from the gun and struck Carmen in the throat. Not a bullet. There were wires. Carmen convulsed. Stopped and convulsed again as the attacker pulled the trigger a second time. He chuckled and pulled the trigger again.

Carmen collapsed.

In a motion as powerful as it was swift, Ellis's face hit the right, front quarter-panel of the Crown Vic.

The dark night went black.

40

Carmen opened her eyes and saw concrete, dirt, and dust. She coughed and blinked away the blurriness and tried to make sense of her surroundings. The engine of her mind was running, but she couldn't put it in gear.

She heard sniffling.

She heard moaning.

Two voices.

Her neck hurt, and a pungent, medicinal odor filled her nostrils. Although she lay on her side, unmoving, the room seemed to spin. Years ago, she suffered from a weeklong bout of vertigo caused by an inner-ear infection. It kept her bound to bed or the sofa, and she thought it would never end.

This was worse.

Jigsaw pieces of memory circulated in her mind, seeking their matches. Where had she been? At the station. No. She had left there. Not alone. Someone was with her. A face flashed on consciousness. *That weasel, Poe. He was with me.* Anger rose in her, then dissolved into concern.

Poe. Where was he? Did he do this? No. Something happened. Another man. A big man, homeless . . . She drifted off for a moment then brought herself back. She tried to bite her lip, hoping the pain would keep her from succumbing to the anesthetic. Wait . . . *what* anesthetic?

A puzzle piece landed face up. She dropped Poe off in Coronado.

Another piece. She had just bent his ear about how much she hated him. He took it on the chin without complaint. A bit of remorse had stabbed her then and poked her again.

A third piece: the homeless man . . . the assault on Poe . . . the electrodes striking her throat. The fire in her skin. The muscle seizure. The hard asphalt of the parking lot. The electricity stopped, and something covered her mouth.

No more memories after that.

She reached for her throat, but her arms wouldn't work. Wrong again. They worked, but they were bound.

The blanket of fog began to lift, letting in the pain.

A heavy thud sounded behind her followed by a groan. A hand seized her arm and pulled her into a sitting position. Carmen looked up and into the face of the man she had seen on the surveillance footage.

His smile chilled her.

He stepped to her side and pulled another form to a sitting position. Carmen turned her head—surprised by the pain the motion brought—and saw Ellis Poe, a large mound of flesh swelling on the left side of his face.

"Wakey, wakey, buddy. Time for a little chat." The man's voice seemed an octave too high for his size.

Poe didn't respond. Their captor slapped the professor's face—right on the jaw injury. Poe's eyes shot opened, and he moaned through the duct-tape gag.

"Ah, there we go." The man turned his attention to Carmen, then reached for her face. She pulled back. "Relax, woman, I'm just removing the tape. I'm not going to hurt you. Well, not yet." He ripped the tape from her mouth, and it felt as if several layers of skin and half of her upper lip went with it. She wouldn't give him the satisfaction of screaming.

She watched as the man took a handful of Poe's hair and lifted his head, seized the tape across his mouth and yanked. Poe had no problem indicating his pain.

Their captor pulled a rustic, rail-back chair over and positioned it a few feet in front of them. To Carmen's surprise, Poe was the first to speak.

"Mitchell Finch, I presume."

Finch cocked his head. "Have we met?"

"A long time ago."

Finch leaned back, crossed his legs and rubbed his chin. "We have a pretty good memory." He stopped abruptly and turned his head as if trying to eavesdrop on a whispered conversation. "Of course. Of course." He clapped his hands. "This is so cool. We *have* met. You're the scrawny kid who tried to interrupt my work. You shouldn't have done that. We're very particular about our work. Still, it was a brave thing to do. Stupid, but brave. You have our admiration."

"Anyone ever tell you that you have a problem with personal

pronouns?" Poe's words were slurred, a result of his injured jaw. Carmen assumed the same sedative she was fighting was used on him.

"We do?" Finch rose and punched Poe square in the nose. He rocked back, then fell over. Muffled gasps came from behind them. Carmen didn't need to turn—even if she could—to know the abducted women were behind her. Finch sat Poe up again. The fury on his face faded. He sat again and studied his new captives.

"This is a real pleasure, Detective Rainmondi. I would never have guessed pretty little Shelly's big sis would become a cop, and a homicide detective no less. Yep, I am impressed."

"Back to the first person, eh?" Poe shook his head.

Finch sighed. "Only a crazy man asks to be beaten, pal."

"*You* think *I'm* crazy?" Poe laughed the best his fractured mouth would allow. Carmen glanced at him. What was he doing? "You should check the mirror."

Finch leaned forward and studied his nails. "Perhaps I should have killed you when we offed Shelly. It wasn't like she was going anyplace. I was just so angry." He smiled. "I may have been a little drunk too. She kept whining about wanting me to pull over. Nag, nag, nag." He sighed. "She made us crash. I stole that car fair and square. You saw it . . . What's your name?"

"Poe. Dr. Ellis Poe."

"Ooh, *Doctor* Poe. I'm impressed." He thought for a moment. "Poe like the painter—" He snapped his head to the side as if someone was whispering in his ear. "Writer. I know he was a writer. Leave me alone."

Carmen exchanged glances with Poe. Finch was howl-at-the-moon crazy.

Finch turned to Carmen and smiled. "Did you know that your sister was my first? A man always remembers his first."

"You must be very proud. Release me so I can shake your hand."

Finch's smile broadened. "Shake my hand. That's a good one, Detective." He raised a finger. "Wait here. I want to show you something."

Wait here? Really? Wait here?

Finch walked to the end of the wide and long room. She watched him go. That's when she noticed the old tools and bits of wood strewn about. Shuffler and Judy had been right. A wood shop. A commercial one, abandoned long ago. She snapped her gaze to Poe. "Stop antagonizing him."

"Why? He plans to kill us anyway. The guy has ruined many lives. He ruined me. He ruined you."

"Focus your attention on getting loose."

"I have been. No luck."

Finch returned with an old cigar box in hand. "I felt bad about beating your sister to death. We took a few things to remember her by."

He opened the box and showed it to Carmen: a lock of hair, an earring, and an old stick of lipstick. The fire in Carmen's belly flared, but she kept it in check.

"She was so pretty. We wish she hadn't made me kill her."

Focus, Carmen. Engage the man. Buy some time.

"You're slipping, you know." She met his crazy eyes without blinking. "You let yourself get caught on camera."

He shrugged. "It doesn't matter. We are almost done—No! It wasn't a mistake. No! I told you, it needed to be done. I had a right! Now, *shut up*."

"You've changed your pattern, Finch. You drugged us. Toxicology showed no drugs in the bodies of the others you killed." Carmen watched his reaction.

"I didn't want you talking during the trip back. Besides, by the time they find your body the chloroform will be clear of your system—" Again, he cocked his head. "Yes, it *will!*" He settled himself then smiled at Carmen. "See, this proves I loved your sister."

Carmen wanted to vomit. "You killed her."

"True. I feel bad about that sometimes, but some good came out of it." He closed the box. "Until that day, I didn't know I could kill someone. Turns out, it's pretty easy, and it makes us happy. That was the beginning for us."

"Where are we?" Carmen grit the question out between her teeth.

"I've forgotten my manners." He grabbed Carmen by the collar and lifted her to her feet. He did the same with Poe. "Let me introduce you to the others. Turn around."

Carmen did. What she saw made her ill. Three women were bound and chained like dogs to a post. Judging by the mess on the floor, they hadn't been allowed to use a bathroom. How long had they been missing? Days. Had they eaten?

One thing was clear: all three had been beaten.

Her eyes moved from the pathetic scene to one that was worse. The unconscious Daniel Templeton had been strung up, naked and hanging by the wrists from a rope tied to an overhead beam. His hands were purple from the lack of circulation and his arms looked out of joint. A short distance away, lying on the floor, was a tall, wooden cross. A workbench stood nearby. On it were several wood dowels, a multistrand whip, purple cloth, and a coil of razor wire.

"First the ladies," Finch said. "Meet Mary, Mary, and Salome, or do you already know their names? The naked man is Dr. Daniel Templeton. Ever heard of him? He's a famous Christian. He's my special guest. He's going to be the center of our little party."

"Why him?" Poe asked.

"We went to school together, Dr. Poe. He was a raging Christian back then. This may surprise you, but people were afraid of me back then. I don't really know why."

Carmen resisted the quip that begged to be uttered.

"Danny was the only one who didn't judge me. He prayed for me. At least he said he would. He's the only one I told."

"Told what?" Keep him talking.

"About the voices in my head. I hear voices. Always have."

"Really?"

"Don't mock us, Carmen. The voices don't like you. They don't want you here."

"I can leave."

Finch frowned. "Don't mock me, woman."

"That's a harsh way to treat a friend." Poe looked from Templeton to Finch.

Carmen knew what Poe was doing. He was drawing attention to himself.

"He said his prayers could deliver me. He lied. And lied.

And lied. I still hear them. He made a promise. No one breaks a promise to us."

"Why not just kill him?" Carmen asked. "You've shown you can do that."

"It had to be this way. It had to be special. Unique. Wonderful. It had to be my way—our way." He smiled at Carmen. "Having you here has made this even better."

He stroked her cheek.

"She's not answering her phone." Bud clicked off his cell. "This isn't like her."

"Maybe her battery died?" Hector was ever the optimist.

Bud snapped a glance at Hector. "Would you put any money on that?"

"Not a penny."

Bud dialed the phone again. "I'm calling dispatch. Maybe we can reach her by radio." That was a dead end, too.

"Come on." Bud rose from the chair in the case room and started for the homicide area. "We're going to talk to the captain."

Five minutes later, Captain Simmons had called Escondido police and asked that a patrol car be dispatched to Ellis Poe's condo. And he sent Heywood to check out Poe's boat.

A short time later, Heywood called. Simmons put it on the speakerphone. "Bad news, Cap. I found Detective Rainmondi's weapon and cell phone. I found Ellis Poe's phone, too. I've got Harbor Police checking Poe's boat and . . . hang on . . . Okay, the boat is empty."

"What about her car?"

"No sign of it." Pause. "Cap, I think Finch has her."

Simmons swore.

Bud felt his strength drain from him. He let the despair linger for thirty seconds, then his training and experience kicked in. "Helicopters, Cap. We got to get helos in the air."

"Agreed, but what direction do we send them?"

"We've been running down possible leads to cabinet shops. We have people in the city and county records working on finding cabinet shops that went out of business in the last five years."

"Why five years?" Simmons stood.

"Property values in the county are still some of the highest in the country. It's hard to imagine property with a decent building on it not selling in five years. Possible, but not likely. We got two hits. One is just outside El Cajon. The second has a lot of buildings around. The El Cajon site is the most likely."

Simmons put out a BOLO for Carmen's car and placed a call to the El Cajon police.

"The shop is outside the city. I looked at a Google map. It's kinda isolated." Bud thought for a moment. "Cap, I don't ask many favors, but I have one."

"You want ABLE to take you there?" The Air Borne Law Enforcement helicopter.

"Yes."

Again, Simmons picked up the phone. When he hung up he said, "We're in luck. Get to the roof."

"On my way."

"Not without me." Hector was right on Bud's heels.

The Eurocopter Astar 3B was one of the SDPD's most useful crime tools and had been called a "crook catching machine." It could travel from the Mexican border to north county in twelve minutes. The trip from downtown headquarters to the east county city of El Cajon would take much less time. The passenger compartment could hold four others. Bud and Hector made use of it.

As the helicopter took off, Bud's stomach sank. And it had nothing to do with the sudden lift off.

Hang on, Carmen, you hear me? You hang on.

Ellis's knees shook so they barely held him up. The sights and smells and sounds turned his stomach. His arms trembled. He had tried to put up a brave front, to show Carmen he was no longer the coward he was when he was eighteen, but terror followed no logic and cared nothing about reputation. Bound hands or not, he wanted to run. To flee across the old workshop and make for the door—bust through it if necessary. It was dark outside. Maybe he could hide. Finch and his fractured mind had other things to worry about.

He doesn't want me. He wants Carmen. He wants the women. He wants Templeton. And he's got them. Maybe he would allow one man to escape.

He felt the urge to cry. To scream for help. To plead for his life. To promise anything and everything if only he could walk out the door. Maybe if he promised to keep everything secret . . .

If Ellis had learned anything since that night in 1985, it was that there were two emotions more powerful than fear: shame and love.

He understood shame. It had been his live-in companion for nearly thirty years, attaching itself to his soul like a leech, growing stronger each day until it left Ellis little more than an egg shell—thin, empty, and fragile.

Templeton groaned then writhed, his toes barely touching the floor. His eyes opened, then widened. Tears poured from his eyes: tears of pain, of fear, of pleading. The tortured man shuddered. Convulsed.

Finch shot toward the man and threw a punch to Templeton's ribs, hitting him like a professional boxer. Ellis heard ribs crack.

Oh God. Please God. Blessed Jesus.

Ellis backed away. He averted his eyes, but they fell on the women, then on the cross, then on the razor wire crown and other instruments of torture. Then on the bruised and bloodied Carmen, standing beside him. It was too much to see, too much to hear, too much to take in. He took another step back, adding two more feet between him and the horror movie he was being forced to watch. And experience.

Carmen swore under her breath, lowered her head, and charged. When one stride away from the behemoth, she screamed loud enough to rattle the windows. Finch had pulled back to throw another punch, but Carmen caught him midswing, just as he rested all his weight on one foot. Ellis heard the air leave the big man's lungs.

He backed away as the two tumbled to the ground.

Carmen landed on Finch, who seemed stunned by the blow and astonished by the viciousness of her attack. She didn't wait for a response. She scrambled to her feet and kicked for all she was worth. The first try landed on Finch's shoulder, the second on the side of his head.

Ellis moved another step closer to the door. This was his opportunity. He wouldn't get another. *Run! RUN!*

Carmen raised a foot, clearly intent on driving the heel of her shoe into the man's skull. She was too late. Finch caught her foot and twisted. Carmen screamed and fell hard, her head bouncing on the concrete surface.

Now. Run. Run. Save yourself.

The room disappeared, replaced by a cool San Diego night. He saw the street on which Shelly was killed. He saw the overturned yellow Camero, heard the vicious rants of a young Mitchell Finch—and watched Shelly crawl from the overturned car as she had that night.

Ellis started for the door, but the vision wouldn't leave his mind. Shelly held out her hand, begging for help as she had in 1985—

No, this was different. She wasn't holding out her hand, she was pointing. Her blood stained face turned to him, her bloody hand pointing behind him. "*My sister . . .*"

Finch laughed. Ellis turned.

"You are no match for us, woman." He towered over her. "I will kill you like we did your sister."

"*Help . . . my . . . sister.*"

Ellis looked at the door.

There was a pounding in his ears. *Thumpa, thumpa.*

Finch laughed. Hideous. Demonic. Cold and terrifying.

Ellis's gaze fell on Carmen. Lovely and brave. Defiant in the face of death. Willing to sacrifice herself for her dead sister, for the women in the room, for Templeton, for the families of the victims and—dear God, for him.

He forced his eyes away and continued to back up.

Thumpa, thumpa.

A glint caught his attention. A sparkle of light from the razor wire crown of thorns. Then he saw the purple cloth, the rods, the whip. Then the cross—the very symbol of sacrifice, of one man dying for the many.

Ellis shook his head. *Run!* He started for the door, then stopped. Carmen screamed.

"No . . . no . . . not this . . . time." Ellis could barely recognize his own whispered voice.

Thumpa, thumpa, thumpa. The walls shook.

Ellis ran. Not to the door, but straight at Finch. He sprinted, pushing his legs as never before, then he lowered his head just as Finch raised a booted foot over Carmen's face. Finch spewed cruelties as he brought the foot down.

It never landed. Ellis hit the behemoth full force in the middle of the back. Pain fired down Ellis's shoulder and into his back. He didn't care. He was beyond caring.

The force of the impact drove Ellis and Finch forward, tumbling until they struck the workbench, sending the items on its used and scarred surface to the floor. Ellis landed hard, his bound hands useless in breaking the fall. He couldn't draw a breath.

Finch bellowed, angry and pained, and bolted to his feet. He picked Ellis up, steadied him with his left hand then drove his fist into Ellis's stomach. The shock and pain were indescribable. Ellis buckled. He was barely conscious when he landed on the cold floor. One kick followed another. He had just enough mind left to think of the battered corpses he had seen.

Thumpa. Such a familiar sound. He wondered what it was as darkness ebbed and flowed in his eyes.

Finch screamed. Ellis looked up to see Carmen on her feet using the only weapons available to her: her feet. She drove a foot into Finch's knee making it buckle. The man staggered to the side.

He shouted at her, fire on his lips, his words rolling through the building.

The names he called her . . .

The fury he displayed . . .

The hatred in his wide eyes . . .

Carmen raised her head. "Bring it, Finch. I've been dreaming of this for twenty-eight years. C'mon! I got more for you! I got something from Shelly just for *you*."

Finch bellowed and moved forward like a train gaining speed for a hill. Carmen tried to kick again, but her injured body betrayed her. Blood poured from her nose and her mouth. Fury blazed from her eyes.

The attempted kick made her unstable. Finch felled her with one blow, a blow that landed in the middle of her face. She crumbled to the ground, her mouth open, gasping for air like a fish on a pier. The sight of the cruelty empowered Ellis. He scrambled to his feet, staggered for a moment, then stumbled forward. He didn't have the speed or the strength of his last attack. He would never be able to move the man, so he took a cue from Carmen and aimed for the knees. His shoulder caught Finch on the side of his right leg.

Finch went down. So did Ellis. For a moment Finch rolled on the ground holding his leg. Ellis used the time to squirm toward Carmen. She teetered on the crumbling edge of unconsciousness.

"Run," she whispered.

"No." He turned his head to see Finch rise, limp to the items of torture scattered on the floor. He bent and picked up the whip. The cat-of-nine-tales. The man's expression had changed. He no longer looked angry. He looked pleased, happy, eager for what came next.

Ellis was spent. He was no fighter. No hero. Just a professor of New Testament studies about to die. Like an inchworm he moved to Carmen and covered her with his body.

Then he closed his eyes.

The first strike of the whip ripped through his shirt. The second laid open his back. The third hit the back of his thighs. He screamed after the first two blows. He had no more strength to scream after that.

"I'm so, so, so sorry . . ." he whispered.

A shattering bang.

Indistinct words: "Don't . . . p-lice." Another strike and Ellis felt his heart hesitate.

A loud pop. Another. Another. Ellis caught a glimpse of Finch backpedaling, then falling on his back—across the large, wooden cross lying on the floor.

The whip never struck again.

Ellis exhaled but couldn't manage to inhale.

Blackness.

White.

Peace at last.

EPILOGUE

Soft lips touch his.

Vague forms hover overhead.

Indistinct voices.

Darkness.

~

Brighter light overhead.

He's on his right side.

Pain.

People talk. A voice comes over an intercom.

He's in a bed.

New darkness.

~

New light.

Ellis opened his eyes. A familiar form in a chair.

Open door.

Letters on window by door. ICU 3W.

Soft, electronic voice. "And the Padres drop their season opener to the Dodgers."

"Figures," he said.

Darkness again.

People near him. Talking. Someone touches his shoulder. Words. Soft. Confident.

Praying.

Someone is praying for him. Ellis opens his eyes to see two blurry figures standing there, and one in a chair.

"Last rites?"

A familiar voice chuckles. "Um, you're not Catholic."

"Oh." A moment later. "Hi, Dr. Bridger, Dr. Dunne."

"Good to see you awake, Dr. Poe. You had us worried." Bridger's image came clearer.

"It's my only skill." He started to roll on his back, but Adam stopped him. "The doctors say you're not ready for that yet. Maybe another day or so."

The events poured back into his mind. "Carmen! How's Carmen?"

"Ease up, Cowboy, I'm here." The person in the chair rose. Her face was swollen, both eyes had been blackened, and a plastic splint was taped over her nose.

"You look lovely."

"Really? Shall I get a mirror for you?"

"No." Ellis smiled. "I've had enough . . . shock for awhile . . .

"Emotions are funny things," Ellis said as he poked at what the nursing staff called Jell-O. "I'm happy and devastated at the same time."

Carmen nodded. "It's how people deal with trauma. It doesn't work well. You just have to ride it out."

"So he's dead? He's really dead?"

"Bud and Hector each put two rounds into him. Finch was as big and as strong as they come, but not even he could take four bullets in the chest and keep going."

Ellis decided he wasn't hungry and pushed the hospital meal away. At least he could sit up now, but even the cushioned bed hurt his back. Plastic surgeons had been eyeing him like an award-winning paper in a medical journal. "What was it they used to find us?"

"FLIR. That stands for Forward Looking Infra Red. Finch had us out in the backwoods of east county. The engine of my car was still hot when they flew over. Even in a FLIR image a Crown Vic looks like a Crown Vic."

Ellis thought about that as Carmen continued.

"Good police work saved our bacon. That and high-end technology and some luck."

"It was probably much more than that, Detective. Much more."

"You gonna go all spiritual on me?"

He shrugged and was surprised by how much the simple act hurt. "It's who and what I am."

"I suppose." She rose. "Well, you've had all of me you can take."

"Nah, I have a high threshold for such things."

She chuckled and walked to the door, then stopped. "Can I get you anything?" She'd asked the same thing every day of his week in the hospital.

"No, I have my books."

She lowered her gaze then raised it again. "I've been thinking . . ." She struggled with what she wanted to say. "You saved my life."

"Nonsense. I just distracted him so you could take your turn."

She took a deep breath. "That's the point. I'm pretty good at handling myself, but the best I could do was annoy Finch."

"You had your hands tied behind your back. It's hard to fight that way."

She shook her head. "I landed some good kicks and barreled into him hard enough to cripple most people. He just popped back up madder than ever."

"He was crazy."

"My point is . . . Look, even if I faced off against him both hands free, I wouldn't have stood a chance." She hesitated.

"What I'm saying is this: You couldn't have stopped him back in 1985. You couldn't have saved my sister."

"I could have reported it."

"You've got that right, and don't think I've forgotten that you didn't. I'm not going to let that go."

"I understand."

Carmen walked from the room.

Two weeks and three operations by plastic surgeons later, Ellis stood at his bed, dressed and ready to leave the tiny hospital room behind. Movement at the door drew his attention. Carmen stood in front of a group Ellis knew well: Bud Tock, Hector Garcia, and Joe Heywood.

"You've come to arrest me?"

"Nope, we figured you would like a real meal." Bud grinned. "You like Mexican food?"

"I live in San Diego. Of course I like Mexican food."

"Good," Carmen said. "The chief is buying us lunch at Jimmy Chen's Authentic Mexican Restaurant. Feel up to it?"

Ellis cocked an eyebrow at the name. "Yes. I could go for some real food."

"You gotta try the beans." Bud's grin was broad.

As was Carmen's grimace. "Oh, brother."

Ellis and the others walked into Jimmy Chen's and Carmen led them to the back room. The place was filled. He saw Adam Bridger and his wife Rachel. The crowd included the families of the victims. The sight of Doug Lindsey's family moved Ellis to tears.

He stepped into the room.

The crowd applauded.

All except Carmen Rainmondi.

DISCUSSION QUESTIONS

1. The greatest day in Ellis Poe's life was his conversion experience. That was quickly followed by the worst day in his life: witnessing a murder. Why would God allow such a thing to happen to a new believer?

2. Ellis Poe chose isolation. What is there about regret that puts distance between us and others?

3. How has regret affected you or someone you know?

4. Ellis invested himself in the lives of others but, knowing what you do about the event in his past, do you have trouble respecting him?

5. Carmen Rainmondi's sister was murdered changing her life and her plans forever. Have you had an event that changed the direction of your life? If so, how do you deal with it?

6. Carmen is not a person of faith so we might understand why she stews in her sadness and anger, but what excuse does Ellis have?

7. Ellis gets drawn into the investigation. How do the events change him?

8. Ellis is once again torn between turning his back on the situation but is unable to do so. What factors keep him from avoiding involvement?

9. There are several horrible murders in this story, all tied to a series of biblical events. Did these scenes make you see the death of Christ differently?

10. There is much evil in the world and we see some of it in this book. Why does God allow such evil to exist?

11. How do Carmen and Ellis ultimately deal with the negative emotions and regrets that have haunted them for so long?

12. Can you overlook Ellis's inaction as a teenager? Is it right to expect him to react as an adult? Could you forgive him?

13. Does a refusal to deal with personal guilt affect others?

14. If God were to suddenly appear in Ellis's office what do you suppose He'd say to the professor?

15. If God were to make a similar visit to Carmen in her home, what would He say to her?